PRAISE FOR

Fair Is the Rose

"Wonderful writing and a terrific story. *Fair Is the Rose* explores living, breathing people with heart-wrenching conflicts and one woman with a faith that shines. The reader is transported. Be sure to have a box of tissues close at hand."

—FRANCINE RIVERS, author of *Redeeming Love*

"A colorful tapestry woven from painstaking research, a rich, vivid setting, and compelling, wonderfully real characters. With excellent writing and a keen understanding of human nature, Liz Curtis Higgs delivers a first-rate, fascinating historical saga. As big and bold a story as the Galloway landscape where it takes place and the hearts of the people who inhabit it."

—B. J. HOFF, author of *Cadence* and *An Emerald Ballad*

"*Och!* What a *guid buik!* Once again Liz Curtis Higgs transported me to eighteenth-century Scotland and caused me to lose my heart to Jamie, Leana, and Rose. I couldn't help but yearn for all three to find lasting love and happiness. The next installment can't get here fast enough to suit me."

—ROBIN LEE HATCHER, author of *Catching Katie*
and *Beyond the Shadows*

"*Fair Is the Rose* is an absolutely stunning sequel to *Thorn in My Heart*. I was transported back in time to my ancestral Scotland and relished every moment. An exceptional work!"

—LINDA LEE CHAIKIN, author of *Yesterday's Promise*

"Liz Higgs's writing resonates with romance and the inward struggles of the human heart. You can almost hear the tunes rising o'er the brae."

—PATRICIA HICKMAN, author of *Fallen Angels*
and *Nazareth's Song*

Fair Is the Rose

Fair Is the Rose

LIZ CURTIS HIGGS

WATERBROOK
PRESS

FAIR IS THE ROSE
PUBLISHED BY WATERBROOK PRESS
2375 Telstar Drive, Suite 160
Colorado Springs, Colorado 80920
A division of Random House, Inc.

All Scripture quotations are taken from the *King James Version* of the Bible.

ISBN 1-57856-127-2

Library of Congress Cataloging-in-Publication Data
Higgs, Liz Curtis.
  Fair is the rose / Liz Curtis Higgs.
      p. cm.
  ISBN 1-57856-127-2
  1. Scotland—History—18th century—Fiction. 2. Triangles (Interpersonal relations)—Fiction.
3. Inheritance and succession—Fiction. 4. Brothers—Fiction. 5. Sisters—Fiction. I. Title.
  PS3558.I36235F35 2004
  813'.54—dc22

                                                                    2003025341

Printed in the United States of America
2004—First Edition

10 9 8 7 6 5 4 3 2 1

GALLOWAY, Scotland
1789
by Benny Gillies

River Nith

Dumfries

...naclellan
...lloway

...och
...Ken

Urr Water

Milltown

Lochend

...hie

Drumcultran

Auchengray

Lowtis
Hill

Newabbey

Haugh of Urr

Threave

Dalbeaty

Criffell

Carlinwark
Loch

Keltonhill

Kirkbean

Kirkcudbright

Solway Firth

Highlands

Dundrennan

Lowlands

The rose saith in the dewy morn,
I am most fair;
Yet all my loveliness is born
Upon a thorn.

CHRISTINA ROSSETTI

One

Never wedding, ever wooing,
Still a lovelorn heart pursuing,
Read you not the wrong you're doing
In my cheek's pale hue?
THOMAS CAMPBELL

Newabbey Parish Manse
October 1789

Rose McBride pressed her back against the paneled wall, her gaze fixed on the man kneeling by her sister's bedside. She could not see Jamie McKie's face at that late hour. Only his sleek brown hair, tied at the nape of his neck, and his favorite blue waistcoat, crumpled from a long day of waiting for his son to be born. Moments after the child had made his entrance into the world, Jamie had appeared in the birthing room and sent her heart spinning.

He'd not come to see *her*, but Rose would see her fill of *him*. Aye, she would.

A peat fire burned low in the grate, barely warming the chilly room. The minister's spence served as a parlor during the day and as a bedroom and study in the evening. 'Twas the last place her sister had expected to give birth; when her labor had started in the middle of services, Leana had had little choice. Though Rose's knees ached from crouching in the same position for several minutes, she dared not move and risk discovery. Her beloved Jamie had yet to spy her hiding behind the high-backed chair in the darkest corner. She intended to keep it that way.

Now he was leaning toward her sister, Leana. Touching her hand, then caressing his son's wee head. The catch in his voice said more than his words. "Leana, will you forgive me?"

Nae! Rose bit down on her lower lip, fighting tears. *'Tis Leana's fault, not yours, Jamie.*

She could not hear the whispered words that followed, but her eyes told her more than she wanted to know. Leana brushed aside her damp blond hair and put the babe to her breast while Jamie stood gazing down at her, his growing fondness for Leana palpable even from a distance. Rose averted her gaze, though the tender image lingered. Why, oh, why hadn't she left the room with the others?

All at once they both laughed, and Leana's voice carried across the room. "One has found a way to come between us."

Rose swallowed hard. Did Leana mean the babe…or her?

"Nothing will come between us again," Jamie said firmly.

He means me. Rose clutched the back of the chair, feeling faint. Why would he say such a thing? *You love me, Jamie. You ken you do.*

Jamie entreated her sister with words no woman could resist. "Will you give me a chance to prove myself to you?"

Prove yourself? Oh, Jamie. Rose sank to the floor on her knees, not caring if they heard her, not caring if she drew another breath. Jamie, the handsome cousin who had kissed her that very morning, was prepared to put her aside like a dish of half-eaten pudding.

"We shall begin again," she heard her sister say. "Now then, tell me about your dream."

"So I will." A chair scraped against the wooden floor.

Much as Rose tried to resist, Jamie's voice, low and familiar, drew her like smoke to a flue. He spun a far-fetched story about the night he left his home in Glentrool and slept on a stony cairn among the crushed berries of a leafy Jacob's ladder plant. Then he dreamed of a mountain, he said, taller than any in Galloway and bright as a full moon in a midnight sky. Winged creatures moved up and down the mountainsides like stairsteps, and a voice roared like the sea.

"What did this…this *voice* tell you?" Leana asked.

When Jamie did not respond, Rose shifted to see him better, her curiosity aroused. In a twelvemonth, Jamie had not mentioned such a dream to her.

"Leana, it was a voice like no other. Wondrous. And *frichtsome.* The words clapped like thunder: 'Behold, I am with you wherever you go. I will never leave you.'"

Leana gasped. "But, Jamie—"

"Aye, lass. The same words you whispered to me on our wedding night."

Nae! Rose pressed her hands to her ears at the very moment a sharp knock sounded at the door. Startled, she fell forward with a soft cry, her hiding place forgotten.

Leana's voice floated across the room. "Who's there, behind the chair?"

Rose drew back, her heart pounding beneath her stays. But it was too late. Taking a long, slow breath, she stood to her feet and did her best to look penitent.

The peat fire lit Jamie's astonished face. "Rose?"

Shame burned her cheeks. Before she could find words to explain herself, the door creaked open, and the coppery head of their house-keeper, Neda Hastings, appeared.

"Leana, I've come *tae* see ye get some rest…" Neda's words faded as she caught sight of Rose. "There ye are, lass! I *thocht* ye'd wandered off tae the kitchen."

"Nae." She could not look at Jamie. "I…I wanted to see…the baby."

"Come, dearie," Leana murmured, stretching out her hand. "You had only to ask."

Gathering her skirts and her courage about her, Rose crossed the wooden floor to Leana's bedside, barely noticing the others as her gaze fell on the tiny bundle in Leana's arms. "Isn't he a dear thing?" While Leana held back the linen blanket, Rose smoothed her hand across Ian's downy hair, as rich a brown as Jamie's own. "'Tis so soft," she whispered. Had she ever touched anything more precious? His little head fit perfectly within the cup of her hand.

"Would you like to hold him, Rose?"

Her breath caught. "Might I?" She bent down, surprised to find her arms were shaking. She'd held babies before, but not this one. Not Jamie's. "Ohh," she said when Leana placed the babe in the crook of her arm. "How warm he is!"

Rose held Ian close and bent her head over his, breathing in the scent of his skin, marveling at how pink he was. And how small. Deep inside her a longing stirred to life, as if some unnamed desire had waited for this moment to arrive. All of her sixteen years Rose had feared motherhood; the miracle in her arms put such foolish concerns to rest. Her mother had died in childbirth, yet Leana had lived, and so had her babe. "My own nephew," Rose said gently, stroking his cheek. "Ian James McKie."

No wonder Jamie was enchanted. Leana was not the one who'd stolen Jamie's heart this night; it was Ian, his newborn son.

Neda came up behind her, resting her hands on Rose's shoulders, peering round her to look at the babe. "Ye'll make a fine *mither* someday. Suppose ye *gie* Ian back tae yer sister afore he starts to *greet.*"

"Aye." Rose did as she was told, chagrined at how cool and empty her arms felt.

"The *auld* wives say," Neda cooed, tucking Leana's bedcovers in place, "the child that's born on the Sabbath day is blithe and bonny and good and gay. Isn't that so, Mr. McKie?"

Jamie smiled down at his son. "Ian is all those things."

When Jamie lifted his head, Rose looked into his eyes, hoping she might find his love for her reflected there. "I'm sorry, Jamie. For hiding in the corner."

"No harm was done, Rose." His steady gaze confused her. Was he glad she was there? Or eager for her to leave?

Neda picked up the candle by the bed and waved it toward the door. "Go along, lass. And ye as well, Mr. McKie. Leana needs a bit *mair* care and a *guid* deal o' sleep. We'll bring yer wife and babe *hame* tae Auchengray soon."

Rose took her leave, pretending not to notice as Jamie bent down to kiss her sister's hand, then her brow, then her mouth, where he tarried longer than duty required. *Oh, Jamie.* Had his affections shifted so quickly? In a day? In an hour? Rose closed the door behind her, shutting out the worst of it. Her empty stomach squeezed itself into a hard knot, even as her chin began to wobble. She would not cry. She would *not.*

The hall was pitch-black, the last of the candles snuffed out by the thrifty minister's wife, who'd shooed her household off to bed an hour ago. Rose halted, unsure of her way in the darkness. Was that her green cloak hanging near the door or someone else's? She would need its thick woolen folds for the journey home.

Behind her the spence door shut with a faint click of the latch.

"Rose?"

Jamie. She could not bring herself to answer him, though she sensed him closing the distance between them, his footsteps echoing in the empty hall. His hand touched her waist. "Rose, you must understand…"

"I do understand." Her voice remained steady while the rest of her trembled. "Now that she has given you a healthy son, Leana is the one you love."

"Nae, Rose." Jamie grasped her elbow and spun her about. The heat of his fingers penetrated the fabric of her gown, and his eyes bored into hers. "To my shame, I do not love Leana. Not yet." He lowered his voice, tightening his grip on her arm. "But I will learn to love your sister. By all that's holy, I must, Rose. She is my wife, the mother of my son, and—"

"And she loves you."

He dared not disagree, for they both knew it was true. "Aye, she does."

"Well, so do I." Swallowing her pride, Rose reached up to caress his face, reveling at the rough feel of his unshaven skin. "And you love me, Jamie. You told me so again this morning, you said—"

"Things I should not have said on this or any other Sabbath." Jamie turned away, releasing his hold on her. "Something happened this day, Rose."

"Aye. Your son was born—"

"Before that, I mean. I had a discussion with Duncan." He hung his head. "More like a confession."

"Duncan, you say?" Neda's husband, the overseer of Auchengray, was a good man and kind. But unbending when it came to certain matters. "Whatever did you confess to him?"

"The truth." The relief on Jamie's face was visible even in the dim entrance hall. "I promised Duncan...nae, I promised God that I would be a good husband to Leana and a good father to Ian. I must keep that promise now. You ken I must." He stared down at the flagstone floor, his voice strained. "Let me go, Rose. Please."

"Let you *go?*" Her throat tightened. "But, Jamie, I love you. After all we've been through, how can you ask such a thing of me?"

"Because you love your sister."

She cringed at the reminder. "Not as much as I love you."

Jamie looked up. "You've loved her longer though. Every day of your life."

"Not this day," Rose protested, though they both knew she didn't mean it. Hour after hour she'd held Leana's hand, pleading with her not to die, praying for her with Neda and the others. Aye, she loved her sister. But she loved Jamie as well. How could she possibly let him go?

He took her hand and led her toward the hall bench, pulling her down onto the wooden seat next to him. "Rose..." His voice was as tender as she'd ever heard it. "I saw you with Ian. You were born to be a mother. And someday you will surely be one. But first you must find a husband of your own."

"*Please,* Jamie!" Did he not understand? Did he not *see?* "*You* should have been my husband. And Ian my son—"

"*Nae!*" He fell back against the wall with a groan. "I beg you, do not say such things, Rose. 'Tis too late for all of that. God in his mercy has forgiven my unfaithful heart, and I will not disappoint him—or Leana—again."

Her heart sank. "Instead you will disappoint me."

"Aye, it seems I must." Jamie turned toward her, his face a handbreadth away. "Forgive me, darling Rose. You were my first love; I cannot deny it."

His first love. But not his last. She closed her eyes. He was too near.

"I may never care for Leana as I have for you. But I must try. Don't you see?"

"I..." She could hold back her tears no longer. "I only see that you don't want me."

"As my cousin, always. But not as my wife." His grip tightened. "You must let me go, Rose. For Ian's sake."

She stood, tugging her hands free to wipe her cheeks, looking away lest he see the sorrow in her eyes. "You ask too much of me, Jamie. You ask…too much." She fled for the front door, stopping long enough to fling her cloak over her shoulders before disappearing into the fog-shrouded night.

Two

Of all the joys that lighten suffering earth,
what joy is welcomed like a newborn child?

CAROLINE SHERIDAN NORTON

Leana clutched the babe to her breast and sank deeper into the heather mattress, realizing she'd used the last of her energy making Jamie feel welcome by her bedside. How attentive he'd been, with his gaze fixed on hers and his constant touches, gentle but firm, as though he were at last laying claim to his wife and child. *Please God, may it be so!* Jamie was gone to Auchengray now, leaving naught behind but his scent on Ian's linen blanket. She smiled, remembering his response when she'd worried over how she must look after her travail: *You look like the mother of my son.*

Mother. It was too much to take in all at once. The blessing and responsibility of her new role drifted down onto her shoulders like an invisible mantle from on high. "Mother," she whispered.

Neda's freckled brow knotted with concern. "Ye miss her, I ken."

"Aye." A shadow fell across Leana's heart. "Though 'twas not my mother I was thinking of just now."

" 'Tis yer own duties that fill yer thoughts then. *Weel* and guid. Ye've no need o' *unheartsome* notions on this blithe day." Neda steadied the pitcher as she poured hot water into a shallow porcelain basin, tipping her head away from the rising steam. Her features remained unlined despite her fifty-odd years, but the slump of her shoulders bespoke her age well enough. " 'Tis a shame yer mither did not live tae see this *granbairn* o' hers. Agness McBride would be mair than pleased *wi'* her daughter's labors." She put aside the pitcher, then soaked a small square of rough linen in the water and wrung it out with hands that stayed chapped and red no matter the season. "Ye did *verra* well, lass." Wiping Leana's forehead, then her cheeks, she added with a chuckle, "Born on a Sabbath *nicht* in a parish manse, yer son is bound tae be a minister someday."

"Aye, perhaps." Leana tipped her chin as the wet cloth swept round her face, which had grown fuller in the last few months. If only she had Rose's lithe neck! But Leana resembled their mother, a broad-cheeked, fair-haired Scotswoman, who had died giving birth to Rose sixteen years past. In her stead, Neda had offered a mother's calming presence and caring touch, seeing to Leana's every need, serving as maid and midwife from the moment Leana's labor began during Reverend Gordon's sermon. To think, the child was born in the man's own home, in his own spence, in his own *bed!* The dour minister might never recover from the shocking sight of a bevy of female congregants taking flight from their pews, with Mistress Gordon leading the charge.

Leana looked down as Ian stirred in her arms. His features were still pink and pinched, his eyes closed tight in the flickering firelight. "*Baloo,* baloo, my wee, wee thing," she sang softly, then brushed her lips against his velvety head. The smooth plane of his forehead and fullness of his lower lip were so like his father's, tears sprang to her eyes. *Jamie, my Jamie.* Perhaps now she might dare speak the truth of her love abroad after months of pretending not to adore the husband she'd claimed. God had forgiven her for how it had all come about, of that Leana was certain. Rose was less generous with her mercy.

The damp cloth put aside, Neda slid her hands beneath the wriggling babe. "Will ye let me take him, lass? Gie ye *baith* a proper bathin' this time?"

Leana hesitated, hating to lose the warmth of him, the slight weight of him pressed against her. Holding Ian was like holding Jamie's heart; she was not willing to let either one move beyond her reach. "Only for a moment," she said, releasing the lad with some reluctance. "Put him close by the hearth so he won't become chilled."

Neda clucked at her, shaking her head. "Already the dotin' young mither, *oot* tae spoil yer son." Nonetheless, she did what Leana requested, wrapping the child in a thick plaid and tucking him in a basket near the glowing peat. "Just 'til yer mither is scrubbed and dressed in a clean shift," Neda assured him. Her eyes shone with a grandmother's pride. Turning her attention to the master bed, she quickly saw to Leana's comfort, lifting her weak limbs to bathe her, bidding her stand only long enough to slip the shift over her head, then whisking off the bed linens and replacing them with fresh ones. Leana raised no objection when Neda slid the family Bible between the two thin mattresses, knowing the woman meant only to safeguard mother and child while they slept. A harmless old custom meant to keep away the fairies.

"See how little time yer bath took?" Neda chided her, brushing the last of the tangles from her damp hair. "Rest a moment while I tend tae Ian."

Leana watched, enthralled, as Neda bathed the child from crown to toes using her bare hands and the last of the soapy water, slipping her fingers between the soft creases of his flesh, ignoring his whimpers of protest. "Hush, little one," Leana murmured. The hour was late and the Gordon household long since retired, the reverend and his wife having found refuge in a spare bed up the stair. Neda patted the babe dry while Leana cooed, "She's almost finished with you, lad." At last, newly wrapped and smelling sweeter than ever, Ian was delivered to her waiting arms, where he settled into an exhausted sleep.

"See ye do the same, Leana." Neda regarded her with a look that brooked no argument. "From time oot o' mind every mither kens she must sleep *whan* her babe does or *niver* sleep at all. 'Tis why I'll not stay here in the spence this nicht and risk keepin' ye awake wi' me snorin'. But ye can be sure I'll be oot in the hall if ye need me." She showed Leana how to rest on her side with the babe cradled just so, a rolled blanket pressed against his back to hold him safely in place. "Ye'll not nap long afore young Ian will need nursin'. Did ye...that is, have ye had a go at that?"

"Aye, when Jamie was here with me," Leana admitted, her neck heating. "It went well, I think."

Neda said nothing for a moment, eying her. "Will ye be wantin' me tae find a village woman? Bring her tae Auchengray as yer wet nurse—"

"Nae," Leana said decisively. "Perhaps the gentry prefer to let a stranger nurse their children, but I..." She lowered her gaze, at once self-conscious. "I'd rather manage on my own."

"Guid." Neda nodded, looking relieved. " 'Nurse yer *bairn* this year, and do yer work next year,' goes the sayin'. 'Twas what yer mither did whan ye were born. God rest her soul, she could not do the same for wee Rose. But ye grew like a summer melon from yer mither's milk."

Leana touched her rounded cheek, fretting at the fullness she found there. "It seems I'm growing still."

"*Och!* Ye've the face o' a woman now, 'tis all. And if I may be *sae* bold, Mr. McKie seemed quite taken wi' yer *sonsie* face this nicht."

Leana pressed her lips tight to hold back a smile. Could it be true? "I must confess, my husband does seem…changed."

"Mair than ye ken. This mornin' outside the spence door Duncan prayed the man tae his knees."

Leana gasped. "*Jamie?* On his knees?"

"If I tell ye mair, I'll risk me own husband's ire, but I'll say this much, Mistress McKie." Neda smoothed her hand across Leana's brow, bending over her bed to whisper the rest of it. "Yer Jamie has pledged tae do right by ye and tae honor his marriage vows, whate'er it may cost him."

Whate'er it may cost. Leana let the words sink in, past the doubt that had built a hedgerow round her heart, beyond the scars of old wounds. Less than an hour ago, in this very room, Jamie had begged her forgiveness, sincerity written across every feature of his handsome face. He had said—had he not?—that nothing would come between them again. He had pleaded for a chance to start over, to begin anew.

And she had agreed, not counting the cost.

"But it will cost him Rose."

" 'Tis not yer concern, Leana," Neda said with a note of resolve, moving toward the door. "Jamie kens the cost and has called on the Almighty tae gie him strength." Her chin jutted out, challenging any naysayers. "Wrong has prevailed *lang* enough at Auchengray. Right will soon reign o'er that household, or yer husband will answer tae mine." The muffled bang of the door punctuated her charge as Neda disappeared into the hall.

Leana stared at the fire, almost too exhausted to sleep. Images of her dear sister nagged at her conscience. Rose holding Ian. Rose gazing at Jamie. Rose leaving the room alone. *Forgive me, Rose.* How often had she said those words? On her wedding day. On the day she knew she was carrying Ian. And a hundred other days besides. If Jamie honored his vows now, as he had promised he would, Leana feared she might say the words forever. *Please, Rose. Forgive me.*

Sleep came but soon departed. Awakened by Ian's cry, Leana shifted her body to accommodate him, guiding his tiny, insistent mouth to her breast. She shivered beneath the heavy plaid, longing for a warming pan to skim across the bedsheets or a hot brick wrapped in cloth to nestle at her feet. No matter. She had Ian in her arms, and he was enough to warm her heart if not her body. The night passed slowly, interrupted by another feeding, then the need for a fresh linen blanket for Ian. Leana drifted in and out of sleep, her legs aching with a dull pain, as though she'd run all three miles to Auchengray and back again. As was customary, Neda had buried the afterbirth the moment it was delivered, then assured Leana that her body would mend in due course. "Next time 'twill be easier," Neda had declared. Leana cared not how difficult it might be, if God would only provide a brother or sister for Ian someday.

Night turned to gray morning. She awoke to the sounds of the Gordon household stirring to life and a firm tap at the spence door. " 'Tis Neda, come tae see *aboot* the new mither." The housekeeper bustled into the spence holding a basin of steaming water. A maid bearing a candlelit breakfast tray was close on her heels, followed by another wide-eyed lass with an armload of towels. In short order mother and child were examined, changed, and fed, with their faces scrubbed clean and the bedding set aright.

"You're a very efficient nurse," Leana teased as the woman yanked the curtains aside to let in what little light the day had to offer. " 'Tis clear why Father never calls for a doctor from Dumfries."

"Och!" Neda tied back the thick folds of fabric. "Yer *faither* is sparin' his coin, that's all." Lachlan McBride's miserly ways were common knowledge among his fellow bonnet lairds with whom he did business. No one suffered from his tightly drawn purse strings more than his own household. "Speakin' o' yer faither," Neda reminded her, "ye're tae expect him at nine o' the clock for a peek at his new granbairn."

Leana sat up straighter in bed, making sure she was modestly covered and the babe's face easily viewed. Any visit with her father, however brief, was a trial from which she seldom emerged unscathed. She would hold her head high this day, however. In January the kirk session had pronounced her a wife, and *yestreen* the Lord had declared her a mother.

She was still arranging the folds of her bedding when her father's voice boomed from the hall. "Daughter, I trust I may enter and see this grandson of mine."

"Aye, Father." She wet her lips, a nervous habit. "Do come in."

The door banged open. Neda and the others flew from the room like hens, arms flapping, their voices unnaturally high. Lachlan McBride marched in, his greatcoat dusting the floor behind him. He pulled a chair by the bedside in a single broad sweep and sat with some ceremony, brushing the dust from his trousers. The silver threads stitched through his ebony hair glistened in the candlelight. If he could mint them, Leana knew he would.

She offered him a slight smile. "As you can see, Ian James McKie has arrived safe and sound."

Her father eyed the drowsy babe with mild interest. "So he has." He touched Ian's head as though to make certain the boy was real, then drew his hand back. "Tell his father there'll be no running off to Glentrool with my grandson. Ian must be raised at Auchengray. If the lad is to inherit my land someday, 'tis only right he think of it as his home."

"I'll tell him," Leana said, uneasy at the prospect of conveying such a message. Jamie chafed under Lachlan's tight reins, pulled more taut each day they remained in Newabbey and away from his own beloved parish of Monnigaff. Lachlan, both uncle and father-in-law to Jamie, served no one's interests but his own.

Her father then leaned forward to peer at her. "Quite a commotion you caused at the kirk *yestermorn*."

"Forgive me, Father," she murmured. "A woman cannot choose when and where such things will happen."

"When you insisted on going to the Sabbath services in your delicate condition, do you recall how I cautioned you against it?"

Leana remembered his words exactly—"not prudent"—but merely nodded.

"Aye, and now you've converted Reverend Gordon's household into a coaching inn for the week. If you'd listened to me, your son would've been born at Auchengray, and you'd be comfortably settled in your own box bed at home. Am I right?" he barked, ignoring the babe, who wriggled in her arms. "Tell me, Daughter, am I right?"

"Aye, Father." Leana forced herself to meet his gaze. "You always are."

Three

One truth is clear,
Whatever is, is right.

ALEXANDER POPE

"W hat is *right*, Jamie McKie, and what is *fair* are not necessarily the
same."

Jamie watched in silence as Rose stamped about the orchard. It had
been a difficult three days since Ian's birth. One minute the lass was
tender and resigned, the next tearful and quarrelsome. "From the moon
tae the midden" was how Duncan described her moods. In the twelvemonth Jamie had loved her, ever-changeable Rose had seldom shown
him the same disposition twice.

The afternoon sun cut a wide swath across the gardens and fields of
Auchengray, burnishing the October landscape to a golden sheen. He
should have been in the sheepfolds with Duncan, preparing the ewes for
their fall breeding. Or off visiting Leana and Ian at the manse in
Newabbey. Instead Rose had pleaded with him to help her harvest
apples, and he'd agreed, determined to bring their sparring to an end.

You ask too much of me, Jamie.

And you, Rose, of me.

"Hold this, will you?" Rose thrust a woven willow basket into his
arms and began plucking yellow pippins from the nearest branch, dropping them into the basket, bruising the fruit as she went. Her gingham
gown was cinched tight at the waist, displaying her figure to best advantage, and she'd woven her silken hair into a thick braid that danced
about her waist. Young Rose knew how to capture and keep a man's
attention.

"As I was saying, Jamie, you may think it *right* to give your heart to
Leana, but I do not think it *fair*. Have I not forgiven you for what happened on Hogmanay? For marrying my sister instead of me?"

A common refrain. "Aye, you have, Rose. But you've not forgiven Leana."

"What sister could overlook such sinful behavior?" She flapped her hand, dismissing any response. "Never mind all that. 'Tis the present that concerns me, Jamie. And the future."

Keeping his irritation in check, he put the basket down with a thud. "My present and future both rest with Leana and Ian. As to your own future, what of your plans to attend boarding school in Dumfries? Has your father not arranged things? And paid your tuition in advance?"

"So what if he has?" Rose threw down the apples in her hands, tossing her long braid like a whip. "I'll not have my father ruling my life." Her dark eyes narrowed. "Not like he rules yours."

At the cruel reminder Jamie clenched his hands into fists, longing to hit something. Lachlan McBride's stern features seemed a worthy target. Or the bearded face of Evan McKie, his own twin brother, whose murderous threats had sent Jamie fleeing to Auchengray. Aye, he could plant a fist on either of their stubborn jaws and feel justified.

Rose, peering intently at him now, clearly sensed she'd spoken amiss. The pointed look in her eyes softened, and her words turned sweeter. "Poor Jamie. 'Twas thoughtless of me to mention how Father has taken advantage of you." She brushed the dirt from her hands and stepped closer, nudging apples from her path with her toe until there was naught between them but a slight autumn breeze. "Will you forgive me? Please?"

The lass presented a bonny enough picture at arm's length. But standing so close, with wisps of her dark hair tickling his chin and the warmth of her body heating his own, Rose was irresistible. Mustering all his strength, Jamie took a step backward and swallowed his regret before she could hear it in his voice. "Of course you are forgiven, Cousin. I fear my conduct of late has confused you."

"*Confused* me?" She gaped at him. "*Crushed* me is nearer the mark."

"I am sorry, Rose." He would keep saying those words until she believed him. "Truly sorry for…"

"For loving me, Jamie?" She stepped closer, beseeching him with her eyes. "Are you sorry for that?"

"Oh, Rose. You ken better." A heady scent of heather wafted from the folds of her gown, stirring memories he was trying hard to forget. Was there something he might say to appease her? He stared at the canopy of golden leaves above him. "Perhaps…perhaps if Leana had not survived the birthing…" Even saying such a thing made his face grow hot with shame. "Perhaps then…our future together might have been different, Rose."

"*Might* have?"

"Would have," he hastened to amend, his guilt increasing. "After a year of mourning, you and I would have married, certainly. As it is, I must do the honorable and right thing."

"'Tis right, aye. But 'tis not fair." She started to pout, then bit her lip instead. "And all these months I thought you loved me."

Och! Did the lass never tire of hearing it? "I *did* love you, Rose. From Martinmas to Hogmanay and every day since, I said those words and meant them."

Hope rose in her face like the sun. "Do you love me still?"

He looked away, barely noticing the blackbirds picking at the discarded apples strewn at their feet. How could he respond and not hurt her? To reveal the truth—yes, despite all, he still cared for her—would confound Rose further. To insist otherwise—no, he loved her sister instead—was less than honest at the moment and would cut his dear Rose to the quick.

One choice remained. "I cannot love you, Rose."

"Jamie, please—"

"I cannot," he said again, as much to convince himself. "Leana has honored our marriage vows from the first. 'Tis time I did the same."

Rose looked up at him, her face awash with tears. "Then what's to become of me, Jamie?"

Everything inside him wanted to embrace her, comfort her, and tell her he didn't mean a word of it. Tell her he loved her still, would always love her and no one else. It would be the easy thing to do. But not the right thing.

"Rose, there will be another man for you. A better man."

She turned her back to him. "I could never love another."

"Aye, you will, Rose. A man with the freedom to love you in return." He took hold of her shoulders, if only to keep her from facing him again. "Rose, shall I talk to your father? Persuade him to find you a proper suitor?"

"Nae!" He heard the conviction in her voice. And the disappointment. "If I'm to have a husband, he will be of my choosing. Not Father's."

An unlikely event, though Jamie could not blame her for wanting it so. "Then I pray you'll find a man worthy of you, Rose." *Soon.* He stood back, releasing her. "I must go. Duncan will be waiting for me in the sheepfolds." Without another word, he strode off toward Auchengray Hill, sensing her gaze glued to his departing back.

Jamie deliberately shifted his attention to the rough ground beneath his boots. One misstep and he would find himself sprawled atop a protruding root hidden under the leafy carpet. He walked with more confidence when the east-side orchards gave way to the gardens nestled against the hill behind the whitewashed stone farmhouse that served as the mains of Auchengray. The view was worth admiring as he passed by: a physic garden full of herbs; a rose bed pruned for autumn; tidy heaps of ash fertilizing the kitchen garden where turnips and cabbages would appear next summer. Surveying the neatly tended rows, he imagined Leana kneeling there with a basket of well-sharpened tools by her side. She often hummed as she worked, even sang to her roses. "As my mother did," she'd once explained, though he hadn't asked why.

Jamie shook his head as he turned and started up the hill, ashamed of how little regard he'd shown his wife. Had he ever praised Leana for her gardening abilities? Her skill with a needle? Her talents in the kitchen and stillroom? *Nae.* He'd been too distracted by her younger sister. In truth, Leana was everything Rose was not. Leana appeared pale next to her sister's dramatic coloring. Her demeanor was quiet compared to Rose's lively ways. Leana sewed and spun wool and read books. Rose danced and laughed and did little in the way of work. Squinting through her spectacles to stitch a hem, Leana looked older than her years. Running through the orchard with her braid flying behind her like an ebony tail, Rose looked like a bonny lass of twelve.

Yet it was patient Leana he'd married. Gentle Leana he'd taken to bed. Faithful Leana who'd borne him a son. She had given him everything; he had given her as little as possible. He had yet to tell her he loved her, nor would he do so until he meant it. Leana knew him too well and would see through any insincerity.

Could he love so meek and unassuming a woman? 'Twas his earnest prayer on the day of Ian's birth: *Please, God, let me love her in return.* He would pray without ceasing until the time came when he could say the words aloud and mean them.

Four

So rolls the changing year, and so we change;
Motion so swift, we know not that we move.
DINAH MARIA MULOCK CRAIK

Laughter floated down the hillside, followed by a gruff male voice.
"If it isn't the lang lost shepherd o' Glentrool!"

Jamie glanced up, glad to see Duncan Hastings standing at the crest of the *brae,* and continued his ascent with renewed vigor. He'd fretted over the women in his life quite enough for one afternoon. "Sorry to desert you, Duncan," he called out. Nearing the summit, he grinned at the older man. "I ken you're eager to see my boots covered in sheep dung."

Duncan said nothing at first, merely bobbed his checked wool cap. He wore his bonnet planted farther back on his head so folk could see the bright blue of his eyes. Or so Duncan could see *them,* Jamie decided.

Duncan cleared his throat, shifting his weight as he leaned on his shepherd's crook. "I spied ye talkin' tae Rose a bit ago." There was no censure in Duncan's tone. "Settlin' her down, I suppose. Smoothin' her fleece. And lockin' the gate behind ye, if ye ken me meaning."

Jamie snorted. "Rose McBride is not a ewe."

"*Mebbe* not, lad, but ye handle them *meikle* the same."

"Aye? Then find the lass a *tup* among the gentry of Galloway."

"If I were Rose's father," Duncan said, "I'd see it done this afternoon."

"So would I." Jamie drew an imaginary arc across the rolling land-scape, encompassing a dozen fine properties. "There must be a gentle-man of means in this corner of Scotland who'd claim Rose McBride for a wife. It's time Lachlan did his duty by her."

Duncan shrugged. "Ye ken verra well why the man's in nae hurry tae find his *dochter* a husband. As lang as fair Rose abides at Auchengray, so will hard workin' Jamie McKie. Or so yer faither-in-law thinks."

"Let him think whatever he likes," Jamie said with a huff, starting out for the nearest sheepfold. "The moment Leana and the babe can travel, we're bound for Glentrool."

A smile bloomed on Duncan's weathered face. "Is that a fact?" He clapped Jamie on the shoulder and squeezed hard. "Weel done, lad! Have ye told yer wife this guid news?"

"Nae." He'd not said a word to Leana. Or Rose. Nor had he written to his mother in far-off Glentrool. "I plan to tell Leana tonight when I join her at the manse for supper. For the moment you'll keep it under your bonnet, eh?"

Duncan doffed his cap. "I'll breathe nary a *wird.*"

"To the ewes then." Jamie led the way, their work a welcome distraction. Two short weeks remained before the breeding season began in earnest. The tups were already pastured nearby, their strong scent wafting across the *dry stane dyke*, preparing the ewes for the mating to come. With Duncan's blessing, Jamie had chosen the most promising rams from Jock Bell's farm on Tuesday and herded them home to Auchengray. Now the ewes needed a prudent shepherd's attention. Ignoring the stiff autumn winds blowing down the hillside, Jamie tossed his coat aside, intent on the task at hand. While Duncan held each ewe in turn, Jamie clipped away the wool tags round their tails and trimmed their hooves. It was slow going, holding the knife steady, keeping the ewes calm while he worked.

"Ye're a good *herd*, lad," Duncan said, warm regard in his voice. "Henry Stewart learned ye well."

Jamie released a wriggling ewe from his grasp. "I haven't Stew's patience, Duncan, but I'm grateful for all he taught me when I was a boy. Please God, I'll see the man before he's finished breeding the ewes at Glentrool."

They worked through one sheepfold, then the next, as the sun sank closer to the horizon. Satisfied with his labors, Jamie stood to stretch his legs and shake the tension from his arms. The air had grown cooler still. He was glad to slip into the coat he'd nigh forgotten.

Duncan lifted his face toward the darkening sky. "The gloaming comes, the day is spent…"

"The sun goes out of sight," Jamie finished for him, nudging the man's elbow. "Alexander Hume, is it?"

"Aye," Duncan grunted. "A man o' the kirk, Mr. Hume. From Fife or thereabout."

Jamie knew better than to tease the overseer for reciting a line of poetry. Duncan, wise in the ways of shepherding, was also well read and canny as they came. Though a man of many talents, he was quick to credit the Almighty for all of them. Would that Duncan Hastings were his father-in-law instead of crafty Lachlan McBride.

The two men headed down the hill toward the mains, hurrying their steps as the light faded to a silvery gray. "Tell the family I'm bound to Newabbey," Jamie called over his shoulder as they neared the back door. "I've hardly enough time to see to my ablutions and a change of clothes."

"I'll make yer apologies for ye," Duncan promised as Jamie crossed the threshold, discarding his soiled boots by the door. Heading up the stair in his stocking feet, he called for Hugh, valet to both Jamie and his uncle when the manservant wasn't saddled with other tasks. Appearing with comb and brush in hand, Hugh smoothed Jamie's brown hair into a neat tail and dressed him in a clean shirt, then saw that his waistcoat and breeches were brushed. Jamie's boots, polished to a rich luster by one of the maids, soon rested outside his bedroom door.

"Leana will thank you for this, Hugh." Jamie yanked on his boots, frowning when the mantel clock down the stair chimed the half-hour. He'd spent more time with the ewes than he'd intended. And entirely too much time with Rose.

Hugh nodded toward the hall. "Willie saw tae yer mount, sir. He's waitin' at the back door."

"God bless the man for his trouble," Jamie called out, taking the steps two at a time. "And you as well, Hugh." Moments later he was astride his gelding, Walloch, and thundering down the rural lane that led to Newabbey. The night wind, sharp against his face, cleared his mind of all but the hours ahead. He would see his son again. *Ian.* Leana had chosen the name weeks ago. Could he blame her for doing so when he'd seemed to care so little? He cared plenty now and would make that plain this night. Rising in his stirrups, he called his son's name aloud, announcing it to the countryside, shouting against the wind. "Ian James McKie!" He favored the middle name especially.

Walloch's hooves pounded against the hardened dirt, kicking up dust behind them. The east Galloway earth cried out for rain. Farther west, in the glen of Loch Trool, such dry spells were rare. His last letter from home, a fortnight past, described bright clumps of rowan berries turned scarlet against the changing leaves. His chest tightened at the thought of it. *Home.* Whether his brother Evan would welcome him or not, Jamie intended to return to Glentrool and claim his inheritance before winter.

Not far to his right he heard the meandering waters of Newabbey Pow. The acrid smell of the snuff mill mingled with the fragrant scent from the pines that crowded the northern edge of the road. He crossed the bridge into the village, passing by Newabbey corn mill, fed by the waters of Loch Kindar flowing through a long and sinuous *lade* from the sheep *burn*. The village proper consisted mostly of single-story cottages made of whinstone or granite. On both sides of the street doors were shut tight, and chimneys exhaled peat smoke into the night sky. Even before he saw the candles in the window of the manse, Jamie fancied he could hear Ian crying for him, bleating like a newborn lamb. He leaned down to whisper in Walloch's ear, "Hurry, man! That's my son you're keeping me from."

Less than a quarter mile and he was there, met at the door by Reverend Gordon, a man of high morals and rigid opinions. "Your wife was becoming concerned, Mr. McKie. 'Tis good you're here at last. My grandson Edward will tend to your horse."

Jamie handed the reins to the shy lad who appeared at his grandfather's beckoning, then pulled off his hat and followed the older man into the hall. The heat of a wood fire assailed him, as did the tantalizing aroma of cooked meat. To his left was the dining room with the long table already laid for supper; to his right, the door to the spence where Leana had labored. Did he not know every crack in those panels, every knot in that wood?

Reverend Gordon turned and caught Jamie staring. "Look familiar, lad?"

"Aye," Jamie confessed. "I spent the better part of the Sabbath with my ear pressed against that door."

"No need to wait in the hall this evening." Reverend Gordon pointed toward the spence door, then walked past it, heading toward the back of the manse, talking over his shoulder as he did. "Escort your wife into the dining room at seven, if you will. I'll see to your son's baptism after family worship." Though Jamie knew the lad would be formally introduced to the community on the Sabbath at his *kirkin,* there was no point delaying Ian's baptism. Not when the babe was born under the minister's roof.

Jamie tapped on the door, then entered at Leana's soft greeting. The room felt warmer than the hall, though only a handful of candles lit the corners. Close by the hearth stood his wife, her pale skin lit by the glowing peat fire. She cradled Ian against her neck, nuzzling his head with her cheek, humming as she did, her expression serene.

Jamie stood in place, touched by the gentle tableau. Had his own mother held him so tenderly? One year ago, when he'd arrived at Auchengray, he had stumbled upon Leana in the same pose, holding a neighbor's bairn. How different she looked to him now that she was his wife and the child his son. Her fair hair was gathered into a loose swirl on top of her head. Her figure, more womanly than he remembered, strained at the seams of her blue gown. Yet it was her full mouth, stretched into a smile when she turned toward him, that transformed Leana into something else altogether.

"Jamie!" she said. "You look as if you've seen—"

"An angel." He moved toward her slowly, almost reverently. "I've seen angels, you ken. In my dream at the cairn."

"Oh, Jamie." She blushed as she held out Ian for him to see. " 'Tis only your wife, grateful for clean hair and a fresh gown."

Touching her elbow, he stepped closer and peered at the sleeping infant, marveling at the tiny fists, the strongly drawn brows. His chest swelled until it ached. *A kind wife. A fine son.* More than he'd hoped for and a great deal more than he deserved. "Ian looks content," he said, then met her clear gaze again. "And so do you." Jamie led her away from the hearth, his fingers pressed against the small of her back. "Neda has been giving me favorable reports. I trust she's telling me the truth."

"Neda could never do otherwise," Leana reminded him as they perched side by side on the edge of the bed. She eased Ian into the crook of her arm, brushing his tiny mouth with her fingertip. "Ian and I are well cared for here, but in truth, I'm eager for home."

"So am I," Jamie agreed, filled with a sudden resolve. The time had come to tell her of his plans. "Eager to go home, that is."

"Home?" Leana looked at him, her confusion evident. "But you only just arrived."

"Not home to Auchengray." His tone was low but firm. "Home to Glentrool."

Five

Stay, stay at home, my heart, and rest;
Home-keeping hearts are happiest.
HENRY WADSWORTH LONGFELLOW

Home to Glentrool. The notion steeped inside Leana like tea brewing in a pot. A new life without her father's undue influence. A grandmother for Ian. And Jamie all to herself. *Och!* Was it possible?

"As soon as both of you are strong enough—perhaps before Martinmas, long before Yule—I'll hire a post chaise to take us west across Galloway, along the Solway coast to Creetown and Monnigaff, then north to the glen of Loch Trool."

Leana smiled at the picture his words drew. "Then you've told Father your plans?"

"Nae, I have not." He glanced away for a moment. "But I will soon enough."

Her father's voice prodded at her conscience. *There'll be no running off to Glentrool with my grandson.* To share that news with Jamie now would spoil their evening together; to wait until another day meant striking a flint to her father's temper and to her husband's as well.

"Jamie…" She pulled the babe closer, as if he might provide the strength she needed. "I'm afraid Father expects us to remain at Auchengray."

Jamie's eyes narrowed. "For how long?"

"For good."

Jamie bolted to his feet and faced the door as though he could not bear to look at her. "Did you agree to this?"

She rose as well, running a nervous hand over Ian's silken hair. "I would never agree to anything on your behalf, Jamie."

Her husband spun round, frustration coming off him in waves. "But you agreed to tell me."

"Aye," she whispered, her eyes beginning to fill. "To my shame, I did."

"How like Lachlan, to put so burdensome a task on someone else's shoulders." He shook his head, clearly disgusted, as he paced the floor. "'Tis no fault of yours, Leana. You've done naught but your duty, as I must do by my own father. Alec McKie will not take kindly to the heir of Glentrool being raised three days' journey from our lands."

"You'll talk to Father then?"

"Nae, I'll simply *tell* the man," he fumed. "There'll be no discussion on the subject." When Jamie turned to look at her, his expression softened. "Come, lass. As Duncan would say, dinna *fash* yerself. You'll come home to Auchengray on the Sabbath, as planned, then home to Glentrool before Yule. For good." He rested one hand on hers, the other on Ian's head, binding them together as he had on the birthing night. "'Twill be just the three of us, Leana."

Relief swept over her like a *freshening* wind off the Solway. "You ken what the *Buik* says: 'A threefold cord is not quickly broken.'"

"Aye." The hint of a shadow crossed Jamie's features, then was gone. "Aye, the three of us," he repeated, offering a faint smile at last. "Reverend Gordon tells me our son will be baptized this night."

"So he will. One of the housemaids promised to watch over him while we break bread with the Gordons. Ian has already enjoyed his supper." She eased the babe onto her shoulder and rubbed his back in small circles as she moved toward the hearth, listening for the last bit of air to escape from his stomach. "Willie brought our old cradle yesterday. Might you help me get him settled? It's difficult for me to bend down just now."

Jamie hastened to assist her, though his eyes widened as she pressed the bundled infant into his arms. "You can manage," she assured him. Seeing how carefully he knelt beside the cradle, Leana resisted the urge to correct him—*Keep his blanket wrapped tight! Mind his wee head!*—though she offered a silent prayer of thanks when Ian was in his bed. The cradle made of oak had once held her mother, then her, and then Rose. Now, lined with plain linen and decorated with a sprig of dill for protection, the sturdy wooden cradle welcomed the newest offspring of the McBrides.

"I've handled many a newborn lamb," Jamie confessed, rising to stand by her side. "Still, I've never held anything so dear to me."

"I feel just the same." Leana slid her hand in the crook of his arm, taking pleasure in the solid warmth of him. "You'll make a fine father, Mr. McKie."

"And you, a finer mother." His broad hand, grown callused from his ceaseless labors, covered hers. When he inclined his head, she accepted the silent invitation, leaning into him, closing her eyes as she sank against his shoulder. Exhaustion seeped through her bones like treacle.

The loud knock at the door startled them both. "Mistress McKie?" A young woman's voice. "Time for supper."

Leana straightened, touching a hand to her hair as she reluctantly moved away from Jamie. "Come in." She nodded at the housemaid as she entered. "The child's asleep and shouldn't need me for an hour or more." Leana paused at the doorway and glanced over her shoulder, apprehensive about leaving Ian. She'd not stepped outside the room for three days, most of which she'd spent cradling him in her arms. Could he manage without her?

The dark-haired maid curtsied, dipping her white cap in Leana's direction. "Yer bairn will be weel looked after, Mistress McKie."

Jamie brushed away Leana's concerns like cobwebs as he guided her across the hall. " 'Twill be good for you to spend an hour with your husband." His breath against her ear soothed her even more than his words. On the night of Ian's birth Jamie had promised her that he was a changed man; the proof strolled beside her into the dining room, his arm circled round her waist.

The family stood by their chairs, waiting for the McKies to take their places at the far end of the crowded table. Clusters of candles lit the faces of more than a dozen souls who'd gathered for the meal. The Gordons, their three grown sons—brown haired, brown eyed, and solemn—along with assorted wives and children, hovered over the empty plates, anticipating the supper hour before them. "Good to have you both dining with us this evening," Mistress Gordon murmured as Leana and Jamie eased past her.

"We're grateful for your hospitality." Jamie paused by his chair and bowed to their hostess. "In particular, you've been more than generous to offer the use of your spence for my wife and son."

Mistress Gordon, a small woman with a pleasant, round face and hair the color of lamb's wool, beamed at them. "A healthy child born under our roof blesses the house and all who are in it." She motioned at her husband sitting at the head of the table, his back toward the roaring hearth. "Will you pray, Reverend, before our dinner loses its flavor?"

Leana ducked her head and smiled. *No chance of that.* Mistress Gordon's mutton, a staple at every parish gathering, was seasoned with enough salt and nutmeg to test the hardiest of palates. After a lengthy prayer, the meal commenced in an orderly manner, served by a staff accustomed to life at the manse, where visitors were commonplace. Reverend Gordon presided over the quiet table with a grim expression, arching an eyebrow at one grandson or another wiggling in his seat. A fancy mold of marmalade pudding appeared at the last, with hot custard sauce drizzled over and round it. The children clapped with glee until their mortified parents hushed them. Leana shared the lads' delight at the treat, winking at them as the sweet pudding was spooned into their dishes. Already she could imagine Ian sitting at table, spoon in hand, cheering for his pudding.

Ian. She must not think of him just now, or her milk might stain her gown. Neda had warned her that tomorrow would be the worst day, that her breasts would grow swollen and painful when her milk appeared in earnest. She must meditate on something else, and quickly. Her gaze searched the room and settled on the man seated across from her at the end of the long, linen-draped table. *Jamie.* Aye, she'd gladly look at him for hours. He glanced up from his dish and smiled as a spoonful of pudding disappeared into his mouth. No words were spoken, but much was said across the table.

In a matter of days they would share the same bed at Auchengray. Jamie had not reached for her in the shadowy confines of their curtained box bed for many months, in part because of the babe, but more likely because of his feelings for her sister. Would he ever stop wishing he'd claimed Rose for his bride? Leana lowered her chin, afraid of what Jamie might see in her eyes. Moving to Glentrool this winter would not ease the remorse of what she'd done to her sister, but it might let her breathe again. It might let her love Jamie without apology. She looked up and found Jamie's green eyes fixed on hers, the planes of his freshly shaven face set aglow by the flickering candlelight.

She started when a servant's hand appeared before her, whisking away the last of her supper dishes. "It was delicious," she announced to no one in particular, though Mistress Gordon bobbed her head at the compliment.

Reverend Gordon opened the family Bible and smoothed the pages with his large hands as his deep voice boomed across the cleared table. "Come, ye children, hearken unto me: I will teach you the fear of the LORD." She knew the psalm well, and, aye, she would teach it to her children. But she would start with the first line: *I will bless the LORD at all times: his praise shall continually be in my mouth.* She had praised God when Ian was born. And she would praise him when Ian was baptized this night, when the dour minister doused his thumb in spittle and sprinkled the babe's head thrice. Bless the Lord she would, for mightily had God blessed her undeserving womb.

Leana tried to pay attention, though like the minister's sermons on the Sabbath, his words were long on affliction and short on mercy. The younger Gordons, despite many pointed looks from their fathers, fidgeted throughout the hour until at last their grandfather put aside the Buik and folded his hands to dismiss them with a final prayer. The assembly rose at the conclusion of the blessing, the visiting family members drifting toward the front door, collecting coats for the short walk home.

Jamie and Leana tarried in the darkened hall, waiting for the minister to join them for the private baptism. Without a word Jamie moved closer to her. Leana's heart quickened as elbow brushed against elbow. By accident or intent, their hands met among the folds of her gown. Leana held her breath. Jamie's fingers laced through hers. Hidden by the fabric, a thousand unspoken words were shared in a single clasp.

Jamie, I love you. That was what she would say if she could. *I will always love you.*

Though the hall was faintly lit, she could still distinguish the lines of his handsome face. Strong nose. Tapered jaw. Bold brow. Some new emotion decorated his features this night. Tenderness perhaps. A willingness to be loved by her. For the moment it was more than enough.

Six

The rose is sweetest wash'd with morning dew.

SIR WALTER SCOTT

Hush," Rose whispered, "or Father will hear you!"

Four tiny kittens, mere weeks old, tumbled about inside her sagging apron. Rose clutched them to her waist as she darted back into her bedroom and nudged the door closed with her shoulder. Most of the household was still asleep, though dawn would soon sweep aside the curtain of night and usher in the Sabbath. Her plan was simple: Bear the kittens safely to the village, then seek out her friend Susanne Elliot. Surely the grocer's daughter wouldn't refuse so dear a gift.

"A newborn babe and a litter of kittens will not both thrive under the same roof," her father had announced yestreen, a sour look on his face. "I'll see that Duncan drowns them in the burn before nightfall." Rose had cornered Duncan in the kitchen minutes later and begged him not to do Lachlan's bidding.

"Yer faither is right," Duncan had cautioned her. "Wi' yer nephew comin' home after services in the morn, there's nae place for *kittlins* at Auchengray. 'Tis ill luck, and ye ken it weel, lass."

Aye, she knew the superstition but could not bear the cruel sentence. "I'll find a home for them, Duncan," she'd vowed. Now holding the corners of her apron in one hand, she grasped Leana's willow basket, pilfered from the stillroom, and placed it on the seat of her sister's reading chair. A small stack of unread volumes—Richardson, Burney, Haywood—stood in a neglected pile by the window. Leana would have little time for books now that she had Ian to care for. And Jamie.

I cannot love you, Rose. His words still bruised her heart. How was it that her sister had a husband and a babe to call her own, and all she had was a lap full of kittens?

With a petulant sigh, Rose released the contents of her apron into the cloth-lined basket. The furry bundles, no bigger than Jamie's fist, rolled on top of one another, tiny claws unsheathed. Two of the kittens were painted with gray stripes, one was as orange as a harvest moon, and the last, her favorite, had coal black fur with white-tipped paws. Watch them drowned? Nae, she would not. Rose tossed aside her empty apron, hastily bathed her face, then braided her hair as the faint light of day appeared in the casement window.

Jamie would think her rescue efforts childish. "Then I shan't mention it to him," she announced to the mewling kittens, her spirits sagging. Jamie had loved her once and now insisted he did not. She had not loved him at first, and when love finally came, it came too late. "So unfair," she murmured, covering the basket with a loose cloth to muffle the sound. It was hard to imagine life without Jamie at the center of it. Nae, it was impossible.

She'd told him that if there was to be another man, she would choose him. *Nae. Let the man choose me.* She would not let her heart be broken again, pining after someone she could not claim. For a twelvemonth she had ignored the other lads in the parish. Much as it pained her to confess it, perhaps the time had come to let them have a look at her.

Susanne Elliot was the perfect person to advise her, a dear friend since they were eight years of age, when they'd giggled incessantly behind the *dominie's* back at the village school. They'd confided their secrets to each other and poured their dreams into each other's hearts. Aye, Susanne would be just the one to point out an eligible man in the parish. Someone to take her mind off Jamie. Someone to mend her heart.

Rose sneaked out the front door, the borrowed basket in one hand, her skirts gathered in the other to spare them being dampened by the dew. The slate-colored sky hung low with clouds, and the air smelled of wet leaves and pungent peat smoke. Sheepdogs barked in the distance, unaware of breaking the Sabbath silence. She pulled her wool cloak tighter and shot a wary glance over her shoulder. Might someone be watching from the windows? Rose fairly ran toward the end of the lane, where Willie, the *orraman* of Auchengray, waited with the two-wheeled chaise. Driving her to the village whenever she required it was among the odd jobs that landed on Willie's aging shoulders. So did keeping secrets from the laird, though all the servants had mastered that skill.

Willie guided Rose into the small carriage, then eased down beside her, nudging old Bess forward with a familiar command. The mare took off with a jolt, sending them rocking back and forth on the springs until at last Bess found her gait. Rose pulled the basket closer while Willie loosened his grip on the reins and settled against the cushioned seat. "Have ye warned the Elliots tae expect ye sae early in the morn?"

She dismissed his concerns with a blithe toss of her braid. " 'Twill not be so early by the time we arrive. Eight o' the clock, I'd say."

Willie grunted, surveying the willow basket that danced on her lap. The short ride east to Newabbey passed without incident, despite the threatening clouds that shrouded the countryside. The village consisted of one long, meandering street with a row of houses tucked along either side, perhaps fifty in all, each one with a name by the door. Bridgeview. Abbeyside. Millburn.

Bess clip-clopped up to the Elliots' cottage—Ingleneuk—whinnying as she did, shaking the mist from her dun-colored mane. Round the door grew an old yew, tended by loving hands that had coaxed the evergreen branches to bend and twist. Bright red berries stood in stark contrast to the dense green foliage, where a blackbird perched, stabbing at the berries with his bright yellow beak, ignoring the newcomers. Willie tugged on the reins and brought the mare to a gentle stop, then turned to fix his rheumy eyes on Rose. "Whan yer faither asks why ye've left for the kirk lang afore the rest, what'll I say tae the man?"

"Tell him I wanted to help my sister prepare for the kirkin of the babe." Rose handed Willie her basket while she jumped down from the carriage unassisted. "I am, by Leana's choice, Ian's godmother. The duty falls to me to see him presented today, aye?"

Willie nodded. " 'Tis a meikle task, being the *kimmer*. Ye'd best keep those kittlins far *awa* from the babe."

"That's why you brought me here first, Willie. Tell Neda I'll be waiting for her at the manse." She waved him off, then tapped on the grocer's front door, donning her most persuasive smile. It *was* rather early in the day to pay a visit.

Mistress Elliot swung the door wide. Her mouth stood agape as well. "R-Rose?" The middle-aged woman's gaze followed the departing chaise, then shifted to the basket and its noisy contents. "Whatever have you brought us, lass?"

Rose flicked aside the cloth. "Kittens! Aren't they dear?"

Susanne's mother eyed the basket askance as she motioned Rose into the low-beamed cottage. All was as tidy as a widow's cupboard, the rooms scrubbed for the Sabbath, the hearth swept clean. The aroma of a cooked breakfast—bacon, porridge, and bannocks—hung in the air. Mistress Elliot, as slender as her husband was round, shook her head. "You'll have a time of it, Rose, if you mean to leave those kittens here. Mr. Elliot won't allow the beasts anywhere near the shop."

Rose smiled. Unlike her own father, Colin Elliot had a soft heart where his daughter was concerned. "Might I speak with Susanne?"

"She's about to have her breakfast. Come bide a wee while. You look as though a saucer of tea would do you good."

Rose followed the woman into the dining room, where the table was laid. Stout candles like beeswax soldiers marched down the center of the table, and pewter plates shone like silvery moons. Her mouth watered at the fresh bannocks and jars of gooseberry jam displayed on the sideboard. "If it's not too much trouble…"

"Och!" The woman waved her toward a chair. "What's another mouth to feed? Susaaaanne!" Mistress Elliot disappeared into the kitchen while Rose found a hiding place for her basket. The kittens would need feeding as well.

Susanne hurried into the room, a wooden *spurtle* in her hand, her face more flushed than usual from stirring the hot porridge. The girl's brown eyes shone at the sight of her. "Rose! You've come to Ingleneuk to break your fast with us, have you?"

"So it seems. I've also brought you a present." Amid much squealing the litter was introduced and a scheme duly hatched for their safe upbringing. Susanne and Rose tucked them in a dry corner of the *byre* amid the lowing cows, where they left the kittens circled about a bowl of fresh milk. The lasses returned to the table moments before Susanne's brothers bounded into the room, shoving one another into their seats before they realized they had an unexpected guest.

"Miss McBride!" breathed Neil Elliot, his expression torn between dismay and wonder at finding her there. Neil was two years older and two hands taller than Rose, an awkward though earnest young man, who'd fancied her from childhood. February last they'd drawn each other's names in the Valentines Dealing, from a bonnet full of names passed about a circle of friends. Each lad and lass pulled out the name of someone to be his or her sweetheart, claiming them for a year. Rose had brushed aside the sentimental custom, since her heart had Jamie's name written on it at the time. Things were different now. Seated at the Elliots' table, she could at least be polite to Neil.

"Mr. Elliot," Rose said demurely, lowering her lashes. She remembered describing Neil once to Jamie—"crooked teeth and more hair than one of our collies"—and how it'd pleased her to see Jamie's look of relief. As if Jamie could ever have lost her to poor, bumbling Neil! Though he surely was an amiable fellow. And he did seem more than a little taken with her.

"Miss McBride," Neil said again, sketching a slight bow. "I'm glad…that is, we're *all* delighted…to have you join us."

"Sit you down, lad." His father, presiding at the head of the long table, waved his butter knife toward an empty chair. "No need to stand on ceremony with a neighbor you've kenned all your life." The grocer turned his large, cabbage-shaped head toward her and smiled affably. "Have a rasher of bacon, Rose. Sold most of what I had on Friday at the Dumfries market, though I kept some back for our Sabbath breakfast. Right good it is."

Rose dutifully ate, taking small bites and minding her manners, aware that Neil Elliot was watching her every move. She could not help but notice that his suit of clothes fit him rather smartly. His teeth weren't as crooked as she'd remembered, and his thick auburn hair was tamed into a handsome tail at the nape of his neck. Not that he could hold a candle to Jamie, she reminded herself, stealing another glance across the table. But a girl could do worse than the eldest son of Colin Elliot, a prosperous grocer with farmland outside the village.

Listening to the family's good-natured banter, Rose noted the affection Neil had for all of them and they for him. How different breakfast was at Ingleneuk compared to the austerity of Auchengray! Though not as boisterous as his younger brothers, Neil held his own, watching her all the while, as if seeking her approval. Susanne didn't seem to notice, but her father did, grinning behind his jam-covered bannocks.

When the meal came to a close, Rose dabbed the corners of her mouth with a napkin, then folded her hands in her lap and smiled in Neil's direction. "Mr. Elliot, I—"

"Neil," he corrected her. "My father is right. Formalities are hardly needed between old friends."

"Neil, then." Her cheeks warmed beneath his steady gaze. Och, how strange it felt to have another man look at her so! "I am bound to serve as my nephew's kimmer this morn and so must take my leave."

Neil bolted to his feet. "Might I walk you to the manse, Rose?"

"You might." Rose pretended not to see the blush of pleasure that colored his neck or the look of astonishment on Susanne's face. Though the arm he offered shook, his step was sure as he guided her toward the door.

Rose bade the family farewell, then followed Neil into the street. Despite the gloomy skies above, the day was off to a promising start. Four kittens had been spared a gruesome fate, and her own gloved hand rested on a manly forearm.

Tentative with each other at first, they spoke briefly of the weather and of the kirkin to come. "He's a healthy lad, I hear," Neil said, then colored slightly, as if discussing such things might not be proper for someone outside the family.

"Verra healthy," she assured him, trying to put him at ease. Did Neil want children of his own someday? Might she test the waters without stirring too deep? She smiled up at him as they walked toward the manse. "Now that you're eighteen, will you be joining your father in the grocery business? Or do you have other plans for your future?"

"Plans?" His mouth fell open, then just as quickly shut. "Aye, my plans are to settle in Newabbey. To…to marry. Start a family." Neil looked straight ahead as he spoke. His flat tone of voice gave away nothing.

"I see." He wanted children then, though perhaps she had misjudged his interest in her. "And who's the bonny lass you hope to claim as your bride?" She pulled a name out of nowhere, baiting him. " 'Tis no secret you favor Grace McLaren."

"Grace? Och, I barely ken the girl!" Neil fumed, pulling Rose to an abrupt stop. He planted himself in front of her and captured both her hands in his, ignoring the curious stares of nearby villagers. "See here, Rose McBride. You ken verra well—"

"I ken nae such thing," she teased, slipping her hands free from his grasp. She'd judged him correctly; he did care for her, it seemed. Still, it was one thing to walk out arm in arm yet quite another to let him declare his intentions so publicly. And so soon. She lowered her voice. "Suppose we save those words for a more private time and place."

A look of triumph shone in his brown eyes. "Suppose we do, Rose." Neil resumed their walk, launching into a description of his last trip to market in Dumfries, no doubt hoping to impress her.

"I will be in Dumfries come January," she confessed, "attending Carlyle School for Young Ladies. Perhaps you might visit me when you come to town for market day."

"Aye," he said, though with little enthusiasm.

Och, Rose! Whatever was she thinking, making such an offer? Too bold by half, not at all proper for a lady. She looked away, ashamed of herself. "Forgive me if I've offended you."

"Offended me?" He laughed, patting her hand. "Lass, 'twas the thought of you leaving Newabbey that gave me pause."

Oh.

Moments later Neil deposited her at the manse gate with a gentlemanly bow, pressing a kiss to the inside of her wrist, just above her glove, before releasing her. The intimate gesture brought a flush to her cheeks—not of pleasure but of embarrassment. "Thank you, Neil," was all she managed before she spun away, running the last few steps, her heartbeat matching her rapid knock on the door. If she was not very careful, Neil Elliot might presume too much.

The manse door swung open. "Your sister awaits and the babe as well." Mistress Gordon beckoned her inside, glancing over Rose's shoulder as she did. "Young Elliot, is it?"

"Not really. You see—"

"I see a fine young man and a fair young miss." A knowing smile decorated the woman's plain face. "Such things often lead to marriage banns, you ken. And perhaps children of your own someday."

Children. Aye, Rose wanted those. She watched Neil saunter toward Ingleneuk, his broad shoulders thrown back. Might Neil Elliot be the man to make her a wife and a mother? She stood there, letting the possibility sink in, feeling her heart sink with it. Jamie was the husband she'd truly wanted. And she'd hoped her babe would bear the name McKie.

Yet hope could not live where it was not welcome.

Let me go, Rose. Please.

Seven

Where did you come from, baby dear?
Out of the everywhere into here.
GEORGE MACDONALD

H ere you are, Rose." Leana delivered the infant, heavy with sleep,
into her sister's waiting arms. "Your nephew is clean and fed,
ready for his walk about the village for the kirkin." She rested her hand
on Rose's shoulder and was glad when her sister did not pull away.
"Bless you for doing this."

" 'Tis the babe who receives the blessing today, not me." Rose traced
Ian's eyebrows with her fingertip. "I am only his kimmer."

Her sister had not stopped gazing at Ian since she'd walked into the
spence. "He has Jamie's mouth," Rose said at last, smiling to herself.

"Aye, and his broad forehead." Leana brushed back the downy tuft
of hair that fell across his brow. She'd done the same for his father a time
or two. *And so has Rose. Many times more.*

A familiar ache swelled in Leana's heart. Had Jamie put Rose aside
for good, as Neda had assured her yestermorn? "See for yerself, Leana,"
she'd said. "Yer sister nae longer hides the lad's heart in her pocket."

Leana prayed it was true. Loving Jamie came easily; trusting him
had proven difficult. Though he'd not taken Rose to his bed, Jamie had
lavished her sister with tender kisses and constant endearments, month
after painful month. Had he indeed changed? Leana would never wish
Rose one moment of unhappiness. But Ian needed a good father and
she an honest husband. Surely the Almighty would provide another
suitor for Rose.

Leana enveloped her sister and son in a loose embrace, gathering
them close to her. *Please see to their needs, Lord, for I love them both.* For
a long moment the two sisters stood in silence, breathing in the milky
scent of the slumbering babe between them. "The laird and servants of

Auchengray will pound down our door shortly." Leana pressed her cheek against Rose's, a habit from childhood, then released both sister and child. " 'Tis time we made ready for them."

She'd already packed the few personal items Neda had brought to the manse for her during the week—a spare gown, linen shifts, stockings, and the like. Leana was grateful for the small task of packing since a new mother was not permitted to work in any fashion until she was churched. Had it been only a week since Ian was born? The cradle waited for the journey home, empty except for a small pillow, a Galloway custom meant to keep the babe safe from harm until he was returned to his oaken bed.

"Be a good lad for your auntie, aye?" Leana pinned a tiny bag of salt to Ian's blanket, an auld wives' method of warding off witches. "She will make you a splendid kimmer."

Rose looked up, truly meeting her gaze for the first time since she'd arrived. "I'm an unmarried girl, the only requirement."

"Nae, that's not so. Godparents must also bear good luck about them." Leana tucked back the wispy strands of hair along her sister's brow. "No one is luckier than a dark-haired lass like you."

"Lucky?" Rose stuck out her lower lip. "You are the one with a husband and a child, Leana."

She tried not to hear the hint of envy in her sister's words. "Your time is coming, Rose. God will provide."

Both sisters turned at the sound of a male voice in the hall, then a knock at the spence door. Jamie, his face flushed from the ride, stepped into the room and swept his hat from his head. "What a grand sight. My son in the arms of his kimmer and my wife in her favorite gown."

"With a new sash." Leana pressed a hand to her waist to show him, then wished she hadn't drawn attention to the thickness she found there. No whalebone corset could undo the damage that nine months had wrought. She waved her hand toward the door and prayed Jamie hadn't noticed the changes in her figure. "If you might store my things in the chaise, I believe we're almost ready to set out."

No sooner had Jamie disappeared with her trunk than Neda bustled through the doorway, followed by Eliza, a sandy-haired lass of fifteen years who served as lady's maid to Leana between endless domestic duties. "Ye're wearin' somethin' new wi' yer auld gown," Neda said, approval in her voice. "Yer faither will follow shortly. Eliza, see what ye can do wi' Mistress McKie's hair."

A brush was located, and efficient Eliza went to work, smoothing her mistress's blond strands into a becoming twist, chattering away all the while. Rose sat on the edge of the bed cooing at Ian, while Jamie wrapped a handful of smoldering peat in a bit of leather. Duncan tended to the last of her parcels, directed by her father, who seldom missed an opportunity to give orders. In the midst of such hubbub, Leana could do little more than press a hand to her stomach to quell her nerves.

Mistress Gordon appeared at the door, her starched white cap in place for the Sabbath. "The kirk bell is about to toll the hour," she announced. "Best be about your business while there's time."

They arranged themselves in order, then Rose proceeded from the room first, clutching Ian against her as she headed for the stair. To assure any newborn a prosperous future, tradition required that he be carried up three stairsteps before venturing out of doors. Lachlan McBride stood waiting for them at the bottom step, a determined look on his face. "I'm here to make certain no detail is overlooked for my grandson's kirkin."

"Especially a custom involving riches," Leana whispered to Jamie, who walked hand in hand beside her. Her husband acknowledged her comment with a wink and a warm squeeze of her fingers, an unexpected pleasure.

They watched Rose ascend and descend without mishap, then followed her through the hall while the household lined the walls on either side, smiling and calling out, "God bless the bairn," in honor of the occasion. Once through the door, the party aimed toward the kirk, mere steps away.

Gray as the sky was, Leana blinked at the raw light of day. Her sensitive eyes had grown accustomed to dim interiors and the soft glow of candles during her week of confinement. As her vision adjusted, she discovered a blur of faces waiting for them, most familiar, some not. It seemed the whole village lingered in the street, delaying their Sabbath duties to watch the familiar ceremony unfold.

Jamie threw his pouch of still-hot peat onto the street behind them, warding off any mischievous fairies who might spirit Leana away to nurse their own fairy children in some distant glen. He brushed the ash off his gloves, then claimed her hand once more. "Much as they might want my wife, they cannot have her."

My wife. Her mouth formed a timorous smile as she walked forward, happier than she could ever remember.

Just in front of her, Rose performed her role of kimmer with relish, holding her head high, giving a regal nod to favored neighbors along the way. The Auchengray household began the first of three turns round the kirk, traveling the same direction as a clock, not *widdershins*. Leana breathed a prayer with each step—for Ian's good health, for Jamie's newfound faithfulness, for Rose's future happiness, for her father's willingness to let them leave for Glentrool before Yule. Jamie intended to press Lachlan for his blessing that evening at supper. She feared how her father might respond but dared not dampen Jamie's resolve.

All at once Elliot Elliot, Susanne's youngest brother, broke free from his mother's grasp and ran up to Rose. His brown trousers, handed down from an older brother, were already too short by a handbreadth, and his wrists protruded well beyond his neat cuffs. Mistress Elliot would no doubt see both hems lengthened by the next Sabbath. "You had breakfast at my house today," said the boy twice blessed with the family name. He yanked at Rose's sleeve and jostled the baby. "Now it's your turn to give *me* some food."

Leana could not hide her surprise. Whatever had prompted Rose to join the Elliots for breakfast? Her sister had said nary a word about visiting Ingleneuk that morning. Then Leana noticed Susanne's oldest brother, Neil, regarding Rose with frank adoration. *Ah.* Already a prayer answered.

Her sister turned, her cheeks as rosy as her name. "Neda, if you would, please." Neda handed the eager lad a sweet cake flavored with arrowroot and vanilla and a bit of hard cheese, which he gobbled down beneath Rose's watchful gaze. "What say you, Elliot?"

"God bless the bairn!" he crowed, and all within earshot applauded.

The gift from the babe had been offered and received and the child blessed, a portent of good things to come for young Ian McKie. The family circled the kirk twice more, then were greeted at the door by a somber Reverend Gordon, his face as dismal as the sky.

"Mistress McKie," he intoned, handing her a lighted candle. "Enter into the kingdom of God." Leana, Jamie, and Rose were ushered inside and directed down the narrow aisle until they stood before the raised pulpit with its turnpike stair. From his lofty post the minister prayed at length, calling down a blessing on mother and child, then led the congregation in reciting a verse from the book of *Paraphrases*.

> My soul and spirit fill'd with joy,
>   my God and Saviour praise;
> Whose goodness did from poor estate
>   his humble handmaid raise.

As the last echo of their voices faded, Leana watched Rose present Jamie with the babe, as befitted the kimmer's duty. 'Twas the father who would see the child blessed by the minister and held up for the congregation's inspection. The ebony centers of her sister's eyes, wider than ever in the dim sanctuary, shone with unshed tears. "Behold, your son," Rose whispered, holding Ian before her like an offering.

Leana released Jamie's hand with some reluctance, taking a half step backward, giving him room to cradle his arms beneath Rose's. Leana observed their bent arms touch, then tarry. Jamie did not move. Nor did Rose. Though she could not see Jamie's face, the look her sister gave him burned like coals freshly stirred to life.

Nae! Leana stared down at the floor. The candle in her hand shook, spilling wax on the flagstones beneath her feet. *Please, Jamie!* She could not bear to look at her husband or her sister or the son she'd borne seven days past.

Nothing had changed after all. Jamie could never care for her. Not when he still loved Rose.

Help me, Lord, for I cannot bear it.

A tear dripped to the floor and landed beside the candle wax as Leana fought for composure. The words she'd spoken when the first pangs of childbirth had brought her to her knees returned to taunt her now. *Jamie, I love you. I've always loved you.* How foolish she must have sounded! How foolish she must look now, unable to hold her head up at her own kirkin.

"Leana?" It was Jamie's voice. "Leana, what is it?"

Eight

Is it the shrewd October wind
Brings the tears into her eyes?
Does it blow so strong that she must fetch
Her breath in sudden sighs?

WILLIAM DEAN HOWELLS

Leana raised her chin, pretending it did not quiver. The room swam into focus: Jamie holding their son, Rose taking her seat in the family pew, Reverend Gordon staring hard at her across the top of his spectacles. Leana blinked, feeling disoriented. "Wh-what am I to do?"

"You are to sit," the minister informed her. "The precentor is ready for the gathering psalm."

Jamie tipped his head toward the nearest pew, and she dropped into it, her face hot with shame. Whatever must Jamie think of her, standing there like a statue? He placed Ian in her arms, then eased down next to her, sitting closer than was proper in the sanctuary. She held the babe to her chest, tucking Ian's head in the curve of her neck, her thoughts racing all the while. Perhaps she'd imagined the desire that had flowed between Jamie and Rose. Was it fear that conjured such scenes in her mind?

The service began, and Leana did all that was expected of her—standing, sitting, singing psalms, reciting verses—praying it would end quickly. Ian was growing restless, and her swollen breasts ached. Most of all, she longed to be home. *Soon,* she told herself, drawing strength from Jamie's nearness.

When the benediction was spoken, the congregants rose to stretch their stiff legs and wander out of doors, looking for a suitable spot where they might partake of the dinners they'd brought from home. Pickled beef and mutton pies were pulled from baskets and pails, as Leana and the others made their way through the crowd of well-wishers, many of whom reached up to touch the babe's blanket as Ian passed by. The threatening sky and skittish breeze did little to dampen the high spirits of the villagers for whom a healthy babe was a cause for rejoicing.

As the new family walked toward the chaise, her father fell into step beside them and appraised his grandson. "He behaved well."

"Aye, Uncle," Jamie answered for them both. "My mother in Monnigaff will be most eager to see her granbairn."

Leana stiffened. *Not here, Jamie. Not yet.*

Lachlan McBride waved his hand in an expansive gesture, as though he were scattering coins instead of words. "Tell my sister the doors of Auchengray are always open to the McKies of Glentrool."

Jamie's eyes narrowed. "I had something rather different in mind. Leana and I—"

"Look forward to visiting with them." Leana spoke with such haste that both men stopped in their tracks and turned to stare at her, prompting her to add, "Wherever that visit might take place."

Her father shifted his gaze to Jamie, then back to her. "Leana, if you are thinking of traveling to Monnigaff, you are barely fit for a short carriage ride to Auchengray, let alone an arduous journey across the moors and braes between here and Loch Trool."

"Perhaps I'm not ready at the moment," she agreed. "But I will be soon."

"Verra soon," her husband added, his voice taut. "We will speak more of this after supper, Uncle." Jamie pressed his hand against the small of her back and steered her toward the waiting chaise. Though he did not speak, his boot heels made sharp dents in the sod.

"Jamie, I'm sorry." She ducked her head to avoid the hard look in his eyes. "I should not have interfered."

"If I am to be laird of Glentrool, I must first be laird of my own family, aye?" When she nodded, he leaned closer and spoke in a gentler voice. "Trust me to handle things with your father, Leana. He will not like my decision, but he will learn to accept it." Jamie patted the curve of her back once more, then released her, raising his voice and her spirits with it. "Come, dear wife. Willie stands ready at the carriage, and Bess seems anxious to head home to her bag of oats."

The wide-eyed servant held the babe while Jamie guided Leana into the chaise. She gritted her teeth to keep from crying out in pain. Her father was right: She was in no condition to travel to Glentrool.

"Here's yer bairn." Willie relinquished Ian into her embrace. "Been *mony* a year since I held sae dear a bundle."

Leana cradled the child against her as Jamie straightened his tri-cornered hat and yanked his gloves in place. "I shall follow close behind on Walloch, should you need anything," he told her. "As to your sister…" He looked about, scanning the parishioners scattered around the kirkyard. Leana knew the moment he spotted Rose, for his posture stiffened, and the last trace of a smile disappeared.

Rose was engaged in conversation, looking up at Neil Elliot from beneath the brim of her bonnet. Laughing, flashing her teeth, twirling a tendril of hair round her finger—even from a distance Leana could see her sister's formidable charms on full display. But for whose benefit?

Jamie watched but a moment before he stormed off in her direction. "Rose! Your sister has waited long enough. Come now, at once."

Leana watched Rose make her apologies to Neil, then grab her skirts and parade past Jamie, her chin pointed straight forward. The two exchanged nary a word as they marched toward the chaise. By the time they arrived, both were red faced.

"You're to walk ahead, Rose," Jamie reminded her. He mounted Walloch as Willie urged Bess forward with a crack of his whip. Rose flounced down the main thoroughfare of Newabbey, not looking over her shoulder to see if the others followed suit, while Jamie rode along-side the carriage. "See that you keep up with her, Willie."

The orraman pulled the chaise in line behind Rose as thunder rumbled in the distance. Duncan and the other servants, who'd started for home ahead of them, would be spared the worst of it. The kirkin party might not be so fortunate. As the rising winds lifted the brim of Willie's bonnet and blew wisps of hair about Leana's face, she prayed they'd not pass a soul on the road. On the day of a babe's kirkin the family was obliged to stop and greet any and all who came along. They clattered past the corn mill at the edge of the village, crossed the bridge over the Newabbey Pow, and pressed on for Auchengray. As the rural road grew narrower and the ruts deepened, the carriage jostled about, bouncing Leana hard against the side. She cried out, awakening Ian, whose wail brought Jamie galloping to her side.

"Whatever has happened?" The carriage halted, and Jamie peered at the babe's pinched features, now the color of fresh-scrubbed beets, his toothless gums bared as though he were in agony. "Is he harmed?"

"Only hungry," Leana murmured, brushing her cheek against Ian's velvety head to soothe him. "The moment we reach Auchengray I'll see he's fed." She glanced down at her tight-fitting bodice, laced up the back as befitted the gentry, and wished it were a peasant woman's dress with fastenings in front she could untie herself. She'd stitch such a gown before the week was out, to be worn in the privacy of her own home.

Willie had given the mare a signal to continue when a figure glided out from the tall pines that edged the road. An older woman in ill-fitting, colorful garb. Not a Gypsy, for the face below her tattered bonnet was pale, the eyes a piercing blue. Leana thought she looked familiar, the sort of woman one noticed on market day lurking between the stalls, age-bent fingers hovering over the bushels of ripe fruit. Noticed, then soon forgot.

The stranger shuffled toward the chaise, her sharp gaze pointed at Ian. "I heard the greet of a newborn babe, did I not?"

Leana's pulse quickened at the voice. Not a stranger after all, but Lillias Brown, a wise woman—a *wutch,* some said—still keen on the auld ways. She lived in a stone cottage planted among the wild moorlands north of Auchengray and seldom ventured onto a public road.

Willie gripped harder on the reins. "Widow Brown, is it?"

The old woman shrugged, not taking her eyes off Ian. "*Fowk* call me Lillias." Since she refused to attend the parish kirk, Lillias was not permitted to receive communion. Most folk gave her a wide berth if they passed her on the road. Leana shrank from the edge of the carriage seat, pulling Ian tight against her.

Undaunted, the crone drew closer and smiled, revealing a crooked row of teeth. "Will ye not gie me a look at him?"

Despite her qualms, Leana could not refuse, not on the day of the child's kirkin. Lillias Brown was counted among their neighbors, however odd her ways. Leana unwrapped the blanket round Ian's face, holding him a bit higher so the woman might see him.

Lillias stared, her smile soon fading into a fierce scowl. She shook her head, backing away, and muttered something in Gaelic.

Leana thought she might be asking for the customary bit of cake and cheese. "W-we have no food to offer you, I'm afraid."

"Och! I wouldna *tak* it if ye did." The woman spun toward the woods and disappeared among the branches thick with pine cones, her departure punctuated by an ominous roll of thunder and a nervous whinny from Bess.

Rose, who'd stood speechless through it all, now hurried back to the chaise, her mouth agape. "Why did you let her look upon Ian? That woman has the evil eye, you can be sure of it!"

Leana held up her hand, dismayed to find it shaking. "Dearie, there is no need for such drama—"

"Drama, is it?" Rose's color was high and her voice with it. "You are afraid as well, my sister. Don't pretend you aren't! 'Tis a grave thing to refuse a gift of food from a bairn on his kirkin."

"Rose, you're frightening your sister," Jamie cautioned, dismounting as he spoke. "Willie, you ride Walloch while I see my wife and cousin home in the carriage." The exchange was quickly made, with Jamie seated in the middle, a McBride sister crowded on either side.

Leana was ashamed to admit how grateful she was to feel his strong shoulder pressing against hers as he held the reins, urging Bess forward. Lillias Brown *had* unnerved her, with her barbed gaze and her decided frown and her refusal of food, even though they'd had none to offer. By rights, Lillias should have walked a few steps with them, blessing the bairn with her favor. Much as Leana longed to discount the old customs, some beliefs were more troublesome to put out of mind, a curse on her babe chief among them.

"Do not worry yourself further." Jamie bent his head toward hers.

"We will *flit* from this neighborhood by autumn's end, far from that woman's influence. Be comforted in knowing the lad is baptized and kirked and therefore belongs to Almighty God and no other."

"Aye," Leana agreed, looking up at the darkening clouds. "I shall remember."

Nine

Why was an independent wish
E'er planted in my mind?
ROBERT BURNS

Nephew, I'll not hear of you taking my grandson on so perilous a journey." Lachlan McBride waved his hand dismissively, as if the matter were settled. "Auchengray is your home now. 'Tis time you accepted that fact."

Jamie gripped the mantel, where the clock ticked with dreary persistence, reminding him of the late hour. Nearly ten. The storm had subsided, leaving a few raindrops still tapping on the windowpanes. Inside the crowded spence that served as Lachlan's bedroom and study, the stale air smelled of beeswax and old books. Leather-bound ledgers, their spines cracked from constant use, lined his narrow desk. A round sterling tray with a decanter of whisky remained untouched that night. Half the household had drifted off to sleep by now. But not his uncle. Nor Jamie himself, not until he had made his intentions clear.

"I've done my duty by you, Uncle Lachlan. Even you cannot deny it." His face felt hot like the peat fire by his boots. If only his words were as sharp as an iron poker. "The time has come for me to attend to matters at Glentrool."

"I'm certain Rowena has things well in hand." Lachlan smiled, a crooked line drawn across a face weathered by sixty Scottish winters. He ran his hand back and forth over a rough spot on the mahogany table beside him, all the while staring at the carpet as though remembering something. "My sister has a talent for managing a house."

"Aye, and everyone in it." Jamie pushed himself away from the mantel to pace the floor of the small room. His mother took great delight in ordering others about—her husband, Alec, included. Jamie had vowed never to marry so willful a lass as Rowena McKie, and indeed he had not; Leana was as pliable as a willow branch. He turned toward his uncle and reminded him, "Mother sent me to your door a year ago, intending that I remain at Auchengray only long enough to marry one of your daughters."

Lachlan's hand stilled, though he did not look up. "You nearly married them both, lad," he said. "Sorting out such irregularities took time."

"Time?" Jamie paused to stare at the man seated before him. "Seven months of caring for your flocks are what it took! Seven months that have come and gone, Uncle. My debt is paid, and my life is my own."

"Is it, now?" Lachlan sat back in his chair, appraising Jamie with eyes as cold as a gray, wintry sky. "Duncan trusted your husbandry skills enough to let you choose the tups. Will you not stay the month and see our ewes bred?"

Jamie's shoulders sank. Only a churl would leave in the midst of breeding season. "Through October then. For Duncan's sake."

Lachlan propped his elbows on the arms of his chair and made a tent with his fingers, tapping them in time with the clock. "Even if Leana and the babe were fit to travel by Martinmas, which I doubt, your assistance would be missed at the *feeing* in Dumfries when we hire new shepherds. So would Leana's careful tending of my ledgers."

"But if we wait 'til late November, the weather—"

"Aye." Lachlan cut him off. "Another good reason to wait 'til spring."

Jamie spun on his heel. *"Spring?"*

"After all the work you'll do to breed them, you'll want to see the lambs birthed, aye?"

When Jamie was too stunned to respond, his uncle pressed his advantage. "In any case, Auchengray cannot afford to lose Leana, Eliza, *and* Rose all at once. The lasses are vital to the running of this household, and you ken it well."

"Rose?" Jamie looked at him askance. "But she won't be going with us."

"Och! Of course she won't." Lachlan wagged his head. "Rose is bound for school in Dumfries in January. Or have you forgotten?"

"Nae," he groaned. "I remember." Jamie sought the nearest chair and dropped into it, a dull pain thudding behind his temples. Lachlan

McBride had an answer for every argument and little concern for a son-in-law's wishes. To his shame, Jamie had bowed to the man's persuasive ways before, with disastrous results. He did not intend to do so now. Despite his headache, a plan took shape in his mind.

"Suppose Eliza remains here at Auchengray." Jamie kept his voice steady, without a hint of pleading. "Once Leana and I leave with Ian, you'll have three fewer mouths to feed and Eliza's undivided attention to her tasks."

Lachlan regarded him with one eyebrow arched, an expression quite like the one Jamie often saw on his mother's face when she thought him clever. His uncle said nothing to Jamie's suggestion at first, then slowly nodded. "Aye, you have more than enough maidservants at Glentrool. Eliza could remain with us."

"You see? We'll hardly be missed." Jamie masked his relief. They could leave the day after Martinmas and arrive by the Sabbath. However gray the mid-November skies might be, they'd not yet be thick with snow. Feeling generous at the prospect, Jamie added, "Mother will no doubt be writing you within a fortnight after we arrive, begging you to take us off her hands."

"That reminds me…" Lachlan patted his waistcoat, as if in search of something. "Rowena sent you a letter." He withdrew a folded paper and shook it open with some effort. "As you can see, one of the servants carelessly broke the wax seal, but all the pages seem to be in order."

Jamie claimed the letter, his blithe mood fading. "How would you ken if they're in order, Uncle, unless you've read them yourself?" Biting back his anger, Jamie scanned his mother's words that covered each page with swirls of black ink.

> To James Lachlan McKie
> Wednesday, 7 October 1789
>
> My dearest son Jamie,
>
> We delight at the blithe news of Ian's birth. I trust Leana continues in good health and the babe as well.

Jamie's grip on the letter tightened. "How is it she's already heard the news? Did you write my mother before I did?"

Lachlan gave an indifferent shrug. "She is, after all, my sister. 'Tis my right to pen a letter at her grandson's birth."

"Aye," Jamie grumbled, "and see that it's delivered by courier rather than by post so you might hear back from her at once." Whatever the contents of his uncle's letter, it had not paved the way home.

> Alas, here at Glentrool your father has developed a worrisome cough. Sheltering your new son under the same roof would not be wise, I'm afraid.
>
> Since Evan is looking toward Wigtownshire for land, spring might be best for your return to Glentrool. Once your father is well again and your brother and Judith are settled far to the south, you and your family will find a warm welcome here...

Jamie glanced up at Lachlan, whose features remained impassive. Clearly Lachlan had read the contents and already knew how their meeting tonight would end: with the McKies forced to remain at Auchengray through the lambing season.

Please God, 'twill be a short winter. Jamie stood, determined to strike a blow at Lachlan's most vulnerable spot: his *thrifite.* Though the money box was not in sight, it was seldom far from Lachlan's mind. "If we tarry here through the spring lambing, Uncle—and I warn you, we'll not stay a moment longer—then 'tis only right that you raise my wages."

Lachlan straightened in his chair, his features alert despite the hour. "Aye, that's fair enough." A light shone in his eyes like that of silver coins held up to the moon. "Suppose I pay you so many shillings for each ewe that survives the winter and so many shillings for each lamb that survives its birthing. What say you to that, lad?"

Jamie could hardly agree to so vague an offer. "How *many* shillings?"

"Come now." Lachlan held up his hands in protest. "Without my ledgers tallied before me, I cannot give you an exact price, Jamie. We'll work out a suitable arrangement before the first snow. For now, let us agree that you and your family will remain here through spring." Lachlan did not offer his hand to seal the bargain but instead rose to his feet and turned toward the bed, signaling the end of their discussion.

Jamie left the room without another word. If his uncle would not be bound to their agreement, then neither would he. He'd been caught in a vicious trap of words last Martinmas when he'd asked if he might have Rose's hand in marriage and Lachlan had said, "You might." The treachery of the man! He'd later shaken his finger and said, "There is no promise in the word *might,* now is there?" The memory of it still stuck in Jamie's craw.

"Then we *might* stay through spring," he muttered under his breath, stamping up the stair without a care for the slumbering household, his mother's letter clenched in his left hand. He flung open the bedroom door, nearly crashing it against the wall as he did, then shut it behind him with a satisfying bang.

"Jamie?" Leana's voice floated across the darkened room. "Did something go amiss?"

"Aye." He tossed the letter and then his waistcoat atop a leather trunk. Hugh would put his clothes aright in the *morn's morn.* For now, Jamie wanted naught but the solace of his bed. He blinked, his eyes adjusting to the light of a single candle, and took a deep breath of the clean, heather-scented air, a welcome change from the closeness of the spence. He shook out the tails of his shirt as he confessed to Leana, "'Twas worse than I expected. Your father thinks we should stay 'til spring."

She gasped. *"Spring?"*

Her response so echoed his own, he almost smiled. "If 'twere your father's opinion alone on the matter, I would brook his displeasure and leave before Yule." He yanked off his boots and dropped them on the floor, then retrieved the letter and held it aloft. "Alas, my mother has made the same request."

Leana slipped to the edge of the box bed and drew the candle closer. "Come, read me her words." Her bare feet shone pale against the wooden floor. The lace-edged hem of her nightgown was whiter still. 'Twould be good to have her sharing his bed again. Next to the hearth slept Ian in his cradle, mere steps from his mother. Odd to have their infant son so near. Might he wake them at all hours? Would they never have a moment to themselves again?

When Jamie sat down beside her, the bed boards groaned. "You'll be missing the Gordon's fine mattress."

"Nae, I will not." She slid her hand inside the crook of his elbow and pressed her cheek against his shoulder. Her hair fell round her face in waves of gold. " 'Tis my husband I've been missing."

Husband. Jamie swallowed his shame. Before Ian's birth, he'd been anything but an attentive husband. "Suppose we save the letter for the morn." Dropping the papers on the bedside table, he slid his arms round Leana, pulling her closer until her head nestled below his chin. She released a small sigh as he kissed the crown of her hair, then tipped her head back so he might kiss her brow as well. When he did so, the forgotten sweetness of her skin overwhelmed him. *Leana.* Memories of their first week as husband and wife returned unbidden, awakening a desire long neglected.

"Jamie." She straightened, brushing the hair from her eyes, though she did not look up to meet his gaze. "You ken that I cannot…"

Of course he knew. Did she think him so base? "Speak no more of it, Leana." He stood long enough to perch the candle on top of the tall dresser. Its feeble flame would not disturb their slumber yet would light the way if Ian awoke needing attention. Sliding beneath the covers, Jamie watched his wife settle into a comfortable position and resisted the impulse to touch her hair, the soft curve of her shoulder, the hollow of her neck.

"Sleep well," she whispered, her words already slurring.

He lay still in the darkness, wide awake yet exhausted, his hands jammed behind his head. This business of being husband to Leana and father to Ian required a patience he did not know if he possessed. " 'Tis like handling a ewe and her newborn lamb," Duncan had explained earlier in the week. "Dinna be *roarie* or hasty wi' yer movements. Make certain the *twa* have a chance tae get weel acquainted. Niver mind the time o' day; if they're tired, let them baith sleep."

He listened as Leana's breathing sank into a deep, slow rhythm. *Sleep then, my wife.*

Jamie woke to a pale, gray dawn filtering through the curtains. Leana had been up and down all night but now slept peacefully by his side with Ian cradled next to her. Watching them, a sense of purpose rose inside him: While Leana saw to their son's needs, he would care for the ewes, see them well fed and well bred. Duty alone would keep him tied to Auchengray until spring—not his uncle's tricks, nor his mother's concerns. He would remind himself of that duty each morning as he rose before dawn to join Duncan in the pastures.

The blue gray days of October came and went, each shorter than the last. Jamie labored in the sheepfolds, returning home at suppertime, his clothes soiled, his muscles aching from hard work and the damp, chilly air. Leana made certain hot water and a clean shirt were waiting for him, though dark circles beneath her eyes and a tremor in her hands hinted at the strain of mothering a babe who'd grown colicky.

"I'll sleep through the night when Ian does," she promised one evening, her tired gaze again drawn to the hearthside cradle. "His colic will not last forever. No more than two or three months, Neda says." She patted Jamie's rough cheek. "Perhaps 'tis best we cannot leave for Glentrool 'til spring."

He nodded but said nothing, distracted by an uneasiness that crawled up his spine like bindweed climbing a garden wall. *Leave now.* That was the gist of it. A sense of urgency growing inside him. *Leave now. Flee to Glentrool.* Of course it was not possible, not practical, a ridiculous notion. His place was here at Auchengray helping Duncan. Supporting his wife. And avoiding Rose, who *blethered* on about Neil Elliot, even as she batted her eyes in his direction whenever Leana was too busy with Ian to notice.

Jamie tried to ignore Rose, though she seemed to grow bonnier with each passing day. Duncan said Jamie had chosen the better path. Or had it been chosen for him? By his mother, by his uncle, by Leana, by the babe? *Nae.* Such thoughts were fruitless. Hard work was his only

hope, and duty his only salvation. He would toil as a common shepherd, counting the hours and days until spring returned to Galloway
and set him free—free from Auchengray and its endless labors, free
from the constant distraction of *loosome* young Rose, free to love his
wife without a shadow of regret.

Ten

If I speak to thee in friendship's name,
Thou think'st I speak too coldly;
If I mention love's devoted flame,
Thou say'st I speak too boldly.
THOMAS MOORE

Rose waited until her father's attention was fixed on Reverend Gordon expounding from the pulpit before she unfolded the note, then bent closer to read it. *Meet me at the abbey. Friday afternoon at two.* Though Susanne had pressed the folded paper into her hand at the kirk door, the words were written in her brother's hurried scrawl.

Neil Elliot was pursuing Rose in earnest; of that there could be no more doubt. Since the Sabbath morning of Ian's kirkin, Neil had called for her at Auchengray on a half-dozen occasions. Even Susanne had hinted at the two girls becoming sisters someday. "By marriage and by law!" her friend had said, eyes bright with happy tears. *Dear Susanne.* Rose neither encouraged nor discouraged her, so uncertain were her feelings toward Susanne's older brother.

Rose looked up to find Neil staring at her across the pews. His eyebrows lifted in a silent query, easily discerned: *Did you read the note? Will you come to the abbey?* Pretending not to notice, she glanced down and busied herself arranging her skirts round her ankles, while a growing sense of guilt gnawed at her soul. The poor lad was quite besotted. And she was not. Though Neil was handsome in his own way, his smile paled next to Jamie's broad grin. Neil was polite, yet his *kintra* ways could not match Jamie's manners, polished in Edinburgh. When Neil clasped her hand, it felt warm in hers but did not build a fire inside her the way Jamie's touch did.

She knew it wasn't fair to compare them. Jamie was her first love;

any man would seem a paltry choice after him. But surely she should feel *something* for Neil by now.

All round her, voices rang in tuneless praise with the first psalm of the morning. Rose moved her lips by rote, but her thoughts traveled a few steps north to Sweetheart Abbey. Should she meet Neil there and confess her uncertainty? It seemed the honest thing to do. They were friends, were they not? *Friday afternoon then.* She looked up and found Neil still gazing at her. Waiting for an answer. She nodded slightly. *Aye. Friday.*

The sun hung low in the sky, skimming the treetops, bathing Newabbey in slanted bars of pale gold. Rose, with her insides wound as tightly as a spring, crossed the bridge on foot, then waved at the miller, Brodie Selkirk, sweeping his doorstep. She'd told Neda she was off to buy hazelnuts for the morrow, Hallowmas Eve. Neda, distracted with festive preparations, had let her go without a quarrel since Auchengray's small harvest of nuts had already been plucked and put to use a month earlier.

On the grassy rise behind the corn mill the lads of the parish were busy stacking fuel for the bonfire to be kindled at dusk the next evening. The mound of broken timbers and barrels, peat and heather, whin and dried ferns had grown to the size of a haystack. A trio of children skipped past, their heads and feet bared to the cool air, their dirty faces bright with glee as they sang the familiar rhyme of the day.

> Hallowe'en, the nicht at e'en,
> The fairies will be ridin'.

Fairies, aye, and witches, too. On Saturday night, hilltops all over Scotland would be ablaze with fires meant to chase away the powers of darkness. Rose intended to be safe inside the walls of Auchengray, far from the reach of Lillias Brown and her ilk.

The door hung open to the grocer's shop. "Mr. Elliot!" Rose sang out as she stepped inside. She could hear the grocer in the back room, whistling as he went about his business. He'd come to the front soon enough. At her feet wooden crates filled with root vegetables were displayed in neat rows, while legs of cured mutton swung from the beams above her head, the meat wrapped in muslin. The pungent aroma of spices permeated the small shop: the rich note of cinnamon, the musky scent of sage, the sweet smell of rosemary. Rose leaned over a shelf to catch a whiff of nutmeg just as Mr. Elliot appeared, his round middle swathed in a white apron stained with the evidence of his trade.

"Miss McBride," he greeted her. "What a surprise to find you in the village."

Rose pretended not to see his broad wink. Had Neil told his father about their tryst? "I'm on an errand for Neda Hastings." She looked about, then asked, "Have you any hazelnuts left?"

"Och!" He waved a meaty hand at her. "I sold the last of my filberts an hour ago."

"Never mind, then. I'll think of something." Rose pursed her lips, picturing the woodlands north of Auchengray, replete with hazels. Might there be some nuts left among the wild shrubs there? An eerie place, to be sure, the most untamed corner of the parish. Yet the hint of danger only added to its appeal. If the weather held, she would slip out the back door in the morn's morn and see if she might find a few stray hazelnuts still nestled in the branches. At the moment she had another matter to attend to; the grocer's son was waiting for her.

"I'm off to the abbey for a stroll." She swept out the door and into the street, calling her farewell to Mr. Elliot. Her eye trained on the abbey's tall central tower, she hurried toward it, holding her skirts above the muck, greeting many a familiar face as she passed by. "Miss Taggart," she said, nodding. "Mr. Clacharty."

At the end of the street, north of the manse, loomed the red sandstone ruins of *Dulce Cor*—"sweet heart," as the monks of old had named their abbey. Heaven served as its roof now, and sod its floor. The graceful arches of the transepts and nave had held their ground for five centuries, even though many of the abbey's stones had been carted off to build cottages or dry stane dykes. She was but six when a society of gentlemen subscribers had pooled their resources to save the abbey from further decline. Her father, of course, had refused to contribute. Too generous an act for so *glaumshach* a man.

Rose slipped behind one of the stout pillars and peeked across the broad expanse of the abbey. Despite the autumn sunlight, the stone was cold beneath her hands. When she spotted Neil Elliot standing by the high altar with his back to her, she took a deep breath, then stepped out from her hiding place and glided toward him. "There you are," she said, keeping her tone light.

Neil turned at once and held out his hands to greet her. "My dear Rose." His face shone like one of his father's polished apples, and his gaze enveloped her from her boots to her braid. "Bonny and fair and all that a man could want."

"Neil!" She looked away, embarrassed by his frank appraisal. "You must not say such things."

His laugh, deeper than she remembered, echoed off the abbey walls. "And why not say them, when they are true?"

Her cheeks grew warmer still. "But we have no understanding." She kept her head down, afraid of what she might see in his eyes. "That is, you haven't spoken to my father."

"Easily done, lass."

Och! She'd said the wrong thing altogether. "Neil, I'm afraid we… that is…"

"I brought something for you." He stepped back, his words rushed, as if he sensed what she intended to say. Digging for something in his coat pocket, he explained, "Mother borrowed the recipe from a cousin in Edinburgh, who bakes these every Hallowmas Fair." He produced a lump of cloth, then unwrapped it to reveal a generous square of gingerbread. "Even with two cups of treacle, 'tis not as sweet as you, my Rose."

Her mouth watered at the sight of it. Neda seldom baked gingerbread. "I suppose she made it with fresh cream and green ginger."

Neil pinched off a corner and held it to her lips. "See for yourself."

She ate the bite of cake from his fingers, savoring the flavor. "Mmm, delicious."

"Aye." He smiled down at her. "Delicious." He fed her another piece, then folded the cloth and pressed it into her hands. "When you enjoy the rest, remember the one who gave it to you."

"I will," she said, already regretting her enthusiasm. "Neil, we must talk."

"But first, we must walk." He drew her hand into the crook of his arm. "Winter will be here soon enough. Golden days like this one should not go to waste." Leading the way at an unhurried pace, he steered them toward the grassy field that wrapped itself round the abbey. They strolled for several minutes, speaking of little beyond the fading colors of autumn that surrounded them. The air was crisp yet clear, fragrant with the scent of burning leaves. Sheep bleated in a nearby pasture as Neil guided her along the crumbling dyke that edged the property.

Passing beneath one of the stone archways that led to the cloister, Rose slowed her steps, even as her heart quickened its pace. She could keep the truth to herself no longer. "Neil," she began, moistening her dry lips, "it was good of you to invite me here."

" 'Twas good of you to come." He stopped and turned toward her, his earnest expression cutting her to the quick. "You ken how I care for you, Rose."

"I do," she admitted, meeting his gaze, difficult as that was. His brown eyes shone with a love she feared she could never match. "I think of you as the kindest of friends."

"Friends?" he protested, sliding his hands along her arms. "Susanne is your friend. I thought I was rather more than that."

"Aye…well…," she stammered, watching in disbelief as he bent his head toward hers, his mouth nuzzling her ear. Whenever had Neil become so bold?

"I wonder if you ken the auld tune that's running through my head," he murmured. His breath warmed her skin as he sang.

> Some say that kissing's a sin,
> But I say that will not stand.

He chuckled. "Now you sing the rest of it, lass."

Rose could not move her head, so tightly did he press his cheek against hers. She whispered the last two lines of the verse, her voice trembling.

> It is a most innocent thing,
> And allowed by the laws of the land.

"Just so." He kissed her. Softly at first, then with more conviction, circling his arms round her waist, pulling her closer before she could stop him, before she could think.

A male voice floated across the cloister. "Congratulations."

Jamie.

Rose yanked herself free and spun about. "Cousin! I didn't expect… I'm surprised to…see you."

"Obviously." He strode toward them, scowling at them both.

She took another step away from Neil. "Wh-whatever brings you to the abbey?"

"You didn't arrive home soon enough to suit your father, so he sent me with the chaise. When I looked for you at the grocer's, he suggested I might find you here. And so I have." His scowl grew more pronounced. "I trust the marriage banns are to be read on the Sabbath morn."

Before Neil could respond, Rose blurted out, "Nae! Things are not at all what they appear."

"On the contrary," Neil countered, "they are quite as they appear." He pressed his hand firmly in the small of her back. "You can be sure I will speak to Mr. McBride when the time is right."

Jamie's eyes narrowed, assessing him. "And when would that time be, Mr. Elliot?"

"Is Monday soon enough, sir?"

Eleven

What will not woman, gentle woman, dare
When strong affection stirs her spirit up?
ROBERT SOUTHEY

When Jamie shifted his gaze in her direction, something flickered across his face. "What do you have to say for yourself, Rose?"

"Jamie, we need to—"

"Leave at once. I quite agree." Jamie thrust out his elbow, an invitation she dared not ignore. "Mr. Elliot, my uncle will expect you for dinner on Monday at Auchengray. One o' the clock. You will either explain your behavior to his satisfaction, or you will make an offer of marriage. Is that understood?"

Neil squared his shoulders, a look of determination in his eye. "Monday it is, sir."

"Monday," Rose repeated, too numb to say more.

The men offered each other polite but curt farewells, then Jamie led her across the abbey grounds to the chaise, his stride long and his temper short. "I see you wasted little time finding a suitor, Rose." He sent Bess forward with a click of his tongue. "Would that you had chosen someone with more…discretion."

"I was not the one who did the choosing." She stared at the grocer's shop as they passed, imagining herself as a grocer's wife. "Neil chose me."

"He also chose to kiss you beneath the wide October sky, where anyone might see you."

"You were the only one who saw us, Jamie."

" 'Tis a good thing I arrived when I did, for the man seemed most intent about his business."

Rose touched her lips, remembering. Their kiss was so brief and unexpected it could hardly be called pleasurable. But *intent*…aye, 'twas that.

Jamie glanced at her sideways, as if gauging her reaction. "Leana mentioned that you've entertained Mr. Elliot at Auchengray rather often of late."

She gave a slight lift to her shoulders. "We walked the braes together. Chatted over tea and oatcakes. Not formal visits. Neil just…appeared."

"And was made welcome." Jamie fell silent, turning to watch the road as they rounded a bend. The chaise bounced hard when they hit a rut, throwing them both off balance. Jamie caught Rose by the arm to steady her and released her just as quickly.

After a considerable silence she feigned interest in a flock of noisy fieldfares plucking berries from the hedgerow so she might study Jamie without his noticing. The man was behaving very strangely. Was he angry? Concerned for her reputation? Or did he still care for her, if only a little?

"Lass…" He cleared his throat. "If your father has not instructed you on courting manners, then I must."

Ah. The corners of her mouth twitched at the prospect of such a lesson from Jamie of all people. "I suppose kissing a suitor in public is not acceptable."

"Indeed it is *not.*"

A laugh slipped out before she could catch it. "James Lachlan McKie, you kissed me dozens of times when we were courting!"

"But not in Sweetheart Abbey," he shot back.

She splayed her fingers and began tallying the places where he *had* kissed her. In the byre. Behind Auchengray Hill. On the road to Newabbey. Beneath the yew in the garden. Among Leana's roses. By the shore of Lochend. In a shepherd's *bothy.* "And the first time you kissed me was standing in a pasture surrounded by sheep," she finished, having long since run out of fingers on which to count.

"Most of those were *after* we were betrothed," he insisted.

"Aye, but then came January and all the months that followed until this one." *Stop, Rose.* But she could not hold back her words nor stem the lingering hurt that fueled them. "What about those kisses, Jamie? After you married my sister?"

He took a long breath, then exhaled. "They were…inappropriate."

"*Misbehadden,* as Neda would say?"

"Aye, most improper." His face was blotched with color. "God forgive me, I had no right to kiss you, Rose."

"I did not resist a single one," she reminded him, feeling guilty for pressing him so.

When he looked at her, the sorrow in his eyes was unmistakable. "I was the one who could not resist, Rose. If there is any blame to be assigned, look no further than me."

I dare not look at you at all. She gazed down the road toward Lowtis Hill, trying to sort through her feelings. Jamie was determined to honor his vows. She could not help but admire him for it, though it cost her dearly. The sad truth was, Jamie would never be hers. Remembering his kisses only made things worse.

Neil Elliot then. A solution of sorts. Would he ask for her hand? Would her father deem him worthy? Could she love such a man?

Jamie nudged her with his elbow. "You're being verra quiet, Rose. 'Tis not like you."

She told him the truth. "I'm thinking about Monday."

"I was a bit...short with Mr. Elliot."

"Short?" Rose rolled her eyes. "You gave him no choice in the matter. Though I believe he'd made up his mind to propose long before you arrived."

After a moment's silence, Jamie asked, "Have you made up your mind as well?"

Was that regret she heard behind his question? "I've not made my decision yet," she admitted, folding her hands in her lap as the gates of Auchengray came into view. "Would you mind if I married a grocer's son?"

"Mind? Nae." He shook his head, as if saying the word was not enough to convince either of them. "Marry whom you like."

Rose paused, listening to the tone in his voice. Jamie was no longer angry. Nor was he worried. His shame had come and gone. Disappointment, perhaps? Nae, this was something else. Her eyes widened. Surely he wasn't *jealous* of Neil Elliot? Impossible, considering Jamie was in every way superior. Nae, he could not be jealous.

When they arrived at the steading, Willie helped her down, looking about the chaise for a sack from the grocer. "All the way tae the village and back and nae hazelnuts tae show for yer trouble?"

"Colin Elliot didn't have a one," she told him. "I'll hunt for some in the morn's morn, for I'll not see you disappointed round the hearth on Hallowmas Eve."

"Och!" Willie shooed her off. "I've nae need tae put filberts by the fire. That's a custom for young fowk. But if ye might pluck a handful or twa, the herds will be grateful. Won't they, Mr. McKie?"

"Aye." Jamie raised his eyes toward the front windows of the mains, where Leana stood, gazing down at them. "We'll all be grateful."

'Twas the last day of October. Already a cold November wind nipped at its heels.

After a hasty breakfast of bannocks and jam, Rose dug through a dresser drawer and unearthed an old apron. She borrowed a needle and thread from Leana's basket while her sister was busy with the babe, tacked the hem of her apron to the waistband, then stitched together the sides to create a single, roomy pocket. Tying the apron over her oldest gown, she slipped out of doors and headed toward Auchengray Hill. In all her sixteen years she had not explored the wild moorlands and dark forests alone. One of the shepherds might have kept her company—Rab Murray or Davie Tait—but 'twas too late now. She'd have to manage on her own.

A pale morning mist swirled about her skirts as she scanned the pastures in the distance. Neither Jamie nor Duncan came into view as she nimbly climbed over the crest and struck out across the rough fields headed for the forests east of Troston Hill. The uneven ground sent her tumbling to her knees more than once, and prickly weeds tore at her skirts. Her spirits lifted when she spied a line of oak trees along the banks of March Burn. A hazel grove waited just on the other side of the narrow stream. The rising mist softened the bright colors of the oak leaves, creating a muted blend of burnt orange, golden yellow, and pale brown. Rose felt an acorn beneath her foot and kicked the hard nut with the toe of her boot, sending it flying across the ground. When she moved into the cool shadows of the forest, she paused as her eyes adjusted and her ears sharpened.

The hazels, with their pinkish brown leaves, stood just where she remembered them from a school outing long ago. Rose searched through the nearest shrub, dismayed to find the squirrels and jays had nearly picked them clean. With some effort she located a few remaining clusters, ripe and ready to eat. She chose two particularly fine hazelnuts—firm, dark, and meaty—and slipped them inside the small, hanging pocket tied round her waist. *One for Neil, one for me.* Moving deeper into the hazel grove, she harvested each shrub diligently, tugging off the leafy frills round the few nuts she found, then dropping the filberts into her capacious apron, singing to keep her spirits up.

> I luved ne'er a laddie but one,
> He luves ne'er a lassie but me;
> He is willing to make me his own,
> And his own I'm willing to be.

She sang out the last words, her voice carried off by the wind whistling through the grove, when a twig snapped behind her, followed by a low chuckle. "There's mony a way tae claim a man's heart—willin' or not. And Lillias Brown kens them *a'*."

Rose whirled about, clutching the corners of her sagging apron. "Mistress Brown!" Brightly garbed, with her gray-streaked hair pinned on top of her small head, the widow appeared to have dropped from the tree like overripe fruit. Rose gaped at her. "Wh-whatever are you doing here?"

The older woman laughed again, holding up a small basket. "Same as ye, Miss McBride. Collectin' the last of the hazelnuts." She patted the necklace made of nuts draped on her bosom. "Some fowk eat them, and some put them in pairs by the fire, divinin' the future. For me, the fruit o' the hazel serves a deeper purpose." Her gaze swept over Rose's apron. "I see ye've claimed mair than yer due."

"Only what is fair." Rose refused to be intimidated, though she had to press her knees together to keep them from shaking. Across the woman's brow was the trace of a scar, faint but jagged. A wutch-score, folk called it, made by some desperate soul who'd sought protection from Lillias and her *cantrips*. Rose hid her right hand beneath her apron and slipped her thumb between her first two fingers. The sign of the cross would keep her safe. "These woods are common to all who live in the parish, Mistress Brown."

"Aye." Lillias stepped closer. Rose, without meaning to, stepped back. "Newabbey parish is home for me as weel, ye ken. My cottage, Nethermuir, is not far from here, beside Craigend Loch." She waved toward the west. "As a raven flies, hard and fast, 'tis but an hour's walk."

"I see." Rose could not resist a second glance at the woman's odd jewelry of polished hazelnuts strung on a black velvet ribbon. "Did you…ah, make your necklace?"

"So I did, lassie. Only a wise woman kens the how and why o' *sic* a thing." Lillias began fingering the smooth filberts like beads on a rosary, grasping each one in turn, moving her lips yet not uttering a sound. Her eyes drifted shut, and her mouth went slack.

The forest grew strangely silent. Rose felt the hairs lift on the back of her neck.

" 'Tis the power o' the hazel," Lillias whispered, her eyes still closed. "It changes the verra air ye breathe." She released the necklace, then rested her hand on top of it and opened her eyes. "Whan I came upon ye, Rose McBride, ye were thinkin' aboot a man. A man willin' tae marry ye, aye?"

Neil! Too stunned to speak, Rose made a small noise of assent.

"As I see it, he is willin', but ye are not."

Rose swallowed, taking another step back. "I am…uncertain."

"Because ye fancy *anither.*" Lillias grasped the necklace, her eyes focused elsewhere. "A man *wha* canna *luve* ye."

A wind with the hint of winter in its breath passed by. *I cannot love you, Rose.*

"This verra nicht ye'll divine yer future husband." Stretching out a withered hand, Lillias plucked a pair of hazelnuts from her basket and added them to Rose's apron. "The nuts, the mirror, the apple—ye ken the auld ways, d'ye not?"

Rose nodded. She put little store in them, but, aye, she knew them.

"Dinna miss the chance tae learn what yer heart already kens." When Lillias touched her hand, Rose was shocked by the warmth of the woman's bony fingers. "There is *ane* man for ye, lassie. And ye ken his name well."

A voice not her own whispered inside her, *Jamie.*

"Nae!" Rose turned and fled across the burn and through the oak woods, her heart racing faster than her feet. Little wonder her neighbors called Lillias Brown a wutch! None but a daughter of the *deʾil* himself would plant so *braisant* a notion in a girl's mind. Jamie belonged to her sister now. There was no going back.

Rose dashed around clumps of gorse and outcroppings of rock until she slowed to catch her breath, gasping for air in ragged gulps. She dared not tarry. It was rumored Lillias Brown could change into a hare or ride a cat like the finest steed or fly through the air in a kitchen sieve. "Rubbish!" Rose had once said. Now she glanced over her shoulder, fearful of what she might see behind her.

Naught but bright trees and a pale blue sky, thanks be to God.

Easing her pace, she set her sights on home and the hours ahead. 'Twas Neil Elliot she would think about this Hallowmas Eve. Neil and no other. She would look for his image in the mirror at midnight, and hope that the apple paring spelled out his name. For if he asked for her hand come Monday, she must know her heart. And she must have an answer.

Twelve

The look of love alarms
Because 'tis fill'd with fire.
WILLIAM BLAKE

M ind the fire!" Neda cautioned.
Jamie poked the dried kale stalks into the burning peat until
the torch was duly lit, then handed the bound stalks to a servant lad,
who ran off to join the others gathering out of doors. Walking the
boundaries of one's property, torches held high, was a time-honored
means of protecting the household from calamity, a custom even the
kirk could not snuff out. Next Hallowmas Eve Jamie planned to be
lighting torches for Glentrool; this October his duties remained at
Auchengray.

"That's the last o' them." Neda plunged her torch into the fire,
motioning at Jamie to do the same. "Your uncle will be anxious tae get
started, afore we lose the light o' day *athegither*." Jamie followed her out
the door, keeping his smoldering kale well away from curtains and
clothing, and found his place among the two dozen family members
and servants assembled on the lawn.

Lachlan gripped his torch like a broadax and barked out orders.
"See that you're the same distance apart. Keep your torch in your right
hand. Hold it up, I tell you, or you'll set the shrubbery on fire!" No one
laughed at the man, however *pensie* his behavior.

When Jamie looked back to make certain Leana was in place, he
could not help but notice Rose as well. Dressed in a blue gown, her hair
cascading down her back, she looked like the Queen of the Fairies herself. His hand clenched the rough kale stalks, the memory of watching
Neil Elliot kissing Rose still fresh in his mind. How dare the lad take
advantage of her innocence!

His conscience pricked him. *Righteous anger, is it? Naught else?* Jamie swerved toward the front, swinging the torch in an arc and scattering sparks across the lawn. He had no claim on the lass, nor she on him. Let Rose kiss every man in the parish if she liked! Leana was his concern now. When he felt a light tap on his shoulder, Jamie swung his head round, prepared to give Rose a good scolding.

Instead Leana stood behind him, holding out her left hand. "Look what I pulled from an oat stalk earlier." She held her torch closer to illumine the seeds in her palm. "Seven seeds from a single stalk."

"Seven children then," he murmured, feeling his pounding heart ease.

"That's what the auld wives say." She waved her hand through the air, scattering the seeds. "If you put any stock in such things."

Jamie eyed her in amazement. "You do not?"

"Almighty God is the one who blesses a womb," she said in a tone of quiet confidence, brushing her hand across her skirts. "If the future holds seven bairns for us, Jamie, I shall welcome every one. 'Tis not a handful of seeds that tells me that but a heart full of faith."

Jamie swallowed, overcome by her simple assurance. "You are too good for me, Leana," he said at last.

"Nae, I am far from virtuous. Or have you forgotten our wedding night?" Her smile was tinged with sadness. "Walk on, Jamie. Hallowmas Eve awaits."

The gloaming faded into a black, starless night as the household began their slow procession, keeping close to the dry stane dykes that marked the boundaries of Auchengray proper. The earth was spongy and uneven, littered with stones. Jamie put down each booted foot with care, keeping one eye on Lachlan's stiff back and the other on the murky ground before him.

"Thrice and done," Lachlan announced at last, tossing his kale torch onto the stony ground. "Duncan, see that the shepherds circle the pastures. As for the rest of you, away with your fires and make to the kitchen." Leaving their torches behind in a small bonfire, the servants ran laughing into the house, eager for the household festivities to begin.

"Jamie?" Leana stepped next to him, sliding her cool fingers inside the curl of his hand. "I promised Neda I'd help with the turnip lanterns. Will you join us?"

They followed the path to the back door, stepping from the black shroud of night into a warm, cheery kitchen smelling of freshly baked gingersnaps and ripe apples. Young and old stood about the square wooden table in the center of the kitchen, eying a heap of yellow and orange turnips. The last of the crop harvested from Leana's garden, they'd been left in the ground to grow plump and thick skinned, better suited for carving than for eating.

"Choose yer favorite," Neda instructed, handing Jamie a stout blade. "Mr. McKie will cut off the top." Eyes wide, the younger ones were allowed to pick first, wrapping their arms round the turnips and bringing them to Jamie so he could slice off the top quarter. In turn, Leana handed them blunt knives and steered them toward a large iron pot with orders to scoop out the centers. Though Neda would cook the *neeps* and mash them with butter and white pepper for their Sabbath supper, this night the turnips would serve another purpose: scaring away the goblins and beasties said to roam the hills and glens of Galloway.

"Take care not to push your knives through the skin," Leana cautioned them, "or Mr. McKie will have no room left to make a face." His skills with a sharpened dirk were put to the test when it came to carving eyes and mouths into the overripe vegetables. Some of the faces were frightening, but most were comical, with noses askew and crooked smiles. Leana shook her head in disbelief, pointing at one of them. "What sort of creature is that?"

Jamie gave a slight shrug. "A friendly one." 'Twas best the younger lads did not learn the grisly truth behind the custom, filtered through the centuries from the ancient Druids who'd gathered at Carlinwark to sever the heads of their enemies. Hardly a story for innocent ears. Let them fill their turnips with candlelight and banish the darkness of auld Scotland.

"Jamie, I must see to Ian's welfare," Leana said, looking toward the hall. "When Duncan and the shepherds come back from their rounds, they'll be *dookin'* for apples with the servants. Be a good husband and fill the wooden tub for Neda, won't you?"

Jamie squeezed her hand, assuring her he would do whatever was needed, and sent her up the stair. The shallow tub sat on the kitchen floor, wide enough to float a peck of apples, so it took several trips to the well to fill it. Rose busied herself breaking off pieces of the Hallowmas bannock for all to partake, while Neda polished the pippins until they shone. Hauling in his last pail of water, Jamie was joined by Duncan and the returning shepherds, who filled the kitchen with noise and merriment, scattering ashes on the floor from the bonfire. "This is Halloweven," one sang out, and another joined in, "The morn is Hallowday."

"Och, such a *stramash!*" Neda fussed, grinning all the while. "Ye'll have ashes in yer hair afore ye're done." She bent down to stir the water with her wooden porridge spurtle, sending the apples bobbing along the surface. "Who'll be first tae dook his head?"

Rose volunteered at once. "I will." She wrapped her hair in a linen towel, then tied another round her neck and knelt beside the tub on the brick floor. "Truth lies at the bottom of a well," she announced, taking a deep breath. The wise wags insisted if folk captured an apple between their teeth that night, they'd have the power to see the days to come. Down into the water she went, chasing one apple after another until she pinned one to the side of the tub and sank her teeth into it amid much cheering. She rose, holding the apple aloft, and whipped the linen from her head. Her hair unfurled like a flag from a rampart, signaling victory, and her eyes were bright with triumph. "Your turn, Cousin Jamie. Or do you have no wish to see what your future holds?"

"I ken verra well what it holds." *And so do you, Rose.* "Let someone else take my turn."

Brushing off his cool response with a toss of her head, she invited Annabel to have a go at the apples instead. A red-haired serving lass, tall for her fourteen years, Annabel served as lady's maid to Rose, along with performing every other household chore Lachlan found for her to do. The girl dooked her head and came up with nothing in her mouth except water. Jamie leaned against the door to the larder, content to watch the others soak their shirts and drown in laughter. Rose stood across the room, polishing her apple on her sleeve, her gaze unfixed. Thinking about Neil Elliot, no doubt.

At ten strokes of the mantel clock, Leana appeared, her tired features telling Jamie what he already knew: Ian's colic had not abated; his muffled cries could be heard above the din in the kitchen. She made her way across the crowded room, reaching for his hand. "Jamie," was all she said, resting her head against his shoulder.

When the gathering moved to the dining room hearth, leaving a sopping mess behind, the servants carted along bowls of nuts and treacle scones, hot tea for the lasses, and warm ale for the lads. Jamie found a quiet corner where Leana might sit comfortably and nicked a scone from the tray, breaking it in half to share with her. She smiled at the gesture. "You fed me black bun on Hogmanay."

"So I did." His memories of that New Year's Eve were awash with too much whisky and ale, a mistake he would not make again. "Eat well, my wife." He broke off a corner and popped it into her mouth, aware of Rose brushing past them as she moved toward the hearth.

" 'Tis Nutcrack Night," Rose proclaimed, holding up two hazelnuts. "Gathered from the forest along March Burn."

A gasp went through the assembly, Jamie's among them. Whatever was Rose thinking, harvesting nuts in that forsaken place? She'd never have confessed it had her father been in the room. No wonder Lachlan was eager to send her off to boarding school; she'd been given too much freedom of late. As he watched her move toward the hearth, his neck grew warm, guessing what she had in mind. One hazelnut would be named *Rose.* But what of the other one?

Her eyes gleamed as she bent over the grate and placed the hazelnuts next to it—not close enough to catch fire, but near enough to burn slowly, telling a tale as they did. If the nuts fretted and fumed, rolling about in the heat, the lad and lass were considered ill matched, and the faithless one would jump away. If the nuts remained close and burned steadily until they were reduced to ashes, the two named were a good match and meant to marry. Rose called out a simple rhyme, and others joined in.

> If you hate me, spit and fly,
> If you love me, burn awa.

Willie teased her, "Will ye tell us the laddie wha shares the fire wi' ye, Rose?"

" 'Tis Neil Elliot," she announced, then ducked her head when the assembly clapped with obvious delight. "Promise you'll not tell the man, or you'll scare him away."

Jamie stared at the pair of filberts. 'Twas good news, was it not? He had begged Rose to let him go, and she had.

As the feasting continued and others added their hazelnuts along the grate, Jamie noticed how exhausted Leana looked. "Shall we be off to bed?" he offered. She stood at once, her blond head nodding. When they reached their room, Ian's crying had ceased, though they were met at the door by a bleary-eyed servant.

"He's all yers," the maid whispered, disappearing down the hall.

The couple tiptoed inside the bedroom lit by a single candle near the cradle. Leana smiled down at Ian while she unlaced her dress, then reached for a volume of *Clarissa* that had rested on the mantel untouched for weeks. "Will you read aloud to me while I see to Ian's supper? I cannot keep these borrowed books much longer."

"If you like." Jamie sat on the edge of the bed, opening the leather-bound book where a feather had marked the place. "Letter 216," he read, his voice warming to the task. "From Mr. Lovelace to John Belford, Esquire. Now have I established myself for ever in my charmer's heart." A vision of Rose flitted through his mind but was swiftly dismissed.

"Go on, dear husband." Leana settled into an upholstered chair, Ian nestled at her breast. "I'm listening."

Jamie read for an hour or more, until Ian was well sated and Leana nigh asleep. He lowered the child into the cradle with exceeding care, then helped Leana to her feet and pressed a kiss to her forehead. "Shall I call Eliza to dress you for bed?"

"Nae, I can manage." She looked at him through half-closed eyes.

"Though I confess, I'm thirsty from nursing. Might you have Eliza bring me a cup of buttermilk?"

"I'll get it myself," he said, glad to find some simple way to please her, and hurried down the stair. Voices no longer rang through the house. The hour was late; perhaps they were all in bed, the servants included. As Jamie turned at the bottom of the stair, bound for the kitchen, a footfall in the dining room caught his ear. He paused, his eyes drawn toward the glowing hearth where a figure hovered over the peat fire. *Rose.*

Curious, he drew nearer the doorway, careful not to make a sound nor to be seen. No candles were lit in the room; the fire alone illuminated Rose's face. She was staring at the hazelnuts straggled across the flagstone hearth. Many had cracked open or rolled into the fire but not the two that Rose was studying. They were reduced to two small mounds of ashes, so close they were nearly one. *As Rose and Neil will be.*

When her skirts rustled, Jamie looked in time to see her produce an apple—no doubt the one she'd caught between her teeth at the earlier dookin'—and begin peeling it with the same knife he'd used for the turnips. She sliced away the skin with short, measured movements as the peel grew into a long curl like a ragged red ribbon. If it broke, some said, the cantrip would be broken as well, and she would not marry for another year.

He watched in grim fascination as the last of the apple skin was cut free. She pinched it between her thumb and forefinger, then held it aloft, letting it dance in the firelight. As the clock began to chime the hour of midnight, Rose turned her back toward the door and swung the paring ever so slowly round her head. Once. Twice. Still it had not broken. She circled her head once more, then flung the apple peel over her left shoulder with a slight cry, spinning round to see where it landed.

It had landed at his feet.

"Jamie!" Though she walked toward him, it was the paring on the floor that held her attention. "What does it spell?" she breathed. "Tell me the first letter of my true love's name."

He could not bring himself to look at it.

She stepped beside him, their shoulders almost touching. He heard a sharp intake of air. "I don't understand. 'Tis a *J*. Do you see the shape of it? Straight at the top, then a long curl of a tail."

Reluctantly he looked down at the floor, where his own initial stared up at him. "This means nothing, Rose, and you ken it well. A silly rite of the season."

Even in the faint light of the fire, he could see her blush. "Aye, but I thought…that is, I expected…"

"The letter *N* for Neil?"

"Nae, Jamie." She glanced toward the tarnished looking glass over the hearth. "I'm afraid I expected you. For when I looked in the glass, I saw your reflection over my shoulder. You ken the meaning of that, don't you?"

"Aye." The auld wives said when a lass ate an apple in front of a looking glass at midnight, her intended's face appeared over her left shoulder. "But what of the hazelnuts?" He pointed to the hearth. "Yours and Neil's remained side by side."

"Nae, they did not. One of them jumped into the fire soon after you and Leana went up the stair." She turned to look at the ashes. "Those were another pair of hazelnuts that I…that I found in the woods. One named for me and the other named…for you."

The heat drained from Jamie's face. However he might ignore them, three omens on Hallowmas Eve were three too many. "Do not speak of this, Rose. Not to anyone."

"You can be certain of it." She inched her toe from beneath her skirt and nudged the apple peel until it spelled a different letter. "I shall not tell a soul."

Thirteen

I should have known what fruit would spring
from such a seed.
GEORGE GORDON, LORD BYRON

Rose pulled a handful of wool across the sharp teeth of her paddles, then lightly brushed the cards first in one direction, then the other, rehearsing what she would say if Neil asked for her hand in marriage that afternoon: *Aye. Nae. Aye. Nae.* Mere hours remained, and she still did not have a proper answer.

The gray November light did little to warm the second-floor sewing room where Leana sat before her wooden wheel, spinning at a weary pace. Rose eyed her sister, a wave of sympathy swelling inside her, Neil forgotten for the moment. "I ken why Ian suffers every night with colic."

"Oh?" Leana lifted her foot from the treadle. "And what would my young sister ken of such troubles?"

" 'Tis no fault of yours," Rose hastened to add. "On the day of Ian's kirkin, did you not see the way Lillias Brown stared when you held up the babe, cursing Ian with her eyes, frowning at his sweet face?"

Leana shook her head, resuming her spinning. "Colic comes from poor digestion, not strange looks or unkind words." The wheel spun beneath her hands as she guided the wool, drawing it into a slender thread. "Besides, 'twas weeks ago we crossed her path. I make my tea with rose hips now and try to keep calm while I'm nursing Ian. Neda says the lad's body will sort things out soon enough."

Rose slapped her paddles together in frustration. "You cannot sleep, you barely eat, and Jamie drags about like a soul untethered."

"Rose!" Leana swung round on her three-legged stool, her chin trembling. "I am well aware of my husband's exhaustion. And of my own. Lillias Brown is responsible for none of it. Especially not Ian's discomfort." The strain in her voice hinted at a week of sleepless nights.

"Many a babe in Scotland suffers with colic." Leana turned to face her wheel again, though not before Rose noticed a spot of pink on each cheek. "I have begged Jamie to be patient and would ask the same of you."

Mortified, Rose leaned forward to stroke Leana's back. "I have no quarrel with you, my sister. Only with Lillias Brown." Rose knew the wutch's ill treatment of Ian was not what truly concerned her. It was the seed the old woman had planted in her own heart, one Rose knew she must not water or nurture: *There is only ane man for ye, lassie.* The two hazelnuts came from the wutch's hand; the omens in the apple peel and looking glass were another matter, not easily explained. Did Lillias's powers stretch as far as Auchengray?

No matter what spells the wutch might cast, Jamie was not hers to choose this day. Neil Elliot, however, was. *Then choose, Rose.*

She yanked her paddles apart and tore at the rough fibers—carding the wool back and forth, back and forth—giving vent to the struggle raging in her head. She enjoyed Neil's company but did not love him. They would live comfortably but never know great wealth. He thought of her as charming. She thought of him as safe.

Aye then? Or *nae? Heaven help me, what should I do?*

"Rose, mind your work," Leana said gently.

With a guilty start, Rose looked down at the wool she'd been carding, now hopelessly tangled among the sharp teeth. "Och! 'Tis no use." She stood in a huff and threw aside the paddles, shaking the curly remnants from her apron. "Wool is the very last thing on my mind."

"What *is* on your mind, Rose?" The wheel slowed to a stop as Leana spun about, her blue eyes filled with compassion. "You've been so *kittlie* the last two days. Will you not trust me with your secrets anymore?"

Jamie had spoken with their father about Neil's visit, but no one else in the household knew why the young man was joining them for dinner. Rose had sat quietly through services yestreen, avoiding Neil, avoiding Jamie, keeping her own counsel. If she told her sister, would Leana understand? Or simply be relieved to have her out from under Auchengray's roof—and away from Jamie—with due haste?

When Leana reached out for her hands, wrapping them in hers,

Rose could no longer keep the truth to herself. "Neil Elliot may very well propose today."

"Oh, Rose!" Leana did not mask her elation, or her relief. "He's a commendable young man. Have you decided? Will you accept?"

She felt a sting between her eyes, warning of the tears to come if she was not careful. "I…don't know." Rose recited a litany of his many good qualities, hoping she might convince herself in the process.

Leana saw right through her. "But you've not said that you love him, Rose."

She looked away, ashamed. "Nae, I have not."

"Listen to me, Rose." There was a note of urgency in her sister's voice. "You do not want a marriage without love."

Like yours. Leana not only cared for Rose's happiness, it seemed; she also wanted to spare Neil.

"He must cherish you, Rose, and you him. 'Tis not the fashion these days to marry for love. Most marry for land, or silver, or convenience, or bairns."

"I *would* marry for children," Rose confessed. "After a month with Ian, I long to be a mother."

"And I pray you will be someday. But choose the father with care. The children will grow and leave, but the man will be with you all the days of your life." Leana pressed a light kiss on Rose's brow, then stood. "Come now, where is my blithe and bonny sister?"

"Not so bonny today." Rose stood as well, frowning at her plain attire. "Neil Elliot has seen every gown I own twice over."

A smile bloomed on Leana's face. "What if you wore my claret one?"

Rose gaped at her. "Are you certain?" It was the gown Leana had worn on her wedding day.

"It hasn't fit me for many months," Leana reminded her, pressing a hand to her waist. "Neil Elliot will think you've had the tailor fashion a new gown just to please him. Whatever your decision, you'll want to look your best." She steered her into the hall. "We'll have Annabel press it for you."

Within the hour Rose stood before the looking glass mounted over her dressing table, ducking her head to take it all in. The wine-colored gown was a perfect fit. She'd had Annabel pull the laces tighter, accentuating her small waist and blossoming figure, then piled her black tresses high on her head to make her appear more sophisticated. A grown woman, not a *green* lass of sixteen. She dared not touch any rouge to her cheekbones, or her father would banish her to the washstand. Instead she pinched her cheeks hard and sank her teeth into her lips, hoping they might appear rosier as well.

A knock on the door sent her spinning toward it. "Aye?"

Annabel called, "Miss Rose, they're here."

They? Rose hurried into the hall, the rustle of her petticoats a distinct counterpoint to the male voices booming up the stair—among them a jovial one that belonged to the grocer from Newabbey. *Mr. Elliot!* She backed away from the top step, her heart in her throat. Neil's father had not come to deliver the necessary foods for their Martinmas feast. *Nae.* He had come to do business with her father. *Marriage business.*

"Baith father and son," Annabel confirmed, peering down the stair at the commotion in the front hall. "My, aren't they a pair? Look, here comes Neda tae collect ye."

The housekeeper reached the top step. "'Tis guid that ye chose sae fine a gown this day," Neda said with a broad smile. "Baith Mr. Elliots will see what a loosome bride ye'll make."

Father and son stood side by side, watching Rose descend the stair. Why did she feel as though she were a loaf of sugar to be bought and sold at market rather than the daughter of a prosperous bonnet laird? The elder Elliot wore a bright blue waistcoat with silver buttons. Neil's suit of clothes were cut to a smart fit, though his hair cried out for scissors. If she married the man, would that task fall to her?

"Mr. Elliot." She offered her hand as any lady of quality would. Colin Elliot obliged, looking amused as he bent to brush an airy kiss across her fingers. Neil followed suit, taking his time, pressing his lips to her skin with uncommon tenderness. *Dear Neil.* He truly did care for her.

"Enough with your highborn manners, Rose." Her father, standing behind their guests, glowered at her. "We are not dining at Maxwell Park. Gentlemen, if you'll join me at table, I'll see our meat served."

Rose grasped her skirts to calm her nerves and trailed after the men into the dining room, where Jamie and Leana stood waiting by their chairs. Brightening at the sight of her in the claret gown, Leana stretched up to whisper in Jamie's ear. He offered a smile as well, brief though it was. If Jamie admired the dress Rose wore, his expression did not tell her so. Neil's face, however, was an open volume, with an earnest declaration of love written across its pages in a plain, sure hand.

Rose bowed her head for prayer, grateful for any diversion. Please God, she would know what to say to Neil when the moment arrived.

While her father intoned a lengthy blessing on the food, her thoughts drifted back to a Sabbath conversation beyond the Elliots' cottage door. *Suppose we save those words for a more private time and place.* Without meaning to, she'd welcomed an offer of marriage from the first. Now that time and place had come.

Rose blinked back tears while three maidservants swept into the room bearing dishes of steaming hotchpotch. The pungent aroma of stewed mutton and well-seasoned vegetables set her stomach churning. While the lasses ladled the thick soup, Rose watched naught but Jamie, praying she might find sympathy there. Her cousin glanced up in time to catch her staring at him, imploring him with her eyes, *Do something!* She noticed the faint lines across his brow. Was it concern? Or irritation?

"So, Uncle." He looked toward the head of the table where Lachlan McBride busied himself with his soup. "As the Elliots are here at my invitation, when might we address the issue at hand?"

Oh, Jamie! She'd hoped he might stall the proceedings, not hurry them along. What was the man thinking? She held her breath and gripped the round spoon next to her untouched plate as her father prepared to speak.

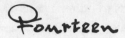

Fourteen

So comes a reckoning when the banquet's o'er,
The dreadful reckoning, and men smile no more.

JOHN GAY

T is nothing that concerns you, Jamie." Lachlan McBride's words were a slammed door. "Mr. Elliot and I will discuss the matter later. In private."

Colin Elliot started to make a comment, then glanced at his son, who shook his head without shaking it, so slight was the movement. Jamie must have noticed, for he shifted his gaze to Rose, who'd seen it as well. From one corner of the dinner table to the other, unspoken words hung in the air like stale peat smoke.

Her father seemed oblivious to the awkward lull in conversation, consuming his soup with noisy relish. After a lengthy pause, Mr. Elliot introduced the subject of Martinmas, which led to a spirited discourse on the changeable nature of weather and market prices. By the time her father called for the last course, Leana had disappeared to tend to Ian, and Jamie had returned to his ewes, leaving Rose to fend for herself. She offered a wan smile when necessary and ate her cranberry tart in silence, while the men talked all around her. Soon they would talk *about* her, and that would be exceedingly worse.

When Eliza and the others came in to clear away the last of the pewter plates, Lachlan stood to his feet. "Mr. Elliot, join me for a dram. I believe these two can entertain each other." His eyes narrowed. "From a respectable distance, of course." The two fathers disappeared behind the spence door, shutting it firmly behind them.

It seemed the men had taken all the sound from the room with them. Rose and Neil sat mute, eying each other across the empty table. Even the north wind, which had rattled the panes all through dinner, had fallen quiet.

Neil spoke first. His voice cracked, as if he were a *hauflin* no older than twelve. "R-Rose? W-will...ah, that is...will you..."

In his timid question came her certain answer: *Nae. I will not.*

"Mr. Elliot," she said tentatively, then stood and began again. "Neil, we must come to some understanding."

"Aye, Rose, we must." Neil vaulted to his feet and skirted the table, ignoring her father's edict. A moment later he stood beside her, taking in great gulps of air. She tucked her hands behind her skirts before he could reach for them, though he touched her elbow and confessed, "I...I should not have...have kissed you, Rose. But you seemed so..." His freshly shaved face turned scarlet. "So...taken with me. So interested. When I told my father about...about our walk through the abbey..."

Her eyes widened. "Whatever did you tell him?"

"Well, that I...that we kissed. That I intended to marry you. He agreed to speak to Mr. McBride at once. To..." He looked away, unable to meet her unflinching gaze. "To discuss the terms of your...bride price."

"My *price?*" She had not even given him an answer yet, and already they were discussing financial matters. "Do you intend to purchase me like a ewe at Keltonhill Fair?"

"Rose! I—"

"Would you have my hand and not my heart?"

"Nae!" His eyes flew open in shock. "I would have them both, Rose. In truth, I...I thought I *had* your heart."

Oh, Neil. "Forgive me, Mr. Elliot."

His eyes widened in confusion. "Will you not even call me *Neil?*"

Rose dropped her hands to her side, taken aback by his obvious despair. Amends must be made. "I do care for you, Neil."

His head shot up, hope lighting his brow. "You do?"

"Aye, as a friend." She hastened to add, "Or a brother. As a lad I've kenned all my life."

His countenance fell. "But not as a husband."

Biting her lip to keep from hurting him further, she only shook her head. "The fact is, I'm too young—"

"Och! I would wait for you, Rose." He tugged on her elbow, pulling a hand free for him to clasp. "A year, if need be. Twa, if you like." Neil squeezed her hand with a firmness born of desperation. With his other hand he touched her cheek. "You're the bonniest lass in the parish. As fair as any *flooer* that e'er bloomed in Scotland."

"But I'm not the flower for you," she said, stepping back, tugging her hand free as she did. "I'm far too headstrong and full of opinions. You'd be miserable in a fortnight, Neil. Besides, you deserve a lass who loves you alone. And I…" She glanced away, swallowing her pride, speaking the truth at last. "I love another."

Behind her, the spence door banged open. "What's that you say, Rose?"

Father. She froze, afraid to answer. How much had he heard? He walked across the room with Neil's father close behind. The two men— one older, one younger by a dozen years—positioned themselves between the young couple, oblivious to their strained expressions.

Her father pressed a forefinger to his lips, as though considering something. "I'm certain I heard you use the word *love* with young Elliot here. Am I to assume you're ready to move forward with the arrangements his father and I have discussed?"

She nearly fainted. "Arrangements?"

"Aye." Colin Elliot beamed, obviously pleased with himself. He held up a parchment between two stout fingers. "As this marriage contract states, Neil is the eldest of my children. My property—the shop, cottage, and farmlands—will belong to him someday, which well pleased your father." The men nodded at each other. "Since I've enough silver in my thrifite to meet the price set by Mr. McBride for your hand, there was little left to do but drink to your guid health and give you both our *blissin.*"

"Blessing?" Her lips were so parched she could barely form the word. "Perhaps…" Rose sought Neil's gaze, pleading for him to speak. "Perhaps your son might explain."

"But I am the one who is confused, Miss McBride." Neil's bewilderment was clear, from his knitted brow to the nervous manner in which he tugged at his waistcoat. "I thought your intentions matched mine. That you loved me, as I do you."

"Och!" Her father jerked his head to the side, as though he might spit on the hearth. "She's confessed her love once, lad. Press her no further. Marriage has little to do with love and meikle to do with carrying on the family name."

Neil grimaced. "When your daughter spoke of love a moment ago, sir, 'twas not directed at me."

"Who then?" Lachlan barked, staring hard at Rose, then back at Neil.

"She...did not say."

"Aye, but she *will* say!" Her father planted his foot a step closer, scowling as he did. "What manner of man would woo my daughter without my knowledge or permission?"

"None," she hurried to say, grateful for a slender thread of truth to offer. "No stranger has wooed me, of that you can be sure."

"So you've no other suitor than young Elliot here?"

She shook her head. "No sir." Jamie was many things, but a suitor was not one of them.

Her father persisted, "And you do not wish to marry this prosperous grocer's son?"

Rose looked away, unable to bear another glimpse of Neil's pain or her father's fury. "Forgive me," she murmured.

Collin Elliot threw up his hands. "Is there to be a wedding this Yule or not?"

"Not," Neil answered, his shoulders sagging. "Come, Father. 'Tis best we take our leave. Whatever family business the McBrides have to settle, 'twill not involve us."

Rose's apology was ignored by all three men, who turned their backs on her and made their way into the hall. Staring at the hearth, her hands clasped before her, Rose heard their voices fade out the front door, carried away by the strong winds. It was just as well, for though the words they spoke were true, they were not kind. *Thoughtless. Immature. Flindrikin.*

The front door banged shut. Rose swallowed the knot of apprehension that threatened to choke her and prepared to face her father's wrath. He came directly, his coattails flapping behind him, his gray eyes ablaze.

"What the de'il were you thinking, lass? Playing our young neighbor for a fool and his father as well!" He stormed about the room, his fist raised as if he were General Hawley at Culloden Moor. His voice rose with it. "Do you not see? The disgrace you've brought to my doorstep with your capricious behavior will leave a black mark no amount of silver can scrub clean."

"Father, Neil and I were naught but friends—"

"*Friends?*" He spun on his heel. " 'Twas not the word young Elliot used. He said he *loved* you, Rose. You can be sure he's ground that sentiment into the dirt beneath his boots by now. 'Tis a long ride back to Newabbey with a sullen father and a broken heart."

She gripped the wooden back of a chair for support and stared out the window at the bleak, gray sky. "I did not mean to hurt him."

"What *did* you mean to do then?" He walked in front of her, blocking her view with his menacing stance. "Dishonor the Almighty? Shame this household? Or did you hope to make a certain cousin jealous enough to forget his marriage vows?"

"I did no such thing, Father!" Her heart leapt into her throat. "Jamie belongs to Leana, not to me. You of all people ken why that's so, Father."

Lachlan McBride did not flinch at her clear accusation. " 'Twas the will of the Almighty." He spoke with such conviction she almost believed him. "The burden falls on me to find you a proper husband. How can I manage, Rose, when you confound me at every turn? Pining after your married cousin for months. Trifling with a neighbor's son and refusing his honest offer of marriage." He glanced at the mantel clock, then shook his head with a decided frown. "The village gossips will not soon let go of this meaty bone, I can promise you that."

His gloomy prediction trailed after her the rest of the day like a cat slipping into the house unseen, getting underfoot, disappearing round corners. Might the *glib-gabbit* women of the parish put abroad a story that she was a *tairt* no worthy suitor would consider? If so, her marriage prospects would be ruined.

Rose fell into a fitful sleep that night, dreaming of the Newabbey kirkyard draped in a moonless mist, its headstones poking from the ground at odd angles. Perched atop the graves were cats of every hue, calling to one other in high-pitched yowls. When Rose stepped into the nightmarish scene, their whiskered faces pointed toward her. In a fierce and frichtsome chorus they screeched out her name.

"Nae!" She sat up, suddenly awake, flailing at the curtains of her box bed until she spied the faint glow of the taper on top of her dresser. The light dispelled the last vestiges of her dream but not the uneasiness that had settled over her. Whatever the hour, it was still too early to rise and dress. She climbed into Leana's old reading chair with a volume by Defoe clutched in one hand, the candle in the other, and tried to concentrate on the plight of beautiful Roxana. But the words swam on the page, and the story thread grew tangled. When blessed sleep tugged at her eyelids once more, Rose replaced the taper and slipped under the covers. Please God, she would not dream again this night.

The new day arrived draped in pale silver with no wind to stir the chilly air. Rose dressed, giving little thought to her choice of gown. No suitor would darken her door today. Annabel helped with the last of Rose's buttons and plaited her hair in a thick braid before sending her mistress down the stair, her steps slower than usual.

Neda greeted her at the breakfast table with a look of mild concern. "Ye've not slept weel, lass. 'Tis not like ye tae have plum-colored smudges 'neath yer eyes." When Rose described her nightmare, Neda's gaze sharpened. "Dreamin' o' cats, ye say?" She clucked her tongue, stirring the porridge more forcefully. " 'Tis an ill omen, Rose. Someone has in mind tae do ye a bit o' harm."

Rose looked at her, aghast. Not Jamie? Or could it be Neil, with his wounded pride? "A man, do you think?"

"Nae." Neda spooned out her breakfast. "Mair likely a woman."

One name came to mind. "Lillias Brown," Rose breathed, a chill skipping down her spine.

"Och!" Neda banged her wooden spurtle against the metal pot, making an awful noise. "What business have ye wi' sae *wickit* a soul as the Widow Brown?"

"None at all," Rose hurried to explain. "We saw her the afternoon of Ian's kirkin. Do you recall her strange mumblings that day?"

"Aye," Neda grumbled. "*Unco* words indeed. Keep far awa from that woman's path, and see that ye niver seek oot her counsel." Once Rose assured her she would do no such thing, Neda's taut features relaxed. "Mebbe yer dream meant ye'll soon be seein' the kittlins ye took tae Miss Elliot's *hoose*."

"Maybe," Rose said, lifting a spoonful of hot porridge to her mouth and almost burning her lips. She hastily put down the spoon and reached instead for a mug of milk, grateful for the cool, sweet taste. Susanne's admiration for her older brother knew no bounds. Would she be vexed at the news? Or might Susanne simply roll her eyes, knowing Rose's capricious nature as she did?

Before Rose emptied her porridge cup, a knock at the door sent her scurrying to the front of the house, patting a napkin to her mouth. Johnny Elliot, the middle son in the grocer's family, stood waiting in the hall, holding out a letter. "For Miss Rose McBride," the lad said. Two missing teeth spoiled the formality of his delivery, but his expression was as solemn as a session clerk's.

Rose took the letter, her heart quickening. "Might you wait while I read it, Johnny? I may want to send you home with a response."

"Aye." He looked about the hall for somewhere to sit, while Rose unfolded the letter, leaning toward a window for light as she began to read.

> To Miss Rose McBride
> Tuesday, 3 November 1789
>
> Rose,
>
> However could you wound my brother so? I trusted you to
> treat him fairly. It seems my faith was misplaced. Neil is
> inconsolable, and my father is stamping about the house in
> a fine temper.

Rose fell against the wall. 'Twas worse than she'd imagined. Susanne's words cut like scissors sharpened on her own thoughtlessness.

> Should you feel compelled to visit, I fear you will find no welcome at our door, nor can I continue to call you my friend with any sincerity.

Her eyes growing moist, Rose stared at the letter in disbelief. Were they no longer friends? Could Susanne possibly mean that?

> It grieves me to write this after so lengthy a friendship, but I feel I must convey the depth of my disappointment and the firmness of my resolve.
>
> With regret,
>
> Miss Susanne Elliot
> Ingleneuk

Rose pressed the letter against her heart. *Please, God, not Susanne.* To think of losing her affection forever! And not only Susanne. If the grocer's daughter put her aside, so might the other girls of the parish. How had it come to this?

Johnny shuffled his feet, his discomfort obvious. "Will you be wanting to write my sister?"

"Aye." Rose brushed away her tears. " 'Twill take me only a minute." She flew up the stair to her room, where her writing desk contained all she would need to pen a letter—except, it seemed, the right words to soften Susanne's heart. She stared at the paper, the ink seeping into her fingertips as she gripped the pen too close to the nub. When Neda tapped at the door, Rose knew she could delay no longer.

> To Miss Susanne Elliot
> Tuesday, 3 November 1789
>
> Dear Susanne,
>
> You and your family have every right to be unhappy with me. Without meaning to, I led your brother to believe my

heart was his for the taking. I am deeply sorry for disappointing him and hurting you as well.

Susanne, you are my dearest friend in all of Galloway. Please accept my sincere apologies, or I shall leave for Dumfries in January with a very heavy heart.

Yours in friendship,

Miss Rose McBride
Auchengray

She cast a sprinkling of sand across the page to dry the ink, then shook it clean and folded it into a square. A stick of wax touched to the candle's flame to seal it, and the letter was finished. Rose found Johnny waiting at the bottom step, staring up at her room as if willing her to hurry. After pressing a coin into Johnny's palm for his trouble, she tucked the letter into his coat pocket and patted it with a silent prayer for mercy.

"You were good to wait, lad. Kindly see that your sister reads my letter."

"I'll try," he said, dipping his head. "Though I cannot promise she won't feed it to the fire, Miss McBride. Susanne's that unhappy with you."

Rose sighed wistfully. "I ken she is, Johnny." *And so is her father. And so is my father. And so is poor Neil.* She pointed him toward the door so he might not see fresh tears pooling in her eyes.

Fifteen

Kindle a candle at baith ends
and it will soon burn out.
SCOTTISH PROVERB

O ch, lass! There's no shame in weeping. 'Tis how every mother in
Scotland waters her kitchen garden."

Leana dabbed at her eyes with the hem of Ian's cotton gown, being
careful not to wake him. Even after two months, the babe's sleeping
pattern had no rhyme or reason to it, and his colic had yet to disappear. "Jessie, you are a good friend to listen to my woes on a cold
December day." Few neighbors could cheer her like plain-speaking
Jessie Newall.

The young woman waved her hand dismissively, shaking her mass
of red hair as well. "Haven't I raised Annie these two years?"

Leana observed the round-faced child toddle about the front parlor
of Auchengray. A low-beamed, square room on the west side of the
mains, it was cluttered with chairs, small tables, and a narrow guest bed,
giving young Annie much to explore. She was dressed in the warm
woolen jumper Leana had knitted for her as a birthday present. The
blaeberry dye had held fast, its purplish hue a bonny complement to
Annie's orange-marmalade locks, so like her mother's. Her spirits lifting,
Leana watched Annie climb into a high-backed chair, then turn round
and sit down, poking her sturdy legs out straight, clapping her hands,
and beaming with pride at her accomplishment.

"Well done," Leana murmured, wiping away the last of her tears.

Jessie eyed her. "I ken it well, that wearisome feeling. You cannot
hold up your head at the breakfast table, yet you cannot keep to your
pillow at night."

"Aye." Leana offered her a shaky smile. "Watching you with Annie
months ago, I did not realize mothering could be so…" She could not

bring herself to say the words that came to mind: *Difficult. Exhausting. Lonely.*

Jessie said it for her. " 'Tis hard, Leana. Motherhood is not for the woman who hates wearing a soiled gown or eating cold porridge." She smoothed a hand over her rounded belly. "Alan Newall had better prepare for many a sleepless night when this one arrives."

Leana studied the look of contentment on her friend's face and wondered how, if the Almighty blessed her own womb again, she would ever care for two bairns. Alan and Jessie had their small farm on top of Troston Hill to manage, as well as Annie to chase after, another wee babe in the house come February, and a flock of blackface ewes lambing in the spring. "However will you do it all?" Leana wanted to ask, though she knew the answer: *Long days. Steady work. Short nights.*

Jessie's gaze met hers. "I must call at Auchengray more often," she said, her tone lightly teasing. "You've grown rather melancholy since you married Mr. McKie."

"Have I?" Leana feared her wan smile did little to dispel the notion. "Jamie is not to blame, poor man. He keeps busy with the flocks."

Jessie's brows, bright as her hair, arched in surprise. "Too busy to see to his wife's pleasure?"

Leana dropped her chin to hide the heat climbing her neck. The things Jessie Newall could say without blushing! "My pleasure is of little concern when we are both so tired by nightfall."

"So that's how it is." Jessie rose to walk the floor, scooping up her daughter and planting Annie securely on her hip as the two circled the room together. "When was the last time Eliza brushed your hair 'til it shone?"

Leana touched her hand to the plaits wrapped round her head. "My *hair*?"

"Aye, and that gown." Jessie paused to look at her and made a face. "Practical, I'm sure, but 'twould appear you've worn it for a month."

"Two," Leana confessed, looking down at the wrinkled fabric. "The bodice laces in the front, you see. I made it especially—"

"Good, then make another." Jessie nodded with satisfaction. "And stitch a new shirt for Jamie while you've a needle in your hand. No wife sews a finer *sark* than you do, Leana. See that he thanks you for it. Properly." She gave a broad wink, then whirled about while Annie squealed with delight, her cherub face shining.

"Anything else that needs doing?" Leana did not try to hide her exasperation. If her friend meant to lift her spirits, her words were having the opposite effect. Leana had plenty of work to do without adding more to the list. If Jamie had not reached for her since she returned home from the manse with Ian, what did it matter? They were both too exhausted to care. Weren't they?

"Listen to me, Leana." Jessie spun to a stop, pulling Annie into a tight embrace. The child's chubby legs twined round her mother's waist, as Jessie rested her chin on her daughter's curls, watching Leana all the while. "Love the man, tired or not. He needs to ken you've forgiven him completely for that foolishness last winter with Rose."

Leana started to object but swallowed her words instead. Jessie spoke naught but the truth. "I will love him," Leana promised, ignoring the fear that coiled in her stomach. Fear that Jamie might reject her. That deep in his heart he still preferred Rose. "Tonight I'll don a different gown for supper and send Eliza looking for my brush."

Jessie smiled broadly. "Well done, lass. If my advice proves worthy, I'll count on you to send me a box of your best *tablet* for Yule."

"Done." Leana laughed. Already her heart felt lighter. "We've butter and sugar enough to make you a sweetie. I'll have Jamie bring it round before the Daft Days are over."

That evening Leana was true to her word. From the clothes press she chose a gown she'd not worn since last winter, then had it aired and pressed. While Ian napped, Eliza washed Leana's hair in lavender-scented water, rubbing it dry and brushing it until it gleamed like molten gold. Leana nursed Ian once more and then slipped on her gown, delighting in the feel of silk on her shoulders. "Lace me with care, Eliza. My waist is no longer as small as my sister's, and for good reason." She smiled at Ian, already asleep in his cradle. "A verra good reason."

No bride felt more beautiful than Leana did, gliding down the stair toward supper. Her slippered feet barely touched the floor. The rustle of her gown made a music all its own. When she swept into the room, everyone present turned to gape at her. But only Jamie's opinion mattered. In a twinkling she had his undivided attention.

"Can this be my good wife?" His eyes widened first, then his smile, as he stretched out his hand, beckoning her forward. "Come, Leana. Tell us what occasion we're to mark this night, for surely you did not dress so bonny for my sake."

"Yours alone." She took the seat next to his, touching his hand as she did. Rose sat across the table from them, silent. Leana felt nothing but sympathy for her sister, for the incident last month with Mr. Elliot was most unfortunate. Perhaps in Dumfries Rose would be introduced to a kind gentleman who might sweep away any memories of Neil. *And of Jamie.* Leana glanced toward the head of the table, where her father gave her a cursory appraisal before directing the family to bow their heads for prayer.

Moments later the maids served plates of cock-a-leekie soup made from chicken simmered in veal stock, flavored with leeks and prunes. Leana supped with care, not wanting to stain her gown with the rich broth. Later, when she swallowed the last bite of almond cake, Leana caught her husband watching her with a roguish gleam. *Oh, Jamie!* She folded her hands in her lap while the plates were cleared, clasping her fingers tight to keep them from trembling.

Family worship, an hour-long evening ritual, seemed interminable. Prayers and psalms were spoken and sung and the large Buik spread open with due reverence. When Leana's mind began to wander, she searched her heart for a verse on which to pin her thoughts. *In the multitude of my thoughts within me thy comforts delight my soul.* Aye, the Almighty *had* comforted her, even delighted her, through the long, lonely months when Jamie did neither. Tonight she would know the comfort of a husband. And the delight, please God; she would know that as well.

At last the closing prayer was said and the tapers snuffed. Climbing the stair with Jamie, Leana shivered at the icy December wind whistling past the windowpanes.

He slipped an arm round her waist, pulling her close. "Are you cold, lass?"

"Not for long," she said, surprising them both. Jamie's laugh was a welcome sound and her flushed cheeks a hint of things to come. They undressed by candlelight, their gazes locked amid the flickering shadows. Ian, fast asleep in his cradle by the hearth, was still close to their hearts, yet far from their minds at the moment.

She slid between the sheets of their cozy bed, stretching her limbs to touch the wooden walls that encased them. Jamie climbed in and closed the thick bed curtains behind him, blocking out the last of the candlelight. A velvety darkness surrounded them. Not a sound could be heard, save for Jamie's steady breathing. And her own, not so steady. The close quarters heightened the fragrance of lavender in her hair, of heather in the mattress, of the spicy soap on Jamie's skin, freshly shaved before supper.

Holding his smooth face in her hands, Leana planted kisses along the razor's path. On his cheek, on his chin, on his neck. Inhaling the welcome scent of him, tasting his salty skin. "Love me, Jamie." She'd whispered the same words all seven nights of their bridal week in Dumfries. Perhaps they might have the same effect.

He pulled her close for a lengthy kiss, pausing long enough to ask, "Are you sure? Are you…well?"

She smiled at his concern. "Ian is two months old now," she reminded him, wrapping her arms round his shoulders. "I am verra sure, my husband. All is well."

Through the folds of the curtain, through the wooden box bed panels, the wail of an infant pierced the night air.

"Och!" Jamie fell away from her, banging his fist on the wall behind his head. "Did the babe hear you speak his name? Is that what's to blame for this?"

Leana sat up, as disappointed as he was. "Let me see what I can do, Jamie."

He rolled aside so she might crawl out, scowling at the ceiling as he did. " 'Tis not your fault, Leana. The Almighty created bairns to fill every minute of silence testing their lungs. Or so it says in the First Book of Discipline."

"On what page would I find that?" She touched his shoulder before turning toward the hearth and their demanding son. Ian refused to be soothed. Nursing him eased his hunger, but then his colic sent him kicking his legs against her, bruising her hip in the process. Jamie watched with mounting frustration, wanting to be helpful, yet clearly wanting his wife.

"I'm sorry, Jamie," she said, pacing the floor with Ian draped over her shoulder. It was the one position that earned her a reprieve from the endless crying. "Don't wait up for me. Go to sleep while he's quiet."

Jamie fell back against the mattress. "And when will Ian be quiet long enough for us to share a bed?"

"Soon," she promised, keeping her voice low as she took another turn about the room. "You'll have your wife back soon, Jamie."

But it was not soon.

Not in a month of December nights did Leana have Jamie all to herself. If Ian fell sound asleep, so did Jamie. If Jamie was wide awake, Leana could not keep her eyes open. When both parents were willing to lose an hour of sleep for each other, Ian was prepared to lay claim to it.

"Ne'er have the Daft Days been more properly named," a bleary-eyed Jamie announced one morning over a saucer of strong tea. "I've not had a single lucid thought in weeks. Even the ewes are more canny than I."

Duncan slapped him on the back, nearly knocking the saucer from his hand. "Ye've a lang way tae go tae be daft as a sheep, lad. Instead ye're a new faither wi' a healthy son."

"Aye, healthy," Jamie grumbled, putting his tea aside to head for the byre and his first tasks of the day. " 'Til supper, Leana," he added, barely looking over his shoulder as he disappeared through the back door of the house into the frosty air.

Leana frowned at her own tea grown cold. She'd stitched a new gown to please her friend Jessie and her husband as well and had worn it that morning. Had Jamie even noticed? When Neda's hand tapped her shoulder, Leana looked round, knowing her feelings were poorly hidden.

"While Ian catches his mornin' nap, Mistress McKie, suppose ye join me in the kitchen. We'll make a pan o' tablet tae bless the neighbors. Take a few boxes tae their doors afore we usher in the year 1790 on Hogmanay." Neda looked down at her, compassion lining every feature. "Might that be a blithe pastime for a *wabbit* young mither?"

"Aye." She rose to her feet, pressing her hands into the small of her back, stiff from too little sleep. "Shall we ask Rose to join us? The girl has so few days left at Auchengray."

"If ye like," Neda said. " 'Tis a guid tongue that says nae ill, or so me mither taught me. Yer kindness toward Rose has not gone unnoticed."

Leana's smile was faint but genuine. "I love my sister, Neda, though the last year has been difficult."

"Och! Nae need tae confess yer sins tae me, lass." Neda stepped into the larder, still talking over her shoulder. "Nor tae yer sister. Only tae God."

"Which I have done," Leana admitted, grieved at how often she'd begged God for forgiveness concerning Rose. "Many times."

"Yer sister flits to Dumfries on Monday next," Neda reminded her, emerging from the larder with a crock of butter in one hand, a small loaf of sugar in the other. " 'Til then, I ken ye'll be guid tae the lass, for she needs ye *sairlie*."

"I am her only sister," Leana agreed.

"Mair than that." Neda pursed her lips. "Ye're her only true friend."

Sixteen

One heart
must hold both sisters,
never seen apart.
WILLIAM COWPER

O ne will never hold it all," Rose groaned, tossing a handful of linen towels in the leather traveling case at the foot of her bed. "Whatever can they mean by 'one small trunk'?"

Leana breathed a quick prayer for patience. It had been a long morning. Dresses and petticoats, shoes and bonnets remained scattered all over the room, enough to fill four small trunks. Rose had worked herself into a high color and had run out of servants willing to do her bidding. Neda wisely kept busy in the kitchen, Eliza was nowhere to be found, and Annabel had fled from the room in tears. Leana alone remained to see the task finished before sending Rose on her way to Dumfries.

"Perhaps an exception might be made." Leana adjusted her spectacles to review the letter from Carlyle School for Young Ladies. The instructions for new students were numerous and detailed, and the language brooked no argument. Neither did the bold hand, which outlined the personal items that were—and were not—permissible. Lachlan McBride had no doubt chosen the boarding school for its severe restrictions. Had Rose even read the letter? Did she know what awaited her on Millbrae *Vennel?*

Leana pulled off her spectacles and slipped them into her pocket tied beneath a small slit in her skirts. "I'm afraid your schoolmistress states her wishes quite plainly, Rose: 'One small trunk allowed each student.'" Hoping to forestall another outburst, Leana offered an explanation. "The school is situated in the very heart of Dumfries. Without the benefit of a steading like ours, storage space for twelve students must pose quite a challenge."

"But what am I to *do?*" Rose whined, a fistful of dress fabric in each hand. "They're daughters of the gentry, Leana. Think of the costumes their parents will have delivered to the school's door! If I'm to be there all spring, I'll need more than these old gowns."

Leana spied the truth lurking beneath her sister's prickly behavior. 'Twas not the lack of clothes that vexed Rose. It was bidding farewell to Auchengray, and leaving Jamie in particular. She gazed out the window, where a dusting of snow carpeted the sill. "Dearie, take your favorite winter gowns now. When you come home for Easter, you can exchange those dresses for lighter spring ones. I feel certain that's what the other lasses will do."

Appeased, Rose went back to folding cambric shifts and woolen stockings, while Leana tucked pouches of dried lavender deep into the corners of the trunk. "For a sweeter scent," Leana explained. *And so you won't forget me.* A needless concern, no doubt, but persistent. More than a sister or friend, Rose was almost a daughter, so involved had Leana been in her upbringing. Though having a quieter house held some appeal, the notion of not seeing her sister for weeks at a time grieved Leana. Even with Ian in her life. Even with Jamie.

The longest Rose had ever been gone was the week she'd spent last winter at their Aunt Margaret's house in Twyneholm. The week Rose prepared to marry Jamie. The week the lass came home to discover the worst news of her young life.

I trusted you, Leana! I will never forgive you!

Leana shuddered, remembering. For a twelvemonth the two sisters had avoided any further discussion of what had taken place on that dark night when Leana became a bride and Rose did not. Perhaps it was better that way.

"Which is better?" Rose asked. "The jade green gown or the rose-colored one?"

Brushing away her musings, Leana inspected the fabrics draped across Rose's winter-pale skin. "Save the green for spring, when you'll have a bit more color in your cheeks." She glanced at the clothes press, weighing a possibility. A peace offering, of sorts. A benediction. "What if I sent you with my best gown instead?"

Rose's eyes grew round. "The claret?"

"It looked lovely on you the last time you wore it. Unless…" Leana watched her closely. "Unless the memories the gown stirs might upset you."

"Memories?" Rose rolled her eyes. " 'Tis only fabric, Leana."

"Why not take it then?" Lifting her cherished gown out of the press, Leana shook out the wrinkles, admiring again the intricate embroidery. She recalled the white silk chemise she had worn underneath it, cool against her skin. And the look on Jamie's face when he had first clapped eyes on her dressed in her rich new gown. Her sister considered it naught but fabric and needlework. For Leana, the claret gown meant a great deal more. But if it sent Rose to Dumfries with a lighter heart, 'twould be worth the sacrifice.

Carefully smoothing the gown for packing, Leana tucked the last of her regrets inside the folds and managed to fit the dress into Rose's overflowing trunk. "Hang your gowns out to air 'til a maid can get to them, dearie. They've grown musty in the press."

Rose posed in front of the looking glass, holding her head in a regal manner, as though an invisible string had come down from heaven and attached itself to the tip of her nose. "Perhaps this spring Father will buy me another gown or two."

" 'Tis the betterment of your mind that prompted Father to invest his silver in your education," Leana reminded her, consulting the letter once more. "You will be studying Latin and French, arithmetic and bookkeeping, dancing and social etiquette, music and art—"

"Och!" Rose exclaimed, turning away from the glass. "If you consider gum flowers, net purses, and shell work *art.*"

Leana smiled behind the letter. "Geography, then. History. Ah, here's something that will please Neda: pastry making and preserves."

"The only thing I care to preserve is the small circle of my waist." Rose whirled about the looking glass as if to make her point. "Tell me, will birthing a bairn ruin my figure for good?"

Leana slowly folded the letter, more aware than ever of the roundness of her breasts and hips and the tightness of her stays. "When a child swells a woman's body, you can be sure it expands her heart as well."

Rose spun to a stop in front of her, all pretense gone from her expression. "Is it worth it, Leana? The months of waiting. And the labor. And the pain. Are you...glad to be a mother?"

"*Glad?* Oh, Rose, that's not the half of it. Loving Ian as I do only makes me love his father more."

"I see." Rose looked down, plucking at the ribbon round her waist.

"And I think...that is, I hope Jamie has begun to love me. A little." Leana prayed her next words would not fall among thorns. "Have you...forgiven me yet, dearie? For loving Jamie?"

Rose lifted her head, a glint of tears in her eyes, a thin edge to her voice. "For stealing him, you mean?"

At last it had come, her hour of reckoning, prompted by her own foolish question. Leana took a long, steadying breath. "I did not mean to steal him, Rose." Nonetheless, she'd done so, goaded on by their father. On Hogmanay, the day of the wedding, Lachlan McBride had made Leana's future abundantly clear: *It is Jamie, or it is no one.* Leana had chosen Jamie, thinking he loved her. Thinking Rose did not love him. Never in her life had Leana been so mistaken. "I blame only myself. No one else."

Rose frowned at her. "Then you admit 'twas your fault."

"Aye, just as I confessed to you the very hour you arrived home from Aunt Meg's, remember?" Leana's shoulders sagged. "Though 'twas not my fault you were delayed by the snow. And not my idea to be your proxy for the wedding."

Rose moved closer, her eyes filled with anguish. "But it *was* your idea to be Jamie's doxy. For the bedding."

"Not his doxy, Rose. His...*bride.*" Leana choked on the word. "Don't you see? That night in the box bed I thought he knew it was me, Rose. And that he...that he wanted me there." She bowed her head in confession. "Instead he thought I was you."

"It *should* have been me." Rose sank to the floor like a discarded dress. "Jamie was the husband I was meant to have. Don't you see? I tried to love Neil Elliot. I *did,* Leana. But he isn't...he isn't..."

He isn't Jamie. "Please forgive me, dearie. This autumn has been very hard on you." Leana reached out a tentative hand, hoping a gentle touch might console her, but Rose jerked her arm away. "I'd hoped we might part on a sweeter note. Why fret over this now, Rose, when you have a whole new life waiting for you?"

"Because it's not *fair*. Because I *am* going away, leaving all I love behind. You have Jamie and Ian and Auchengray, and I have *nothing*." Rose wiped her tears away as quickly as they formed, her gaze still pointed downward. "I've never had a mother. Nor a husband. Who knows if I'll ever have children?" Her voice fell to a ragged whisper. "All I have is you."

Leana reached for her. "But I love you like my own child, Rose."

"'Tis not *my* love you want." Rose avoided her embrace. "'Tis Jamie's." Her dark eyes narrowed. "Have you ever heard Jamie speak those words to you, as I have?"

"Nae, I have not," Leana said faintly. *Not yet.* Somehow Rose knew that sad truth. Knew, and wielded it like a weapon sharpened by months of resentment.

Rose stood and shifted her attention to the looking glass, straightening her neckline. "I suppose once I'm gone to Dumfries, you'll expect Jamie to forget me."

Leana came up behind her, resting her hands on Rose's shoulders, gratified that she did not pull away this time. Though her sister had gravely wounded her, 'twas naught but justice meted out long after the crime. "Jamie could never forget you, for he *does* love you, as his cousin. And I love you, as my sister."

Rose turned away from her reflection but not before Leana saw a look of deep pain, like that of an abandoned child, move across her sister's features. "You cannot love me," Rose said, her voice broken. "Not when I still love Jamie."

"You're wrong, dearie." Leana squeezed her shoulders tight, fighting a fresh spate of tears. "I cannot stop loving you, Rose, any more than I can stop loving my husband. 'Tis my responsibility to love you both, a task I dare not put aside. For the gifts and calling of God are without repentance, and my heart would ne'er let me do otherwise." She aimed Rose toward the door. "Come, we've kept the man waiting long enough. For 'tis Jamie who'll deliver you to your new life in Dumfries." *Then, please God, let him come home to me.*

Seventeen

I do perceive here a divided duty.

WILLIAM SHAKESPEARE

I'm ready, Cousin!" Rose called out, hastening toward the chaise, her green cloak vivid against the wintry background.

Jamie watched her approach with misgivings. When she arrived at his side, breathless from hurrying, he noticed that, though her face was pink, he saw shadows there as well, and her eyes had a furtive look about them. Driving Rose to Dumfries was not a duty he'd chosen; rather it had been assigned by Lachlan at breakfast without any opportunity to protest. "How is it that I'm the one to escort you?" Jamie asked her, curious to see how she might answer. "Your father should claim the honor of depositing you at Mistress Carlyle's doorstep and seeing you settled, Rose."

"Aye, he should," she agreed, pretending to pout. "But this is the Monday he meets with Mr. Craik and the Society for the Encouragement of Agriculture. He wouldn't miss their gatherings for all the world." She rested one gloved hand on the chaise. "Shall we climb in then?"

Jamie had no intention of giving in so easily. "What of Willie? He's taken you round the parish for many a year. Why not today?"

"Willie isn't himself just now." She leaned closer and confided, "He ate a rather generous portion of Neda's plum pudding at supper last night, with altogether too much caudle sauce."

Jamie could not argue the ill effects of wine mixed with rum, having suffered once as a boy from such overindulgence. "A small serving is good for the stomach, but in large doses…" He left the rest unsaid, catching sight of Duncan and one of the menservants dragging Rose's cumbersome trunk across the lawn. "Here, let me see to that."

Duncan grunted as the three men heaved it into place behind the seat. "Ye'll need help pryin' it oot o' the chaise whan ye get tae Dumfries."

"'Twill not be the only trunk arriving at Carlyle School today," Jamie assured him, slapping the man's back good-naturedly. "I'll find a younger lad to assist me."

"Och!" Duncan flapped a hand at him. "Younger mebbe but nae stronger." He glanced at the others, then inclined his head toward the steading. "Might I have a wird wi' ye, Jamie?"

Begging Rose's pardon, Jamie followed Duncan several paces from the chaise, then stopped with his back toward Rose. "What is it, man?" He kept his voice low. "Something with the ewes?"

"Aye, a certain ewe wha's aboot tae put herself in an *unchancie* situation." Duncan shot a pointed look at Rose. "'Tis not wise for a married man tae be ridin' alone wi' a lassie."

Jamie shook his head and used Duncan's own words to assure him. "Dinna fash yerself. 'Tis a cousin's duty I'm about, not a lover's."

Duncan tipped his head back, eying him from beneath the brim of his wool bonnet. "Have ye told Leana that? Might put her mind at ease."

Jamie heeded the man's sound counsel, trotting toward the mains with a slight wave to Rose. He knew he'd find Leana in the kitchen with Neda, preparing a meal he'd be sorry to miss. Pickled mutton and bannocks, already packed in the chaise, would have to suffice for their dinner. Dumfries was nine long miles away on a January day with a mere handful of daylight hours—dreary, gray light at that—and a biting wind. Though the snow had stopped, the roads were bound to be *slippie*. He had some errands to do for her father while in Dumfries as well. The sooner away, the sooner home.

"Leana," he called down the hall, stamping the snow off his boots at the threshold. When she appeared at the kitchen doorway, her hair caught up in a white cap, her blue eyes wide with concern, he quickly closed the distance between them. "Not to worry, lass. I only meant to say in parting…" Feeling foolish, he grasped her hands, warm from cooking, and held on to them, rubbing his thumbs over her tapered fingers. "Well, I wanted to be verra sure you understood that nothing improper will come of today's journey."

She did not blink an eye. "You mean with Rose."

"Aye," he said, swallowing his relief in a great gulp. "I've told her many times what was once between us is nae more, but your sister is not easily persuaded."

"How well I ken the truth of that." Leana drew his hands to her mouth, kissing the rough back of each one. "I love you, Jamie. And I love Rose, though today in particular she may not be convinced of that. I trust you'll both act in an honorable manner." She squeezed his hands, this time not so gently. "Be assured, I'll be praying from the moment you leave." She lowered her gaze, her pale lashes fanning across her cheeks. "Hurry home to me, Jamie."

"Never doubt it." He pulled her into his arms and kissed her thoroughly, not caring that they stood in full view of the servants, who tittered behind their aprons. Finally lifting his mouth from hers, he murmured, " 'Twill be long past dark when I come riding up to the house. Warm the bed for me, lass."

Without another word, Jamie headed for the lawn, eager to have the ordeal with Rose over and done. He'd endured a difficult two months since Hallowmas Eve, much of it spent avoiding Rose's gaze at meals and keeping his distance whenever they crossed paths.

She waited a stone's throw from him now, standing near the chaise, where a handful of loyal servants stood shivering in their threadbare cloaks. "We must arrive by two o' the clock," Rose reminded him, holding out her gloved hand. "The *lowpin-on stane* awaits." Jamie assisted her without comment, guiding her boot onto the mounting stone that enabled her to step into the carriage. She swept aside her skirts, settled onto the cushioned seat, then patted the space next to her. "Come and keep me warm, Jamie, for the brick at my feet has already lost its heat."

"Then I'll have Neda find you another," he said evenly, nodding at one of the servants, who flew toward the house, no doubt grateful for any task that would take him withindoors. Jamie climbed onto the chaise with ease, sitting as far to the right as he could, mindful of the very real danger of being bounced out of the carriage, for the springs were ancient and stiff with cold.

The manservant appeared moments later bearing a hot brick from the kitchen hearth. He placed it beneath Rose's boots, then carted off the other brick as Rose bade cheerful farewells to those round her. "God be wi' ye," they responded, already taking small steps toward the house where Leana and Neda stood at the window waving.

Jamie faced forward, the reins held loosely. "On with you, Bess." The auld mare fell into a steady pace, her harness bells jingling a cheery rhythm.

Rose did not wait long to begin her usual chatter. "If 'twere Willie sitting here—"

"Which it could still be," Jamie offered, preparing to tug on the reins.

"Nae, nae!" Rose argued, waving her hand. "The man is too ill to travel. I made sure of that."

Jamie looked at her askance. "You did *what?*"

Flustered, she clasped her hands. "I mean, I knocked on his door and made certain he truly *was* ill."

"I see." Jamie believed her because he wanted to. The thought of Rose, his innocent young cousin, growing into a woman unafraid of *swickerie,* like her Aunt Rowena, soured his stomach. Rose had merely inquired after Willie's health; she hadn't tampered with his plum pudding.

An uneasy silence stretched between them until Rose began again as if naught had happened. "As I was saying, if Willie were sitting beside me, 'twould feel as though the last year had never passed."

Jamie stared straight ahead. If he said nothing, might she change the subject?

"Willie and I rode side by side like this on a snowy Wednesday in late December, headed for my Aunt Meg's in Twyneholm." She looked about the fields and woods. "You remember, Jamie. 'Twas the week before the wedding."

"Rose…" He sighed heavily. "I will not spend this journey discussing circumstances that cannot be changed."

"Fine," she said with a dramatic wave of her hands. "Let us speak of Ian then, for he is the sweetest child."

Jamie relaxed, pleased to expound on his favorite subject. "Ian can hold up his head now and roll onto his back. And the lad studies his hands by the hour, as though ten fingers were a miracle of creation. Which, of course, they are. And his smile—och, Rose!—'tis an altogether grand thing, that toothless smile of his. Leana insists he saves the best ones for me."

Rose nodded as he spoke, encouraging him to continue. Her eyes gleamed in the forenoon light, and her mouth fell open slightly, distracting him. Jamie deliberately looked away, realizing the power she wielded over a man, intentional or not. So comely a lass as Rose could not help being desirable any more than he could change the color of his eyes. But she could be resisted.

As he signaled Bess to follow the main road to Dumfries, Jamie's thoughts turned elsewhere. To Leana, pale yet radiant—his wife, whom he'd kissed not an hour ago. Aye, he would think of her and not her sister. There was no hardship in that, for to be loved by Leana was pleasure enough for any man. *Warm the bed for me, lass.*

They rode along in silence, stopping to pay the toll, greeting passing travelers heading southwest from the burgh. An icy wind whipped the snow about the carriage wheels as Bess plodded past Craigend Loch. Rose pulled out their dinner, offering him thin slices of pickled mutton, which he plucked from her fingers without touching her. When she broke the bannocks into manageable pieces and popped them into her mouth, he did not let himself watch. 'Twas more prudent to think about chewing and swallowing and little else.

As they approached the outskirts of Dumfries, he glanced at his pocket watch, relieved to see they were on schedule. "Almost there, with a *bittie* of time to spare."

She nodded but did not speak, her gaze pointed toward the mean cottages of Brigend. Beyond the village lay Devorgilla's Bridge across the River Nith; on the other side waited Dumfries proper. "Ian will be four months old when I see him next," Rose said at last, drawing Jamie's eye to her again. "I've been away from home for a single week but not four weeks in a row. However will I manage, Jamie?"

He heard the thread of concern running through her words, the apprehension in her voice. Suddenly Rose was no longer a temptress or a nuisance but a frightened young woman facing a new and uncertain life. "Come now, Rose," he said as gently as he could. "You've a whole new world to explore and another household to bend to your bidding."

"Is that what I do?" Rose sniffed, touching a handkerchief to her nose. "Then Auchengray will be thankful I'm gone. You especially."

Jamie was at a loss to respond. He *was* thankful. Life would be easier without her, though he would never tell her so. Might he find some way to send her off with a smile? "Rose, you will be missed by all at Auchengray."

Her dark eyes sought his. "Are you sure?"

Slowing the chaise as they approached the bridge, he gave her his full attention long enough to speak the truth. "You stole my heart, Rose, for a year and a day. It belongs to another now, but you will always be my beloved cousin."

Despite the shimmer of tears, a smile bloomed on her bonny face. "Oh, Jamie. You always did know just the right thing to say."

Eighteen

Love is the emblem of eternity:
it confounds all notion of time:
effaces all memory of a beginning, all fear of an end.

MADAME DE STAEL

arm the bed for me, lass.

Leana shivered as the words unfurled inside her, wrapping a bright ribbon round her heart. *Warm the bed.* The last thing Jamie said before he left. Clever man, to put such a notion into her mind. She'd thought of little else since.

Later that evening Ian would be three months old to the hour. Jamie might not remember that, but she did, as well as the good and the bad that had followed. For three months she'd been a mother but not fully a wife. Ever mindful of the babe by their hearth and the sister in the next room, Leana had not attended to her womanly duties. Out of sheer exhaustion. And a modicum of fear. Fear that he might no longer find her desirable. Fear that he never had.

Now it seemed her fears were grounded in falsehood. 'Twas not a warming pan or a heated brick Jamie wanted in his bed that night. 'Twas her, Leana McKie. He'd said so. *Warm the bed.*

Hours would pass before he returned home, so she took advantage of the last rays of afternoon light and immersed herself in a new sewing project, hoping it might distract her. She curled up in the window seat of her second-floor sewing room, with Ian napping in the cradle at her feet, and plunged a freshly threaded needle into fine cambric. But since it was a sark for Jamie, it hardly took her mind off the man. She soon imagined his long arms filling the sleeves and his strong shoulders straining the seams, and—

"Leana!" Neda's head poked in the doorway.

She was so startled she stabbed herself hard enough to draw blood.

"Och!" Pressing her fingertip between her lips to stanch the bleeding, she looked up at Neda, sensing her pale cheeks blooming with color.

"Lass, are ye expectin' Jamie for supper or later than that?"

She pulled away her finger with a smack. "He did not mention his supper. Only his bed." Now she *knew* her face was red, because Neda was laughing, a great cackling sound.

"He mentioned that, did he? Guid for Jamie." Neda pressed a hand to her chest as her laughter subsided to a chuckle. " 'Tis a new year, lass. Yer sister has flitted tae Dumfries, aye? Though I love the girl like me own, 'tis best she's gone for a season. Ye and yer man need tae begin again. *Spleet-new.*"

Leana could not dispute the wisdom of her advice. A blank calendar of days lay open before them. If ever there was a time to script a new life across its pristine pages, that time was now. Beginning tonight when Jamie walked through Auchengray's doors.

"Neda," she said softly, "can you help me? I almost don't know where to start."

The housekeeper perched on Rose's carding stool. "Suppose Duncan and I kidnap Ian for a few hours tonight. Ye fill the babe wi' yer guid milk first, then let yer auld Neda walk the floor wi' him 'til ye're ready tae claim him again." She grinned. "Nae need tae be hasty."

Leana watched the babe stirring in his cradle and could not keep from smiling. "Aye. Nine o' the clock. Jamie should be home by then." She looked up and winked at Neda. "I'll have to see to my husband's supper as well."

"Och! Soon as the lad hears what ye've planned for him, he'll swallow his mutton pie whole."

When Lachlan rang the supper bell at seven, Jamie had not yet appeared. Neda's mutton pies were served and eaten, though she set two aside for Jamie, should he arrive hungry. Family worship filled out the hour before Leana did as she was told, nursing Ian until his round body could hold no more, then bathing them both until mother and son smelled sweet as dried lavender.

Neda gathered the child in her arms, tucking his head under her well-padded chin. "We're off tae the third floor. Knock whan it suits ye and not a minute sooner."

Feeling at loose ends without Ian to care for, Leana brushed her hair with long strokes, taking deep breaths to match, calming her spirit. She and Jamie would begin again. Aye, spleet-new. She tarried near their bedroom window, listening for the jingle of Bess's harness. When at last she heard it and saw the lantern light bobbing along the drive, Leana flew like the wind down the stair and out the front door, not caring if she wore no cloak, not caring that it was the dead of winter. Her hair streamed behind her. Her arms stretched forward, bidding him come. "Jamie!"

He pulled the chaise to an abrupt stop and leaped to the ground, scaring Bess, who backed up a step and whinnied, scolding him. He hardly noticed, leaving Willie to attend to the mare while he headed across the frozen lawn toward his wife, walking at first. Then running. "Leana!"

His arms were round her before he finished saying her name. The fierceness of his embrace lifted her off the ground. When his mouth found hers, she buried her hands in his hair and held him there. She'd forgotten how wonderful his kisses were. She would not forget again. *Jamie, Jamie.* After long moments her feet touched the ground, but just barely.

Jamie's voice was rough. " 'Tis good to be home, Leana." He circled his arm round her waist, holding her tight against his side as he drew her toward the gaping front door.

She looked up, asking what had to be asked. "Did all go well with Rose?"

When his gaze met hers, she had her answer. "Your sister is where she belongs, Leana. And so are we." As they approached the threshold, Jamie paused long enough to slip his other arm behind her knees and sweep her off the ground.

"Jamie!" She gasped and threw her arms round his neck, fearing she might tumble to the ground. But he held her fast.

"I'm a year and a day late, lass." He kissed her again, gently this time, and carried her through the entranceway. "Welcome home, my bride."

A cluster of servants stood in the hall, their eyes as wide open as the door. Eliza was the first to curtsy. "Mr. McKie, there are mutton pies waiting in the kitchen."

"Guid." Jamie strode past with Leana clinging to his shoulders, bound for the stair. "I'll have them for breakfast."

Leana did not remember breakfast. She only remembered all that came before it, and when she remembered those sacred hours, her heart nearly burst with joy.

" 'Tis a blissin tae see ye sae blithe." Neda slipped a knuckle under Leana's chin before the lass had a chance to hide her embarrassment. "Ye as weel, Mr. McKie."

"Aye." Jamie grinned, concealing nothing.

All three of them stood in the front parlor, where Ian was being introduced to his new crib. Fashioned by Willie from a fallen oak on Auchengray land, it was a clever bit of carpentry—neither so low that Ian could climb out later, nor so high that he'd get hurt if he tumbled out. Leana lowered the child into his sturdy bed, lined with a woolen mattress, and was relieved when he did not fuss at his new surroundings.

Neda's coppery head bent over the crib. "Now then, look at our guid boy, smilin' up at his mither and faither from his new bed," she cooed. After a moment of play, Neda gathered his soiled linens and turned toward the door to the hall. "He's all yers, dearies, for I've a house tae manage. Take yer time gettin' tae the sheep, Jamie. Duncan says he can handle things this mornin'."

"Bless you, Neda," he called after her. "For everything." Jamie crouched down and offered his hand to Ian. A look of wonder came over his face as the babe grasped one of his thick fingers and shook it like a rattle. "What a grip the lad has!"

"Aye, he's strong," Leana agreed. "Like his father."

Jamie looked over his shoulder at her, warming her with his steady gaze. "Nae, 'tis his mother's strength I see. For it seems the lad will not let go, no matter how foolishly I try to pull away."

Leana pressed her lips tight, holding back the tears that seemed ever present of late. "Holding on was all that I could do, Jamie. And all I wanted to do."

"I'm grateful, lass. More than I can say." He eased his finger free from Ian's tight clasp and rubbed the boy's stomach before rising to his feet to look at her. Jamie's eyes were a bit bleary from their short night, but his smile was as potent as ever. "Now that I have my hands back, let me put them to good use." He cradled her face and drew her to him, tipping her head back, planting kisses where he pleased until he landed on her mouth, where he lingered long.

When at last they eased apart, Jamie looked down at their son, happy in his new crib. "You're a lucky boy to have such a good mother. And I am a blessed man to have such a fine wife."

I love you, Jamie. She could no longer bring herself to say it aloud. The risk was too great. Instead she whispered, "Thank you," and took his hand, squeezing it.

He lifted her hand to his mouth and tenderly kissed her fingers. "You have waited much too long to hear this. But I could not say it until it was true, until it meant something." He paused, perhaps to be certain she was listening.

Her heart stood on tiptoe.

"I love you, Leana."

Oh, Jamie. She could not speak. Joy flooded through her. And with that joy came the words she longed to say. "I love you, Jamie. I will always love you."

"You always have, Leana." He kissed her again, then said in a low voice, " 'Tis forever to my shame that it's taken me so long to return it."

She shook her head, blinking away tears. "Shame is not forever, Jamie. But this is." She pressed his hand to her heart. "Love is the banner that hangs over the gates of eternity. Not shame, Jamie. Love."

"Aye." He leaned back for a moment, studying her. "Leana, I will not have you thinking this is because of what happened last night."

Her whole body sighed with relief. 'Twas precisely what she'd feared. "How well you ken me, Jamie."

"Aye, so I do." A grin flickered across his face, then he grew serious again. "You deserve more from me than a night's passion and idle words easily forgotten. 'Tis respect that you deserve. And so you shall have it. The Buik commands us, 'Let us not love in word, neither in tongue; but in deed and in truth.' Tell me, Leana. How may I prove myself?"

She responded at once. "Love our son."

"Och!" His features softened. " 'Tis already done. The lad ran off with my heart the night he was born. Three months and a day, aye?"

He remembered. Patting her cheeks dry, Leana turned to Ian. "Do you hear that, sweet boy? Your father loves us both!" *God be praised.*

Jamie was as good as his word. All that week his genuine regard for her showed in his eyes, in his actions, in his words. He touched her cheek in passing. He complimented her gown, even though he'd seen it many times before. He brought home small gifts when errands sent him to the village—silk ribbons for her hair, a doeskin ball for Ian. Jamie's love enveloped his wife and son like a thick plaid, comforting them, protecting them.

Up the stair and down, the servants sensed a change at Auchengray. The dour atmosphere that Lachlan sustained with scowls and severe pronouncements gave way to laughter in the scullery and a lightness in the hall. Even the harsh winds and bitter cold of January could not dampen the blithe spirit that fell upon the household. Leana, who'd learned to live without hope, now embraced it with both arms. Jamie loved her, truly loved her, in word and in deed.

Thursday evening the three of them sat beside the hearth after family worship. Ian was livelier than usual at that hour, so they delayed tucking him into his crib and let him roll about on a blanket by the warm peat fire. Leana caressed the child's bare feet, enjoying the feel of his tiny toes. "Let us see, Mr. James McKie, if your mother taught you properly as a child." She held Ian's big toe between two fingers. "This is the man that *brak* the barn." Wiggling the next toe, she continued, "This is the man that stole the corn." She looked up. "Your turn, Jamie."

He gamely grabbed the child's third toe, which disappeared beneath his thick thumb. "This is the man that stood and saw." He moved to the next toe. "This is the man that ran awa." Leana joined him in pinch-

ing Ian's tiny little toe, while the child squealed with delight. "And wee
Peerie-Winkie paid for a'!" Jamie's deep laugh rolled across the slate
floor. "You've not one foot but two, Ian McKie. Suppose we start on the
other." He looked up at her then, his features lit by the firelight, his eyes
glowing with affection. "What say you, Leana?"

She smiled, too happy to think. "I love you, Jamie. That's what I say."

"D'ye hear that, laddie?" Jamie made a comical face, to Ian's amazement. "Yer mither luves me! And ye ken a *saicret?* I luve the lass too."
He tickled Ian's feet with his rough beard, then kissed Leana soundly,
tickling her skin just the same.

Nineteen

Standing with reluctant feet
Where the brook and river meet,
Womanhood and childhood fleet!
HENRY WADSWORTH LONGFELLOW

I do not consider that 'standing,' Miss McBride. 'Tis more properly called 'slouching.' *Levez-vous, s'il vous plaît.* Stand up, if you please."

Etta Carlyle held court amid a circle of young women, her own posture that of a British soldier of superior rank. The thin carpet beneath Rose's feet offered little warmth, nor did the coal fire in the hearth. A pine mantel was one of the room's few adornments. Two uncurtained windows facing Millbrae Vennel ushered in the meager winter light, barely dispelling the general gloominess of the square, high-ceilinged room that smelled of tallow. 'Twas a tidy enough place but decidedly grim. Rather like the schoolmistress.

A dozen pairs of eyes were fixed on Rose as Etta Carlyle admonished, "Taller, Miss McBride."

"Yes, *mem.*" Rose stretched her head higher, hoping her spine might elongate as well. The silver-haired dowager pursed her lips, then moved on without comment, leaving Rose to wonder if she'd managed to please the woman. Mistress Carlyle's deep-set gray eyes, cold as granite, were now trained on another newcomer at the school, a wheyfaced girl from Torthorwald parish.

"Do not hold your arms so stiffly, Miss Herries. See how Miss Johnstone holds her elbows at a pleasing angle? *Oui.*" Round the room her instructions were quite the same—sparse with praise, replete with correction, sprinkled with French, ever comparing the lasses to one another and seldom favorably. Not that *lass* was a word Etta Carlyle permitted beneath her roof. Nor the word *aye.* "We look to London, not Edinburgh, as our model," the schoolmistress had explained on the first day. "The young ladies of Saint James say 'yes,' not 'aye.' We shall do the same."

Rose gazed about the room, resisting the urge to roll her eyes. To think she'd fretted over which gowns to pack! The assembled daughters of Dumfriesshire were, to phrase it kindly, plainly dressed. Their gowns were cut along somber lines, without a thread of Belgian lace to lighten the muted grays and browns, and they wore their hair wrapped in tight nests perched on their heads. Rose, dressed in Leana's rich claret gown, with her hair in wispy ringlets she'd tamed with rose water, felt like a bright-feathered kingfisher among a flock of gulls.

The schoolmistress broke into her thoughts. "Take your seats in the classroom, ladies. I've prepared a lecture on establishing a proper beauty regimen. In alphabetical order, please. Miss Elizabeth Balfour. Miss Mary Carruthers. Miss Margaret Herries. Miss Sally Johnstone."

Rose followed the others into the adjoining room, where four long tables dotted with glass inkpots awaited them. She pinched her lips shut to keep from smiling. *Beauty regimen?* 'Twas hard to imagine what instruction Mistress Carlyle might offer on that subject.

The Johnstone lass, who brought to mind a pretty brown wren, whispered over her shoulder, "Perhaps *you* might teach this class, Miss McBride."

Rose merely smiled in response, aware of the pride swelling in her breast. "Favour is deceitful, and beauty is vain," her father would say, quoting the Buik. Chastened by the unspoken words echoing in her head, Rose took her seat in the second row, scraping her chair against the unpainted wooden floor. The plaster walls were whitewashed, without adornment except for the sconces. Next to the single front window hung an oil portrait of a young woman—the schoolmistress as a girl? Nae, she'd never been so bonny. The painting might be of her daughter or of a noteworthy pupil from lang *syne*. The girl's posture was admirable and her hands gracefully folded; perhaps she was there merely to set a good example.

Sally Johnstone leaned sideways to catch Rose's ear. "You belong at Queensberry. 'Tis more fashionable than Carlyle."

Queensberry. The name alone sounded promising. Rose kept her eyes to the front lest the schoolmistress take note. "Is it also more costly?"

"Aye," Sally moaned. "My father wouldn't hear of sending me there."

Nor mine. Naturally, Lachlan McBride had chosen the school requiring the least amount of silver.

Mistress Carlyle began her lecture without preamble. "The secret of preserving and maintaining beauty can be found in three disciplines: cleanliness, temperance, and exercise." She made it clear they were to react with surprise and delight, as if every word she spoke were a revelation.

Rose chafed under such expectations. Where were the lessons in history or mathematics? She did not need to be told that cleanliness "kept her limbs pliant" or that frequent tepid baths did away with "corporeal impurities." Such words the woman used! Let others be moderate at table; Rose relished Neda's cooking to the fullest, with no ill effects. And breathing the fresh, bracing air of the countryside was the very definition of Rose's life at Auchengray.

"But avoid the dews of evening," the schoolmistress cautioned, "when the imperceptible damp saturates the skin, exposing you to the worst maladies our Scottish air has to offer. *Prenez garde.* Take care. Lest you visit the graveyard too soon."

Rose looked dutifully concerned, even as she remembered scampering across the hills in the gloaming, bareheaded and barelegged, chasing ewes that had wandered from the fold. Picturing Auchengray's blackface sheep conjured memories of a certain shepherd who'd escorted her to Dumfries, depositing her onto Mistress Carlyle's doorstep with due haste. Was he so very grateful to be done with her? After five long days did he even miss her? She yearned to see everyone at Auchengray, Ian especially.

"Miss McBride!" the schoolmistress said rather sharply. "Might you tell us where your thoughts have traveled? It is apparent from your unfocused gaze that they have long since left this assembly."

Rose stood, clasping her hands in front of her waist, as she'd been taught. "Begging your pardon, Mistress Carlyle. 'Tis the bobbing heads of those passing by the front window distracting me. I shall endeavor to do better." Rose took her seat, proud of herself for not succumbing to her *kenspeckle* habit of stretching the truth far beyond its borders. She *had* glanced out the window earlier, had she not?

"*Bien.* Good. Your desire to see more of Dumfries is about to be assuaged, Miss McBride." The schoolmistress smiled. Though it did not alter her stern features, it did improve the day's prospects. "It is time we explored the environs that will serve as your home this spring. We shall embark on an outing after the midday meal and stroll one of the main thoroughfares of our royal burgh."

A ripple of excitement moved through the schoolroom. Rose could not keep her own delight from showing. She'd already borrowed the *Dumfries Weekly Journal* from the basket on Mistress Carlyle's desk, reading the broadsheet late one night by candlelight. Though most of the political rhetoric gave her a headache, reading words like *Sir* and *Viscount* made her heart skip a beat, while the advertisements plucked at her purse strings. A new bridge across the River Nith was in the planning stages, as well as a new prison, which made her squeamish. But a playhouse, not far from the school, was also in the offing, and that was promising indeed. Spring and autumn court circuits were held in Dumfries, and two weekly markets, and three annual fairs…oh, the possibilities!

But first, the midday meal. Boiled, sliced potatoes, sparingly seasoned, and salted codfish garnished with dried parsley were placed before each young lady seated round the linen-draped dining table. Colorless, nigh to tasteless, the food was dispatched without comment. Rose was too eager to cross the threshold to think about her stomach. She'd visited Dumfries several times but always in the company of family. This was different and altogether more exciting, for Dumfries was home now, if only for a season.

A few minutes before one o' the clock, wrapped in her green cloak with her leather gloves pulled on tight, Rose and the other lasses ventured down the narrow Millbrae Vennel toward Saint Michael Street, holding their skirts as they stepped round puddles and refuse. Brick houses stood on either side of the narrow alley, crowded together, with the occasional *close* offering a glimpse of the barren winter gardens behind them.

Lizzie Balfour, a delicate creature with enormous blue eyes, fell into step beside her. "Have you ever seen so many dwelling houses? 'Tis nothing like Moffat."

124 LIZ CURTIS HIGGS

"And even less like Newabbey," Rose agreed, trying not to stare back at the children who pressed grimy faces against their windows to watch the flock of ladies. When the residents of Carlyle School reached a wider thoroughfare, they found themselves sharing the street with gentry and commoners alike. One baldheaded man had the badge of a beggar pinned to his tattered clothes, while other passersby were well shod and wore fashionable hats. Her ears twitched at the strange accents that whispered of places she'd only imagined—Glasgow to the northwest and Edinburgh to the northeast, each a journey of some eighty miles. More than once the clipped, unmusical speech of a Londoner caught her ear.

"We will worship at Saint Michael's this Sabbath," Mistress Carlyle announced. "*Dieu est en toutes choses.* God is in all things." She swept her hand upward toward the towering red sandstone church surrounded by gravestones taller than any soul buried beneath them. "Turn here, if you will, ladies. Let us see what Saint Michael Street has to show us."

Curiosity pulled Rose forward, with little concern for the damp chill of January seeping through her cloak. Beneath her feet, mud and muck gave way to neatly fitted flagstones. The buildings round her grew in stature and grace, with ornamented windows and arched doorways, neatly swept front steps and polished glass panes. Leana had seen these houses as well, Rose reminded herself. During the bridal week her sister spent with Jamie in Dumfries, her sister had no doubt walked this very street. Leana had been too ashamed to describe the sights when she and Jamie had returned to Auchengray. A miserable day for them all. Rose forced her thoughts into the present, refusing to ruin her outing with such dreary recollections.

"Nith Place is the fashionable quarter of Dumfries," Etta Carlyle explained, lowering her voice in deference to the neighborhood's genteel residents. She nodded toward Irish Street. "At the foot of the close leading to George Inn, you will note the Assembly Rooms, where gentlemen convene to play cards and drink tea. When court is in session this spring, ladies of quality will gather there for balls and exhibitions." She looked over her charges with a steady gaze. "Perhaps some of you will be introduced to society inside those elegant rooms."

Perhaps not. Rose turned away rather than see the hopeful looks adorning their faces. By their eighteenth birthdays they would no doubt be married to older, uglier men with stout purses and figures to match. She shook her head, as if to dislodge the terrible thought, and walked with deliberate steps, following the others.

"*Allons.* Let us press on, ladies." Their schoolmistress waved her hand through the air. "Mill Street will lead us home."

Carlyle School was hardly home, but 'twould serve a useful purpose through Whitsuntide. Amid the confines of its drab walls Rose would polish her manners, sharpen her domestic skills, and learn more of the French language that trilled prettily off her tongue. When God saw fit to bring a gentleman of distinction across her path, she would know just what to say to him: "*Je suis prête.* I am ready."

Twenty

A strange volume of real life
in the daily packet of the postman.
DOUGLAS JERROLD

L ook at this, Jamie. Rose is learning French."
      Leana held out the letter she'd received from Carlyle School,
slipping off her spectacles. "Though I can pronounce the words, I cannot begin to make sense of what they mean. Can you?"

"Oui," he said, chuckling. "Aubert Billaud, our cook at Glentrool,
came to us from Marseilles, so Mother pressed him into teaching me his
native tongue. As well, I had instruction in French at university." He
winked at her. "The auld alliance between Scotland and France will
remain as long as our countries face a common enemy."

"England," she said, smiling at his jest.

Jamie studied Rose's letter. "*Le monde est le livre des femmes.* The
world is woman's book," he translated at last, running his finger across
the paper. "Rousseau's words. A fine student, our Rose."

Our Rose. The lass had been gone a mere ten days, and already Jamie
missed her. Leana could read it in his eyes, which drank in the contents
of Rose's letter like a thirsty man. She could see it in the smile tugging
at the corners of his mouth and hear it in his voice, filled with admiration. Not for *our* Rose, but for *his* Rose.

Leana could not stop herself. "Does her absence grieve you?"

"Grieve me?" Jamie looked at her in amazement. "Nae, Leana. I'm
happy for her. And relieved for us." He reached across the table and
squeezed her hand, his gaze warming. "Leana, if I think of Rose as our
older daughter, rather than as a charming young lady, I'm able to…well,
'tis better that way."

"I see." Leana smiled at his candor. *Dear Jamie.* She'd misjudged
him again. Jumped to conclusions. "I should have known you had

things well in hand," she confessed, collecting the letter to read again later. "If you'll excuse me, I'll away to the kitchen to prepare a *noony* for your son."

Jamie chuckled. " 'Tis all the lad does: eat."

"And sleep," Leana reminded him. Now that Ian's colic had settled, the babe dozed several hours at a time between his night feedings. Grateful for the respite, Leana was slowly regaining her strength. If her body did not feel quite her own yet, at least it did not feel like a weary stranger's, dragging through a twilight existence of nursing and changing and bathing their son. Perhaps tonight her husband might turn to her again in the darkness of their box bed and find her wide awake. And more than willing.

Jamie stood, stretching his arms and rolling his shoulders like a large, graceful cat. "Did I mention I'm to visit Dalbeaty with your father Thursday next? Something about assessing the value of a property there."

"In Dalbeaty?" Leana gave the notion a moment's thought. "A favor for Duncan, do you suppose?" Two of the Hastings's grown daughters lived outside the small village eight miles southwest of Auchengray; perhaps they were considering moving to another farm.

Jamie shrugged. "When I asked the same question, your father seemed a mite *dootsome.*"

"I ken that look well." Leana wiped the smile from her face and assumed a vague expression so like her father's that Jamie laughed aloud.

"You've captured him exactly, lass."

"Then he's hiding something. My father is seldom uncertain, particularly when it comes to property." She glanced at the window. "I hope 'twill not be such a *weatherful* day as this for your outing. Do see that you're warmly dressed."

"Aye, Mother," he teased, then leaned forward to kiss her. Hugh had not shaved him that morning, so Jamie's beard felt rough against her skin. She did not mind in the least. "Much can happen atween now and next week," he murmured, kissing her once more before he turned toward the door. "Come, I'll escort you to the kitchen. Neda may have deduced something of my duties in Urr parish."

They stepped into the room arm in arm and discovered Neda

standing atop a small ladder, reaching for a copper-bottomed pot swinging from the rafters high above her head. "Mr. McKie!" Neda called out
in relief, easing back down to the floor. "Ye've arrived in the nick o' time
to spare an auld woman a nasty fall."

"So I see." He lifted the heavy cooking pot from its hook and
handed it down to her. "Whatever are you making in such a large pot,
Mistress Hastings?"

"Applesauce." She pointed to a basket of pippins with wrinkled, yellow skins. "Been down in the cellar too long, I fear. Duncan will feed
them tae the pigs if I dinna put them tae better use. Yer laddie will thank
me for makin' applesauce, I ken."

"So will his mother." Leana claimed a paring knife and reached for
the first fruit of many. "Tell us, Neda: What business does my father
have in Dalbeaty next week? Jamie's expected to accompany him."

Neda eyed them both while she scrubbed the pot clean in steaming
hot water. "I've not *jaloused* the meanin' of it, but it might involve a
woman."

Leana gasped. "A *woman?*"

"A certain widow by the name o' Douglas." Neda heaved the pot to
the dressing board and began drying it with her apron. "Duncan found
a ledger entry in yer faither's hand. 'Purchase of five milk cows for
Edingham,' it says. My daughter in Dalbeaty kenned the rest o' the
story. Edingham is a fine farm in Urr parish. Home tae Mistress Douglas and her three sons. What unco interest yer faither had buyin' the
woman livestock, I canna say."

"Nor can I." Leana glanced at Jamie, who shook his head.

"Mebbe afore ye go, the laird o' Auchengray will deem tae tell us
mair. 'Tis mony a mile from here tae Dalbeaty. But ye ken what they
say." Neda winked as she reminded them, "Greedy folk have lang arms."

"But it appears Father *gave* her the cows," Leana protested.

"*Och!* For naught? Ye ken yer faither's ways better than that, lass."

"Neda is right," Jamie agreed. "Lachlan McBride seldom gives a gift
without expecting to gain by it." He consulted his pocket watch, then
headed for the door. "Mark my words, there's some swickerie at work
here. If my uncle is not forthcoming before our journey south, I'll see that

you both have all the details come Thursday next." Jamie touched Leana's sleeve in passing, warming her with his eyes. "I'll see you at supper, lass."

He disappeared down the hall, his broad shoulders turning at the stair even as Neda turned her blithe expression on Leana. "'Twould seem yer man has finally come o' age."

"Now, Neda," Leana chided, reaching for another apple. "Jamie was twenty-four when he came to Auchengray. Old enough to be counted a man."

"God niver measures a man by inches nor by years." Neda scooped up the apples Leana had pared and cored, dropped them into her clean pot with several cupfuls of water, then hung the pot over a well-banked fire. "'Tis not the calendar that makes the man but the days he spends wi' his eye tae the Buik and his ear tae the Almighty."

"Jamie has been more attentive to such matters of late," Leana agreed. "He borrowed Father's copy of *Mortification and Sincerity* by Low and a book of sermons as well."

"A guid beginnin'." Neda stepped into the larder and brought out a block of sugar, which she crumbled between her fingers and added to the cooking pot. Already the sweet aroma of overripe apples filled the close confines of the kitchen. "Whan he lives what he reads and means what he says, then will yer Jamie be the faither Ian requires." She smiled across the fragrant steam. "And the husband ye deserve, Leana."

"What of Rose? Does she not deserve a proper husband?" Leana's hands stilled. "'Twas not her fault for losing Jamie. 'Twas mine for taking him."

Neda clucked at her like a hen fussing at its chick. "I'll not see ye dwellin' on the past, Mistress McKie. Though yer sister does merit a bit o' concern, I'll grant ye that. Ye heard the letter she wrote to yer faither. *Fu'* o' pride, her words. Learnin' this and accomplishin' that."

"But she's in school!"

"Aye." Neda stood before her spice chest, fishing out a stick of cinnamon from the marked drawer. "And do they not teach ye in *scuil* tae inquire after yer elders? Tae care mair aboot others than yerself? Rose didna ask how Ian had grown nor how Annabel was gettin' along wi' her gone. Her letter was *Rose McBride,* from first wird tae last."

" 'Tis always been so, Neda. Otherwise she would not be our Rose." Leana deposited another handful of pared apples into the simmering pot. "Suppose I fix a bit of cereal for Ian, then write Rose a long letter filled with all the parish blether. 'Twill keep her mind on us for at least the quarter of an hour 'twill take her to read it."

"Yer luve for yer sister puts us all tae shame, lass." Neda patted her arm, sprinkling cinnamon on her sleeve. "Lemme see tae yer lad then. He'll be wantin' his noony."

While Neda went off to fetch Ian, Leana got on with her tasks, spooning the last bit of breakfast porridge into a small cup, thinning it with boiled milk, sweetening it with a sprinkle of sugar, and then strain-ing the mixture through loosely woven muslin. From the moment Neda arrived with him in her arms, Ian was elated to see his mother, waving his arms and legs, squealing with anticipation as Neda sat down and tried to hold him steady long enough to tie a cloth about his neck.

Leana laughed at his antics. "Let me nurse the poor lad for a few minutes to calm him, or he'll wear his porridge rather than eat it." Neda busied herself elsewhere in the kitchen while Leana put Ian to her breast, a clean apron draped across them both for modesty's sake. She brushed her knuckle along his cheek as he sighed like the contented child he was. "Such a good lad." His silky cap of hair was already grow-ing darker like his father's.

When Ian seemed more settled, she eased him from her breast and quickly laced up her dress. "Time for porridge," Leana called, at which Neda appeared with some worn linens to catch the worst of it. The housekeeper pulled a chair close to Leana's so their knees touched, then planted Ian in her lap. Leana scooped up the cup and a tiny silver spoon, a gift from Jamie's mother. "Mmm, mmm." Leana opened her own mouth, hoping he might mimic her. When he did, she slid the spoon-ful of porridge between Ian's lips. And prayed.

He sucked at it. Wrinkled his nose. Sampled it again. Widened his eyes, then his mouth. Another bit disappeared.

"More?" Leana offered the child scant spoonfuls while she and Neda praised him thoroughly. Before they finished, all three of them were covered with runny porridge, though most of it landed on the linens, which Leana whisked away. "You've made a good start, Ian McKie."

Neda patted his plump arm. "Weel done, lad."

Leana called to Eliza to take him up the stair for a quick bath and a well-earned nap while she saw to her own ablutions. She then went in search of the writing desk Jamie had presented her on Hogmanay, their first anniversary. 'Twas where she'd left it, perched on the sideboard in the front room of the house. Dragging a small table nearer the window, Leana lit a candle, then lifted out a sheaf of paper, reveling at the fine texture of it. Jamie had been most generous.

Where to begin her letter to Rose? Her pen paused over the paper until she feared it might drip, and so Leana blotted it again. They had not parted on the best of terms; perhaps that was the place to start.

> To Rose McBride
> Wednesday, 13 January 1790
>
> My dearest sister,
>
> I am so very sorry that our last words before your departure for Dumfries were not kinder ones. Forgive me for anything I might have said or done to ruin what should have been a happy occasion.

Happy for whom, Leana? Though she would never let Rose hear her say it, Leana was relieved to have her in Dumfries and away from Jamie. Was it wrong to want him all to herself?

> Both of your letters were enjoyed by the whole household. As you might imagine, Jamie was most impressed with the French phrase you included. When you come home for your first visit at the end of the month, I fear the two of you will be speaking a language no one else will understand.

A slight chill ran along her arm. Perhaps she sat too close to the frost-covered window or the fire needed tending. Shivering yet again, Leana gathered a plaid from atop a nearby chest and wrapped it round her, then perched on the chair once more and took up her pen.

> Ian grows more amiable by the hour. Truly the lad is
> made in the very image of his father. I hope you will dis-
> cover the joy of bearing children someday, Rose. Mother-
> hood is a pleasure no letter can adequately describe.

She paused, dipping her pen in the ink. Would stories of Ian interest her sister or rub salt in an open wound? Did Rose care about her at
all, or was their friendship no more than a memory, and a distant one
at that? Leana's hand hovered over the paper as she prayed for the words
to write and the strength to write them.

> Dear sister, let there be no uncertainty between us. I
> love Jamie and Ian with all my heart. But I love you as well,
> Rose. Nothing, however grave, could alter my fondest affec-
> tion for you...

Twenty-One

Then came your new friend:
you began to change—
I saw it and grieved.
ALFRED, LORD TENNYSON

Here she comes!" Lizzie Balfour leaned her forehead against the icy window, her eyes and mouth agape, as the other lasses crowded round her. "Will you *look* at that gown? Red as rowan berries, and velvet besides."

"Aye." Margaret Herries breathed the word out, her hand pressed against the bodice of a dress the color of oatmeal. "My mother would ne'er let me be seen in so vainglorious a thing."

Sally Johnstone turned away from the second-story window. " 'Tis how the ladies of quality dress at Queensberry."

Rose quickly took Sally's place, squeezing between the others until she was pressed against the panes, her gaze riveted to the street below. A dark-haired young lady of obvious means approached the door to Carlyle School on the arm of an older gentleman—her father, no doubt. At the foot of Millbrae Vennel stood a coach-and-four, the ebony carriage sides gleaming, the brass lanterns polished to a high sheen. It was as fine a coach as the one belonging to Lord and Lady Maxwell, their parish neighbors at Maxwell Park. Rose felt no prick of envy at seeing such a display of wealth, only an eagerness to know more.

"Whatever brings her *here* of all places?" Rose wondered aloud, watching as Etta Carlyle greeted her newest pupil. They'd been informed an hour earlier that another young lady would be joining them, taking the place of poor Mary Carruthers, who'd developed a frightful cough and was sent home to recover. After the morning lesson on deportment, the schoolmistress had sent the girls up the stair to put aright their sleeping room. Twelve narrow beds lined the walls, each with one small trunk at the foot. Only one bed lacked such baggage, though it appeared an impressive replacement was being carried through the front door at that very moment.

Sally's voice floated over their heads. "Her name is Jane Grierson."

"Grierson of Lag?" 'Twas all Lizzie could do to say the name. "From Dunscore?"

"The very one," Sally confirmed, "however many generations removed."

Rose gaped at the others. *Sir Robert Grierson!* The infamous persecutor of the Covenanters and a Jacobite as well, known to every soul in Galloway and feared by most. Though he'd been dead some sixty years, his reputation stretched far beyond the grave. Was the stunning creature below a great-great-granddaughter, perchance? Or a more distant relation?

"My mother wrote to warn me she was coming," Sally said, her tone one of cool superiority. When they fussed at her for keeping secrets, Sally explained further. "I received her letter only this morning. Miss Jane Grierson enrolled at Queensberry last term, then was discreetly asked to leave after Yule."

Rose couldn't stop herself. "Asked to *leave!* Whatever for?"

Sally's pale eyebrows arched. "No lady would be interested in such details." After a dramatic pause, she broke into a fit of laughter, her haughty expression forgotten. Spreading her arms as if to draw them all closer, Sally added in a stage whisper, "She's eighteen, you ken. Older than any of us and exceedingly more…ah, experienced. Mother hinted that Miss Grierson slipped away on more than one occasion and came back smelling of whisky."

A collective gasp rose from the group, Rose included. It was hard to say which was more scandalous: traveling the streets of Dumfries unescorted or drinking whisky.

"Does the schoolmistress know all this?" Lizzie asked.

Sally shook her head. "You can be sure she does *not*, or Miss Grierson would ne'er have been admitted. Though as my maid oft says, 'Silver makes all easy.'"

From down the stair came the bang of a door closing and cultured voices in the hall trading pleasantries. Startled from their perch by the window, Rose and the others flew about the room, straightening bedcovers and tidying trunks, their eyes like saucers from sheer anticipation. After a fortnight together, friendships were beginning to emerge, though Rose had yet to find one young lady with whom she might share her heart's deepest secrets.

Footsteps on the stair heralded the arrival of Jane's trunk. Two footmen in pristine liveries paused in the doorway, bearing between them a finely tooled leather chest. "Place it there, if you would." Rose indicated the abandoned bed next to hers. She suddenly wished the sheets were whiter, the linens less coarse, and the sconces more abundant.

After the footmen bowed and disappeared into the hall, the girls could do nothing but wait until they were invited down the stair. Having already made the stark room as neat as possible, they saw to their own appearances, pressing their gowns smooth with damp palms and playing lady's maid for one another with comb and brush.

" 'Tis foolishness to carry on so," Sally said, fretting over a knot in her hair ribbon. "She is a girl from a good family. All of us may lay claim to that."

"But none of us has so lofty a name as Grierson." Lizzie, attempting to add some roses to her cheeks, pinched them hard enough to make her wince. "Nor do we have sufficient silver to buy so magnificent a gown."

Rose kept her thoughts to herself. Wasn't *McKie* a worthy name and Glentrool a vast estate with silver aplenty for velvet and satin? *McKie* would not be *her* name though. That chance had come and gone.

Etta Carlyle's imposing form appeared in the doorway, her tailored gown the color of ink, like a mourning dress. Only the pearl buttons marching down the bodice relieved her somber appearance. "Ladies, Miss Jane Grierson awaits your acquaintance at table. We will have an early dinner, then proceed with our French lessons. I've no need to tell you of her family's standing in our community. You will, of course, offer her a most gracious welcome." She waved them down the winding stair, closing the door behind them. The air filled with the rustle of their skirts, the soft footfalls of their padded slippers, the gentle hum of their voices as they glided into the dining room.

Jane Grierson stood by her place at table, her rich brown hair piled on the crown of her head in a magnificent mass of twists and curls, her elaborate gown a splash of red in a room devoid of color. But it was her eyes that caught Rose's attention. As dark as her own and every bit as lively, Jane's eyes sparkled with mischief, challenging anyone who might think to change her ways to think again. When a brilliant smile bloomed on her face, the effect was complete.

Rose adored her at once and without reservation. Here was the friend she had longed to meet, the woman whose soul matched her own. Vibrantly alive. Eager to experience all the world had to offer.

When Rose smiled back at her, Jane laughed, a low and throaty sound that belonged to a woman, not a girl of eighteen. "Come and sit beside me, dark-eyed lass. 'Tis plain we're to become fast friends within the hour."

The others took their places, shifting to make room for Rose, whose assigned chair stood elsewhere. Not a soul cocked an eyebrow, not even Mistress Carlyle. How strange that Jane Grierson had singled her out! And how grand. After a lengthy blessing, seats were taken and dishes served in proper silence. All through dinner Rose and Jane exchanged glances, both suppressing the urge to laugh aloud. Truly they were cut from the same cloth. When the marmalade pudding was cleared away and conversation invited, the two young ladies burst into words, as if struck by lightning.

"Your name," Jane demanded, "for I know you've been told mine."

"Rose McBride of Auchengray," she said as proudly as she could. "My father is a bonnet laird, with four hundred sheep scattered across the hills of Newabbey."

Jane grinned. "Well done, Rose McBride. One must make the most of one's family." Jane eyed her rose-hued gown, then leaned forward and said in a conspirator's voice, "I see you fancy bold colors and superior fabrics. We're nigh to the same size. Borrow anything of mine that catches your eye. My mother plans to send me a fresh trunk of gowns every fortnight."

"A fresh trunk…" Rose could not keep her jaw from dropping, then snapped it shut. "You are too generous, Miss Grierson."

"Call me Jane or nothing at all, for I shall call you Rose. Aye?"

Rose glanced over her shoulder at the schoolmistress seated at the far end of the table. "Be warned, there are words that Mistress Carlyle will not permit us to use. *Hoot* is one of them. And *aye* and *lass* and *laddie* and *meikle*—"

"*Losh!*" Jane muttered.

Rose cringed. "That one especially."

"Then we must be very sure Etta the Grim does not hear us." Jane pressed her napkin to her mouth to hide her broad smile, then tucked the linen beside her plate. "Do you know why I've been banished to Carlyle School when Queensberry is more suited to my station?"

Rose narrowed her eyes playfully. "I can guess."

"Whatever you're thinking, you can be sure I was guilty of it."

"And proud of it as well," Rose teased her, amazed to find herself so at ease and so bold in her speech. What a spell this young woman cast to engage another's trust in an instant! Rose looked about the room, not surprised to find every head turned in their direction. 'Twas difficult to read their faces. Curiosity? Envy? Or concern? Much as she was honored to have caught Jane's eye, Rose wondered how it might affect her growing friendships with the other girls. Jane trusted her, it seemed. Could she trust Jane?

Rose asked in her most sincere voice, "Will you not admit what brings you to Carlyle? If we're to be good friends, Jane, I must know more about you." She lowered her eyes and then her voice, praying no one would overhear. "'Tis only fair, for I have a scandalous story to share with you as well."

The corners of Jane's mouth twitched in amusement. "You must tell me every detail some evening when we can gossip to our hearts' content. Just as I shall make my confession to you in a quiet hour of the night."

Jane rose to her feet at the schoolmistress's command, with Rose and the others hastening to follow suit. *"Parlons français?"*

"Oui," Rose agreed, smiling. "Though it appears you already speak the language."

Rose soon discovered that a mastery of French was only one of Jane's countless accomplishments. The young lady was equally adept at geography, attributing her knowledge to many hours spent hiding under the eaves with her father's *Geographiae Scotiae.* She brushed off any praise of her mathematical skills, saying she'd stolen her older brother's schoolbooks. Her grasp of history was blamed on eavesdropping whenever foreign visitors knocked on her father's door. Jane could expound at length on the revolution under way in France and oft quoted the more ribald poetry of Robert Burns, pretending not to notice Etta Carlyle's stern expression.

"The verse of Mr. Alexander Pope is better suited for a lady's delicate ears," the schoolmistress said. "Certainly more appropriate than the scribbled lines of a poor ploughman."

Jane came to his defense at once. "But Mr. Burns is my neighbor in Dunscore parish and well regarded in the literary circles of Edinburgh." Her eyes twinkled. "Furthermore, Reverend Kirkpatrick welcomes the Burns family to services on the Sabbath. A more worthy poet cannot be found in all of Dumfriesshire." She sighed expansively. "Still, if 'tis Mr. Pope's writing you prefer, you shall have it." Jane drew herself up, clasping her hands at her waist. A slight smile played about her lips as she began her recitation.

> See sin in state, majestically drunk,
> Proud as a peeress, prouder as a punk;
> Chaste to her husband, frank to all beside,
> A teeming mistress, but a barren bride—

"Miss Grierson, that is quite enough!" Etta Carlyle clapped her book shut with a noisy thump. None in the classroom dared laugh aloud and so hid their smiles behind their hands, while the schoolmistress continued her lecture, extolling the virtues of Oliver Goldsmith and William Cowper, without further reference to the works of Mr. Pope. Or Mr. Burns.

Rose could not bring herself to look at Jane, knowing her composure would unravel. No other woman of her acquaintance—not Susanne Elliot, not Jessie Newall, and certainly not Leana—had so keen a sense of humor or so fearless a manner of displaying it. Were Jane's family not of such high station and her father's wealth not so substantial, she would be turned out on the street by good society. Instead Jane's antics were tolerated, even celebrated in some circles. Though not by Etta the Grim, of course.

Each evening when the last candles were snuffed out and the curtained sleeping room lit by the hearth alone, Jane's husky voice would reach out to Rose, teasing her with details of her many daring escapades. Stories of rides on horseback at midnight and whisky drained from a gentleman's decanter. Tales of afternoon picnics with *bacheleers* and carriage rides to Glasgow without benefit of a proper chaperon. Queensberry, Rose discovered, was the last of three establishments that had opened its doors to Jane, only to close them behind her a few weeks or months later.

"Carlyle is your *fourth* school?" Rose asked in amazement.

"Since January last." Jane laughed softly. "Perhaps it's best we not discuss what happened in 1788."

"You've already told me more than I can fathom." In the darkness Rose could barely discern Jane's form, huddled under a thin blanket. That morning Mistress Grierson had delivered a luxurious goose-down blanket for her daughter; Jane refused to use it if it meant the rest of the girls shivered through the night.

Jane yawned. "They say turnabout is fair play, Rose. You hinted at some scandal. What have you done in your young life that might curl my toes?"

"'Tis not what *I* have done but what my family has done that's scandalous." Rose propped herself up on one elbow, peering about the room to see if others were listening. Except for slow, steady breathing, not a sound could be heard nor a raised head seen. "My cousin, James

McKie of Glentrool, came to Auchengray, fell in love with me, and asked me to marry him."

"Rose, that is not scandalous. Cousins often marry."

"Aye. But as you see, I am not married. The day of my wedding I was stranded in Twyneholm in a snowstorm. My father proceeded with the wedding, insisting my sister, Leana, serve as the proxy bride."

Jane sat up at once. "A *proxy!* In this day and age? Losh, what foolishness. What sort of sister would agree to that?"

"The sort who wanted Jamie for herself." Rose dropped her voice to the faintest whisper. "Leana not only wedded him; she bedded him."

Jane gasped. "Then he must have loved her as well. Och, poor Rose!"

"Nae, he did not love her! He thought I was the one in his bed."

"He thought *what?*" Swinging her feet over the side of the low bed, Jane bent over until their faces were a handbreadth apart. "Rose, do you mean what you are telling me? That your sister stole the man you love and claimed him as her own, pretending to be you?"

"Aye. He confessed he'd had too much ale and whisky at the bridal. 'Twas long past midnight when Leana sneaked into his room, knowing very well Jamie was expecting me to arrive any minute." Rose sniffed, teary all over again. "There's naught to be done, Jane."

"*Wheesht!* There is always something that can be done to remedy so unjust a situation." Jane slid back under her covers. "Though the hour is too late for such considerations, know that the wheels of my mind will be spinning, young Rose. Your sister will not have the last word on this. Mr. McKie was meant to be yours, and so he shall be, or my name is not Grierson."

Twenty-Two

Trust him not with your secrets,
who, when left alone in your room,
turns over your papers.

JOHANN KASPAR LAVATER

Jamie captured Lachlan's elbow the moment they both dismounted, prepared to be rebuffed. "A word with you if I may, Uncle."

"A word?" Lachlan McBride stared at him in disgust. "We've been riding for nigh to an hour, Nephew, enjoying a spell of dry weather and a freshening wind. Why wait until now to mention this 'word' of yours?"

Jamie deliberately showed the man his back, hitching Walloch to a wooden post near the mains while he bridled his own temper. The man had blethered the entire journey without giving Jamie a chance to ask the time of day, let alone an important question. He'd dreaded this outing for more than a week; the last hour had reminded him why. When Jamie turned round, Lachlan's scowl was waiting for him. "Uncle, I want to be verra sure I understand the purpose of this visit to Edingham."

"Och! I've already told you. We're here to walk the boundaries of Mistress Douglas's farm, see the lay of it, assess the steading and the mains, and determine what value might be assigned to the property."

Jamie wrinkled his brow. "If 'tis rent income you're trying to establish, shouldn't that be the heritor's responsibility?"

"Ye've missed the point." Lachlan smiled, a grim line carved across his sharp-edged features. "She *is* the landowner. Edingham belongs to her alone."

Confused, Jamie stared at him. "Then why would she not consult—"

"Wheesht!" Lachlan's eyes cut him like a dirk. "The Widow Douglas consulted *me*. 'Tis my opinion she values."

"All fine and good, Uncle. But why am I here?"

Lachlan's jaw jutted out. "Because you are my nephew, my son-in-law, and the father of my only male heir." He inched nearer. "Because 'tis imperative to me that our neighbors in Galloway make your acquaintance and extend to you their trust." When he stepped closer still, his sour breath preceded him. "Because I thought you might prove useful today. Concerning her sons in particular."

The man's words were naught but heated air on a cold January morning; he'd revealed nothing new. Jamie dared not shrug, but he made certain his tone of voice did. "Very well, Uncle. I am at your service." Weary of squirming beneath the blade point of Lachlan's gaze, Jamie surveyed the mains of Edingham and its farm steading. Granite and slate formed the gable-roofed house with its dressed windows and corniced entrance. The steading was nearly the size of Auchengray's, but the square plan of the stables and byres presented a tidier appearance, a fact he could hardly pretend not to notice. "Mistress Douglas has a well-tended property."

"Aye, she does." Lachlan chuckled, though he did not sound amused. "You'll have time enough to examine the buildings later. First, you've a family to meet."

Before they reached the entrance, the front door swung open. A woman of some forty years perched on the threshold. With her short, round figure, ruddy face, and fawn-colored gown, she looked so precisely like a goldfinch that Jamie was prepared for her to burst into twittering song.

"Mistress Douglas," Lachlan said, hand outstretched, lengthening his stride. She no doubt heard the cordial note in Lachlan's voice and marked him as a pleasant man. Jamie heard his warbling for what it was: the smoothest of deceptions. His uncle continued, "I am delighted to see you again."

Again? There *was* that business with the five cows, a transaction to which Lachlan had not confessed. Did he think Duncan wouldn't take note of the ledger entry?

They were ushered through the doorway, where they put aside the plaids that had kept them warm astride their mounts. His uncle spoke using overstated gestures, common to hawkers and horse traders at

Keltonhill Fair. "James Lachlan McKie of Auchengray, my nephew and namesake, I am pleased to introduce you to Mistress Morna Douglas of Edingham, whom I have had the delight of seeing at more than one social gathering in Galloway."

Jamie heard little after *McKie of Auchengray.* Glentrool claimed his allegiance, not a bonnet laird's farm in Newabbey, however prosperous. Three months, four at most, and he'd bid Auchengray good riddance. For the moment he would be polite to this woman and smile as he bowed, for the plump bird had a kind face.

"Mr. McKie." Her voice was soft and high, like a child's, and her hands fluttered about her face. "How good of you to come." She blinked her eyes so often he thought at first she'd caught a bit of lint in her lashes. "Mr. McBride tells me you have a clever way with numbers and a keen eye for land." The widow beamed at Lachlan. "As your uncle is a trustworthy and honorable gentleman, I must assume he speaks the truth."

"You leave me no choice, Mistress Douglas. For were I to disagree with his praise, I would be calling my uncle a liar." Jamie turned toward Lachlan, letting his eyes say what his lips could not. *Liar.* It felt good to simply think the word in his direction.

She picked at her sleeve, her gaze darting toward an open doorway. "My sons are waiting in the parlor and eager to meet you." The widow led them into a room so densely furnished there was little room to sit. "Mr. Douglas was fond of carpentry," she explained, waving them toward a small, upholstered settee. "Always fashioning something whenever he could find the wood."

Amid the flotsam of tables and chests, three young men rose as one. Taller than their mother, muscular where she was soft, they looked anything but eager for this meeting. Wary, Jamie decided. Suspicious. They had something in common then.

"Mr. McKie, this is my oldest son, Malcolm Douglas, who celebrated his twentieth birthday December last." Malcolm bowed slightly, and his mother curtsied with him. Habit, perhaps. "And Gavin Douglas, my middle son, who will be nineteen in April." Another paltry bow. "And my youngest, Ronald Douglas, who is newly seventeen." He brushed the hair off his forehead.

Jamie bowed properly to all three, already aware he'd have a hard time keeping them straight, so close were the lads in age, size, and features. Curly, matted hair the color of wet clay. Freckled skin without much evidence of a beard. The broad backs and rough hands of farm laborers. Despite their mother's diffident manner, it seemed she worked her sons as hard as Lachlan worked him. Jamie sensed the three of them assessing him as well and found himself squaring his shoulders. "My own property is in Monnigaff parish," he said, avoiding Lachlan's stare. "Glentrool is the estate of my father, Alec McKie."

Malcolm, the oldest, seemed surprised. "So you'll be leaving Auchengray?"

"Not for some time," Lachlan answered for him smoothly, "for as you might imagine, since I have no sons of my own, James is invaluable to the running of the farm." Lachlan had the nerve to clap his hand on Jamie's shoulder, though it did not remain there long. "Suppose we see to your mother's property, lads, for that is why we've come."

The widow's mouth flew open. "Will you not take some refreshment first?"

" 'Tis dry for the moment with a fair sky." Lachlan glanced out the window. "I suggest we take advantage of the weather and walk the boundaries now."

"Very well, Mr. McBride," she said demurely. "As you wish. My sons will escort you while I tend to matters in the kitchen."

The men trooped out the door, Malcolm leading the way. From the moment they emerged into the cobblestone yard of the steading, Malcolm began pointing out its features—the *doocot* and granary, the barns and the byres. His voice rang with the pride of their accomplishments. Even in January there were a good number of farmworkers busy about their duties. "We raise black cattle for market," Malcolm said, though 'twas hardly necessary to mention it when the beasts stood about the fields.

Jamie took note of various details as they strode about the steading, calculating the price such a property might command. Surely that's what this secretive business was about: selling Edingham. Lachlan insisted it belonged to the widow, not the sons, already an odd arrangement. Did they intend to pocket their profits and sail to America as so many in Galloway had already done? Would the poor woman be forced to join them? It was not at all clear what this family's plans might be.

Climbing to a higher vantage point, the men were better able to survey the land, a rolling terrain of hills and mosses. To the east stood the granite remains of Edingham Castle. Once a tower house, now a ruinous shell, the keep appeared to be guarded by an enormous elm and held together with an overgrowth of ivy. A single gable rose from the rubble, its two blank windows staring into the Urr parish countryside. Portions of the other walls remained, and in the far corner a turnpike stair climbed into thin air.

" 'Twas built for the Livingstones in the sixteenth century," Malcolm explained, walking up beside him. "But they were hardly the first to claim the property. We've found Roman coins in the peat mosses."

Jamie turned toward him, ignoring the others, who continued on. Perhaps he might draw the lad out before Lachlan paid attention to their conversation. The air off the Solway was brisk, tinged with salt, blowing hard against his face. "Tell me, Malcolm." Jamie kept his voice low. "Do you ken what interest my uncle has in your property?"

The younger man's eyes narrowed. "Shouldn't you be asking him?" Malcolm stalked off before Jamie could respond. No help to be found there. Either the lads didn't know, or they didn't approve of Lachlan's presence at Edingham. No matter how mannerly his uncle might be with the Widow Douglas, it was apparent he had no genuine feelings for the woman or for her sons.

Jamie stamped across the hard soil, kicking at loose rocks as he went. He'd had a dull headache since they had left Auchengray; now it pounded at his temples. The pain did not ease when they returned to the house for a late dinner. Potted herring, smoked beef rump, roasted partridge—fish, flesh, fowl—were spooned onto their pewter plates in alarming amounts. The three brothers shoveled down their food with little concern for etiquette. Jamie ate what he could, though the dishes were not seasoned to his palate. Neda had a more deft hand with spices; the Douglases' cook reached for pepper in lieu of anything else.

After swallowing a round of shortbread so dry he feared choking,

Jamie was relieved when Lachlan seemed about to end their visit. His uncle offered a second lengthy grace—more intent on impressing the widow than on blessing either the Lord or the meal, Jamie suspected—then rose before the others could push back their chairs.

"I believe I left my gloves in your spence," Lachlan declared, already heading for the room. "Jamie, tell them something of our flocks at Auchengray. I'll not be a moment."

Jamie did as he was told, describing the long, coarse wool of the blackface breed, their mottled faces, the curved horns on both tups and ewes, until his uncle's lengthy absence became awkward. "Suppose I find my uncle *and* his gloves," Jamie offered, standing.

With the family half a dozen steps behind him, Jamie arrived at the door to the spence in time to see Lachlan shuffling through a stack of papers. Whatever was the man looking for? His uncle spun round at once, waving the gloves he'd no doubt pulled from his coat pocket moments earlier.

"There you are, lad. I feared you might tarry at table for another hour." He strode out of the room without a word of explanation, calling for their mounts.

After strained farewells, the two rode north toward home. His uncle's self-satisfied demeanor so sickened Jamie he could not carry on a civil conversation. Instead he rode in silence while Lachlan talked endlessly of cattle and sheep, of market prices and rising fuel costs.

Only when they made the final turn into Auchengray did his uncle broach the subject of Edingham. 'Twas not a comment he offered nor a question but a simple command: "On the Wednesday next, we shall visit Edingham again, Nephew." If a badger could smile, it would look like Lachlan McBride. "Truth be told, I believe the Widow Douglas enjoyed having two gentlemen with guid manners at her table."

Twenty-Three

Jane borrow'd maxims from a doubting school,
And took for truth the test of ridicule.
GEORGE CRABBE

'Twas the last Monday of January, as damp and dreary a winter's day as any Rose had seen in Dumfries. An icy rain pelted the windowpanes of the kitchen as the young ladies of Carlyle School attempted to create puff paste. Their schoolmistress had engaged the veteran baker from Drumlanrig Castle to teach them.

"A cool day is best," the cheerful woman insisted, her sleeves already covered in flour. She nudged back a loose strand of toffee-colored hair with her shoulder, then talked them through the process. "Sift the flour, add the salt, then make a little well for the lemon juice and a bit of water. Not too much!" The sticky mess became a stickier dough, which needed to be rolled and folded and dotted with butter and rolled again. "This is called the first turn," the baker said. "We've two more turns to do."

Not a groan escaped anyone's lips, but Jane's eyes did a slow roll. When the baker was busy helping another pupil, Jane whispered in Rose's ear, "What do you say we strike out on an errand this afternoon?"

"In this weather?" Rose gave her a quizzical look. "What errand?"

Jane's mouth curled into a sly grin. "Have you heard of the Globe Inn?"

"*Heard* of it?" Heat traveled up Rose's neck. " 'Tis where Jamie proposed to me on Martinmas."

"So that's where it happened." Jane eyed her, compassion plain on her face. "I've not forgotten, Rose. And neither should you. When Jamie McKie sees your pretty self at week's end, I have no doubt he will seek to amend the situation. Seeing the very spot where he proposed should give you all the courage you need to remind him of it."

Rose shook her flour sifter, even as she shook her head. "We cannot possibly visit the Globe, Jane. 'Tis a public house and no place for gentlewomen without an escort."

"Indeed," Jane said evenly, plunging her hands into the dough as the baker strolled past to assess their labors. "Leave everything to me."

Not long past three o' the clock, their lessons for the day behind them, the two were bundled in their cloaks and heading north on foot toward the High Street. Though the rain had stopped, a cold wind appeared to take its place. "The school overlooks Queensberry Square," Jane explained, "though we'll stop there only long enough to drop this off." She held up a slender volume with streaks of flour ground into the grain of the leather. "*A New and Easy Method of Cookery,* written by the schoolmistress at Queensberry. I was meant to leave it in her able hands, but by some coincidence it ended up in my trunk." She winked knowingly. "I truly cannot imagine how it landed there, for I do not intend to cook a single meal in my lifetime."

Rose sighed. "I will have to cook many a meal unless I marry well."

Jane, her cheeks reddened by the wind, looked down at her with mock disdain. "And why would you marry otherwise, my dear? Your Jamie is a man of means and quite capable of hiring a good cook. Let us make quick work of our errand. I promised Etta the Grim our visit to Queensberry would include a severe reprimand by my old schoolmistress, which seemed to please her to no end. 'Take an hour then but no more' were her last words." Jane hooked Rose's arm in hers and pulled her closer as they crossed the slippery flagstones of Nith Place. "Five minutes for Queensberry. And the rest for the Globe."

Rose tried to swallow her fears, but they caught in her throat, straining her voice. "The innkeeper must know your family. Won't people recognize you there?"

"Aye, they will." Jane's deep, rippling laugh rolled out more smoothly than pastry. "That is to our advantage, Miss McBride, for Mr. Hyslop will tuck us in the Globe's snuggery where we can sip whisky without threat of discovery."

Rose could not speak, so stunned was she with Jane's audacious plan. *Whisky!* Aye, she had tasted it, and Neda always stirred some into her *het* pint for Hogmanay. But to sit sipping whisky like a man…*och!*

Rose prayed the Queensberry's schoolmistress would not let them come and go in so brief a fashion, detaining them until it was too late to visit the Globe. Perhaps Mr. Hyslop would not welcome a bonnet laird's daughter without her father. Or better still, the proprietor might be otherwise engaged, and Jane would have no means of securing a table. Two young women of quality drinking alone in a tavern? Unthinkable. And also, Rose realized with a twinge of guilt, deliciously tempting.

Shaking off the cold mist that wrapped itself round their shoulders in a ghostly embrace, Rose and Jane hurried up the street, ducking their heads to ward off the worst of it. Rose found herself laughing, whether from nervousness or excitement, she could not decide. What a *bauld* friend she'd found in Jane Grierson! They passed English Street, heading toward the Midsteeple. The masonry courthouse with its pointed white cupola was a bittersweet reminder of the day Jamie had proposed to her. Hadn't she stood at the base of those very steps searching for her father and Duncan? She hurried past it now, noting the time on the clock face. If they were to return to Millbrae Vennel before the skies grew dark at half past four, they must make haste.

The newly erected stone pillar, dedicated to Charles, Duke of Queensberry, pointed upward like a slender finger. It stood amid a vast, open market square, frozen and deserted. "And there's the school." Jane pointed to an elegant corner building as she dragged Rose in that direction. "This will take but a moment. Mistress Clark will be drinking her tea at this hour. Only a foolish servant would disturb her for the return of a book." Jane knew the schoolmistress's habits well. They no sooner had rung the bell and presented themselves to the head servant than the soiled cookbook was plucked from Jane's gloved hands. A curt word of thanks was followed by an abruptly closed door.

Jane brushed off his poor manners with a sweep of her long cloak, as the two spun about and made their way back down the High Street, bound for the Globe at a brisk pace. "Rose, 'twill be an adventure you'll not soon forget."

"Aye, if I live to remember it." Rose shivered, for a dozen reasons. With the wind against their backs and the path downhill, they had to slow their steps to keep from falling. Rose spotted the Globe at last and felt her heart squeeze into a knot. In that very inn Jamie McKie had spoken the words that changed her life. *Say you'll marry me, lass. I've waited a lifetime for you.*

Memories swirled round her like mist: the love she'd seen in Jamie's eyes that day; the greed she'd spied in her father's; the disappointment that surely had shone in her own. For she had not loved Jamie then. Instead she'd prayed he might marry Leana. *Och!* 'Twas a mistake she would not make again, throwing away a perfectly good proposal of marriage, waiting for some elusive feeling of love. Her love for Jamie had bloomed too late. And his love for her had faded too soon.

"Miss McBride!" Jane tugged on her elbow. "A more melancholy countenance has ne'er been observed in the vicinity of the Globe. Cheer up, lass. A wee dram will put the roses back in your cheeks. *Attendez voir.* Wait and see."

They slipped through the narrow wooden doors, greeted first by a wave of warm air, then by the strong scent of whisky and ale, punctuated by the sound of tankards banging on tables. Instinctively Rose backed toward the door, her eyes darting about the crowded entranceway. A young tradesman stared her up and down, his impudent brown eyes gleaming. She hastily set her sights elsewhere. Wasn't that the very thing Father had warned her about? "Your bonny face may open doors better left closed, Rose." She stole a quick glance in the lad's direction, distraught to find him still eying her beneath his coppery lashes. She longed for a husband, aye, but this man did not have the look of a bridegroom about him.

Hovering behind Jane, Rose stared at the damp tendril of hair that clung to the back of her friend's neck and listened to her chatting with the patrons as though she knew them, as though the braisant woman breezed through the door of such establishments without an escort every day of her pampered life. Words of caution Rose learned one Sabbath long ago echoed through her conscience: *Let not thine heart decline to her ways, go not astray in her paths.*

Rose longed to be daring, to be different, to explore the world. But not like this. "Jane." She aimed her gaze at the floor, "I think it best we leave."

"Too late, fair Rose, for here's Mr. Hyslop to escort us to our table."

The proprietor, a ruddy-faced man with a barrel for a chest and fore-arms the size of tappit-hens, waved Jane forward. "*Oniething* for a lady. And her friend," he added, leering at them. "And who might this be?"

Jane answered before Rose could stop her. "This is Miss McBride."

Mr. Hyslop peered at her. "Ye wouldna be Lachlan McBride's dochter?"

"Aye." Shame flushed her face to the roots of her hair. Mr. Hyslop's family resided in her own parish. No doubt he would feel duty bound to write her father a letter and inform him what a tairt he had for a daughter. *Heaven help me!*

He shifted his attention to Jane. "Ye'll be wantin' the snuggery, I venture."

Jane pulled off her gloves with great ceremony, obviously enjoying his amusement. "'Tis the only proper place for two gentlewomen."

"Aye, if ye say, 'tis so." He rubbed his bearded chin, the curly brown hairs thick as wool. "The door's closed, Miss Grierson. Could be the room is spoken for. Unless a certain poet has laid claim to it, I'll see the patron finds another room."

The beefy proprietor tapped on the snuggery door, eased it open, and stuck his head inside the room. "Well, if it isna Rabbie, sharin' a dram wi' Alastair Waugh!"

"Mr. Burns," Jane mouthed to Rose, as if all her concerns might melt away at the thought of meeting so notable a character.

The innkeeper pushed the door open further, stepping aside so the parties might catch a glimpse of one another. "Gentlemen, I've twa special guests who'd be pleased tae have use o' the second table, if ye'll allow it."

A man with dark, soft hair and eyes like pools of chocolate stood at once and bowed. "Miss Grierson, I believe. You are quite welcome to either table." He was perhaps thirty years of age and robust in appearance. Though Rose knew the poet was a farmer in Dunscore parish, his man-ners more bespoke a drawing room than a milking parlor.

"Mr. Burns, Mr. Waugh, I am pleased to introduce to you Miss Rose McBride." Jane tipped her head toward her. "From Newabbey."

As if stuck with a pin, the other gentleman bolted to his feet. "Mr. Alastair Waugh of Dumfries at your service, ladies."

Rose moistened her lips, lest they crack when she spoke, and stared forlornly at a decanter and two well-drained glasses on a table stained from years of use. "You are most generous, sirs, but I fear we've interrupted you."

"Not at all." The poet waved his hand toward the empty table and chairs. "'Tis merely a birthday we're celebrating, Miss McBride." He eyed them both. "Rest assured, dear ladies, we're kintra folk and harmless as they come."

"Harmless?" Jane repeated, offering a dazzling flash of teeth. "Because you reside in the country?"

"Nae, miss." His smile bore an equal measure of charm. "Because we are both married men."

Twenty-Four

We married men, how oft we find
The best of things will tire us!
ROBERT BURNS

"Poor Jamie, you look exhausted." Leana ushered him into the house, slipping off his coat and dispatching a servant for hot water. "Where is Father? Did he not ride home with you?"

"Nae, lass." Jamie dragged the tricornered hat off his rain-soaked head, grateful for a dry house and the prospect of a bath. "Morna Douglas welcomed us to her table for dinner again. 'Twas an invitation I declined, but your father was quick to accept."

Leana nodded, as though considering that bit of information, but said nothing. Jamie was relieved she didn't ply him with questions, for he had few answers. Her father's interest in the Widow Douglas seemed little more than neighborly, but one could never be sure with a *sleekit* man like Lachlan McBride. All afternoon Lachlan had pored over her ledgers—in full view of the widow this time—and at considerable length. His uncle had muttered to himself as he added figures in his head and jotted notes in a small volume he kept hidden beneath his waistcoat. The brothers came and went, no doubt making notes of their own.

While the widow was away preparing tea and her three sons busy elsewhere, Jamie had pressed him for an explanation. "Is there some purpose for this second visit, Uncle?"

Lachlan had drawn himself up, as if preparing for a fight. "The Buik says 'tis pure religion and undefiled before God to visit the fatherless and widows in their affliction."

Jamie was proud of himself for not quoting the rest of the verse about keeping oneself unspotted from the world. Lachlan McBride worried more about a single blemish on another person's moral fabric than the mass of black marks that sullied his own. How the *hatesome* man had fathered a good and gentle soul like Leana was beyond Jamie's ken.

She stood before him in the hall now, looking up expectantly. Her hair, freshly washed and brushed, gleamed in the candlelight. "How fine you look," Jamie said, touching her cheek. "The gathering at the Drummonds' is still planned for this evening, aye?"

Her joyful expression told him all he needed to know. Indeed, who deserved an outing more than Leana, confined to the house for months with Ian? A few hours of merriment at nearby Glensone would provide a welcome respite from winter's bleak sameness. "If you aren't too tired to escort me," she quickly amended. "And if you won't object to going out again in this wretched weather."

"Not to worry. We'll take the chaise." He captured her hand in his and turned toward the stair. "Come and tell me what our son has been about this *dreich* day." Leana followed him up to their bedroom, where a tub of hot water and a clean suit of clothing awaited him. Jamie tossed aside his damp, filthy attire and sank into the steaming tub, while Leana pulled her chair a modest distance away.

Her voice rang with maternal pride as she described Ian's progress. "I read to him this morning. Of course, he can't begin to understand a word, but he babbles along as I read."

"Aye, I've heard him when he coos," Jamie agreed. "Sounds like he belongs in the doocot."

"And look at the rattles Neda made for him." She held up the dried gourds with painted faces. "Berry juice, Neda said she used. 'Tis a blessing to have such a thoughtful woman under our roof. I wish your mother lived closer so Ian might ken the love of his grandmother, too."

Jamie scrubbed his arms with a rough cloth, grinning broadly. "Rowena McKie has many admirable qualities, but I cannot picture her as a doting *granmither.*"

"Have you ever seen her with a babe in her arms?" Leana was clearly challenging his assessment. "Her own grandchild, that is, not another's?" When he shook his head, she laughed. "Wait 'til we ride up to the gates of Glentrool this May and tuck Ian in your mother's arms. Children have a way of turning sensible women into Scotch pudding."

He gazed at her across the rising steam. "So I've noticed."

"Aye, well." She ducked her head, a becoming shade of pink coloring her cheeks. "Suppose I see to the lad's supper while you dress." With that, Leana was away to the nursery, a small storage room down the hall that she'd claimed for Ian. Jamie had watched her direct the servants over the last week, preparing the room. She often scrubbed the surfaces herself to be certain they were clean enough for their curious son, who explored things as much with his mouth as with his eyes and hands. No father could want a more dedicated mother for his child than Leana.

With his chin scraped smooth and the bathwater grown cold, Jamie unfolded himself from the narrow wooden tub and stood, rubbed his skin dry with a linen towel, then pulled on his clothes. The clean shirt felt good against his still-damp back. Hugh, who'd gone after the boots Jamie had discarded by the door, reappeared holding them at arm's length, the leather polished to a rich mahogany. Jamie motioned toward the bed. "Just leave them there. And see if you can't do something with this neckcloth, will you?"

Hugh lit two more candles, for the winter sun had set long ago, and put Jamie's cravat to rights. The manservant, his graying hair pulled into a sleek tail, fashioned the same style for Jamie, tying his brown hair in place with a bit of ribbon.

Leana stepped back into the room bearing a drowsy-eyed boy. "Look, Ian. Doesn't your father look *braw?*" She'd no sooner propped up the child in her arms than his head drooped to the side. Laughing softly, she turned Ian about and draped him against her shoulder, where he let out a muffled sigh and collapsed into sleep. "Rest assured, lad, Mr. McKie is a sight to behold."

"So is Mistress McKie." Jamie said the words easily, meaning them at last. She had no need for Rose's dark beauty or *speeritie* personality; for Leana was her sister's superior in a dozen ways. She had a sweet nature, a kind tongue, a patient spirit, a keen mind, a trusting heart. Above all, Leana was filled with unquenchable faith. And she loved him far more than he deserved.

Now he was doing his best to return that love, in every manner at his disposal. With gifts, with affection, with words, with deeds. Was it enough? Did she believe him when he confessed his love for her? Did she sense it in his embrace, feel it in his touch?

Perhaps his eyes gave away his thoughts. For after she handed over the sleeping child to Eliza, waiting silently behind her, Leana turned to him and said, "Tonight I am not a mother, nor a wife duty bound to her household. I am a woman, Jamie, and yours alone." The frank longing in her eyes spoke louder than her words, pulling him across the room.

He closed the door on the startled maidservant and drew Leana against him, then kissed her soundly. Aye, she knew that she was loved. Before the night ended, he would make certain of it.

"Jamie," she whispered at last, smoothing her hand along the back of his neck, "we're expected for supper at six."

"Aye." Somewhere on his person was a pocket watch. He fumbled to find it. "We must leave at once, I'm afraid." Jamie straightened, releasing her from his embrace but not from his gaze. "When we return home, good wife, we shall have our own midwinter festivities, you and I. Consider this a formal invitation."

They arrived at Glensone with little time to spare. The elder Drummonds were already ushering guests into the dining room when Peter, their son of twenty years, greeted Jamie and Leana at the door. "Our closest neighbors, yet the last to arrive," Peter teased as he relieved them of their wet cloaks. "Come, we've saved a place for you at table."

Candles brightened the four corners of the low-ceilinged room. At the hearth, pine logs were ablaze, the welcome heat drying the damp hems of skirts and trousers hidden by the long, cloth-covered dining table. " 'Tis good that we came," Jamie murmured in her ear, guiding Leana to an opening along one of the narrow benches. Since he'd arrived in the parish, Jamie had given the gossips plenty to blether about, but no more. He was a father now, a husband, and a hardworking head shepherd. Though Auchengray would only be their home for another quarter, Jamie wanted the neighborhood's last impression of the McKies to be a favorable one for Leana's sake.

No sooner was he seated than his stomach growled in anticipation of the feast spread before him. Up and down the table were displayed heaping plates of thinly sliced pickled salmon and roast grouse wrapped in bacon, soft-curd cheeses and sharp-flavored cheddars, freshly baked scones and barley bannocks. Jamie spread his napkin across his lap and waited. Grace before meat.

Peter Drummond stepped behind Jamie to plant a solid grip on his shoulders. "Now the McKies are here, 'tis time to pray."

Mr. Drummond spoke a short grace over the meal, then hands and plates went to work for a jubilant hour of eating and drinking, laughter and spirited conversation. The staid atmosphere of Auchengray's table was noticeably absent at Glensone. When the guests had done their best to polish off every last bite of food, a fiddler presented himself at the door on cue. The red-headed musician struck up a merry rendition of "Johnny McGill" that brought the assembly to their feet to form two lines in the adjoining room, where the furniture had been pushed against the walls.

Jamie took several turns with Leana, as lithe and graceful a dancer as any in the room. Every time he looked at her, the corners of her full mouth were curled upward. How it pleased him to see her enjoying herself, surrounded by friends. He begrudgingly released her when Alan Newall of Troston Hill claimed her for a strathspey.

"Jessie's at home with Annie," the young farmer explained, "preparing for the arrival of our second. The *heidie* lass sent me out the door on my own. To give her a moment's rest, or so she said." Alan held out his hand. "Come along, Mistress McKie. Let's see if I can't do better than your man from Monnigaff." Jamie laughed as the two joined the line in time for the bow and curtsy. A *tassie* of hot punch was pressed into his hands by Mistress Drummond as the fiddler struck the opening notes of "Green Grow the Rashes."

While the others danced, Peter Drummond sidled next to him, hands clasped behind his back, a tentative expression on his face. "If you'll not think me too bold, Mr. McKie, might I inquire as to Miss Rose McBride's...er, health? Is she well? Enjoying school?"

"Aye, she is well." Jamie smiled when he said it, pleased that not even a slight twinge of jealousy stirred inside him. It seemed his feelings for

Rose had faded even as his love for Leana had grown. "My sister-in-law is learning a great deal in Dumfries. I dare say we won't recognize the girl when she comes home for a visit at week's end."

Peter looked away but not before Jamie noticed the spot of color on his cheeks. "Might there be a time when Rose…uh, that is, Miss McBride…would be at home? A time when I might…ah…call on her? At Auchengray?"

Jamie studied the lad's earnest expression. Five years his junior, Peter Drummond was sole heir to an excellent property, as well-dressed and well-mannered a young man as any in the parish. Peter would make a fortunate match for Rose. Particularly after her disastrous blunder with Neil Elliot. Jamie clapped Peter on the shoulder and squeezed hard. "I'm certain a visit can be arranged once Rose arrives home on Friday."

When Alan delivered Leana to Jamie's side a few minutes later, his face was full of apology. "Why did you not warn me of your wife's skills on the dance floor? I *grushed* her toes at least once in every chorus."

Jamie ordered a maidservant to bring a second tassie of punch. "Your farm and ours share the same march, Alan. I thought surely you'd danced with Leana before."

"*Oo aye*, many a time. But not with her husband laughing at me over his punch cup."

"I see." Jamie winked at Leana, then offered a toast, and the men drank to their mutual good health. "Afore it slips my mind, Alan, the bothy in the glen between Troston and Auchengray needs our attention. Stones that have tumbled loose and all. Might you help me set it to rights when the weather breaks?" Since the bothy stood where the properties met, both landowners were obliged to maintain it. Alan agreed, then tossed down the last of his punch and looked round for another lass to trample in a reel, leaving Jamie and Leana standing out of harm's way.

"Rose and I often played in that bothy when we were children." Leana took a sip from his tassie, then described how the girls had set up housekeeping in the rough stone hut and pretended they were married to shepherds.

"And now you're married to a herd who doesn't even have a bothy of his own to offer you for shelter."

Leana smiled up at him, warming him more than the punch ever could. "Your love is all the shelter I need, Jamie." She fished out the watch from his waistcoat pocket and opened the silver case. "The hour is late, and we've another engagement to keep, you and I. Unless you'd rather dance the next jig—"

"Say no more, lass." He set down their cups. "I'll get the chaise."

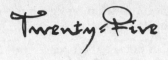

Twenty-Five

In general, pride is at the bottom of all great mistakes.
JOHN RUSKIN

D *ésolé!*" Rose grasped the lace cuff of her gown and wrung it beneath her desk. "I'm sorry, Jane. Truly sorry."

From the front of the classroom, the schoolmistress pinned her with a sharp look. "That is quite enough whispering, Miss McBride."

Jane did not turn in her seat or acknowledge Rose with other than a slight tilt of her head before looking forward once more, leaving Rose no recourse but to do the same. *Och!* How could this have happened? Befriended in a day, discarded in an hour. An hour that began as a clandestine errand and ended with Rose in tears, fleeing the Globe Inn before a drop of whisky had been served or a seat taken.

That fateful Monday evening Jane had followed her out into the frigid evening air, her breath as heated as her words. "Rose, how *could* you be so rude! You greatly offended Mr. Burns and Mr. Waugh."

"But they're *married men,* Jane!"

"Naturally," she'd said, folding her arms across her fur-trimmed cloak. "Unmarried men are to be avoided at all costs."

Standing on the flagstones of the High Street, Rose had listened in dismay while Jane expounded on the merits of being seen in public with men who were properly wed rather than with eligible bachelors. "The first may lead to gossip, but the second could lead to the kirk door. And I, for one, am not ready to marry."

They'd walked home in chilly silence and parted company as soon as they'd stepped inside Carlyle School. Though they had sat near each other at supper, they did not speak. Though their beds were side by side, not a word was exchanged.

Now it was Thursday. Lessons were to end at noontide so that each young lady might pack her trunk and prepare for her first weekend at home. Home was the last place Rose wanted to go, not until the breach with Jane was mended. Rose did not regret leaving the Globe Inn, but she did mourn the loss of her friendship with Jane Grierson. Was there no way to restore Jane's confidence in her? 'Twould be a dreary, lonely spring at Carlyle without *shortsome* Jane to add color to her days.

All through their French lesson, Rose's mind was in a whirl, wondering what novelty might tempt Jane to forgive her. A daring adventure that would prove Rose a worthy companion. An exploration of something unknown to Jane, yet of exceeding interest. And there must be some risk involved. *"Dangereux,"* Jane would say. *Oui.* Dangerous.

Then it came to her. *Lillias Brown.* Rose almost swept her papers onto the floor in her excitement. *Of course!* Jane knew half the residents of the shire, but she'd not mentioned crossing paths with a wise woman. Did they dare visit Nethermuir? 'Twas a frightening notion, which made it all the more ideal. Rose jotted a brief note to Jane, pausing until Etta Carlyle had her back to the class before reaching forward and placing the folded paper beside Jane's hand. *Suppose I took you to meet a wutch? Prepare to leave at noon.*

Rose watched in despair as the note sat there unclaimed. *Please, Jane!* Several minutes passed before Jane picked it up, fingered it without opening it, then slid it inside her book. Rose was certain all was lost until she saw Jane take the note out again and unfold it. It took her friend only a moment to read the words and even less time to spin round in her seat, her eyes wide, her elegant brows arched.

"A *wutch?!*" Jane mouthed.

Rose nodded, keeping her face composed. Time enough for explanations later. Now she must think how the two of them might manage to slip away for a few hours. Rose had enough silver in her purse to hire two horses, and they'd not be gone long enough to require food. Finding Nethermuir would be simple; 'twas along the way to Auchengray, was it not? Beside Craigend Loch, Lillias had said. Anyone in the neighborhood could point the way.

By the time the lesson concluded and the lasses were sent to their rooms to pack, Rose had her scheme well devised. A convincing story for the schoolmistress was all that remained, and Jane was adept at coming up with those. "Tell me," Rose whispered, "for I cannot bear the suspense." She touched Jane's elbow as she followed her into the sleeping room. "What say you to our adventure?"

Jane spun about and gave her a quick embrace. "I say yes!"

"I am forgiven then? For what happened at the Globe?" Rose held her breath one moment longer.

"Completely." Jane squeezed her hand. "You've simply more to learn about life, and I am the very one to teach you."

"So you are." Rose blinked back tears, relieved to be in her friend's good graces again. She briefly described her intentions, then assured her, "We'll return by five. Think of something to tell Etta the Grim."

Jane pursed her lips for a moment, then offered a cunning smile. "I have an elderly aunt in Lochrutton parish whose heart is failing. I'll tell the schoolmistress that I must visit her without delay. And since she's heard so much about you, my Aunt Catherine has requested to meet you as well."

Rose's spirits fell. "I do not think we will have time to see your aunt and Lillias Brown, too."

Jane gaped at her, incredulous. "My aunt is in fine health, silly girl! And she will vouch for us, should some question arise." She glanced over her shoulder at the other pupils, busy with their trunks. "Let us pack at once so they'll not say we've shirked our duties here. Then we'll be off."

Rose watched their plans unfold like a lace handkerchief. Quietly. Gracefully. Unobtrusively. They slipped out the door with their schoolmistress's blessing before one o' the clock, pulling their hooded cloaks tighter about their faces to shield them from the cold and damp. Neither rain nor snow was falling at the moment, but thick, pewter-colored clouds hung low in the sky. Heads bowed, Rose and Jane hurried toward the stables at Whitesands, seeking a pair of horses to hire.

As they neared the bridge and the stables came in view, Jane slowed her steps. "You're very sure you can pay for this, Rose? I fear my father does not trust me with much silver."

"A prudent man." Rose laughed, hoping it might dispel her nervousness. "Aye, my purse will be sufficient." Saying it aloud, Rose swelled with pride. Though Jane's family was wealthier by far, 'twas her own generosity at work this day.

Moments later they approached a stable lad loitering about the horses. Jane held her head high, daring anyone to refuse them. Rose, with her fingers clutched round her purse, worried she might not have enough silver after all. "T-two geldings, please. Saddled for ladies."

Before he could answer, the boy coughed, bending in two. A miserable barking sound, as if he could not breathe. Lifting his head at last, he wiped his sleeve across his face. His eyes were red rimmed, and his shoulders sagged. It appeared he'd not slept in days.

"Poor lad." Rose could not help noticing how young he was. No more than ten. "How long have you been sick?"

He shrugged listlessly. "A day or twa. My brother has it as weel." Waving a weak arm toward the stables, he asked, "How lang will ye be needin' the beasts?"

"Only until five." When he mumbled the cost for half the day, Rose swallowed hard. 'Twould take every coin in her purse, saved over many a season. Despite his wavering steps, the lad saw the ladies well seated with their skirts modestly arranged and sent them across Devorgilla's Bridge at a brisk trot.

"Under no circumstances are we to tarry along the streets of Brigend," Rose cautioned, aiming her eyes straight ahead, pretending not to see the beggars and vagrants, Gypsies and traveling folk crowded along their route. She held the reins tightly, urging the horse forward, ignoring the coarse suggestions tossed at her like refuse from a second-story window. At all costs they had to put Brigend behind them not long after nightfall or risk their very lives.

When the two of them passed the last mean hovel and were breathing fresher air again, Jane threw her head back and laughed aloud, nearly frightening her horse. "I do believe you've aged a year since we first met, Rose McBride!"

"If I have, then so much the better," Rose said, urging her mount forward. "Did you not say I've more to learn about life?"

The incident at the Globe well forgiven and forgotten, the two set off with lighter hearts, despite the foreboding sky. The familiar road undulated across the hilly countryside, a brown ribbon of mud and gravel amid the gray green grass of winter. Keeping a brisk pace, the two were soon a few miles southwest of Dumfries before Jane eased them to a stop, pointing out a familiar landmark. "Goldielea. You've been there, I'm sure. The colonel gives the loveliest parties."

Rose gazed at the grand mansion situated on a pleasant rise. Much as it grieved her, she confessed the truth in a small voice. "I've ne'er been inside Goldielea."

"And here we are, practically in your parish! You disappoint me, Rose." Jane's *tsk tsk* could only be heard as disdain. "Goldielea has much to commend it. A good-sized drawing room, well-fitted library, and eight bedrooms. Plus all the servants' apartments, of course."

"Of course." Rose pressed her gentle horse forward, a heaviness settling on her heart. Had she painted too affluent a picture for Jane, numbering the sheep on Auchengray's hills the very moment they met? Did her friend imagine her living in a distinguished country home like Goldielea or a vast estate like Maxwell Park? Auchengray was commodious enough for their small family but hardly a place one stopped to reflect upon.

This much Rose knew: The future of her friendship with Jane depended on a bewitching encounter with Lillias Brown. Three more miles and they would be at Craigend Loch, knocking on Widow Brown's cottage door. Perhaps the wutch would not be home. Then what? *She must be. She will be.* Rose prayed, begging God to be kind, to be merciful. Surely the admonitions in the Buik concerning witchcraft did not mean a harmless wise woman like Lillias, did they? At once the commands from the Law crowded out all other thoughts: *There shall not be found among you any one that useth divination, or an observer of times, or an enchanter, or a witch, or a charmer, or a consulter with familiar spirits...*

"Rose, whatever are you daydreaming about?"

She shook her head, as if to shake the words loose, though they would not be moved. Might Jane be apprehensive as well? Rose shifted in the saddle to look at her more closely. "Have you any fear of meeting Lillias Brown? Fear of what she might say or do in that cottage of hers?"

"Do you think me a ninny? Very little frightens me, lass. Lead on, for I'm weary of this saddle. My legs are nigh to numb."

"Follow me then." Keeping her eye to the left of the road, watching for the stream that would lead them to Craigend, Rose paid scant attention to the darkening skies above or the winds from the north bearing down on her back. Though it was not cold enough to snow, it was cold enough. When she headed for the narrow burn winding off into a forest, Jane fell in behind her, for the path along the burn did not allow for two abreast.

"Such a meager track! I see why you didn't hire a chaise. You're sure this is the best way?"

" 'Tis the only way," Rose said, a tremor creeping down her spine. She was growing anxious, nothing more. Who knew what tales they might hear, what spells the wise woman might weave? The thick stand of oaks meant Rose no longer felt the wind, but she heard it whistling above them, rustling the bare branches. An eerie sound like unseen creatures whispering. She did not like the color of the sky and so refused to look up again. Nor did she turn to the left or right, afraid she might spy a pair of eyes peering at her from the brush. Foxes, hiding low to the ground, and roe deer, standing stock still lest they be seen, were common in this corner of Galloway. She had no dread of them, but she did not like to think of them watching her, catching the scent of her fear in the air.

"Rose." Jane's voice was sharper. "How long until we reach this woman's house?"

"Almost there." A safe answer, neither truth nor lie. Half an hour later, when the gray surface of the loch shone through the trees, Rose almost wept. "There's Craigend!" she called out, pressing her mount forward. Now she had only to find the wise woman's cottage, and her prayers would be answered. Not by Almighty God perhaps, but answered nonetheless. The trees thinned near the water's edge, especially toward the right. Surely that's where she'd find Nethermuir. To veer left meant they'd find themselves climbing the steep slopes of Woodhead Hill. *Nae.* Lillias would be found going this way.

By the time the two spied the thatched roof of the woman's lonely whinstone cottage, smoke pouring from its chimney, Jane had fallen silent, her favorite means of punishing others who disappointed her. When Rose pointed to the carved sign on the door—Nethermuir—Jane's only comment was, "At last."

Without saying another word, both lasses dismounted, tethering their horses to low branches near the loch. Around them, all was still. Not a bird on the wing stirred the air. Not a squirrel or a rabbit scurried into view. The cottage appeared to have grown there like a tree planted in another century. Narrow-stalked broom bushes nestled close to each end, and stonecrop crawled round the entranceway. Thick ropes of dried grasses hung across the lintels of the small windows, dangling skulls the size of fists bleached white by time and weather. They'd once belonged to hares, by the shape of them. Rose did not look long, though, startled to see bones so gruesomely arrayed.

Propped against the door were several small packages wrapped in cloth. Recently placed there, Rose decided, for no forest debris covered them. She suddenly wished she'd brought something for Lillias. A gift. An offering.

"Shall we get on with it, Rose?" Jane brushed back her hood, touching a gloved hand to her hair. "I've waited long enough to meet your wutch."

Rose caught a flash of color at the window. A furtive movement. "You won't need to wait much longer, Jane." The door began to open as if under its own power. "It seems Lillias Brown is expecting us."

Twenty-Six

Mix, mix, six and six,
And the auld maids cantrip fix.
TRADITIONAL SCOTTISH SPELL

Only twa?" The wise woman gathered the bundles at her feet, muttering over each one, then stood with her arms full. "I thought ye'd bring all twelve, Rose McBride."

Rose gulped. "T-twelve...what?"

"The lassies at yer scuil. Are there not a dozen? Och, but ye couldna bring sae mony horses. Twa is better. And wha is this wi' ye, pray tell?"

Jane's shoulders drew up like a cat crossing paths with another. Even the fur trim on her cloak seemed to stand on end. "I am Miss Jane Grierson of Lag."

The woman's blue eyes lit like candles. "Kin to Sir Robert?"

"Aye." Jane said the word as if 'twere an oath. "See that you don't speak ill of him, old woman."

"Speak ill o' the *deid?* I'm not sae daft as that! Nor am I sae auld as ye think." Lillias Brown backed into her house, pushing the door open wider as she did. "Ye've been oot o' doors lang enough this cold day. Come within *whaur* 'tis warm and dry."

Jane went in first, bending to enter the stone cottage, though her back remained stiff. Rose stayed close on her heels, as if the door might close on its own and shut her out. The two of them stood in silence for a moment, letting the wise woman attend to her packages while they took in their surroundings. The interior was brighter than Rose expected. Candles of every hue and shape burned on pewter plates scattered about the room, lighting a large circle carved into the dirt floor. The wutch's bed was no more than a small cot draped with a worn woolen blanket. Over the head of the bed hung a crudely formed star. It was fashioned from long bones—human, no doubt, collected from some neglected graveyard.

Pressing her hand against her mouth as if it might stem the bile rising in her throat, Rose coughed, then swallowed, shivering at the awful taste. Whatever had she been thinking, bringing Jane here? Such an evil place could hardly strengthen their friendship; instead it would ruin everything.

As Lillias Brown gazed at her, the flickering light of the wood fire traced the wutch-score carved across her brow. "Ye're thinkin' ye're sorry ye came, Rose."

"Oh! Nae, I…I'm…"

"Dinna fret, lassie. I kenned ye'd seek me oot someday." She waved a bony hand in no particular direction. "Whan I found ye pickin' hazelnuts in the wood October last, I saw it in yer eyes. Saw ye'd be knockin' on me door afore lang."

"And here we are." Rose tried to smile and feared it was more of a grimace. "Thank you for opening your door to us, Mistress Brown."

Her gray head wagged back and forth. "Ye'll not be calling me 'mistress,' for I've little cause tae be *mainnerlie.* Lillias will do." She pointed to a pair of three-legged stools near the hearth, placed just outside the earthen circle. "Sit ye *doon.*" While they settled themselves, Lillias slipped her fingers in one of a handful of tins lined across the rough mantel, then threw a dusting of dried greens on the fire. The leaves hissed, turning the flame a brilliant blue, releasing a strong aroma Rose couldn't begin to name. Lillias did that for her. " 'Tis a rare fern. Moonwort." She lit a thick red candle and placed it above them on the mantel. Pulling a third stool near the hearth, Lillias sat down between speechless Rose and sullen Jane. "I ken what troubles ye, Rose. The man ye luve is drawin' farther awa, 'stead o' drawin' closer. Aye?"

Jane came to life with a gasp. "Rose! You told this woman about Jamie?"

"Nae. 'Tis a clever guess."

"*Guess?!*" Lillias's laugh was like the screech of a cat with its tail caught in the gate. Even the ceiling beams seemed to cringe. "D'ye think Lillias Brown pulls her notions oot o' the air that circles her gray head? 'Twas Hogmanay Night. Not the last, but the ane afore it. Ye were tae marry a lad by the name o' James McKie. But yer sister's luve was powerful. Enough tae fool them both. Now there's a bairn that shoulda been yers. And a man that's yet tae be."

Rose's eyes widened. "Yet to be what?"

"Tae be yer husband." Lillias abruptly stood, slipping out the door before Rose could stop her.

Jane grasped her hand, half standing herself. "Rose! This woman is either a true witch or a madwoman. And I don't relish either possibility."

"But I thought you wanted—"

"What I *wanted* was to spend an amusing hour with a silly auld spinster pretending to be a witch. Truly that was all I expected." She aimed a wary glance at the door. "Lillias Brown is the devil's midwife, Rose. Are you certain you want to hear what she has to say?"

Rose bit her lip, staring at the fire burning yellow once more. The old woman, whether wicked or wise, knew the truth about Jamie. And Leana. And her. If Lillias had some means of looking beyond the here and now to a day when Jamie would belong to her…then aye, Rose wanted to know more. Whate'er the cost.

"I do want to hear what she has to say, Jane." She squeezed her friend's hand. "But if you prefer we take our leave, we'll do so at once."

Jane turned her head to survey the cottage once more, with its stacks of parchment and odd piles of weeds. "We'll tarry, Rose. For a short while. Perhaps the wutch has some news for me as well."

"News ye'll not want tae hear." All at once Lillias stood inside the cottage. The door was closed, though they'd not heard her enter. "News o' the sort I'm not keen tae share." In one hand Lillias bore a small oak branch with two acorns still attached and in the other, freshly picked ivy. Laying the oak across Rose's lap, Lillias said simply, "Because 'tis Thursday." She wrapped the ivy round Rose's neck, leaving it loose like a necklace draped across her bodice. "Because 'tis needful." The auld woman sighed, a mournful sound. " 'Twould be better if 'twere Friday at ten o' the clock. But we canna always have what we want." She jerked her head toward Jane. "Can we, lass?"

"What news are you not keen to share?" Jane said sharply, her patience thinning. "If you have something to tell me, Lillias Brown, by all means do so."

The woman laid a wizened hand on Jane's high forehead, working her jaw as though speaking without forming words. "'Tis feverfew ye'll need, though hard tae come by in winter." Lifting her fingers off Jane's brow, Lillias passed her hand through the fire, then reached inside a tall cupboard filled with square boxes. No two were the same size. She clutched a handful of dried stems and flowers and tossed them into an empty bowl, then added steaming water from a kettle on the hearth. "Put yer head o'er the bowl and breathe deep. Ill weeds wax weel, ye ken."

Jane eyed the bowl, suspicion etched across her features. "Since I am not the least bit ill, I'd rather not, thank you."

Lillias stared at her for a long time while the steam continued to rise from the bowl between them. "Ye'll not take what guid I've offered?"

Jane seemed ready to say something, then pinched her lips and shook her head.

At that, Lillias turned toward Rose, dismissing Jane as though she no longer existed. "Then ye *maun* be the one tae tak the feverfew into yer body, Rose. Dinna waste it, for ye'll sairlie need it as weel."

Though she, too, was not suffering from any sickness, Rose stood to do the woman's bidding, weaving a bit as she bent over the bowl.

"Closer, lassie."

Rose leaned farther down as Lillias laid a thin towel over her head, trapping in the pungent steam. The moist heat felt wonderful, clearing her head of the congestion that had settled there a few hours earlier. The feverfew, whatever it was, smelled musty. Bitter. But not evil. Nothing that felt so divine could be dangerous. When Rose lifted her head a few minutes later, blinking as the cooler air touched her hot cheeks, she smiled and took a deep breath, then coughed.

"There," was all Lillias said. "Keep the towel wi' ye on the ride home. Wrap it round yer neck." She glanced at the window. "We've little time left, Rose, but a bit more tae do. Will ye drink some tea if I brew it?"

"Aye." Rose settled onto the stool, eying Jane, who seemed preoccupied studying the laces in her boots. While the widow prepared tea, Rose leaned toward her friend. "Jane," she said softly, "we'll drink this tea, and then we'll hasten home to Dumfries." When Jane looked up, Rose was struck by a terrible sadness in her friend's eyes. As though Jane had seen some dreadful thing but could not name it. "Soon, Jane. I promise we'll leave soon."

Jane nodded absently, her gaze wandering to the bones over the wutch's bed.

Lillias served only one cup of tea. To Rose. "Drink wi' haste, while 'tis hot." The wutch folded her hands, her eyes trained on the cup as Rose brought it to her lips. "Dinna fear what it contains. Naught but black tea, rose hips, and *hindberry*, though the deer ate most of the last afore I could pick it."

Rose nearly burned her lips on the tea, yet felt compelled to drink it. "What is it meant to do?" she asked, wetting her lips to lessen the sting.

"I've already told ye what's tae come," Lillias reminded her. "And ye already ken the truth, for the apple spelled his name, and ye've seen him in yer glass, and the hazelnuts niver lie."

"Jamie," Rose breathed between sips.

"Aye." Lillias consulted the red candle on the mantel. "Yer hour here is nigh tae finished. Have nae worry. I'll bury the melted wax so the spell will not be broken. Instead 'twill grow like a seed in the earth. I've two things ye'll need to tak wi' ye." She reached into her pocket and drew out a blue ribbon from which hung a plain, round stone with a hole through the center. "Since I found it meself, 'twill not have meikle power. Should ye find ane like it by the road, toss this in a loch and wear the new ane round yer neck. Aye? Ye'll remember?"

Rose gulped the last of her tea. "I will."

"Guid, for 'twill bring ye what ye desire most: a fertile *wame*." Lillias removed the ivy, lifting the stiff leaves over Rose's head. Then she lowered the crude amulet in place. "Keep the stane tucked 'neath yer gown." She patted the flat stone, smoothed by water, carved by an unseen hand. "'Tis best if no one kens what ye're aboot."

"But what *am* I about?" Rose put aside her cup and stood, anxious to leave. Jane was rather *fauchie*, and she felt queasy herself.

"Ye're aboot tae become a mither. And a wife."

Despite her apprehension, Rose giggled. "You mean a wife and then a mother."

Lillias said nothing, only reached above her head where dried plants hung from low wooden beams and chose a cluster of pale blossoms. Like Leana, she'd no doubt picked them another season and left them to dry upside down, so the potency remained in the flowers. "Milfoil," the wise woman explained, holding the plant aright. "Yarrow, if ye like." She produced a black-handled knife from her pocket and cut off a smaller stem, then pressed the dried flowers into Rose's hand and closed her eyes. The words she spoke sounded like music. "Say it wi' me, Rose."

> I will pluck the yarrow fair,
> That more benign shall be my face,
> That more warm shall be my lips,
> That more chaste shall be my speech.

"There's more tae it, but none that ye need. Awa wi' ye now, for the nicht draws near."

Without warning, Jane stood to her feet, tugging her hood over her head. "I'm ready," she said in a hoarse voice.

Rose hid the yarrow in a pocket of her cloak, then pulled on her gloves, eager to be off, yet sensing there was more still to be said or done. Some show of gratitude perhaps. "However may I thank you, Lillias?"

Lillias waved her hand toward the long wooden table where earlier she'd unwrapped the bundles collected at her door. "*Leuk* what me neighbors have left me. A sack o' meal. Eggs, butter, rashers o' bacon. A new wool bonnet. Wax candles by the pound." Her wrinkled face creased even more when she smiled. " 'Tis fear, ye ken. They think I'll ruin their crops or sour their cows' milk." Her crooked teeth seemed to grow more yellow. "So then. Have ye brought me a *praisent* as weel?"

Chagrined, Rose looked at Jane. She'd used all her own silver for the horses. Might her friend have a single coin to spare? A fancy hairpin she would not miss? Jane, looking dazed, shook her head, and Rose's heart sank. It was up to her then. When she nervously clasped her hands, the answer presented itself: her gloves. Tearing them off with due haste, she thrust them at Lillias. "My gloves are yours to keep. They're made of good doeskin and will warm your hands until spring comes to Nethermuir."

The wutch took a step backward, her eyes widening. "I'll not have them."

Rose's feelings were hurt. "Because they belonged to me?"

"Nae, nae, lassie." She hesitated, wetting her cracked lips. "Yer gloves have traveled tae a place whaur I *durstna* go. Ye'll bring me anither praisent someday, aye?"

"I will," Rose promised as sincerely as she could. She pulled her gloves back on, then circled her hand through the crook of Jane's elbow. " 'Tis time we were going, dearie."

Lillias stood at the door as they left, her face tipped up toward the approaching night. "Darkness *waukens* the owl," the old woman said, tapping at her brow. " 'Tis a guid visit we had, young Rose. Tak care o' yer friend, for she'll need yer help afore lang."

Twenty-Seven

Danger past,
God forgotten.
SCOTTISH PROVERB

Rose waved a cautious farewell with one hand as she dragged Jane along the forest path with the other. "Mind the roots, Jane. Are you feeling as feverish as you look, poor girl?"

"I do feel warm," she confessed, rubbing her forehead where Lillias had laid her hand. "And strange. Like I've awakened from a nap I never meant to take."

As the lasses approached their waiting horses, the animals whinnied and shook their shaggy manes. Without a stable lad or a lowpin-on-stane to help them mount, Rose did what she could to help Jane, nearly tossing her friend over the saddle. Rose made very sure Jane's foot was firmly balanced in the stirrup and her knee well placed round the pommel. Riding sidesaddle was an art and Jane a master. But not this day when her legs seemed to be made of pudding. If she did have a rising fever, then the sooner they returned to Dumfries, the better. The Grier-sons would collect Jane in the morning and see her well cared for, though a good night's sleep might be all that was required. Jane was healthier than the horse she was riding. 'Twould take more than an outing on a bitterly cold day to stop so valiant a heart.

Rose found a sturdy tree stump and was soon seated on her gelding as well. Guiding the horse to Jane's side, Rose was relieved to find her friend rallying a bit. Jane's eyes were fully open, and she was sitting up straighter. "Shall we make for the road to Dumfries, Jane?"

"Aye," was all she said, though a faint smile crossed her lips.

Retracing their steps was easy at first. The watery shore of Craigend offered a natural pathway to follow and only a scattering of fallen trees to slow them. Once the girls entered the murky forest, however, rotting logs and thorny shrubs seemed to lie in wait at each curve of the icy burn, putting horses and riders on edge, making them both skittish and uncertain. "Careful!" Rose said, hearing the gelding behind her stumble.

"Not to worry," Jane said, her voice a bit stronger. "Carry on, Rose."

" 'Twill not be long until we reach the main road, and then we'll ride like the wind." Instead the wind rode them. Blowing down hard from the Lowther Hills, a wintry blast bade them a harsh greeting as the two lasses turned onto the road bearing northeast, leading to Dumfries. Thick clouds, heavy with rain since morning, at last released their burden. As the first cold drops began to fall, Rose shook her fist at the sky, taking the heavens to task. "Och! Could you not wait until we were safe in our beds?"

Darkness soon fell, and so did a blinding rain. Riding side by side, if only to stay in sight of each other, Rose and Jane pressed their horses into a swift gallop. Hooded wool cloaks served them well against the cold but not against the rain, which crept between the folds of fabric and nestled like icy fingers along their throats, leaving them cold and wet. Rose touched a gloved hand to the linen towel wrapped round her neck. The cloth, heated by her skin, still smelled of feverfew. 'Twas good the wise woman had refused her gloves; clutching the reins, Rose could not imagine facing such fierce weather with her hands bared to the elements. *"Bethankit!"* she whispered, praying that Almighty God would still listen to her prayers.

"Rose!" Jane called into the wind. "Can you see the road?"

"Nae!" she cried. "Pray the geldings find the way." Guided by instinct and the sound of gravel beneath their hooves, the horses avoided the shallow ditches and moved on at a steady pace. By the time Rose and Jane reached the first cottage of Brigend, the wind and rain had both eased considerably, but the cold and damp had not. Rose could not feel her foot in the stirrup, and her hands held the reins with a painful grip. But she dared not stop; she dared not tarry. A storm had kept her from going home once before. Never again.

All through the village stretched rows of crooked windows lit by candles and hearth fires. "Should we find shelter?" Jane's voice sounded hoarse again and desperately tired.

Much as it grieved her, Rose shook her head. "We're almost there. The stables are just over the bridge, remember?" As the Midsteeple bell chimed the hour of five the girls crossed the red sandstone arches into Dumfries, their horses eager to get to their oats.

'Twas the stable master himself, a round hillock of a man, who came marching out of his hovel to greet them. He grabbed the reins of both horses at once. "*Whatsomever* are ye doin', lassies, ridin' in this frichtsome weather? I thocht tae niver see the horses again!"

Rose dismounted, wincing when her frozen feet landed hard on the muddy ground. "We had little choice, I'm afraid. I gave all the silver in my purse to the lad who works for you and promised him we'd return by five o' the clock."

"*Och!*" He exhaled loudly, filling the air with steam. "I'd not have charged ye mair if ye'd stopped along the way." The man helped Jane down, eying her with obvious concern. "As tae the stable lad, I sent him hame wi' an *ugsome* cough."

"He did sound rather poorly," Rose agreed, feeling sorrier than ever for the child.

"Aye, barkin' like a chicken wi' the pip." The man slapped his bare hands together, rubbing them vigorously. "If ye'll not be needin' oniething else, ladies, I've horses tae feed and a family of me *ain* tae see aboot." He led the geldings in the direction of their stalls as Rose took Jane's arm and steered her toward the High Street.

Nigh to running, Rose and Jane made their way to Carlyle School, avoiding the shadowy vennels until they reached the one marked Millbrae. Rose paused to catch her breath and say what needed to be said before they reached the door. "I'm sorry, Jane." She could not even meet her gaze. " 'Twas a foolhardy notion. A wutch's cottage! Whatever was I thinking?"

"You were thinking it would be novel. And dangerous," Jane said between gasps for air. "And it was."

"Too much so."

"Nae." Jane tugged affectionately on her cloak. " 'Twas grand. You promised me an adventure, Rose McBride."

"Aye!" She laughed, her relief so complete she nearly collapsed on the steps outside Carlyle. "You were just so…so *quiet* at Nethermuir."

Jane tarried on the bottom step. "I'll not lie to you, Rose. I grew feverish for a time and did not feel at all myself." She cleared her throat, then swallowed, wincing as though it hurt. "But fresh clothes and a warm bed will set me to rights. See if they don't."

Rose slipped the linen cloth from round her neck and offered it to Jane. "There might be a hint of feverfew left."

Jane laughed. No sound could have pleased Rose more. "Nae, lass. The wutch's herbs and spells are for you alone." She reached up to tap on the door. "You let me spin the story of our day at Aunt Catherine's in Lochrutton, aye? About the salmon we had for dinner and the honey cakes we had with tea and how my auntie is embroidering me a scarf and what the doctor told her yestreen."

"Oo aye!" Rose nodded emphatically. " 'Tis all yours to tell."

When Mistress Carlyle opened the door at their knock and found them standing there, exhausted and soaked through, not a word was said about their late arrival or about their disheveled appearance. "I have done nothing but pray since the first drops landed on our window sill," the schoolmistress confessed. "We shall see to hot baths, then supper, then bed." Escorting them both up the stair, past a dining room filled with their saucer-eyed schoolmates, Etta the Grim was in her element, ordering about her small household staff, opening the girls' well-packed trunks to find gowns that, if not fresh, were at least dry.

"See that your hair is well rubbed with a towel," the schoolmistress cautioned, as servants gingerly carried two large bowls of steaming water into the sleeping room. "We cannot be too careful in winter. Mary Carruthers is still in bed with a fever, you know." She handed the girls clean linens and did her best to appear compassionate. "I'd hate to see two of my brightest pupils spend the rest of the school year beneath their bedcovers."

"Yes, mem," Jane agreed, though Rose detected a thread of sarcasm in her voice. "That would be most unfortunate."

Mistress Carlyle, it seemed, heard something else. "Your throat sounds hoarse, Jane. Are you feeling quite well?"

"Yes, mem, I'm—"

"Come, come, I've the very thing for it. A simple herbal remedy. You've only to lean over a bowl of hot water and draw it into your lungs."

"Really?" Jane looked at Rose, who looked at the floor and bit her lip so hard it bled. "I don't think I'll be needing that," Jane murmured, "but thank you."

The minute the woman left, the lasses fell onto their beds and buried their faces in their pillows, laughing. It had been a very long day; Rose could not think of a more fitting end.

Friday morning dawned with a touch of pale blue behind thin clouds and no hint of rain. "The temperature rose overnight," Mistress Carlyle explained to the whole school over breakfast. " 'Tis an answer to prayer, of course, for you all have journeys to make."

She consulted a list in her pocket, slipping on a pair of silver-rimmed spectacles to read her notes aloud. "Miss Balfour will be some time reaching Moffat and so will not return to us until Tuesday. Miss Johnstone will spend a good part of this day reaching Ruthwell, though I'm pleased to say we'll see her Monday afternoon along with the rest of you. Miss Herries will be enjoying an early dinner today in Torthorwald, while Miss Grierson and Miss McBride will still be in their carriages, traveling in opposite directions. Though very much the same distance, I should think. Nine miles to each of your doorsteps, isn't it ladies?"

"Yes, mem," Rose and Jane said in unison, then winked at each other, unseen by the headmistress, who still had her nose buried in the handwritten list.

When Willie arrived to escort her home, Rose said good-bye to Jane in the parlor, grateful her friend did not spy the common chaise at the foot of the vennel. Next to the Griersons' ebony coach-and-four, the two-wheeled carriage from Auchengray was a sorry conveyance. " 'Tis only three days, Jane, but it feels like 'twill be a lifetime until I see you again."

"You *are* a silly girl, Rose McBride." Jane grasped her hands and squeezed tight, blinking hard. "I will be here Monday, and so will you."

Rose lowered her voice and tried hard to sound stern. "And you'll keep your head dry and your lungs moist?"

"Yes, mem. Round the clock." Jane tipped her head, a wistful expression on her face. "I'm glad to have met you, Rose. What you did yestreen was very brave, and all because you wanted us to be friends again."

"Aye." Rose dropped her chin. "Though it nearly turned out quite the opposite."

"That's not so." Jane pressed her cheek to Rose's and whispered in her ear, "*Nous serons toujours amies.* We will be friends always." They stood very still for a moment before stepping apart, both of them smiling through their tears. Jane touched a sleeve to the corner of her eye. "Wait until Mr. James McKie sees what a month of polishing and refinement has done for his fair, young Rose."

Rose turned toward the looking glass hanging near the door for a swift appraisal. "Do you think Jamie will notice a difference?"

Jane's laugh was low and raspy. "The man will be hard pressed to notice anything else."

Twenty-Eight

Be to her virtues very kind;
Be to her faults a little blind.

MATTHEW PRIOR

J amie, she's here."

He looked up from his reading to find Leana standing in their bedroom doorway, her hands clutching her skirts. The note of distress in her voice was unmistakable. He rose and joined her at once, *Gulliver's Travels* forgotten. "Come, we'll greet your sister together." Taking her hand in his, he led her into the hall, keeping his voice down. "You have no need for concern, Leana. 'Tis you whom I married. Remember that."

Rose's musical laughter carried through the house. They soon found her in the front parlor. At first Jamie could see only the feathers of her high-crowned bonnet encircled by various members of the household, all crowding round her, welcoming her as though she'd been gone twelve months instead of one.

"Jamie!" Rose spun toward him, giving him her complete attention. She swept the servants aside and curtsied, bending to the floor like a seasoned courtier. *"Bonjour, monsieur."*

Hiding his amusement, Jamie matched his bow to hers, brushing his hand across the carpet. *"Bonjour, mademoiselle. Pourrais-je vous présenter ma femme, Léana."*

Rose smiled and glided toward them. "I know your wife very well." She embraced Leana briefly, as one might greet a neighbor, not a sister. *"Enchantée."*

"Whatever are you two saying?" Leana scolded them, smiling. "You'll have us all scratching our heads."

Rose stepped back, folding her hands at her waist. "Fear not, Leana.

Naught but 'good afternoon' and 'may I present my wife.' Phrases one learns in a first lesson. Within minutes I will have exhausted my entire French vocabulary, 'tis so meager."

"Nae, 'tis impressive," Leana said smoothly. If she felt overshadowed by her sister, neither her manner nor tone revealed it.

Jamie marveled at them both. If only he and his brother, Evan, could have behaved so civilly. Seldom were the men in the same room without jabbing at each other with sharp words, if not swords. Though by the time Jamie had fled from Glentrool, Evan had good cause for his anger: With their mother's help, Jamie had tricked their father into giving him Evan's inheritance. Little wonder Rowena McKie didn't urge her younger son to return to Glentrool just yet. *Soon, Mother.*

"I was told dinner will be served shortly." Rose waved toward the stair, her hand mimicking a swallow in flight. "If I might take a moment to attend to my *toilette* before I greet Father."

"Of course." Leana stepped aside as her sister swept past her. "Jamie, I must see to Ian's dinner before our own."

He turned and met his wife's troubled gaze, chastising himself for watching Rose even for a moment. "Your sister is home for three short days," he reminded her. "I intend to stay busy and out of harm's way. By Monday afternoon life at Auchengray will be as it was before your sister waltzed through the door."

Leana's voice fell to a whisper. "I will try not to count the hours."

Jamie circled his arms round her and held her for a moment. "You worry too much, lass. She is still a child, nine years my junior. More polished, aye, and armed with a few social graces. But Rose is not the woman I married, nor is she the mother of my son. You are both those and loved besides." He kissed her brow. "Off you go to feed that ravenous offspring of ours. I'll be waiting for you at table."

He'd forgotten how much attention Rose required; the dinner hour soon reminded him. She kept up a steady narrative of events from the last four weeks, not seeming to notice her father's glowering expression. Lachlan McBride preferred to eat in silence, a practice Rose disregarded as she skipped from one tale to the next like a child eager to show off her birthday presents. Jane Grierson, an older girl she'd mentioned in her last letter, figured prominently in the various stories, though Jamie sensed there was more to be told than Rose was willing to share.

"So, Jamie." She fixed her gaze on him. "What have *you* been doing all month?"

He shrugged, feigning indifference. "Mending the dry stane dykes. Tending the ewes. Loving my wife." He had meant to surprise her; the look on her face told him he'd succeeded. "Leana and I spent a midwinter's eve at Glensone." Jamie smiled at Leana, making sure his love for her was evident and undeniable. When he turned back to Rose, he recomposed his features into a bland mask. "Peter Drummond inquired about you."

She wrinkled her nose. "Peter?"

Jamie looked toward the head of the table, ignoring her response. "What say you, Uncle, to a visit from our neighbor, young Mr. Drummond? We discussed Saturday at four o' the clock when he and I last spoke."

"*Och!*" Lachlan spat out the word. "'Tis a fine time to include the girl's father in such a discussion. Drummond should have come to me first."

"Aye," Jamie agreed, "Peter ought to have done that verra thing. 'Twas a request made in passing. He meant no disrespect." Jamie watched his words bank the heated coals of the man's ire. Rose might not be so easily appeased.

As expected, she cornered him in the hall after the final grace was spoken over the meat. The girl was flushed, almost feverish, and her tongue was sharp. "Jamie, what swickerie is this, pairing me with Peter Drummond?"

"The pairing is not mine," he said evenly. "Peter merely asked if he might call on you. You'd be wise to see what the lad has to offer, Rose."

Her eyes narrowed. "I have no wish to be Peter's wife."

"Then choose another, Rose, for I am blithely wed." Instinctively he stepped back. "See that you treat Drummond with the respect he deserves. I'll not stand by and watch another neighbor humiliated."

He left her there alone in the hall while he sought the quiet sanctuary of the byre. Though she was still as bonny as ever, Rose had changed. And so, please God, had he.

When light appeared in the eastern sky Saturday morning, Jamie was already busy in the farm steading cleaning his shears. Work—hard, grimy labor—would keep his family foremost in his thoughts and Rose far from his side.

Dinner came and went without him, though his absence was noted. Duncan came looking for him in the barn. "Ye were missed at table," he said, kicking the mud off his boots.

Jamie dragged an oil-soaked rag across the blades. "Not hungry."

Duncan grunted. " 'Tis three o' the clock, lad. Have ye not invited Peter Drummond tae pay a call on Rose?"

"The lad invited himself. Anyway, my uncle can handle things."

Duncan folded his arms across his chest. "Lachlan McBride is not the one wha bade him come."

"Speak plainly, man." Jamie tossed aside the shears. "You're here for a reason, and it's not Peter Drummond."

"Nae." A grin stretched across Duncan's face. "I niver can *swick* ye, Jamie. 'Tis aboot Rose."

Jamie shook his head. *Rose, always Rose.* "I suppose she sent you to find me."

"She did not." His smile faded. "My faither once said if the de'il finds an idle man, he sets him tae work." Duncan stared at the freshly sharpened shears, the neat stacks of grain, letting the words sink in. "I'm here because a married man skipped a meal tae avoid a maid."

Heat climbed up Jamie's neck. "And?"

"Ye ken what the Buik says: 'Watch and pray, that ye enter not into temptation.' Are ye prayin', Jamie? Because ye can be verra sure that I am. There's meikle at stake here—"

"I ken what's at stake!" Jamie snapped, irritated at Duncan's suggestion. "You've seen how it is with Leana and me. There's no need to fear I'll go chasing after Rose McBride again."

Duncan clapped his hand on Jamie's shoulder; his fierce gaze fixed on him as well. "Glad tae hear ye say it, lad. Come make Drummond feel welcome then. Offer yer blissin on their courtin'. Let Rose see ye happy for her." He lowered his voice but not his conviction. "'Tis time Rose got on wi' her life and ye wi' yers."

"You'll get no *argle-bargle* from me on that." Jamie rubbed his hand across his beard. "If I'm to greet Mr. Drummond at four, tell Hugh I'll need his razor."

"Done." Duncan released his grip with a smile of satisfaction, then headed toward the mains.

Mindful of the hour, Jamie quickly finished cleaning the last of his shears. The tools wouldn't be needed until June, but once the lambing started in late March, there'd be no time for such chores. By the time Jamie reached the house, Hugh was waiting for him in his bedroom. So was Leana.

She drew him aside while Hugh sharpened his razor on a strop. "Jamie, I'm not certain Rose should see Mr. Drummond today."

He groaned. "Don't tell me the lass has refused him already."

"Jamie, the problem is not Peter. 'Tis Rose. She's not looking well. If you'd joined us for dinner earlier, you'd have discovered that for yourself."

A female voice floated in from the hall. "Discovered what?"

They both turned to find Rose standing outside the doorway, looking a bit unsteady on her feet. Leana clasped her sister's hand and eased her into the room. "Discovered *you,* dearie. How tired you look. Feverish." With her free hand, Leana touched Rose's forehead. "Ah. Warm but not hot."

"Nothing to worry about then." Rose smiled, though not with her whole face. "I...we missed you at dinner, Jamie."

His shoulders sank. "Clearly I cannot miss a meal in this house again, or I'll ne'er hear the end of it. Forgive me, ladies. As Duncan would say, I have meikle to do and few to do for me." Pausing to study Rose's face, he noticed the faint smudges beneath her eyes. She *did* look tired. "Suppose I tell Mr. Drummond to come calling another day. Would that suit you, lass?"

She exhaled, and a genuine smile decorated her face. " 'Twould be *ferlie*. You're so kind, Jamie."

Kind. Kindness had nothing to do with it. He was being selfish, not sensitive, for he wanted Drummond to see Rose at her best and proceed with his suit.

Leana circled her arm round Rose's waist. "Suppose I take Rose down to the kitchen for a cup of tea with honey. 'Twould help her throat."

The women had no sooner started down the hall when Hugh cleared his throat behind him. "Will ye be needin' yer shave, sir?"

Jamie turned to find Hugh holding a steaming towel in one hand, a gleaming razor in the other. "Foolish of me to waste the hot water. By all means, man, do your duty." Grateful for the servant's ministrations and a few minutes of uncluttered thought, Jamie sank into the chair and tipped his head back, exhausted.

Leana found him that way an hour later and woke him with an unhurried kiss on each smooth cheek. "Poor man," she said affectionately, running her fingers through his unbound hair. "Hugh said you fell asleep like a taper that's been snuffed out."

Jamie sat up, groggy and disoriented, rubbing the stiffness in his neck. The room was shrouded in darkness, with only a flickering candle to light their faces. "Whatever can the time be?"

" 'Tis nearing the supper hour."

"Och! What of Peter Drummond?"

"Come and gone. Father explained that Rose was too ill to see visitors today. She's taken to her bed."

Jamie straightened, suddenly alert. "Is she worse then?"

"Aye." Leana's pale eyes shone in the candlelight. "She says her throat aches too much to think of eating supper. I'm hardly a doctor, but the glands along her neck feel swollen."

A sense of urgency launched him to his feet. "Should I ride to Dumfries for a surgeon?"

"Goodness, Jamie! 'Tis not so bad as that. Naught but the common cold, though you can be certain I'll watch her carefully."

He began to pace the floor. "Was it the carriage ride home, do you suppose? The weather has been dreadful all week. Was she out of doors at all?"

"Calm yourself." Leana caught his elbow. "Rose hasn't mentioned any particular reason why she might be sick, though she says not to worry. Come look for yourself." Leana led him down the hall to the room she and Rose had once shared and tapped on the door. "May we come in, dearie?"

A single candle stood by the box bed, where Rose sat propped up with pillows. Her cheeks looked flushed but no pinker than if she'd skipped across the orchard. Relieved, Jamie smiled.

"Do you always greet sick people with such a jolly face?" Her voice sounded thin with a worrisome rasp.

"Better a smile than a frown," he said lightly, clasping his hands behind his back lest he touch her by mistake. He couldn't recall ever seeing Rose so quiet, so subdued. Her newfound confidence was nowhere to be seen.

Leana smoothed a hand across her bedcovers. "It seems your last two days at home may be spent in this room, Rose."

"Aye," she said, falling back against her pillows. "It does."

Twenty-Nine

The weary rain falls ceaseless, while the day
Is wrapped in damp.
DAVID GRAY

"Och!" Neda flapped her dishtowel in the direction of the kitchen window. "Have ye ever seen sae weatherful a Sabbath?"

Leana nodded absently, preparing a tray of tea and porridge to take up to Rose's room. The servants were busy assembling in the hall for her father's stamp of approval before leaving for the kirk. Rain, snow, or sun, Lachlan McBride made certain every member of his household was dressed and shod for services. They might go barefoot any other day of the week, but not Sunday.

"Rose didn't sleep well last night," Leana said, covering the steaming teacup with a saucer. "With the rain falling so hard, she ought to stay home from services. I'll care for her, of course."

Neda arched a sparse eyebrow. "D'ye think ye should? Yer hands are fu' enough nursin' Ian."

"I expect my sister to sleep most of the day, as I've a tincture of chamomile to give her. We'll manage." She gingerly picked up the tray and headed for the stair, climbing one stone step at a time. However did Eliza fly up and down the stair without spilling a drop? When she glanced up, Jamie stood at the threshold, watching her with obvious amusement.

"You'll not think me so *knackie* if I drop this on your foot, James McKie."

He chuckled, stepping back to let her pass. "Your sister is fortunate to have so talented a nurse."

Leana paused at Rose's door. "My skills are limited to what I plucked from my garden last season. Still, I'll do what I can to make her comfortable." She stared at the wood panels of the door. "Pray for the lass, for I fear she had a restless night."

"As did you," he said, compassion in his eyes. "I felt you climb out of our bed several times."

"Forgive me for waking you, Jamie." She dipped her chin, careful not to spill her tray. "I am, after all, a mother. 'Tis my task in life to worry." Offering him a trace of a smile, she leaned on the door, easing it open. "Do you want to see Rose?"

"I've seen *you*, Leana." He planted a kiss on her forehead. "That's all that matters."

She watched him slip down the stair to join the others, enjoying the bounce to his step and the broad line of his shoulders. She had never imagined such a day, but it was here: She not only loved Jamie with her whole heart; she trusted him. Even with Rose.

Reminded of her duties, Leana pushed the door open further and entered the darkened bedroom. Her sister was blessedly asleep, though Rose's breathing sounded congested, and her bedcovers were in a heap. Leana put the tray aside and parted the curtains so she might see to work. Rain fell in sheets against the windowpanes. A good day for sleeping, but the cold and damp did not bode well for healing. Leana folded Rose's blankets down to the end of the bed, then tucked the pillows in place and brushed the back of her hand against her sister's forehead. Fever was the greatest concern. Earlier that morning Annabel had carried up a pitcher of fresh, tepid water, ready for Leana to wipe across Rose's brow if required. One touch to her hot skin, and it was clear the water would be put to use.

"I'm sorry to wake you, Rose." When she lay the damp cloth across the girl's brow, her patient didn't stir. Alarmed, Leana pressed her fingers against her sister's neck, seeking a heartbeat. *There now.* She heaved a sigh of relief and turned the cloth over, pressing it against Rose's forehead, then her cheeks, then her cracked, dry lips. Gingerly pulling open the neckline of her sister's nightgown, Leana was surprised to find a long, blue ribbon hanging about her neck. Tugging on the ribbon brought forth a stone, as plain and ugly as some discarded rock one might find along the road. The smooth hole through the center was its one distinction. Heated by Rose's skin, it lay in Leana's palm like a living thing. Anxious to be rid of it, Leana lifted Rose's head with one hand

and eased the necklace over it with the other, taking care not to tangle the ribbon in her loose, fever-dampened hair.

The moment Rose's head touched the pillows again the girl opened her eyes. "Leana, please." Her voice was hoarse, strained. "Don't."

Leana's first instinct was to hide the beribboned stone beneath her apron, until she heard Neda's voice whispering in her head, "Whaur there are suspicions there is nae love." So she confessed the truth to Rose, holding up the necklace. "I did not like the look of this, dearie. And I feared I might ruin the ribbon with my damp cloth." She placed the stone inside the table drawer, longing to ask what it signified, where it came from. Not from any jeweler in Dumfries, of that she was certain. Perhaps her new acquaintance at school had presented Rose with the stone as a token of their friendship. "Is the necklace from Jane?"

"Jane!" Rose's eyes widened. "Is she here? Is she well?"

Here? Leana freshened the cloth across her sister's brow. *Poor girl!* Perhaps the fever was worse than she'd realized. "I'm afraid I don't ken what you mean, Rose." She kept her voice calm, her touch soothing. "Are you talking about your friend from school?"

"Sick," she murmured, her gaze blank. "Fever."

"I ken you're sick." Leana patted her hand. "And you do have a fever." She rolled up the sleeves of Rose's nightgown and inched the hem up to her knees. "You might shiver a bittie, but I'm going to keep your heavy blankets off and let your body cool on its own." No apothecary had taught her this; she had learned it quite by accident three Novembers past while caring for Janet Crosbie, a childhood friend suffering from pneumonia. Janet, too, had kicked off her many covers, and as a result her temperature had started to drop. Until an irate Mistress Bell, the wife of a local bonnet laird who fancied herself an expert on such matters, had insisted the girl be covered chin to toe in one thick plaid after another. Janet Crosbie was dead by morning.

Leana would not make the same mistake. Nor would she allow a surgeon to come knocking on Auchengray's door with his spring lancets and his bleeding bowls. She would see to Rose's recovery using prayer, common sense, and God's provision from her garden. "I've something to help you sleep, dearie." She handed Rose a small glass of water mixed with a dollop of rum and a tincture of chamomile harvested last summer when she could still manage in the garden. " 'Tis the very thing for your raw throat and that unco cough of yours."

Rose drank it down without complaint, then sank onto the pillows. Her eyes drifted shut. "Fever…few," she said faintly, her voice cracking.

Leana put aside the drained cup. "Aye, you have a fever, too. Bear with me, Rose. You'll feel better soon." Dipping one cloth after another into the lukewarm water, then squeezing out the excess, Leana draped the wet fabric on her sister's arms and neck, on her calves and feet, and all round her face, whispering an entreaty as she put each cloth in place. *Lord, have mercy. Christ, have mercy.* As she finished covering her sister with prayers and compresses, there was a knock at the door, and Neda quietly entered the room.

"We're awa tae kirk now…" The older woman's words drifted off as she looked at the patient, then at Leana, eyes widening with concern. "Ye're sure ye ken what ye're aboot?"

Leana froze, dismayed by the question. What if she did *not* know and her remedies made Rose worse rather than better? Suppose her sister's illness wasn't a common cold but pneumonia? Or influenza? "Oh, Neda." Leana's voice caught. "Please God, I'm doing everything I can."

Neda drew her into a mother's embrace, pressing her head against her shoulder. "Now, lass. Nae one could do better, for nae one loves yer sister mair than ye."

Leana sniffed, dabbing at her nose with a spare cloth as she gazed at her sister. "I pray that's true. I do love my sweet Rose."

"Aye, ye do." Neda rested her hand on Rose's brow, turning the cloth once more. "Read the Buik tae her, Leana. I'll have Duncan bring it up tae the room afore he leaves." She touched a hand to Leana's cheek in parting. "Ye ken the truth and the One wha penned it. Let yer sister hear it from yer lips today, for she needs it sairlie."

Neda slipped out the door, opening it enough for Leana to overhear Ian in the next room fussing a bit, wanting his breakfast. "Sleep well, Rose. I won't be lang." Leaving the door slightly ajar in case Rose should wake and call out for her, Leana hastened to the nursery, where Eliza had Ian cradled in her lap.

The sandy-haired maid glanced up. "Is that yer mither, wee boy?"

Ian's arms flapped like a barnacle goose taking flight. Leana, laughing at his antics, scooped him up and bussed his sticky cheeks with kisses. "Aye, 'tis your mother. As glad to see you as you are to see her."

Eliza stood, for there was one chair in the small room. "I'll awa tae kirk, then, if it pleases ye."

Leana released the quiet girl with her blessing, then put Ian to her breast without delay, grateful for a peaceful moment in the midst of a troubling morning. She stroked his head, delighting in the warmth of his skin, the silkiness of his hair, humming in tune with the sweet little noises he made. A languid half-hour passed without a sound in the house, save Duncan's delivery of the family Bible to Rose's bedroom. Leana rested her head on the high-backed chair and let her imagination carry her to Loch Trool, for her feet would travel there soon enough. Jamie called it the loveliest spot in all of Galloway with its steep green braes and a sparkling loch nestled between them. Not far from the water's edge rose the stony walls of Glentrool, a massive house meant to last for generations. " 'Twill be your home, Ian," she told her son, bringing his tiny fingers to her lips and brushing them with a kiss. "And mine."

True to his pattern, Ian sank back into sleep. Though it wouldn't be a long nap, it would give her time to care for Rose and tidy his room a bit. Not a true cleaning, for it was the Sabbath, but enough to put her mother's mind at ease. She made quick work of it, stacking Duncan's latest present, a set of carved blocks, and Neda's colorful rattles, wiping the surfaces of his crib, sweeping his soiled linens into a basket. "Sleep, my little prince," she said, leaving the door ajar and moving to Rose's room next door.

Her sister was still asleep, as expected. "Not to worry if you don't awaken while I read to you, dearie." Leana settled into the bedside chair. "I'll benefit from hearing it as well." Thoughtful Duncan had placed the thick Bible on the table beside the bed and moved the chair closer, for the book was too heavy to hold in her lap for very long. Fishing out her spectacles, Leana lit a second candle, still squinting at the text as she began to read. She spoke slowly and clearly, on the chance Rose might merely have her eyes closed and be listening after all.

"By faith, we have peace with God through our Lord Jesus Christ."
Leana paused, letting the words penetrate the soil of her heart. *Faith,*
aye. She understood that. But *peace?* How could a mother ever know
peace once a bairn left her breast, once he toddled from her arms into a
dangerous world? Like Rose, toddling off to Dumfries and coming
home ill?

The answers were there, woven through the words: The peace was
from God, and with God, and through God. Leana pressed her damp
hand to the page, praying as she did. *May God grant you that peace,*
dear Rose.

Thirty

A malady
Preys on my heart that medicine cannot reach.
CHARLES ROBERT MATURIN

G*od, help me.* Rose could not even whisper the words, so swollen
was her aching throat. She could pray the words, however, and so
she did. *Please help me.* 'Twas a fool's request, considering she'd turned
her back on the Almighty and crossed the threshold of Lillias Brown's
cottage. *Please forgive me.*

She forced her eyes open. Mere slits squinting at the meager light.
Leana had come and gone all morning—or was it many mornings?
After yanking back the bedcovers, her sister had draped damp cloths
across Rose's bare skin, leaving her trembling, feverish, and alone in the
murky room. Why had Jamie not come to see her? Or her father? Or
Neda? Maybe they had come. Maybe they'd given her up for dead. She
clawed at her bedcovers like one climbing out of a drugged sleep. A tincture Leana had given her perhaps. Was her sister a wutch like Lillias?
Her words had been soft and her touch gentle. But perhaps her intent
was less benign.

Feverfew. Aye, she'd told Leana. Hadn't her sister listened? Hadn't
she understood?

Forgotten words returned in fragments, bobbing through her mind
like boats without moorings. *The wutch's herbs and spells are for you
alone.* Jane's voice. Laughing as she said it. *Choose another, Rose, for I am
blithely wed.* Only Jamie could be so heartless. *My little daughter lieth at
the point of death.* Her father. Or was it Reverend Gordon, reading from
the Buik? Nae, 'twas Leana who'd read to her.

"Leana." It came out on a croak. When no one appeared at the door,
Rose tried another name. "Jane," she struggled to say. But Jane lived in

faraway Dunscore. And wasn't Jane sick too? "Susanne." Nae, she would never come. *Jamie.* She could not even bring herself to speak his name aloud, for then she might weep, which would make her throat hurt even more.

A tap at the door, faint as it was, startled her.

"Rose, it's me." Leana came in bearing a tray. "The others will be home from services soon," she reminded her. "I thought it best to feed you before your bedroom is filled with anxious faces." She put down the tray, then tucked a napkin beneath Rose's chin. "Will you try some applesauce? 'Tis the same as I fed Ian a bit ago."

Rose stared at the cup of strained fruit and her sister, horn spoon in hand. Had it come to this, being fed like an infant? Mortified, she faced toward the wall.

"Please, Rose. You'll need your strength if you're to recover."

She closed her eyes and waited for her sister to grow weary of persuading her. It was some time before Leana put aside her things and tiptoed out of the room. Rose tried to sleep, but sleep would not come. She tried to sit up, but her body would not cooperate. When she stretched out a badly shaking hand toward the abandoned applesauce, she misjudged the distance and knocked it off the tray. The pottery cup shattered, spilling its contents across the painted wood floor.

Leana returned at once. "Poor dearie. You were hungry after all." There was no judgment in her expression, no scolding in her voice. "Let me clean this up, then we'll see about a fresh cupful."

Rose had no choice but to let herself be fed.

"I did this when you were a babe," Leana confided, dabbing at her mouth with a napkin. "Neda helped me tie you into a high-backed chair with one of my sashes. I spooned porridge into your sweet mouth until your cheeks looked like a squirrel's."

Rose waved away the rest. It was too humiliating. And it hurt to swallow.

Leana did not argue but instead wiped Rose's face clean, then found a brush and began pulling it through her sister's hair in long strokes, humming as she did.

Rose did not have the strength to resist her, nor after a time did she want to. With her scalp tingling, she sank deeper into the heather mattress. Her eyelids felt sewn shut. Many minutes passed before voices on the stair caught her ear.

Leana bent closer. " 'Tis the family, home at last. I'll insist they not tarry. Will that suit you, Rose?"

She cared little who visited her bedside or how long they stayed, only that she might sleep. And sleep she did.

When she woke, even the gray shadows in the room were gone, and it was well night. Not a candle was lit, though she heard someone breathing in the chilly darkness. She mustered her strength, straining her voice to speak. "Leana?"

" 'Tis I, Rose."

Jamie. Her heart thudded in her chest. "Oh," was all she managed to say.

"Since you were well asleep, I thought it safe to take my turn by your bedside." She heard the slight smile in his voice. "Leana is quite adamant: one visitor at a time." A scrape of a chair and he drew nearer. "Shall I light a taper?"

"Nae." She swallowed with some difficulty. Surely she must look as horrid as she felt. "Who...else?"

"Neda spent the first hour with you, then Duncan, then Annabel." His voice was low, soothing. "Leana will come knocking any moment if she hears you are awake. You've slept the Sabbath away."

To have Jamie so near, all to herself, and not be able to speak to him was torture. She dragged her hand across the bedcovers, hoping he might clasp it in his. Instead it slid off the edge of the box bed and dangled above the floor.

Jamie lifted her hand back in place, barely touching her. "Poor Rose. You truly are in a bad way." He eyed her with compassion, nothing more. "Were others at your school ill? Before you left, I mean?"

"Jane...Grierson." Every word was an effort. At least she would not have to explain that her sickness came from breathing the foul air of the wutch's cottage. From swallowing her *eldritch* herbs. From riding through a winter rainstorm. Rose counted it a miracle she was not already dead. And what of her dear friend? Had she recovered or grown worse? Rose managed two more words—"Write Jane"—before she sank into a feverish slumber.

When she stirred again, gray sunlight filled the room. Annabel was dusting her dressing table, lifting each item with care, putting it back in precisely the same place: the silver-edged hand mirror, the stiff-bristled brush and ox-horn comb, the wooden box of hairpins, the round tin of face powder, the elegant bottle that once belonged to her mother, now filled with fresh rose water. Rose watched the maid's efficient movements, remembering when the girl had first come to them from Aberdeenshire, timid and clumsy. Since then Neda had taught her to read, to clean properly, to help in the kitchen. Her skills as a lady's maid were less adept, but Rose would see her trained soon enough.

When she said the girl's name in a gravelly whisper, the servant whirled about, her dusting cloth waving like a flag. "Miss Rose! Ye're awake then. I'll find Mistress Leana."

"Nae." Rose coughed, a terrible barking sound. When she'd recovered enough to breathe, ragged as it sounded, she aimed her gaze at the breakfast tray beside her bed. "Drink."

Annabel complied at once, lifting a tepid cup of tea to her lips. "Steady as she goes." Despite the maid's efforts, the tea dribbled down Rose's chin, staining her linen nightgown. "Och! I'm sae sorry, miss."

The door swung open. "What have we here? Is Rose awake, and you've not called me?" Leana's face appeared above Annabel's shoulder, her expression more haggard than usual. "We've not slept a wink worrying about you, dearie. Come, Annabel, let me care for my sister while you finish dusting the room. We're sure to have more visitors, for Rose was missed at services yestermorn."

Rose shook her head, though it made her dizzy, and forced one word past her aching throat. "Nae."

"Nae visitors?" Leana laid the back of her hand along the curve of Rose's neck. "Perhaps 'tis best, for your fever has not passed." She brushed a cool cloth across each cheek and round her chin, dabbing at the spilled tea as well. "Naturally we'll welcome Reverend Gordon. As to the others, suppose I have Neda fill them up with cakes and short-bread, then send them on their way."

Rose was relieved to hear it. 'Twas customary in the Lowlands to visit the ill, to crowd the sickroom until a patient could barely catch her breath. She'd made many such visits herself; in the future she might reconsider. For the moment one matter weighed heavy on her heart, and that was Jane. She must write her at once, inquire after her health, and beg for her forgiveness. To think of Jane feeling this poorly because she'd dragged her off to find a wutch on a winter's day!

She'd mentioned sending a letter yestreen, but Jamie had not understood. Rose spoke more firmly this time. "Write Jane."

"Your friend from Carlyle School? You'd like me to send her a letter?" Leana deposited the cloth into a bowl of water, then dried her hands on her apron. "If you'll tell me what's to be done, I'll gladly scribe it for you." Leana returned a few minutes later with her writing desk, which she perched on her lap. "Now, say only what is necessary. I'll flesh out the rest of it."

For every phrase Rose forced between her parched lips—"Sick too." "Very sorry." "Please write."—Leana penned a full paragraph, reading each one aloud, waiting for Rose's approval. They'd no sooner finished the brief letter when Leana took out a fresh sheet of paper. "Dearie, I've discussed this with Neda…" Her voice trailed off as her earnest gaze studied Rose's face. "We think it prudent you not resume your schooling for a bit. Suppose I write and tell them so, and we'll post both letters at once."

Even nodding her head required more strength than she possessed. Rose lifted her hand briefly, then let it fall. "Candlemas," she whispered.

"Aye, we can enclose your offering for Mistress Carlyle to spend on candles for the school." Leana's pen moved across the paper in graceful sweeps. "Your friend Jane will no doubt be hailed the Candlemas Queen come the morn's morn."

Rose closed her eyes, praying that Jane would travel to Carlyle School on schedule, that after breakfast on the second of February, Jane

would present the schoolmistress with the largest donation of silver—
the Candlemas *Bleeze*—and earn her paper crown. *Please God, let it be
so. Let Jane be well.*

Leana glanced at the window, repeating the oft-told rhyme.

> If Candlemas day be dry and fair,
> The half o' winter's to come and mair;
> If Candlemas day be wet and foul,
> The half o' winter's gone at Yule.

"We'll pray for wet and foul then, shall we? I've had enough of winter, and I ken you have as well. Father thinks it was your ride home in
the chaise that brought on this unco cough of yours."

Let them think what they liked. Rose would hardly dispute it, not
if it spared them from knowing the truth. She alone was responsible for
the sickness that crawled through her body like a serpent, wrapping
itself round her throat until she could barely draw breath.

Thirty-One

I am not the rose,
but I have lived near the rose.

HENRI BENJAMIN, CONSTANT DE REBECQUE

How does Rose fare?" "Whan will she be weel?" "Is yer sister sae fauchie we canna see her?"

A shower of questions greeted Leana each time she stepped outside Rose's room. Household servants, worried neighbors, farm workers—all loitered about the house, getting underfoot and pleading for news. Neda served shortbread and tea, but the well-meaning folk would not be moved, so great was their curiosity aroused by the strange malady come to Auchengray.

Murmuring her thanks, Leana slipped through the motley assembly in the dining room and knocked on the spence door, hoping she might find her father within.

"Enter!" His voice sounded more gruff than usual. She would tread with care.

Latching the door, Leana joined him by the small hearth. He sat in his favorite upholstered chair, its dimensions thronelike, nursing his morning dram. "Father, I've come about Rose."

"Och!" He banged his pewter cup on a thin-legged table, making it dance to his disagreeable tune. "Is nothing else worthy of discourse in this house?"

"You're right, 'tis wearying. But my sister *is* dreadfully ill." Leana folded her hands to keep them from shaking. He'd always affected her thus. She thought nothing of it, for didn't all fathers strike a note of fear in their daughters' hearts? "Neda and I wondered if Rose might remain home this week rather than return to Carlyle School."

He shifted in his chair, the silver threads in his hair catching the hearth light. "But I've paid for the full term. Through Whitsuntide."

" 'Twill be a week, perhaps two, and she will be ready to resume her studies. Rose is doing quite well, with her French especially."

Lachlan McBride snorted. "*Sans valeur.* Worthless. Unless your sister imagines herself an aide to the Comte de Mirabeau." He sipped his whisky in silence, though she noted the smile playing about his lips. " 'Tis amusing to think of your sister in Paris, fending off the mobs, going without meat or bread, when she cannot manage a day without sweets."

Leana tipped her head in acknowledgment. She knew about the revolution in France, of course—'twas the favored topic of discussion from kirkyard to drawing room—but caring for Ian had taken precedence over foreign politics. Perhaps when she and Jamie reached Glentrool, she might have more time for keeping up with such news. "What say you, Father? May we care for Rose under our roof until she is truly well?"

"Aye, if you must. Though I'll expect some reduction in her tuition if she misses more than a few days."

Leana looked down at the letters in her hands, wondering how to proceed. At Rose's request, she'd added a postscript to the one for Mistress Carlyle: *Enclosed you will find your Candlemas Bleeze, with our family's compliments.* Now she must make good that promise. Few things in life were more daunting than asking Lachlan McBride to part with silver. "Father, since the morn is Candlemas, 'tis appropriate that we send a...a small donation for Mistress Carlyle. Tradition, you ken."

He abruptly stood. "My own daughter," he growled, "telling me what's to be done on a festival day." Yanking his thrifite from the broad shelf above his desk, he unlocked the wooden lid and threw it back on its hinges with a thud.

From where Leana sat, the box looked quite full. Colorful Scottish guinea notes and coins in all sizes—copper and silver—nearly spilled over the edge. Stretched across her father's fortune lay a thick, gold cord tied with knots. Had it always been there?

"Send the woman this." He drew out two shillings and tossed them into her lap, closing his money box as quickly as he'd opened it.

"Very well, Father." Leana held the coins in her palm, warming them. A shamefully small gift. She was glad Rose did not have to present it to her schoolmistress in person. "I'll ask Willie to deliver it for us with a letter." She would not mention that it was already written, lest her father accuse her of scheming behind his back.

Lachlan motioned toward the door, the corners of his mouth turned down. "See if Willie cannot take some of those wastrels with him, before they demand to join us at our dinner table."

She kept her tone even and her voice soft. "Father, they're our neighbors, our parish friends. They'll think well of Auchengray and of you if you simply bid them welcome. Thank them for their concern. Urge them to visit another day perhaps, when Rose is better. 'Twould only take a bittie of your time."

He flung open the door without comment and strode into the dining room, waving his arms expansively and greeting their visitors with such a lairdly air that all felt they were standing, not in the mains of Auchengray, but in the gilded rooms of Maxwell Park itself. His smooth words masked the fork in his tongue that prodded them out the door. Within minutes they'd all departed, congratulating themselves for having such a fine neighbor.

Leana, watching from the spence door, was nigh to speechless at his performance. "Father, you amaze me."

He brushed past her, a self-satisfied expression on his face. " 'Tis a matter of giving folk what they want. Recognition. Some acknowledgment of their existence. A nod to their sense of importance, however poorly deserved." He busied himself at his desk, straightening papers that were already neatly in place. "People are made happy by the smallest things, Leana. Take you, for example."

"Me?" She touched her hand to her heart. "What small things make me happy, Father?"

"Ian, for one. Jamie's love, for another."

Leana bowed her head, disconcerted that he would speak of so personal a matter. "My husband's affection is not a small thing."

"Heaven knows you've waited long enough for it. Maybe now you see the wisdom in all that I did for you, Leana."

Her head slowly rose. "All that *you* did?"

"Meeting with the kirk session after your wedding. Seeing that the record was altered so you were marked as Jamie's bride and not as an *ill-deedie* woman."

Leana opened her mouth to object, then shut it tight. 'Twas not fair to call her wicked. But 'twas more than right to call her a sinner. Even so her sin was forgiven and forgotten, for the Buik said God was faithful to forgive sins and to cleanse his people from their unrighteousness. Aye, she was scrubbed clean in the eyes of God. But in the eyes of her father, she would never be clean enough.

"I'm grateful for what you did." And she *was* appreciative, hard as it was to confess. Lachlan's efforts had proclaimed Jamie her true husband and she his true bride, to the satisfaction of both kirk and village. "Father, I pray you are thankful as well for a healthy grandson worthy to be called your heir."

"My heir," her father repeated, his voice flat. "So you say." He waved his hand toward the door, dismissing her. "See that Rose's Candlemas offering is delivered at once. And make certain Willie understands that *two* shillings are to be placed in Mistress Carlyle's hand. The woman is as greedy as she is genteel and will want them both." As Leana departed, he called after her, "You can be sure those coins will line her own pocket and not the candle maker's. Isn't that so, Daughter?"

What had he said earlier? *'Tis a matter of giving folk what they want.* She heeded the man's advice as she closed the door behind her. "I'm sure you're right, Father. You always are."

Candlemas Day dawned anything but dry and fair. Rain fell in sheets on the already saturated earth, swelling the burns to torrents and turning the parish roads into rivers of mud. No visitors braved the elements, not even Reverend Gordon. The household took turns maintaining a sickbed vigil, offering comfort and prayers but mostly wringing their hands.

Though Rose's fever had abated slightly, her cough had grown worse. She seemed to choke on her own phlegm at times and had begun to drool, though Leana made certain she was kept clean and presentable. "Poor dearie." She dabbed a cloth at the corners of her sister's chapped mouth. One minute Rose struggled to take a deep breath; the next her breathing became shallow and rapid. She was losing weight too, for her collarbones poked through her nightgown, and her once rosy cheeks were sunken and colorless.

Leana grew more fearful by the hour. As she sat nursing Ian in his cheerful little room, she bit her lip to hold the tears at bay. *Almighty God, whatever am I to do?* She searched her heart and mind for some neglected remedy. Warm air and bright sunshine were not to be had in Galloway for many months. Rose needed to exercise her lungs, but her coughing spasms were painful to see and worse to hear.

She prayed that Reverend Gordon would find his way to their door come the morn. Across Scotland's parishes, the ministers were often the most educated among their flocks and so did what they could to offer medical advice when needed. Doctors, a rarity in the countryside, were reserved for dire situations. Her father would object to the expense, and she'd disagree with a surgeon's intrusive methods. Perhaps Rose would improve with another night's sleep. Or the minister might come bearing news of a certain cure.

She was seated in the nursery, touching a handkerchief to her nose, when Jamie came looking for her. Her anxious thoughts must have been stamped on her features. "Leana, would you like me to ride to the village and bring Reverend Gordon back with me?"

"Oh, Jamie, I would, but…" Her shoulders sank, listening to the rain thrashing the windowpanes in the hall. "'Tis too dreich a day for man or beast. I fear you might find yourself in a sickbed as well."

"While we are speaking of such things…" He paused and bent to kiss her, then planted a tender kiss on their son's head as well. "'Tis *you* I worry about. Tending to Rose round the clock, then tending to Ian. We might all of us contract this terrible disease, whatever it is. I care not for myself, but I care very much for you and for my son." Jamie pretended to look stern, though his eyes gave him away; he was afraid, just as she was. "Promise me you'll let the others help nurse her back to health. Please, Leana? For my sake? For Ian's?"

She could not resist teasing him a little. "Would you miss me? If I died, if I were no longer your wife? Would you not simply find another?"

Jamie bent his knees, lowering himself until they were eye to eye. Now with his jaw firmly set, he did look stern. And very dear. "I could never find another wife like you, Leana. Nor do I care to try." He leaned forward to kiss her once more, lingering a moment before he rocked back on his haunches, then stood. "Our shepherds say the skies will clear tomorrow. They're seldom wrong about such things. Better weather will bring the reverend and perhaps a respite for Rose."

Brighter skies and Reverend Gordon both appeared soon after Wednesday's breakfast. The laird of Auchengray was already bound for Edingham when Leana escorted the minister to Rose's bedside. Jamie stood, offering the minister his chair, then joined Leana in the doorway.

She clasped her husband's hand, needing his strength. "We're grateful you've come, Reverend Gordon." She resisted the temptation to add, "finally." The minister was a busy man with many souls to attend— some two hundred in the village, another four hundred in the countryside. "Our Rose is not well." Leana looked across the room at her sleeping sister, her heart as swollen with love as the streams were with water. "See for yourself, sir."

Reverend Gordon drew near. Though his brown hair had given way to silver sometime ago, his thick eyebrows retained their color, drawing two dark slashes across his visage. The minister punctuated his sermons with his bushy brows, knitting them together through sobering passages and lifting them heavenward when he delivered a surprising word of grace. At the moment his forehead was creased with worry as he bent toward the box bed, brushing aside the curtains to get a better look. He touched Rose's forehead, then pressed his fingers to either side of her neck. "Worse than I'd expected. Some malady of the lungs and throat. More pernicious than the common cold, I can assure you of that." He let the curtain drop into place with obvious reluctance. "'Tis the sound of her breathing that concerns me most. What have you given her to relieve the congestion?"

Leana outlined the numerous herbal remedies she'd cautiously administered—chamomile to help Rose sleep, wild cherry to suppress her cough, goldenrod and elder for excessive phlegm, mugwort for fever. Each of them was greeted with a grunt of approval.

"You've done well, Mistress McKie." From beneath his coat the minister produced a worn copy of *Primitive Physic, or an Easy and Natural Method of Curing Most Diseases.* "I brought this, thinking it might be of some use to you." He then held up a leather pouch the size and color of a hedgehog. "And this I found on your doorstep. Perhaps you'll recognize the contents."

"Bless you, sir." She tucked the book under her arm, curious to discover what the pouch might contain. Sliding a finger between the leather pulls to open it, she bent to take a whiff, then jerked back, eyes watering. "Och! Feverfew." She sniffed it again, to be certain, then pulled the pouch strings taut. "A more bitter herb you'll not find, though it has many good uses. In truth, I should have thought of it myself. You've seen it in my garden, Jamie. Feathery stems with tiny yellow and white flowerets, like wee daisies."

"If you say so, Leana." He eyed the mysterious bundle. "But this pouch is not from your garden. From whose then?"

The three exchanged glances, though no one offered an answer. Finally Leana said, "I can only assume it was a thoughtful neighbor, someone who saw Rose's condition on Monday and thought feverfew might help her coughing. Which it very well might." She stepped back. "If you'll excuse me, gentlemen, I've an inhalation to prepare."

When Leana turned toward the stair, Reverend Gordon snagged her sleeve. "Tarry a moment, lass." He inclined his head down the hall. "Is there somewhere I might speak with Jamie in private? An empty room perhaps?"

Leana heard two words—*Jamie* and *private*—and her nerves stood on edge. Had her good husband done something wrong? Had she? A quick look at Jamie's face assured her that he, too, was taken by surprise. "If it's not too small, the nursery is empty." She gestured toward the adjacent door. "Neda is busy feeding Ian in the kitchen. You'll have the room to yourselves."

"Fine." The minister steered Jamie past her, no longer meeting her gaze. As she started down the stair, she heard him explain to Jamie,

"Inquiring after Rose's health is not the only task that brings me to Auchengray. I also carry news of a rather unfortunate oversight that requires your attention."

"What oversight?" Jamie said, already defensive.

Leana paused at the landing as Reverend Gordon ushered Jamie into the nursery. Though she did not mean to eavesdrop, her anxious heart would not let her move.

"Now, lad," the minister said as the door began to close. "You ken what the kintra folk say: There is a time to *gley* and a time to look straight."

Thirty-Two

He went like one that hath been stunn'd,
And is of sense forlorn.
SAMUEL TAYLOR COLERIDGE

Whatever are you getting at, sir?" Jamie's heart began to pound. *Unfortunate. Oversight.* Reverend Gordon's words raised more questions than they answered.

The minister pulled the room's single chair away from the wall, dusting the seat with his oversized handkerchief. Annabel had already done a thorough job cleaning the room. 'Twas plain Reverend Gordon was stalling.

"Sit you down, son, for we have much to discuss." His uneasiness was apparent, from the faint sheen of perspiration on his brow to his long fingers fiddling with the buttons on his coat.

Jamie sat, but not comfortably. "What is it, Reverend?"

The minister pursed his lips, pressing a forefinger against them, as if weighing his words. "Early this morning I had occasion to open the kirk session records from December 1788. Looking up another matter entirely, you see." His gaze flickered toward Ian's empty crib, then landed on Jamie. "As expected, I noted the three Sundays on which the banns were read for the impending wedding of James McKie and Rose McBride."

"Aye." Jamie relaxed a bit. That was hardly a newsworthy discovery, nor was it the final entry for the year. " 'Twas indeed James and Rose for the banns. But then—"

"Wait." Reverend Gordon held up his hand to stem Jamie's words. "You were there, lad, and you heard your names cried out in the kirk, did you not?"

"I did." He could not deny the truth. Nor could he deny that he once delighted in hearing his name spoken in the same breath as Rose's. "Go on, sir."

"In truth, 'tis not the banns that concern me," the minister continued. "'Tis the clerk's entry for the last day of the year that gave me pause."

Ah. Jamie smiled with relief. Reverend Gordon had found the change of names noted on their wedding day and had forgotten how that came about. After all, the event occurred some thirteen months past. Much took place in a parish. Who could remember it all? "You mean where it was amended to read 'James and Leana McKie'?"

"Nae," the minister said, his expression darkening. "For then we would have no need for this discussion. I mean the recorded entry in the session clerk's hand, indicating the legal and binding marriage of James and Rose McKie."

"Rose?" Jamie nearly choked on her name. "That cannot be right."

"Right or wrong, that is what appears on the page. Your name and Rose's, in the clerk's own scrawl. There is no other notation."

"But 'twas meant to be changed!" Jamie's voice stretched taut as a hangman's noose. This was no oversight; it was an abomination. "My Uncle Lachlan met with the kirk session in early January and had the record amended." *Or didn't he?* Jamie gripped the arms of the chair and said as calmly as possible, "I'm not certain which day Lachlan met with the session, for Leana and I were in Dumfries that week." *Leana.* The very thought of her hearing this news made his stomach clench. "No later than the sixth or seventh of January, I'd say. Were you not there, Reverend?"

"Aye. 'Twas in fact the fifth of January, the first Monday of the month, when the kirk session regularly meets. I sat in the very room where your uncle presented his case."

"Well then!" Jamie took his first full breath since sitting down. "You ken the truth of it." *All this trouble for naught.* "You have only to strike through Rose's name on the entry for 31 December and write the name of my true bride, Leana, in its place."

"Which is what should have been done," the minister agreed as he shifted his weight from one foot to the other. "But our session clerk...och!" He swatted at the air as if the clerk were a bothersome fly. "Perhaps you remember the man: George Cummack."

"Nae, I do not. Should I?"

"Bit of a dotard, I'm afraid, though he was as sharp as any man in his youth." Leaning back against the closed door, the minister released a heavy sigh. "George was in attendance at the January meeting when your father presented his testimony on your behalf. However, George neglected to purchase a new recording book for 1789, and the one from 1788 had already been shelved in my office."

Jamie's hands grew clammy. "Are you saying he took no minutes of the session?"

"On the contrary, George wrote down every word of it on loose leaves of paper. He assured us he would purchase a bound book at once and copy his notes into the official session records within the week and have them signed and approved."

Jamie leaned forward, holding his breath. "And?"

The minister's shoulders sank. "I am sorry to confess he did not. Nor did he remember to change the entry in the 1788 record."

Jamie fell back as though struck. "How could...that is, why didn't..." His speech stuttered to a stop as the truth reeled round inside his mind. None of it made any sense. If the wedding entry was never changed...if the January meeting was never recorded...

The minister seemed calmer now that he'd delivered his news. He mopped his brow and tucked his handkerchief back into his pocket. "I'm afraid this means that by the law of the kirk, which is the law of the land, you are not married to Leana. You are married to Rose."

Jamie shook his head, slowly at first, then faster, as if he might shake loose the awful truth. "Cummack. He is the one who can fix it. Surely he must answer for this...this 'oversight,' as you called it."

"Therein lies the crux of the problem." The minister was no longer looking in his direction but was staring at his shoes. "Cummack's health was failing. Before the session met again, he quit the parish to live with his daughter. Without procuring a testimonial letter from me, sorry to say."

"*Quit?*" Jamie ground out the word. "And moved where?"

"Eskdalemuir."

" 'Tis in Dumfriesshire, not London," Jamie railed. "A half-day's ride at most."

"His place of residence would pose no concern, if 'twere not for the fact that…" When Reverend Gordon looked up, regret was drawn across every solemn feature. "Och, Jamie, there is no easy way to tell you this: George Cummack died within a fortnight of leaving Newabbey. Without his minutes, the record must remain unchanged."

Jamie's composure shattered. "*But I am married to Leana!* Do you understand me, sir? I care not for your kirk sessions and your record books and your dotty clerks. Leana is my wife and the mother of my son. Not Rose."

"I ken, lad. I do. But the record stands differently."

"Then *fix* the record!"

"That I cannot do, and you ken it well. Where would we be if people changed kirk records to suit themselves? They represent a legal document, Jamie. Even I cannot alter that."

Jamie was stunned to silence. He barely heard the minister's words, spoken in a pastoral tone as though he were officiating at a funeral.

"You must understand, Jamie, how embarrassing this is for me. I married you to Rose, or so I thought. Then I was a witness to Lachlan's testimony concerning Leana and accepted it as valid. And I trusted George Cummack to do his duty: change the name and register your uncle's remarks. Alas, neither detail is a matter of kirk record."

"*Detail?*" His life was being taken away, bit by bit, word by word. "Leana is not a *detail.* She is my *wife.* God help me, *she is the mother of my son!*"

"Aye, she is. 'Tis common knowledge that you hold her in high regard." Laying a calming hand on Jamie's shoulder, the minister continued. "Jamie, your fair cousin is quite ill. Heaven forbid this disease should claim her young life, but—"

"Wheesht!" Jamie shot to his feet. "Do not suggest for a moment that I'm to pray for Rose to die!"

"Nae, nae, lad. I am a servant of the Lord Almighty and would never call down destruction on one of my parishioners. I am only saying that *if* Rose were to die, then the matter could be resolved soon after. You and Leana would meet me in the village, where I would perform a private wedding before the kirk door. In minutes, everything would be as it should be. The parish already considers you husband and wife by habit and repute. 'Twould require a brief notation of your wedding in the kirk session records to put all to rest."

"Another *detail*, is that it?" Jamie's eyes narrowed. "And what if Rose lives? Which, as her minister, you should be praying for above all. What then of my marriage?"

Reverend Gordon lifted his shoulders in a faint shrug. "If Rose should survive, the three of you will be required to stand separately before the kirk session and give testimony."

Jamie's ire turned to ice, starting with his hands. "And what would we be expected to say?"

"Each of you would make a public confession of your intentions concerning the last day of December 1788 so that it becomes a matter of official record. In truth, that's how things should have been handled from the start. When your uncle appeared before us that January eve, however, you and Leana were in Dumfries, and your uncle was most…persuasive."

Jamie grimaced. "I imagine the coins he tossed on your table were quite compelling."

A frown crossed Reverend Gordon's face like a shadow come and gone. "The poor of our parish benefited from Lachlan's generous contribution," the minister reminded him. "And you benefited as well, James. Because of your uncle, you married the woman of your choosing."

My choosing. But he had not chosen Leana; Lachlan had chosen for him. When he did not want Leana for his wife, she was his nonetheless. Now that he wanted her very much, it seemed she was not his at all.

And it was Rose who stood in the balance. Between life and death. Between freedom and bondage. He did not need to guess what she might tell the kirk session. He knew too well. Yet Jamie could not bring himself to wish for Rose's passing, not for a minute. He could only beg for God's will to be done. Left to his own devices, Jamie feared which outcome he might choose.

The reverend moved closer to the door, apparently eager to be away. " 'Tis not arduous, meeting with the kirk session. You will each be asked to describe your role in this…ah, unusual situation, one at a time. Rose will, of course, relinquish any claim on you, past or present, will she not?"

Jamie did not respond.

"After her testimony, you will state your original intention to marry Leana rather than Rose, as your uncle explained previously." Reverend Gordon shook his head. "Such a pity his words were not recorded, or we could spare you this inconvenience."

Jamie stared at him. *Inconvenience? 'Twas* far more than that.

"Then Leana will declare she loved you from the first and that you favored her as well. From the beginning." He splayed his hands. "See how simple it will be?"

Jamie bit his tongue. *'Twill be anything but simple.*

"Come, Jamie. I should pray with Rose before I take my leave." Swinging the door open as though he were set free from prison, the minister motioned him to follow. "I intend to plead for her recovery so the session minutes may be amended with due haste."

Thirty-Three

How does your patient, doctor?
Not so sick, my lord,
As she is troubled with thick-coming fancies.
WILLIAM SHAKESPEARE

Reverend Gordon slapped Jamie's back as they walked toward the
bedroom. "In all my years of ministry, lad, I've seldom seen so
tapsalteerie a wedding as yours."

"Aye, 'twas that, sir."

The minister's tone was sympathetic, his words reassuring. " 'Twill
be good to put all that behind you soon."

By now Jamie was half listening, for as they entered the bedroom,
his attention focused on his cousin. Rose had somehow pulled herself
up to a sitting position and was clinging precariously to the edge of the
bed, a terrified Annabel by her side. Rose's eyes were wide open and her
mouth wider still, gasping for air. Her skin was so pale it looked blue.

"Rose!" Jamie leaped to her side, sliding his arm behind her to keep
her from falling. "Breathe, Rose!" With his free hand, he tore back the
curtains from the box bed, fearing the heavy fabric might suffocate her.
"Annabel, find Leana!"

The minister hastily tied back the bed curtains, eyes wide with
alarm. "Nae, let the maid stay. I'll find your wife. And a doctor as well."
He moved toward the door, his deep voice rolling across the room as
though he'd mounted his pulpit. "Listen to me, Jamie. Rose is gravely
ill, worse than any of us realized. I'll ride to Dumfries Infirmary and
send a surgeon at once."

"Let me ride, sir," Jamie offered, but the minister was already at the
door.

"You're needed here, and they'll not refuse when I tell them what
I've seen." He shot a worried glance at the box bed. "Pray, lad, for there's

none but the Almighty who can save her now." The minister departed, coattails flapping, and thundered down the stair calling Leana's name.

Jamie leaned Rose back against the pillows, only to sit her up again when she seemed to be choking. Something was in her throat, strangling her, smothering her. "Rose, you must breathe. Try again, Rose."

"Jamie!" Leana appeared in the doorway, a steaming bowl in her hands, her face white as linen. "Reverend Gordon said…"

"Aye, aye, 'tis bad, Leana." Jamie motioned her forward, fighting for breath himself. "Come, do what you can, for the healing arts I use on my flocks do not stretch so far as this."

Neda was close on her heels, while the household hovered at the door, their mouths gaping, their eyes full of fear. "Stay put," the housekeeper cautioned them, "and let us do what must be done. In the meantime, ye'll serve yer mistress best on yer knees." They knelt as one in the hall, their prayers rising like the steam from Leana's bowl of herbs.

Jamie stepped back to let Leana and Neda work and averted his gaze as they pulled Rose's knees to the edge of the bed, then rearranged her nightgown. The truth struck him afresh. *She is my wife.* The minister's words rang through his soul: *By the law of the kirk you are married to Rose.*

Rose, who was fighting for her life.

Jamie stared at her, forcing himself to pray without regard to the consequences. *Let her live, Almighty God. According to your mercy, heal her.*

The women stood on either side of her, supporting her beneath the arms. Rose hung there, limp, not moving, not speaking, barely breathing. "Lean over the bowl," Leana coaxed. "That's my guid lass. Breathe through your nose if you can." When Rose's hair fell round the bowl as they bent her forward, Leana said calmly, "Aren't you the clever one, sweet Rose? We won't need a towel, for your own hair will keep the steam where it belongs. Can you breathe now? Just a bittie?"

Jamie marveled at Leana's fortitude, for his own knees were nigh to buckling beneath the weight of worry. Aye, and guilt. Had they done enough? Rose was dreadfully weak and her color ghastly. They should have sent for a doctor sooner. Yestreen. Even Monday. Was it too late? Had they failed her?

Rose coughed, a horrid, gurgling sound, then drew the thinnest of breaths. Leana smoothed her free hand across Rose's back, drawing slow, comforting circles between her shoulder blades, crooning in her ear all the while. "Baloo, baloo, my wee, wee thing."

It was all he could do to look at Rose in such a state, yet here was Leana, singing to her. *Singing.* Jamie made himself watch her gentle labors, even if tears stung his eyes, even if his chin trembled. This was the woman he loved. This was the woman he had married. And this was the woman he would fight to keep by his side.

If Rose were to die...

Nae. He would not think of it, would not consider the possibility. She must not die, or a part of Leana would die with her.

If Rose should survive...

She would survive. She *must* survive.

All of Auchengray did what they could for Rose—Leana and Neda supporting her shoulders, Annabel replacing the hot water, Jamie wiping her brow, and Duncan offering encouragement from the doorway. Leana recited verses aloud, lifting her face to the heavens, as though the Almighty were gazing down on Auchengray and no other household. "I pray thee, come and lay thy hands on her, that she may be healed; and she shall live."

At noontide the servants at the door parted like the Red Sea, and a gentleman dressed in a fine black suit swept into the room, perspiring beneath his periwig from the hasty journey. He wore intelligence like a mantle draped across his sturdy shoulders and possessed a keen eye that surveyed the situation at once.

"Dr. John Gilchrist of Dumfries Infirmary," he said brusquely, shaking Jamie's hand. "Your minister was most insistent that I come without delay." He rinsed his hands in the steaming water before him, then bade Neda take the bowl and table away so he might examine the patient. As he pressed and prodded Rose's face and neck, he barraged Jamie and Leana with questions concerning her age, where she'd traveled of late, what symptoms they'd noticed first, when she'd begun to cough, how long her fever had persisted. "As you can see by the bluish coloration of the skin, the patient is not getting sufficient oxygen."

Jamie could only see that she was very ill. "What's to be done, sir?"

He unfolded his surgical etui, revealing a gleaming collection of ivory-handled instruments: scissors, scalpels, tweezers, a tongue blade, a thumb lancet. "Our first task must be to clear her air passage. This will involve the removal of the obstructing membrane. Not a true membrane, you understand, but a thick, grayish blanket, a preternatural coating of the throat." He polished his spectacles with his handkerchief, then flicked the cloth toward an empty chair near the bed. "Lift her onto that straight-backed chair, if you please. I will need you to hold her very still."

Neda and Leana managed to ease her onto the chair, holding her shoulders against the wooden slats, tipping her head back and stretching her neck a bit, as the physician instructed. Rose moaned, and her eyes rolled back as though she might faint. Or worse. When Dr. Gilchrist wielded the tongue blade, then called for more light, Jamie squared his shoulders and gripped a candlestick in each hand, preparing himself for whatever gruesome procedure might follow.

"Dr. Home of Edinburgh recommends a tracheotomy in such cases. I prefer not to use such invasive measures with my patients unless absolutely necessary." He pinned Leana and Neda with an arresting stare. "If you do not hold her still, cutting an incision in her windpipe will be necessary. Understood?"

Hold Rose the women did, though tears streamed down her neck and down theirs as well. Jamie could do little but hold the candles aloft and pray. Weak as she was, Rose did not have the strength to resist them while the doctor made his thorough examination, but she tried valiantly, wriggling in her seat until they convinced her she must not move.

The doctor used both hands to open her mouth still farther. "Forgive me, lass, for I cannot sedate you. Bear with the pain, for it will be over soon enough, and you'll be breathing once more."

Jamie grimaced as the physician's thin, silver-bladed scalpel disappeared down Rose's throat. As the man worked diligently, efficiently, Leana comforted her sister without ceasing, praying aloud that she might endure what could only be agony. At last the doctor retracted the device and eased his patient forward to take a deep but ragged breath.

"God be praised!" Neda cried, echoed by the servants crowding the door.

Leana continued her ministrations, lifting Rose's hair back from her face, wiping her bloody mouth. "Thank you, Lord," she murmured over and over.

"I'll take a bit of thanks as well," the surgeon said good-naturedly, dispensing advice as he wiped his instruments clean. "Give her tepid liquids by the spoonful. No solid food for at least a week. She will not heal quickly, so put away any thoughts of her returning to Dumfries. 'Tis almost certain that is where she contracted her disease."

Leana glanced at Jamie, as if seeking his support, then asked with some trepidation, "What disease is that, sir?"

The doctor stared at them, astounded. "I thought you knew. Your sister has croup. Though you'll seldom find cases in Edinburgh, 'tis not unknown in Galloway. The sea air, you know. Most often we treat infants for croup, but we've seen several cases this winter among young adults."

"Infants?" Leana's eyes widened. "Is my son in danger? Are we all at risk?"

Jamie felt his hands grow cold at the prospect. Could the day hold any more terrible news? First his marriage was in jeopardy, and now this. *Heaven help us all.*

Dr. Gilchrist pursed his lips for a moment. "You say she arrived home Friday, and her coughing began Saturday? If no one else in the household has presented the same symptoms, you should be safe. We usually see problems arising two to four days after exposure. I will make a second visit next week and see how my patient is doing. Should any additional cases arise, of course I can come sooner." He refolded his leather etui, no larger than a volume of poetry, and slipped it inside his coat pocket. "You know, a stable lad in Dumfries infected a dozen others before we traced its source." He laid a hand across Rose's cheek, his manner clinical but not without compassion. "Might your sister have come in contact with the young man, Mistress McKie? Hiring a horse perhaps?"

Jamie answered for her. "Impossible, I'm afraid. The young ladies of Carlyle School would have no need of a horse. Shall we carry her back to bed now?"

"Aye, for 'tis sound sleep she needs. And feverfew immersed in boiling water round the clock." The doctor smiled at Leana as he adjusted his spectacles. "You were brilliant to think of it, Mistress McKie, even before my diagnosis of her ailment. Feverfew is the oldest remedy in Scotland for croup."

Thirty-Four

You can never plan the future by the past.
EDMUND BURKE

Carefully holding Rose upright in the chair, Leana watched Jamie out of the corner of her eye as he moved about the sickroom like one sleepwalking, picking up discarded linens from the floor, only to move them to another spot and drop them in a heap. "Come, Jamie," she called, warming her voice, wanting him to trust her with his concerns. "Neda has changed the bed linens. Might you help me move Rose into bed?" Leana made sure to catch his eye before she added, "As in all things, dear husband, I cannot manage without you."

She'd meant to encourage him. Instead he stared at her like a man stricken. "Jamie, what is it?"

"Reverend Gordon..." His sigh was sorrow itself. "We must talk later, Leana. In private."

Of course. The minister's discussion with Jamie. *An unfortunate oversight.* She'd completely forgotten their chat in the nursery, lost amid the crisis. "Aye, we'll discuss it later, for my sister requires our undivided attention now."

Working side by side, they transferred Rose into the box bed. Her throat, ravaged by the doctor's scalpel, would not let her speak, but her eyes communicated her thanks. Leana gazed down at her sister, brushing her hair off her brow, straightening her nightgown for modesty's sake, then clasping Rose's pale hands between her own. *I love you, Rose.*

Jamie stood behind her and rested his hands on her shoulders, kneading them ever so gently. "She looks better, Leana."

"Aye, she does." She lifted one hand to touch Jamie's fingers, her other hand still holding Rose's, joining the three of them together, if only for a moment.

"Leana." Jamie gave her shoulders a final squeeze, then stepped round to look at her. "I need to inspect several more of the ewes before I lose the light of day. 'Tis seven weeks 'til the lambing begins."

And in a few more weeks, we leave for Glentrool. Leana was comforted by the prospect. "It hardly seems possible."

"If you remember, your father has promised to pay me so many shillings for each ewe that survives the winter and so many shillings for each lamb that survives its birthing." A weary smile stretched across his features. "I intend to see every ewe thrives and gives birth to twins."

"Och, Jamie! Such a dreamer you are." Leana smiled and motioned toward the door. "Go on then, for I hear your woolly lassies bleating for you."

"Will you mind terribly?"

"I will not. We'll speak of Reverend Gordon's news when you return." She sent him on his way with a tender kiss, then turned to see how Rose was faring. Her eyes were closed, though Leana noticed tears shimmering between her long, dark lashes. *Poor girl.* Her throat surely hurt beyond imagining. "Feverfew, the doctor said." Leana picked up the leather pouch from the bedside table. "Then feverfew it shall be. Whatever generous soul brought this gift to our doorstep, these herbs kept you breathing until the doctor arrived. Perhaps our good neighbor will step forward and let us shower him with thanks."

Rose opened her eyes, then her mouth. She said one word in a whisper so faint Leana could not be sure it was a word at all. It sounded like "her."

"Don't talk, Rose. You ken what Neda would say: Save yer breath tae cool yer *parritch.*" She bent down to press her cheek against Rose's, glad to find her sister's skin neither cold nor hot. "I'll send Annabel back up the stair with warm cloths and steaming water for your inhalation."

When she straightened, Rose lifted her hand, as though she had more to say. Straining, her face contorted with pain, Rose could only manage a single sound: "Jay."

Leana knit her brow. "*Jamie,* you mean? He's gone to tend his sheep, dearie."

Rose yanked on her sleeve, harder than Leana imagined she could and shook her head. "Jay!" she said again.

"*Jane?* Is that what you mean? Your friend from Carlyle School?"

Rose nodded her head, then collapsed as if she'd used the last of her strength on a single syllable.

"Jane Grierson, is it? Forgive me for asking you to say her name twice." Anxious to make amends, Leana arranged her sister's bedcovers, then plumped her pillows. "Willie delivered your letters to the school on Monday. Perhaps we'll hear something from Jane in tomorrow's post. 'Til then, you must rest."

Leaving one taper burning, Leana closed the door and slipped down to the kitchen, where the servants were in a hurry-scurry to get supper on the table by seven. Despite the day's traumas, Lachlan McBride would expect his meal at the proper time when he arrived home. Leana sent Annabel to the sickroom with the steaming bowl, then located Reverend Gordon's copy of *Primitive Physic* and retired to the quiet of her stillroom to see what she might discover among the book's pages.

"Croup," she read aloud. "A disease of the throat accompanied by harsh breathing and hoarse coughing." An accurate description of Rose's infirmity; there could be no doubt. As Leana continued to read, mentally crossing off each recommended treatment, she came to the final notation, a cautionary word from the author: "The poison produced by croup can damage the heart and nervous system and, in severe cases, may result in heart failure."

For a moment Leana feared her own heart might fail. She'd treated Rose as if she were suffering from a common cold! When Jamie had offered to ride to Dumfries for a doctor on the Sabbath eve, what was her reply? "Goodness, Jamie! 'Tis not so bad as that." *Nae, Leana, 'twas worse.* Her pride would not allow a surgeon to darken their door, certain she could heal her sister by herself with herbs and prayers. Though her aversion to bloodletting and opiates had played a part as well, her pride had nearly cost Rose her life.

Forgive me, Father.

Leana closed the physic book and pressed it against her chest. How close Rose had come to death, none could say. *Too close.* Bowing her head over her book, Leana begged for mercy. She tarried in the stillness, not moving, only breathing. *I will wait for the God of my salvation. My God will hear me.* She prayed without words, sensing a weight of silence falling over her.

A light tapping sounded at the stillroom door. Leana opened her eyes slowly and found Neda peeking in at her. *"Pittin' the brain asteep,* are ye?"

"Aye." Leana rested her chin on the book's binding. "I've much to think about, for I've not been the best of nurses to Rose."

"Hoot!" Neda pulled her into the noisy kitchen. "The lass would niver have lived tae see anither Galloway mornin' had ye not cared for her sae ferlie. Dinna be sayin' otherwise, for the doctor from Dumfries called ye brilliant, and so ye are."

Leana put aside her book, shaking her head. "Whatever you say, dear woman. Father is ringing the supper bell. I'd best get to table."

Neda nudged her toward the door. " 'Tis why I came lookin' for ye. Off ye go."

Supper was livelier than usual. Her father, just arrived home from another visit to the Widow Douglas's, had missed the day's events and so plied them with endless questions about Rose's traumatic turn for the worse. Leana noticed that Jamie said nothing about his private conversation with Reverend Gordon, only that the minister rode to Dumfries to fetch a doctor, convinced of an urgent need for the man's services.

"I suppose this surgeon presented you with a bill."

"He did." Jamie produced a folded paper from his waistcoat pocket. "Considering the man saved Rose's life, his fee is more than reasonable."

Lachlan yanked the bill from Jamie's grasp. "I'll be the judge of that." He glanced at the paper, grunted, then put it beside his plate without comment. "What of Reverend Gordon? Did the man have any news to pass along?"

"News?" Jamie scratched his neck. "What sort of…news?"

Lachlan stared at him askance. "The sort any minister worth his stipend discloses while visiting his flock. Come, man, Newabbey has no newspaper. How else is the parish blether to get about, if not from mouth to ear?"

Jamie visibly relaxed. "We had little time for such matters, I'm afraid." Though his high color began to recede, Jamie avoided looking in Leana's direction. "He did our family a great service, galloping off to Dumfries like a wind from the Irish Sea, hard and swift."

"Aye." Lachlan came very close to chuckling. "The minister spared our Rose, but that *puir* nag of his may not recover." He rang his brass handbell again, calling for the pudding to be served. At many a country table, sweets were a luxury reserved for Quarter Days. At her father's table, they were a twice-daily indulgence. "Flummery, is it?" He rubbed his hands in anticipation. "You've added some currants plumped in sack, aye, woman?"

Neda placed a generous portion before her master. "A *mutchkin* o' milk and anither o' cream, egg yolks and rose water, sugar and nutmeg. And, aye, yer favorite currants." She paused for a moment, then added. " 'Tis hot from the fire, sir. Mind yer tongue."

Leana saw a smile twitching at Neda's mouth and hid her own smile behind a spoon. How many seasons had the woman waited to say those words to her father? *Mind yer tongue.* Och, he didn't mind for a moment! The man said whatever he pleased, not caring whose feelings he might hurt in the process.

The threesome finished their supper, then Lachlan read to them from the Buik: " 'I the LORD speak righteousness, I declare things that are right.' And we," Lachlan added, his gray eyes appraising them, "are to do the same. We are to speak the truth. To say what is right and not lie."

Though her father preached what he did not practice, Leana believed those words with all her heart. The manner in which truth was spoken mattered too, and to that end, her watchword was simple: *Speak the truth in love.*

After such a harrowing day the McKies retired early. They tucked Ian in his crib—fed, bathed, and content—and saw to Rose's comfort, spooning tincture of chamomile between her lips, letting it slip down her wounded throat a few drops at a time, lest Rose begin to cough and inflict more pain than the surgeon's scalpel had. Leana left instructions for the maidservants to keep a constant bedside vigil through the night, summoning her at once if there was any reason for concern.

"Goodnight, sweet Rose," Leana called from the doorway, then retired to her own bedroom. Jamie was waiting for her by the hearth, still dressed, an uneasy expression on his face. She hastened to his side and rested both hands on his coat sleeve. "Jamie, I heard Reverend Gordon mention some 'unfortunate oversight.' Is that what's troubling you?"

"Aye, lass." Jamie took her left hand in his, studying her fingers, rubbing his thumb over her silver wedding band. He was quiet for so long she wondered if she might need to find some other way to broach the subject. Then he spoke, and the pain in his voice was unmistakable.

"It has to do with the night of our wedding, Leana. And the kirk session record. Reverend Gordon says there is a discrepancy."

Thirty-Five

Love can hope
where Reason would despair.
LORD GEORGE LYTTELTON

A discrepancy?" Leana did not like the sound of that. "What does the kirk session record show?"

Jamie said nothing at first. He seemed absorbed with her hands, taking his time, pressing his lips against her ring. Turning her hand over. Kissing her palm more tenderly still. When at last he looked up to meet her gaze, she knew the news was very bad indeed.

"The kirk record shows that on 31 December I married Rose McBride."

The light in the room changed, as though all the candles flared at once. Leana was certain she had misunderstood, for to accept Jamie's statement as truth was unthinkable. "The minister is mistaken. That entry was changed. My father assured us that he'd taken care of everything."

"So he did." Tension stretched between each word. "But the change was not recorded as promised. Nor does your father's testimony appear in the session minutes." Jamie carefully explained why. Told her the whole, dreadful story about a man named Cummack. An auld man, dead and buried, who'd taken the truth to his grave.

She listened but could not speak as her peaceful life began to crumble around her. *Please, Lord. It cannot be. It cannot!*

Jamie's expression was grim. "And so it comes to this, Leana: By law, I am married to your sister. To Rose."

"Nae!" She clutched her skirts. "Then you and I are—"

He touched his fingers to her lips, as if stopping the word from being spoken might keep it from being true. "We are husband and wife by habit and repute. That is good Scottish law, Leana."

"Yes, but if the law—"

"Everyone in the parish kens you are my wife. *You*, Leana. Not Rose."

"Aye, but, Jamie—"

"All of Newabbey watched you bloom with Ian month by month." He placed his hand low against her body, as though laying claim to her womb. "No one seeing the son you bore could doubt for a moment that he is mine. As you are. You are mine, Leana."

"But the kirk…" She gasped for air, her throat thick with fear. "Oh, Jamie, tell me they can do something. Tell me this isn't the end!"

"Nae, lass." His voice grew ragged, the words breaking down as he did. "You are…my wife. You are…my love." He pulled her into his arms, crushing her so tightly against him she could not move. "I will not let them take you away from me. I will not, I *will not*."

She clung to him, needing his strength, desperate for his assurance. They stood there for many minutes; the only sound in the room was the crackling of the fire on the hearth and her anguished sobs muffled against his chest. "What's to become of us, Jamie?" she whispered at last.

He released her long enough to look in her eyes, then told her what must be done to appease the kirk session. "My concern lies not with the elders but with Rose. And with Lachlan. Who kens what either of them might say?"

Leana steadied herself, her hands resting lightly on his shoulders, and took a shaky breath. "If we speak the truth in love, Jamie, we cannot fail."

"But if Rose speaks the truth—that she alone was meant to be my bride on Hogmanay—all is lost."

Leana shook her head. "The truth is, she did not love you at first and encouraged you to love me instead. Remember?"

"Aye," he groaned. "Would that I'd listened to her."

"Never mind that now." Leana smoothed a hand across his cheek, a sense of peace falling over her. *O my God, I trust in thee.* "The elders are good men, Jamie. Righteous. And just. They will want what is best for Ian. And for our family, and the kirk, and the glory of the Almighty. We will speak the truth, all of us." She brushed her lips against his in a brief kiss. "Honesty will prevail. It always does."

The corners of his mouth lifted slightly. "Lass, you amaze me. Ever hopeful when there is no cause for hope."

"There is always cause for hope, beloved." Leana stepped back and began to pull the pins from her hair, shaking out the waves as they fell past her shoulders. "Even the grave is not the end."

Brave words, and she meant them. But deep inside, in a well-shaded corner of her heart's garden, a dark seed of fear landed on fertile ground. Once her sister heard the news, she might turn it to her advantage. *What if Rose steals Jamie from me, as I stole Jamie from her?* There was naught to be done but wait for Rose to heal. And then, when her sister was strong enough, tell her the truth. And beg her to be merciful and to do what must be done, for Ian's sake. *And for mine. Please, Rose.*

Rose was markedly improved the next day. Limited to weak tea and lukewarm soup, she nonetheless swallowed all that was offered and nodded for more. "Sic a guid patient I have!" Neda crowed, tucking a bib round Rose's neck and feeding her by spoonfuls.

"Jane," Rose managed to say after her dinner, a bit more clearly this time.

Leana informed her they'd received no news from Dumfries. "But Peter Drummond stopped by this morning to inquire how you are doing. Might you like to see him when he comes again?" Leana was surprised when Rose shook her head no. Her sister had no other prospects, and Peter was an amiable young man of sufficient breeding and income to please their *pernickitie* father. Odd that Rose would refuse his suit, as though she had another in mind. Had she been introduced to a gentleman in Dumfries? Or did she still think she might claim Jamie's heart? The kirk session had opened the door to that terrible possibility. If Rose continued to mend, she would need to be told sooner rather than later. Until then, Leana would shower her with affection and pray their sisterly bond would hold fast.

On Friday morning Rose was able to sit by the side of the bed without support and then, with Leana's help, stand to her feet and walk a few steps. "Bath," she croaked, and so the wooden tub was carried to her room and filled with hot water by a household staff eager to see their mistress healed.

Leana herded all but Annabel out of the room so Rose might have some privacy. While the maid tended to Rose's skin, grown nearly transparent from her illness, Leana washed her sister's hair. She whisked the whites of half a dozen fresh eggs into a froth and poured it over Rose's head. After letting it dry, Leana rinsed her hair with rum and rose water in equal measure and rubbed the strands dry with a towel, draping her hair across her shoulders. "See how it shines! Like a silk cape."

Rose touched her hair and smiled. "Like Jane's." Sitting by the hearth in her old reading chair, she was swathed in blankets, for the February day was predictably cold and damp.

Leana produced a letter from her pocket, hoping it might bear good news. "Look what Willie brought from the village. A surprise, posted from Dumfries."

"Please…read," Rose labored to say, sinking deeper into the cushions. Her sister was far from well; the frailty in her movements and the sparseness of her words pointed to her discomfort.

Leana broke the wax seal—stamped with an elegant *C* for Carlyle— and unfolded the paper, recognizing the schoolmistress's bold penmanship. "What a fine hand she has." She placed the stool from the dressing table next to Rose's chair and sat, arranging her skirts to keep them clear of the hearth. "Now let me read to you."

To Miss Rose McBride
Wednesday, 3 February 1790

Dear Miss McBride:

We were all most distressed to hear of your sudden illness and pray this letter finds your health improving. Though we will miss your lively manner, we agree it is wise you remain at Auchengray until you are completely well. Do let us know when we may expect you. *Nous ne t'avons pas oublée.* We have not forgotten you.

Leana paused to glance at her sister, who looked anything but lively. She'd told their father Rose might be home for a week or two. Looking at her now, Leana realized two months would be closer to the mark.

> Your letter to Miss Jane Grierson has been forwarded to her home in Dunscore parish. She, too, was not well enough to return on Monday, for she suffers from a persistent fever and vexing cough.

"Oh!" Rose pressed her fingertips against her mouth.

Leana put the letter down long enough to lean forward and touch her sister's shoulder. "I'm sorry, dearie. It seems you were right to be concerned about Jane's well-being."

> We have begun our study of Allan Ramsay's *The Gentle Shepherd*. If your father has a copy on his bookshelf, perhaps you can join us in reading the happy trials of Patie and his bonny Peggy.

Neda had read the pastoral play to Leana as a child; years later Leana had read it to Rose. "Remember, dearie? 'Oft when we stand on brinks of dark despair, some happy turn, with joy, dispels our care.'" The words sank into Leana's heart and took root. Did not her own marriage hover on the brink of despair? Every night in their box bed she soaked Jamie's nightshirt with her tears, their passion tinged with sorrow. Rose must heal and quickly, for they could not keep the news to themselves much longer. *Please God, may some happy turn come soon.*

Thirty-Six

Ah, nothing comes to us too soon but sorrow.
PHILIP JAMES BAILEY

'Twas not the weather that had made her ill. 'Twas the stable lad with his dreadful cough. Rose knew that now. Leana and the others would soon know too if they put the pieces together. She vaguely remembered Dr. Gilchrist mentioning it, delirious as she was. Would that she had been unconscious. Would that she could not recall his visit at all. But she could, in frightening detail.

Rose shut her eyes for a moment, assailed with memories. The terror of being pressed back against the chair. The revulsion of the doctor's strong fingers probing her mouth. The agony of his terrible blade touching her throat. *God, help me. God, help me.* She swallowed again, feeling queasy.

"I would see you well, dear sister." Leana stood, assessing her with a practiced eye. "You need more warm liquids, salty ones especially, to heal that raw throat of yours. A tasty beef broth for your supper should do nicely. I've enough feverfew to keep the air round you fragrant for several more days. And I have what I need in my stillroom to make a mint salve for your chapped lips."

Such devotion deserved more, but Rose only managed to say, "Thank you."

Leana was busy looking about, frowning as she did. " 'Tis too cold in here. I'll have Willie double the peat allotted for this room."

Rose raised a brief word of protest. "Father."

"Aye," Leana agreed, smiling. "Father will not approve of such extravagance. I will remind him that I have a renowned physician to answer to as well, for Dr. Gilchrist expects to find a healthier patient when he appears on Wednesday."

Rose felt a sudden chill, though not from the drafty windows. "Again?"

"No need to fret, dearie." Leana tugged the blankets closer round her neck. "I will see that he keeps his surgical instruments in his coat pocket, where they belong. I imagine the doctor will only need to peek down your throat long enough to check his handiwork."

Rose stared at the hard-backed chair, empty and menacing, as if it were waiting for her.

Leana followed her gaze and guessed her thoughts. "I will ask him to examine you here, in this comfortable chair. Not in that wooden one. Better still, we'll relegate it to the ground floor." She waved at the oak chair, as though dismissing it from the room like a naughty child. "Annabel, please place that uncomfortable thing in the hall, and see that one of the men finds a home for it in the front room."

Annabel swatted the chair with her dusting cloth for good measure before carrying it out the door.

"You see?" Leana bent to kiss her sister's head. "Have no fear, sweet Rose. Dr. Gilchrist saved your life when I could not. He brought healing to this house. And he will again."

Rose did not pay heed to the days that followed, for they blurred together without a Sabbath visit to the kirk to mark the end of one week and the start of another. Annabel stayed home with her this time. Her reading skills only allowed a few familiar psalms, but they were a comfort nonetheless. *Lord, be merciful unto me: heal my soul.*

Rose dutifully partook of salt-laden broths and honey-drenched teas, all served at the same warm temperature that soothed without hurting. Leana rubbed her skin with a cream that smelled of melon seeds—"'Tis not meant to heal your throat but to put the moisture back in your skin"—and her bedclothes reeked of feverfew, so often was the steaming concoction brought afresh to her room.

With each day Rose felt a bit better. She could take a deep breath without coughing. She could swallow without cringing. And she could circle the room without losing her balance. Was Jane also healing, she wondered? Perhaps by now her friend had returned to Carlyle School healthy as ever, with her bright gowns and her bold laugh and her dark, mischievous eyes.

When Wednesday came, Rose woke early, restless, with no appetite. Leana knocked on her door at noontide and ushered in a broad-shouldered man with a silvery periwig fitted to his head. *Dr. Gilchrist.* A busy man, judging by the quickness of his steps and the sharpness of his movements. She was grateful he did not reach for his instruments. Instead he drew near, beckoning Leana to hold two candles aloft. "Open wide, Miss McBride. I will not hurt you. Not this time."

Rose held her breath and tipped her head back. *Please don't. Please.* She closed her eyes, though she could not shut out her fears. Stretching her mouth open was torture; the sensation of his fingers pressed against her palate made her feel faint.

"Good, good," he murmured at last, withdrawing his hands, then running them lightly over her throat. "The swelling is down considerably. Your sister makes an exceptional nurse."

Rose opened her eyes and nodded a little, unwilling to force any words past her aching throat. When a few tears slid down her cheeks, she brushed them away, grateful that Leana had asked the others to wait down the stair. 'Twas embarrassing enough to have her sister see her like this, let alone Neda and the others.

Leana eyed them both, then asked tentatively, "Dr. Gilchrist, is there anything in particular I should be doing for Rose? Any problems that might arise?"

Clasping his hands behind him, he rocked back on his heels for a moment, then settled in place, like a tree firmly planted. "There is one possible complication I would be remiss not to mention."

Rose heard one word—*complication*—and her pulse quickened.

"You see, for a young lady to be exposed to a prolonged high fever at the onset of her childbearing years, combined with the ill effects of croup on the heart and other organs…well, 'tis regrettable."

Childbearing. Regrettable. Rose swallowed over and over, despite the pain, trying to quell the sickening sense of dread that grew inside her.

Dr. Gilchrist bent toward her, his eyes full of sympathy. "One cannot be certain of such things, Miss McBride, but 'tis possible the health of your womb has been compromised. You may be unable to bear children."

Her heart stopped. "I'm...*barren?*"

"Oh, Rose." Leana touched her shoulder. "Dr. Gilchrist, can nothing be done?"

"Nae." Rose shook her head. He could not mean what he said. "Nae."

"I am very sorry, my dear."

Rose blinked, but the words were still there, seared across her mind. *Unable to bear children.*

"You are a lovely young lady." He leaned closer, as if that might comfort her. It did not. "I am certain you will make a lovely wife."

She bowed her head. *But not a lovely mother.*

It was just as well she could not speak; no words came, only pain. She felt hollow inside, as if her womb were naught but an empty embrace. While Leana stroked her hair, the doctor continued to volunteer words of comfort, reminding her that, though it was a strong probability, 'twas not a certainty. That her life could be very full, even without the blessing of a child.

"We will pray," Leana said softly, "and trust God to heal my sister's womb."

The physician stepped back, buttoning his coat. "I hope I will be proven wrong someday and that you will appear at my door with a bevy of children in tow. But perhaps it is best you know now, before you consider marriage, so that you and your future husband might be...ah, resigned to the situation."

Rose grabbed Leana's arm, pulling her closer. Her voice was hoarse, urgent. Every word was an effort. "Tell...no...one."

Leana turned her head so their gazes met. "I understand, Rose. No one needs to know."

Dr. Gilchrist offered Rose a parting word. "Miss McBride, you are a fortunate young lady to have survived. Not all who've fought croup have been so lucky." He paused at the door, his hand on the latch.

"Yestreen I left the bedside of a young woman with the same symptoms. Even her coloring was similar to yours. But I arrived too late." He shook his head. "Heart failure. Eighteen years old, as bonny a lass as you, and she is gone."

Same symptoms. Similar coloring. Eighteen.

Rose forced herself to ask. "Where?"

"Dunscore parish. An old family there, of substantial means. They should have sent for me sooner. No one ever imagines how serious croup can become."

Rose held her breath, knowing that once she let go, her tears would not stop. "Who…was she?"

"Jane Grierson was her name. Lovely girl. A pity."

Thirty-Seven

What shall be done for sorrow
With love whose race is run?
Where help is none to borrow,
What shall be done?

ALGERNON CHARLES SWINBURNE

The funeral was on Saturday.

Rose was too ill to attend, but in her heart she traveled north to Dunscore parish, to a house she had not seen, to a family she did not know, to a girl she had counted as a true friend. And she wept without ceasing. Nothing Leana could do or say eased the sorrow. The post from the Griersons was painfully short. *Thank you for your letter inquiring after Jane's health. Alas, our dear daughter has died.*

Guilt gnawed at her day and night. If it were not for her foolhardy notion to visit Lillias Brown's cottage, Jane would be alive, and her own womb might be healthy. No prayer, no supplication could bring Jane back from the grave. *Forgive me. Forgive me.*

To make matters worse, Reverend Gordon had stopped to visit twice of late, asking how soon she might be able to venture out of doors.

"Soon," Rose had said in a guilty whisper. A body had to be gravely ill to miss services.

He'd peered at her across the top of his spectacles. "By the first of the month perhaps? Your sister thought you might be well enough to travel come March. You will be excused from singing the *Paraphrases* for quite some time, but your presence at services would be…ah, prudent."

Would that she were strong enough to travel *this* morning rather than be left alone another Sabbath in an empty house. At least now she could dress for the day and not spend every hour in her nightgown. And she could walk down the stair to take her meals with the family and eat more substantial food. Nothing coarse like venison or sharp-edged like almonds, but Neda's thick stews slid past her scarred throat without complaint.

A cold breakfast waited on the sideboard, prepared the night before. Bannocks and butter, apple jelly and orange marmalade, hard-boiled eggs with thin-sliced ham. "Good morning," she said tentatively. Her voice still sounded rough, like gravel trod by a silk slipper.

Jamie and Leana both looked at her, then at each other. Their exchange was so brief Rose might have missed it. What did it signify? She had not told another soul of Dr. Gilchrist's sorry news and had no intention of doing so. Leana's pity, however carefully masked, was bad enough. Jamie must not know, or any hope she might have of winning him back someday would be dashed to pieces. What man would want a wife who might not give him an heir? And she would never tell her father, for Lachlan McBride would disregard her existence from thenceforth. No more pretty gowns to catch a suitor's eye, for no suitor would seek the hand of a barren young woman. No more schooling, for 'twould be wasted on a *stayed lass.* No more life, not as she'd known it.

Nae, she could not risk so much. A truth not told was not a lie. 'Twas merely a secret. Everyone seated at table this morning had plenty of those.

Rose tucked into her breakfast, suddenly famished. "Do give my friends at kirk my regards," she said between bites, then felt her cheeks grow warm. Her list of close friends had grown short. The Elliots would not speak to her. The Drummonds might not either, for she had refused to meet with Peter. Perhaps their neighbors, the Newalls, might be counted.

"Speaking of friends," Leana began, her expression jubilant, "I meant to tell you, we've word from Troston Hill: Jessie Newall is safely delivered of a son."

Lachlan glared at her. "Not at table, Leana. 'Tis unseemly."

"Sorry, Father." Her sister leaned across her plate of bannocks and said in a low voice, "They've named him Robert Alan Newall. The image of his faither, Duncan says. Alan must be so proud."

One of the advantages of a scarred throat was that no one noticed if you did not speak. *A happy mother. A new son. A proud father.* Until that moment Rose had not known what it would be like to grieve, rather than rejoice, at such news. *Selfish, Rose.* Aye, 'twas. But hard to resist when everything inside her cried out for a child of her own.

She could not do as she wished—bolt from the room and seek solace in her bedroom—so Rose did what she could to keep her composure. She took great pains with her meat, smearing it with apple jelly, then cutting it into tiny squares, easily swallowed. Then she slathered her bannocks until every dry corner was covered in rich, yellow butter. Looking up when spoken to, looking down when not, Rose did not open her mouth again, except to eat, for the rest of the meal.

Despite her hasty departure from table, she did not get very far. Leana followed her into the hall, calling her name. "Might we speak with you before we leave for services?" Jamie came up behind Leana, like an actor appearing on cue, and the two stood side by side, imploring Rose with their eyes. "Please? In your room, if we could."

Rose agreed, if only out of curiosity, and started up the stair. Had Leana told Jamie what the doctor had said? Might the two of them be planning to move to Glentrool after all, encouraged by the break in the weather? Could it be that Leana was expecting again? Another child so close on the heels of Ian seemed unwise. When the three arrived in the room, Rose closed the door, then fell against it, already breathless from the short climb.

Leana spoke first. "Please sit, dearie, for you do not look well."

It was true; her knees would not hold her much longer. Moving to the chair, she eased into its cushioned embrace and tried not to moan with relief. When Jamie and Leana sat down before her, their hands clasped, their shoulders touching, Rose had to admit they made a handsome pair, one dark haired, one fair.

After an awkward pause, Jamie began. "Rose, we'll not tire you with long explanations. Reverend Gordon came to see you before he rode off to summon Dr. Gilchrist. Do you remember his being here?"

"Aye…and nae." She'd spent the last ten days trying not to recall what had happened that painful day.

"We understand, Rose. Best to forget." Leana stood long enough to tuck a plaid round her shoulders, then nodded at Jamie to continue.

"The minister came not only to visit your bedside but also to speak with me about an oversight in the kirk record for December 1788." His gaze did not quite meet hers. " 'Tis about our wedding, Rose."

"But I was not there." Her voice grew faint, from exhaustion or heartache, she could not say. " 'Twas Leana who spoke the vows."

Jamie gazed at Leana with naught but love written on his face. "Aye, she did. And by habit and repute Leana is my wife and Ian McKie, my son, for which I'm most grateful." With a measured sigh, he turned to look directly at Rose now. "But the kirk record says I'm married to someone else." She saw the truth in his eyes before the words reached his lips. "You, Rose."

Her mouth fell open.

"By law, you and I are husband and wife."

Jamie. She felt faint, nearly slipping to the floor before he caught her and set her aright.

Leana clasped her hand, feeling for a pulse. "Och, Jamie. 'Twas too much to bear after her illness and then the loss of Jane Grierson. We should have waited."

"Nae," Rose whispered. *Can it be? Is Jamie mine?* "Please. Tell me how this happened."

The story was so implausible it had to be true. One blunder after another. Misplaced books and forgotten notes. Rose stared at them both, her thoughts reeling. "But what's to be done?"

Jamie described the reverend's expectations: All three of them were to stand before the kirk session and give testimony concerning the events of 31 December. In a tone that brooked no argument, Jamie added, "It's important that we all agree what is to be said."

Rose clung to her hopes, even as they began to slip through her fingers. "And what were you thinking I might tell them?"

Leana leaned forward, the firelight moving across the golden braids curled on her head. "The truth, Rose. God will honor naught but honesty. Tell them that you did not love Jamie when he asked you to marry him. That you wanted him to marry me from the first. Can you do that, dear sister? For we both ken 'tis true."

Jamie's voice struck a firmer note. "The Buik says, 'Trust in the

LORD, and do good.' That means not only what is good for you, Rose, but also for your sister. And for Ian."

Rose turned so that he alone was in her line of vision. "What of you, Jamie? What is good for you?"

He gathered Leana's hand in his. "To have Leana as my wife and as the mother of my son." Then he surprised Rose by clasping her hand as well. "And to have you as my beloved cousin."

Oh, Jamie. Even given the chance to have her as his wife, he did not want her.

"Forgive us, Rose, for not telling you sooner." He looked duly penitent. "We should have included you in our discussions from the first. But you were delirious that day and the next…"

"And sick, dearie. So terribly sick." Leana's voice caught. "Several times that night I feared we might lose you."

She eyed the two of them: healthy, whole, and loved. Everything she was not. Realization, like a chilling wind, rushed over her. " 'Twould have made things easier for you if I'd died."

"Rose!" Leana gasped. "Don't even think such a thing, dearie. I would rather have you alive and happily married to my Jamie, than see you buried in a kirkyard."

Stunned, Rose stared at her sister's face, as open as any lined book. "Can you mean what you say?"

"Aye." Leana lightly rested a hand on each of them. "I love you as much as I love Jamie, Rose. I'll keep saying that 'til you believe me."

Rose looked away, ashamed to confess that her sister's love, however boundless, was not enough. She wanted Jamie's love. She wanted a child to love. *I want what you have, Leana.*

Jamie glanced at his pocket watch, then stood to leave. "Forgive me, Rose, but we'll be late for services if we do not depart shortly. We'll speak more of this later, when you…when you've had time to think things through. Leana, I'll see to the chaise."

Leana gathered her skirts about her. "And I must tend to Ian. He's missed you, Rose."

Precious Ian. "Might I see him? For I've missed my nephew as well." Perhaps holding the child against her heart would help it heal, like a salve placed on an open wound. 'Twas clear the kirk session's mistake would be remedied without delay.

Leana returned shortly with the child sitting up in her arms, blinking as though he'd just awakened. "Look who wanted to see you! Is that your Aunt Rose?"

Seeing Ian eased her pain, if only for an instant. "Such a dear boy. He truly is Jamie in miniature." Grabbing a stockinged foot, no bigger than a hen's egg, Rose gently squeezed it, feeling his wee toes inside the woolen folds. The voice of Dr. Gilchrist echoed through her heart. *Unable to bear children.* "I am glad I have *this* child," Rose declared as though the surgeon were still in the room.

"I beg your pardon?"

Rose looked up to find Leana staring at her, confusion in her pale eyes. "I mean to say, I am glad I have *this* child for my nephew and not some dull lad who does not smile back at his auntie."

"Of course." Leana squeezed Ian tight. "Time to bundle him up for kirk. One cannot be too careful about the weather, though 'tis a pleasant day for February." She glided toward the door, bussing Ian's cheek. "Saint Valentine's Day last year was fine as well. You would not remember it, sweet boy, for you were hidden inside me, eagerly waiting for October to come, just as I was."

Rose stared after her as Leana's voice faded into the hall. Her sister had no cause for concern, for she had Jamie's love and Jamie's son, even if it seemed she did not by law have his name at the moment. That treasure belonged to her, to Rose. *Rose McKie.* Alas, like words scribbled on paper for the Valentines Dealing, the name signified nothing if Jamie did not wish it so.

"The truth, Rose," Leana had insisted. Rose sank back in her chair. The truth was, she loved Jamie still. Even if he no longer loved her.

Thirty-Eight

The wife, where danger or dishonour lurks,
Safest and seemliest by her husband stays,
Who guards her, or with her the worst endures.
JOHN MILTON

Jamie, why are you fretting so? I've asked Rose to speak the truth, and
I believe she will."

Halfway to the kirk, and he could still see the look on Rose's face
when he'd told her. *By law, you and I are husband and wife.* She'd nearly
swooned at the news. Yet even as she'd begun to slip from the chair, he'd
seen a ghost of a smile cross her features. *Nae, Rose. Forgive me, but it
cannot be.*

He lightly snapped his whip across the mare's back, feeling his jaw
tighten. "Rose will tell the truth, aye, but only if it gets her what she
wants."

"Jamie, Jamie." Leana soothed him with naught but the sound of
his own name, spoken in love. "Rose no longer has such designs on you.
Besides, she is not the only one who will testify to what happened, dear
husband. You and I will both have the chance to speak the truth as
well." Seated beside him in the chaise with Ian nestled in her arms,
Leana leaned her head on his shoulder. "God has blessed our union,
despite the unseemly manner in which it began."

Ever punishing herself, this wife of his. "And who's to blame for that
beginning, Leana?"

She did not hesitate. "I am, of course."

"Nae," he chided her. She still did not understand who was truly
responsible. " 'Twas your father's swickerie from the start. You've told me
the despicable things Lachlan said to you that night, the threats he made,
the half-truths he poured in your ear. Cease chastising yourself, Leana.
'Twas your father's lies that sent you looking for answers in my bed."

"But I went there of my own will, Jamie. Never forget that, for I shan't."

He took his eyes off the dirt lane for a moment to meet her gaze. "Do not heap all the guilt on yourself. Had I realized sooner what a fine wife I had, instead of pining after Rose all those months, your sister would have given me up long ago."

"Now, Jamie, 'tis another issue entirely and well behind us."

Her reminder was a prudent one. The two of them had plowed that garden before, numerous times.

"A clerical mistake is *not* your fault, Jamie. Nor mine. Nor Reverend Gordon's. 'Tis not even my father's fault."

"We've no proof of *that* yet," he grumbled, waving his hand in the direction of Lachlan McBride, who rode well ahead of them astride Walloch. The hard ground beneath the chaise's two wheels bounced them alongside rough grazing land, where a flock of goats climbed and leaped about the craggy boulders. "I don't care to be in the room when Reverend Gordon tells your father, do you?"

Leana shuddered. "Nae, I do not. Still, I pray it happens soon. I will sleep better at night when you are my husband and mine alone."

The woman seemed so sure of the outcome. Did she love Rose too much to see the dangers that lay ahead? Better to broach the subject now than tend her wounds later. "Leana, have you given any thought to what we will do if Rose tells the kirk session what truly happened on Hogmanay? Because I have. If I am forced to honor my vows and take Rose as my wife, I will seek a divorce."

"On what grounds, Jamie?" She *had* considered it, for her answer came too quickly. "To our knowledge Rose has not been unfaithful to you. 'Tis the only way the kirk would allow a divorce."

"Then I will leave her here," he insisted, "and take you and my son to Glentrool."

Leana shook her head, laughing softly, though there was no hint of joy in the sound. "You fool yourself, Jamie. Reverend Gordon would never give us our testimonials under such circumstances. The minister of your parish would turn us away at the door and refuse to let us near the communion table. We would be outcasts, unwelcome everywhere we went." She shifted, pressing their sleeping son to her heart. The pain in her voice cut him to the quick. "Jamie, if the unthinkable should happen—please God, it will not—we will all remain here in Newabbey. And I will raise Ian and remember what it was like to be your wife."

"Och, lass." Jamie moved the reins so he could slide his arm round her shoulders and pull her closer. " 'Twill not come to that. I will not allow it." He prayed she did not hear the bravado behind his words. "In the meantime, how will you manage?"

"By keeping my eyes on God, my hands on Ian, and my heart on you."

Overcome, he kissed the top of her head until he could speak. "And what of Rose?"

Leana sighed, her mood shifting. "When Rose was a girl, I would step on her skirt hem so she couldn't get away from me."

"Have you tried that of late?"

"Nae, but I've considered it." She gazed toward Criffell, rising not far to their right. Even on a blue-skied morning, the summit was wreathed in mist. "Something happened to Rose during her time in Dumfries. I'm not certain of any details, but I sense it was unchancie."

Jamie nodded, trusting her appraisal. He'd noticed only outward changes in Rose—how she wore her hair, her newly polished manners. Leana noticed things he could never see.

"To be honest…" Leana brushed Ian's cheek with her thumb, back and forth, clearly struggling with what she wanted to say. "I have come to believe that Miss Jane Grierson, much as Rose spoke well of her, was not the most…ah, virtuous of company. Forgive me for saying so, God rest her soul."

"No need to apologize, Leana. Your instincts are usually right."

"Not always." Her chin dipped and her voice with it. "It could have been our Rose in that grave."

For one shameful instant, he wished it so. *Forgive me, Father.*

"Oh, Jamie." Leana's voice drew taut. "What if Ian had caught croup while I was caring for her? You were the one who recommended we summon a doctor. I'm sorry I held your idea at arm's length for so many days."

"Och! Look who's blaming herself again." He brushed his lips across her forehead. "Slip an extra coin in the poor box, if you like, Mistress McKie, but any mistakes made concerning your sister are more than outweighed by your love for her."

" 'Charity shall cover the multitude of sins,' aye?"

"Like a thick plaid, lass."

Moments later he gripped the reins, holding Leana steady as they rattled across the Newabbey Pow and into the village. Cottage doors and windows were flung open, inviting the milder weather to bide a wee while. Birdsong in the gardens sweetened the air, and touches of green sprouted along the hedgerows. It was far from spring, yet far from winter.

"A perfect Saint Valentine's Day," Leana said, brightening a bit. "Which reminds me, I brought you something for the ride home." She dug inside the pocket of her cloak and produced an apple, red and firm, polished to a high sheen. " 'Twas the nicest of the lot."

She'd given him an apple last February—"My valentine"—along with her whole heart. He had given her as little of himself as possible. Now, it seemed, he might pay for that foolishness.

Leana nudged him with her elbow as the chaise eased to a stop. "You're looking very solemn all of a sudden. Do you not like your apple?"

"I do." Jamie smiled at her, putting aside their worries for the moment. Whatever was to come, Leana was the woman he loved. He would not let her soon forget that fact. "The apple is fine. But I'd rather have a kiss."

"Here?" She beheld their neighbors milling about the kirkyard. Hamiltons, Kingans, McBurnies, and the rest. "In front of the kirk?"

"I cannot think of a better place." He glanced at the kirk door. "For 'tis here I kissed you first. Like this." He held her face in his hands and fitted his mouth to hers. Leana did not resist him. On the contrary, she was rather more willing than the first time. The night of their wedding.

At last she pulled back, though not far. "Jamie, everyone is watching us."

"Good." Jamie kissed her again, more thoroughly than before, until he could feel the heat of her skin rising beneath his hands. He chuckled when he leaned back. "Have I embarrassed you enough for one day?"

"Och!" Leana pressed the backs of her fingers to her cheeks to cool them, smiling even as she ducked her head. "They'll ne'er stop blethering about this, I can tell you."

"I hope you're right." Jamie leaped to the ground with a jaunty spring, then tipped his hat toward their neighbors and walked round the chaise, grinning at Leana. *Let them see who is married to whom and where my true affections lie.* Though the voices round them did seem to grow louder, the tone was merry and the smiles genuine. He paused beside the carriage. "A husband kissing his wife? Disgraceful."

"Scandalous," she agreed. She tucked Ian in his arms, then alighted. "Reverend Gordon might think it improper, though, considering how the record reads."

"A record soon to be changed," he reminded her, escorting his family through the kirk's narrow doors and toward their pew. Jamie prayed that the man who'd married them would be on their side when the time came. *Please God, may it come soon.* The less time Rose had to think and plan, the better.

When the minister climbed the turnpike stair into the pulpit, he cast his stern gaze across all his parishioners, singling out the McKies with a brief nod. Good omen or bad, Jamie could not decide. Two hours later Reverend Gordon followed them out the door and into the bright light of midday, guiding them in the direction of the manse, then pausing at the gate. "We've no need to go inside, or Mistress Gordon will think she's to have guests at table. But I did want to see if you are ready to proceed with that…ah, matter."

"Aye, we are," Jamie assured him. "We've explained things to Rose," he added, certain that would be the man's next question. "When will the kirk session meet?"

"The first of March. I'll announce the meeting next Sabbath. But you're getting ahead of yourself, lad. Your father-in-law must be informed of the oversight as well. 'Twas his testimony that was lost and his silver that did not bear the fruit he intended."

Jamie grimaced. "Sir, my uncle does not weather surprises like this verra well."

Reverend Gordon snorted. "Do you think I dinna ken that? 'Tis why I came to you first, a young man with a good dose of *rummle-gumption,* trusting you to tell the lasses. Now we must inform your uncle as well, though he will not stand before the kirk session. You three are the ones who must testify, for 'tis your story to tell, not Lachlan's." The minister brushed away a spider that had landed on his sleeve, no doubt wishing he could dispatch Lachlan McBride as easily. "Suppose I come to Auchengray this Friday afternoon. At four o' the clock, if it suits. Tell him to expect me. I'll explain about the clerk's bungling and our intent to right those wrongs at our kirk session on the first." He bent toward Leana. "Your sister will be able to travel by March, aye?"

Leana wet her lips, a habit Jamie credited to nerves. "I feel certain she will be ready to ride in the chaise by then."

"Good. And what was Rose's response to the situation, if I may ask?"

"Her response was…" Leana's voice faded away.

"Predictable," Jamie finished for her. "Rose promised to speak the truth."

The truth was, he no longer loved her as he once had. Could she accept that truth and speak it aloud? Or would she cling to a distant vow and demand that he make good on it?

Reverend Gordon grunted his approval. "'Tis the only thing the kirk session asks or requires before God: the truth."

Thirty-Nine

And, after all, what is a lie? 'Tis but
The truth in masquerade.
GEORGE GORDON, LORD BYRON

R everend Gordon here tae see ye, sir."
Eliza curtsied in the open doorway of the spence, then re-
treated toward the kitchen while Leana escorted their visitor into the
small room.

"What's this you've brought me?" Lachlan said in a gruff voice.
" 'Twas a pot of tea I called for, not a minister."

Leana smiled, as though he were teasing the reverend instead of
simply being rude. "Eliza has gone for the tray, Father." She pressed her
damp hands against the folds of her skirts. "Kindly show Reverend
Gordon to his chair, and I'll be glad to pour tea for you both."

The men sat without a word. Their upholstered chairs were drawn
close to the meager hearth, a small table perched between them. "Now
then, Mr. McBride." The minister spoke first, his face much like the
day's weather: cold and gray. "I'll not stay long, but I do have an important matter to discuss with you."

"Aye, so Jamie mentioned." Her father eyed Reverend Gordon with
suspicion. Jamie had only told him to expect the minister to call.
Though Lachlan missed very little that went on beneath his roof, of late
he'd been preoccupied with matters at Edingham Farm and had not
pressed Jamie for further details of the minister's visit. *Thanks be to God.*

Eliza arrived with her tray full of tinkling china cups and saucers and
gingerly placed them on the table. "Sirs." She curtsied again, then
stepped into the hall while Leana poured two cups of steaming black tea.

"I'll leave you gentlemen to your business." Leana joined Eliza in
the hall, longing to find some reason to tarry outside the closed door.
"I'd give anything to be a book on his shelf just now," Leana whispered.

How many times had she leaned against those door panels, eaves-dropping on her father? But she was older now, a respectable wife and mother. One did not do such things.

Eliza's dimples showed. "I canna turn into a book, but I can be a housemaid dustin' in the hall. Ye see for yerself how it needs a rag taken tae it." She flapped her white dust cloth and gave her mistress a saucy wink. "Tae *hearken* at the door is a maid's duty, ye ken."

"Not this time." Leana cast a wary glance at the spence. Better not to have anyone listening to what might be said this day. "You'll please me most if you'll leave the gentlemen to their tea."

"If ye say so." Eliza, plainly disappointed, wandered toward the stair, humming to herself.

Leana turned toward the kitchen. Though she would not eaves-drop, she'd not venture far either. She found Neda by the hearth stirring a pot of muslin kale for supper. Cabbage, barley, and onions swirled round her spoon in a fragrant broth. Leana had told her briefly of the situation that morning, confident the woman would keep the news to herself. "Where are the others?" Leana asked, for the house was quiet.

"If ye mean yer Jamie, he's hard at work in the pastures wi' Duncan. The air may feel like winter, but the ewes will be lambin' afore the month is oot." Neda tossed a handful of salt into the pot, then brushed off the last grains on her apron. "Annabel's busy wi' Ian in the nursery, practicin' her readin'. As tae yer sister, she's nappin' in her room. The puir lass is wabbit, and 'tis but four o' the clock."

"Aye. Dr. Gilchrist said she'd be some time getting her strength back." Leana said no more. Seldom did she think of Rose's health and not remember what else the surgeon had said: *unable to bear children.* She could not imagine a crueler sentence levied on a woman's soul. True to her word, Leana had not told anyone, nor would she. God alone held sway in such matters.

Leana spent a few moments in the stillroom tidying her shelves, then returned to find Eliza's anxious face at the kitchen door. "Mistress McKie! D'ye not hear? Yer faither is nigh tae shoutin' at the reverend!" Her hands twisted round her apron strings. "Should we do somethin'? For I fear they'll come tae blows."

Neda left her spoon in the soup pot and stepped closer to the doorway, her feet soundless on the brick floor. "Ye kenned it might come tae this, lass."

"Aye," Leana confessed. "But I prayed it would not."

The spence door was flung open with a mighty crash of wood against plaster, causing the copper pots to sway from the kitchen beams.

"Leana!" her father shouted with vehemence.

"Coming." She gathered her skirts and all but ran down the hall. Reverend Gordon was nowhere in sight, though she heard the sound of hoofbeats on the lawn. Her father was still withindoors, pacing the floor of the spence. "What is it, Father?"

Lachlan's neck was so swollen inside his collar he could barely get the words out. "I have just been informed that my labors on your behalf January last were for naught."

"I see."

"Do you?" His teeth were clenched hard enough to snap a stick. "Maybe you do, Leana, and maybe you don't."

"Oh." It seemed the safest thing to say until she learned what else Reverend Gordon might have told him. "What's to be done, Father?"

"You will wake your sleeping sister, call your husband in from the flocks, and meet me here in the spence. At once."

At Auchengray news traveled through door cracks like smoke from a fire. By the time Leana informed Neda and reached the door to her sister's room, Annabel was already splashing cool water on her mistress's face.

"Rose," Leana said softly, helping her out of bed. "Father has been told the situation, though 'tis not clear how much he kens." She guided Rose down the stair and aimed her in the direction of the spence. "Say nothing until we join you, dearie." Leana flew out the front door and headed for the byre. The damp ground soaked her calfskin slippers, and a chilling breeze knifed through her linen gown.

Jamie was already heading her way, waving his bonnet at her. "Neda rang the bell," he explained. "I take it Reverend Gordon has arrived."

"And departed. In a huff, I'd say." She took her husband's arm and walked with him toward the house, past the overgrown hazel plucked clean last autumn. "Father is in an *ill-scrapit* mood, demanding to see the three of us without delay."

Jamie kissed her cheek before they crossed the threshold. "Remember, this clerical error is not our doing, Leana. Do not let your father convince you otherwise."

When they reached the spence, the tea tray was gone. Three wooden chairs were lined up with their backs against her father's box bed. Rose sat in one, clutching the sides of the chair and looking faint.

Lachlan paced back and forth before the hearth like a snarling dog tethered to a leash. He stopped long enough to point to the chairs. "Sit."

Leana and Jamie did so, their hands discreetly joined beneath a fold of her skirts. The three of them waited in agonizing silence until Leana started to say something and Jamie tugged on her hand. A warning.

Lachlan planted his feet in front of the grate and folded his arms across his embroidered waistcoat. "I have only now learned of the kirk session's 'unfortunate oversight,' as Reverend Gordon called it. All these months I thought my testimony and my silver had covered your sins. But nae. They've been dragged into the cold light of a winter's day for all the parish to see."

"That's not true, Father," Leana protested. "The whole parish has not been told…" She stopped, realizing what she'd done.

"So." Her father pinned his gaze on her. "This oversight is not news to my family, eh? I thought as much. The good reverend was not so forthcoming with information as you, Leana. What else do you ken of this affair?"

Jamie answered instead. "He told me first, Uncle, for I had the most at stake."

"*Och!*" Lachlan turned on him, livid. "Is my silver not at stake? Wasted on the poor, who do nothing to better themselves. And my name, is that of no value? Do you think I relish the thought of the elders laughing up their coat sleeves at this bonnet laird, whose daughter and nephew have lived without the benefit of the kirk's blessing for more than a year and given him a *bystart* for a grandson?"

"Enough!" Jamie surged to his feet. "Ian is my lawful son. Leana is my loving wife. By habit and repute we are well wed." His words struck like hammers, ringing through the room. "We will fix this oversight come the first of March, and we will wipe the dust of Auchengray off our feet come May."

Oh, Jamie. Leana bowed her head, lest her relief show on her face.

After a weighty silence, Lachlan spoke in a voice that shook with unspent anger. "Do not make an enemy of me, Nephew."

"I would make nothing of you." Jamie's voice was even, a cold blade against Lachlan's heated words. "Reverend Gordon assured me you will not attend the kirk session. Our testimonies—Leana's, Rose's, and mine—are the only ones required."

Lachlan's chuckle was an ugly sound. "Aye? And who will provide the silver?"

"We have no need of silver," Leana replied.

Rose suddenly sat up straight, like a marionette on strings. "The Buik says, 'The tongue of the just is as choice silver.' If I speak the truth, is that not of more value than coins?"

Ignoring her, Lachlan lashed out at Leana instead. "And do you ken the rest of your sister's proverb, lass?" His voice rose. "Well, do you?"

Aye, she did. "The heart of the wicked is little worth."

"And would you call me wicked, Daughter?"

Leana did not bend beneath his anger. " 'Tis what you called me not long ago: ill-deedie. However wicked my behavior may have been on my wedding night, I have freely confessed my sins before God. And before Jamie and Rose. And before you, Father."

Lachlan's eyes, dead until now, sprang to life. "See that you don't confess those sins to the kirk session, or you'll be spending the Sabbath on the stool of repentance."

He turned toward her sister. "The only one innocent that night was Rose. It is she who will testify first. And here is what you will say, Rose. For I will not have you spin a different tale than the one I told January last, or I will appear to have given false testimony. The kirk session does not tolerate liars. I care not which woman ends up in my nephew's bed, but I care very much that I not end up in Dumfries standing before the synod. You will tell the session what I direct you to tell them. Nothing more."

Rose spoke in a voice as small as a child's. "What am I to say?"

Lachlan counted each point on his blunt fingers, making sure Rose heard every word. "You will tell them that you never loved your cousin, James McKie. That you wanted him to marry Leana. That you agreed to the wedding out of obligation. That you changed your mind and ran off to Twyneholm. And that you intended your sister to marry Jamie in your stead."

"But, Father—"

"*That* is what I told them, and *that* is what you will say. Five points, Rose. Repeat them. All of them."

Her voice shaking, Rose did so, counting on her own hand. "But, Father, 'tis not the truth—"

"It is *my* truth!" he snapped. "If you hope to marry well someday, you will abide by my wishes, Rose. Otherwise I have a long list of decrepit auld farmers in this parish who'd pay good silver for a bonny wife like you."

Leana shuddered, thinking of Fergus McDougal, an ill-mannered bonnet laird from the neighboring parish who'd buried his first wife, then appeared at Auchengray two Octobers past looking for a new mother for his children. If her father had had his way, Leana would be well married to Fergus, with his stained teeth and protruding middle, and bearing him more children.

Lachlan McBride's threat was not an idle one, and his daughters knew it well.

He pointed his finger at Jamie now. "You will be next to testify, Nephew, for yours is the other name that appears in the kirk session record."

Jamie thrust out his chin, daring him. "And I suppose you have words you propose to put in my mouth as well."

"Only if you want Leana. And your son. If you do not, say whatever you like. But if you would keep my daughter and grandson as your own, you will repeat what I said on your behalf, which was this: When you realized that Rose did not love you nor want you for her husband and that her older sister was only too happy to join you at the bride stool, you married Leana instead with Rose's blessing."

"Forgive me, Uncle," Jamie said, his words rife with sarcasm, "but how many points was that?"

Lachlan glared at him. "Count them yourself, lad."

Leana stood as well, if only to draw upon Jamie's warmth and strength. "And then I will speak to the kirk session, Father."

"Aye, you will. Yours is the most important testimony of all, Leana, for you have the most to lose: your husband, your son, and your reputation. Listen carefully then. I said that you loved Jamie from the first hour he arrived. That you were certain he cared for you. That your sister came to you, weeping, confessing that she did not love Jamie. That she begged you to marry him instead. And so you did. Say no more than that, Leana."

"I've no need to repeat it," she murmured. "I'll not forget what you said." Leana bit her tongue before a snippet from a psalm rose to her lips—*The wicked plotteth against the just*—knowing that her own sins did not allow her to judge the sins of others.

Lachlan turned his back on them to pour a dram of whisky, then pointed toward the door with his pewter cup, as if he'd grown weary of their company. "I've had enough drama for one evening. Tell Neda I'll take my supper alone in here."

"Alone you shall be," Leana said, slipping an arm through the crook of Jamie's elbow. "For we shall be together. And come the first of March, we shall speak the truth."

Forty

I must not say that she was true,
Yet let me say that she was fair;
And they, the lovely face who view,
They should not ask if truth be there.

MATTHEW ARNOLD

A full moon rose in the eastern sky that first evening in March. In Reverend Gordon's brightly lit dining room a wood fire was ablaze on the hearth, and candles shone round the room, holding the darkness at bay.

"Miss McBride, we will begin shortly."

Rose bobbed her head at Andrew Sproat, dominie of the parish school and the youngest of the three kirk elders sitting across from her at Reverend Gordon's long table. Not yet forty, Mr. Sproat had an earnest look about him. His thinning blond hair allowed momentary glimpses of his freckled scalp, and the spectacles perched on his nose magnified every blink of his blue eyes. He looked the sort to be sympathetic.

Reverend Gordon had yet to take his place at the head of the table, though he was a punctual man and would no doubt walk into the room promptly at seven o' the clock. Perhaps he was conferring with Jamie and Leana, who waited their turn in the hall. Had they considered what she might say? Leana had begged her to be fair, to be merciful. And above all, to be truthful. Aye, but *which* truth would she speak?

The three of them had arrived at the manse earlier than expected. With a fresh wind from the southwest pressing hard against their backs, they'd traveled the road from Auchengray to the village at a sprightly clip, setting the lantern on the chaise swinging. Since Lachlan had refused to allow an early supper, Neda had tucked warm mutton pies into their coat pockets for the journey. Too nervous to eat, Rose and

Leana had given their pies to Jamie, who'd polished them off long before they rode past the snuff mill.

'Twas unbearable, the three of them riding in the chaise—Jamie in the middle, a sister on either side. He'd lavished his attention on Leana, of course. Whispering endearments, assuring her the meeting would end well. When he'd helped Rose alight from the chaise, he'd met her gaze with a kind but distant look in his eyes. " 'Twill be over soon, Rose."

Aye, 'twill.

She folded her hands, covering an unattractive spot she'd discovered on her gloves, and took a steadying breath. Aye, she would be more than fair. She would see justice served.

When Reverend Gordon announced the kirk session meeting from the pulpit Sunday last, he'd requested no more than a quorum be in attendance. Three men. The auld clerk's bungling did not speak well of parish business, she guessed; the fewer who learned of the oversight, the better for all involved.

A useless precaution. The entire parish would soon know the truth.

Like Andrew Sproat, the other two elders busy shuffling their papers were men of good repute, respected in the neighborhood, able to resist strong drink and weak women. Henry Murdoch was a prosperous merchant, a legitimate importer of goods, not a free trader evading the Crown's excisemen. Short in stature, with the keen eye and jaded nature of a businessman, Mr. Murdoch sported thick gray hair that sprang from his head like coils. He would bear the most watching, for his mind was as sharp as his tongue.

She regarded the man next to him with misgivings. Jock Bell was a close neighbor and associate of her father's, yet he knew Jamie as well. Each September, the bonnet laird of Tannocks Farm sold Lachlan tups for breeding Auchengray's ewes. An affable man in rumpled clothing that belied his true wealth, Mr. Bell was seldom seen without his plaid bonnet and blackthorn walking stick. No doubt Jock would favor Jamie's account of the wedding, though she would smile at him nonetheless.

At the far end of the table sat the new session clerk, his record book open, his pen poised and waiting. This was not dotty George Cummack, come back from the grave to err again, but Walter Millar, the kirk elder newly appointed to the clerk's position in late January. A thin, nervous man, whose head and hands seemed too large for his body, he sat silent and alert, as if at any moment something might require his careful notation.

Reverend Gordon appeared and took his seat, his back to the roaring hearth. Not many folk used wood for fuel in Galloway, scarce as it was, but one of the parishioners supplied the manse with cut, dried pine. Rose loved the smell—clean with a sharp tang, not musty like peat. The wood cracked and snapped as it burned, sending an occasional spark onto the flagstone floor, where it cooled in an instant. Like Jamie's love for her, burning hot one minute, turning cold the next. All because of a wee babe. Born across the hall in this very house.

Rose touched a hand to her heart and felt the stone amulet beneath her linen gown, comforted by its solid, unseen presence. Though it made Rose uneasy to think of depending on such a woman's counsel, all that Lillias had promised seemed to be coming true. 'Twas clear she knew how to draw a husband near. Perhaps her cantrips would also heal a barren womb.

"We are ready to proceed," the minister announced, opening the Buik with his usual ceremony, his hand sketching an arc through the air. "A reading from Paul's letter to the church at Ephesus. Herein is the purpose of a gathering like ours this evening: 'That we henceforth be no more children, tossed to and fro, and carried about with every wind of doctrine, by the sleight of men, and cunning craftiness, whereby they lie in wait to deceive.'" He pinned his gaze on the five present, not moving from one face to the next until he seemed convinced each person understood the words and their portent.

Sleight. Cunning. Craftiness. Deceit.

Her father was not in the room, or the minister would have good cause for concern. Rose did not need swickerie. She only needed the chance to tell the truth.

The minister's attention returned to the page, and his deep voice filled the room. "But speaking the truth in love, may grow up into him in all things, which is the head, even Christ." He closed the book with a mighty clap. "Aye, there is our directive."

Speak the truth in love. Leana had said those same words for a fort-night, urging all three of them to be in agreement, to put their love for one another and for God above all. Lachlan McBride had given them a different assignment altogether: *Speak the truth according to my wishes.* If her father were here—and Rose was grateful he was not—she would have a message for him as well: *I will do nae such thing.*

"Miss McBride."

Reverend Gordon's commanding voice made her sit up straighter and aim her gaze across the table to the three elders and the clerk, who sat, hands folded, prepared to listen and judge. "Aye, sir. I am ready to give testimony to the events of 31 December 1788."

"Understand, lass," Henry Murdoch cautioned, "you may be asked to comment on events that happened prior to that date."

She nodded, more than willing to answer their questions. The far-ther back their examination stretched, the stronger her claim on Jamie would appear. "Am I to stand?"

The men looked at each other, then shook their heads. " 'Tis not necessary," the minister said. "This meeting is merely a formality to amend the kirk session records." He rested his elbows on the table, mak-ing a tent with his hands, a pose her father often struck. "Now then, your cousin James McKie first appeared in Newabbey parish in…"—he checked his notes—"October 1788. When and where did you strike an agreement to marry Mr. McKie?"

"Martinmas, the following month. He made his request to my father at the Globe Inn in Dumfries that afternoon in my presence. That evening at Auchengray Jamie and I made our formal pledge of betrothal with the entire household serving as witnesses."

Andrew Sproat studied her through his spectacles. "Did you wet your thumbs and join them, as is custom?"

"We did, sir."

The session clerk's pen scratched across the page of his leather-bound book.

"And were you also present to hear the banns read in Newabbey parish kirk on three consecutive Sabbaths?"

"Aye. My name was the one read. Rose McBride. And James McKie." It felt wonderful to say it aloud. To be reminded, in her own voice, that Jamie was meant to be hers. From the beginning. What she was doing was fair. And right. And most assuredly true. Wasn't that what Leana wanted?

Jock Bell leaned back in his chair. "Tell me, lass, when did you plan to be married?"

"Hogmanay."

"And did you have a gown fitted for this occasion?"

Rose smiled, remembering the first time she'd slipped the rose-colored gown over her shoulders. "Aye, my gown was made by Joseph Armstrong, a tailor from the village."

Reverend Gordon turned to Henry Murdoch. "I believe you've already spoken with Mr. Armstrong."

Her hands grew cool inside her gloves. Though it was customary for the elders to gather information round the parish, the thought of them knocking on doors, inquiring after her own actions, unnerved her. Naught slipped past their watchful eyes. A fisherman mending his nets on the Sabbath or a lad who did not properly respect his father soon found himself before the kirk session, where he might be reprimanded, fined, or locked in the *jougs* at the kirk door, an iron collar tethering him to the outside wall, exposing him to the ridicule of his neighbors. She hoped they'd not unearthed some impropriety on her part, for she was the innocent one. Hadn't her father said so?

Mr. Murdoch nodded curtly. "Mr. Armstrong remembered the bridal gown and both sisters. He was certain 'twas the younger sister—'the dark-haired one,' he said—who was to be the bride. Said she took leave of the fitting to deliver wedding invitations with Mr. McKie."

"Is that how it was, Miss McBride?"

"Aye. Jamie and I delivered the invitations. Together."

Rose eyed the empty chair next to hers, imagining Jamie sitting there glowering at her. Furious. Her brave front began to slip. *Please, Jamie. You ken 'tis true.*

"So then," the minister said. "You traveled to Twyneholm parish one week before your wedding to stay with your aunt, Miss Margaret Halliday, a woman of good standing. A matter of tradition, aye? The bride flits for seven days, then returns for the wedding itself."

"Aye, 'tis."

"But you did not return."

"Nae." She looked away, pierced afresh with a keen sense of loss. How innocent she'd been! Naive. Trusting. It had never occurred to her, not for a moment, that her delay would cost her Jamie…that Leana…that her own father…

Jock Bell nudged her with his words. "Miss McBride, why did you not come home as planned?"

Rose brushed a loose tendril of hair from her damp forehead, delaying the inevitable if only for a moment. "The morning of my wedding we awoke to a terrible snowstorm. Newabbey was not affected, but the roads were not fit for carriage nor horse in Twyneholm."

The dominie tapped his notes. "I can write Reverend Dr. John Scott in Twyneholm parish to verify that point, if necessary."

Reverend Gordon held up his palm in response, his gaze fixed on Rose. "What was your expectation? That your family would go on with your wedding with a proxy bride? Or that your cousin would in fact marry your sister with your blessing?"

Touching the round stone beneath her dress, as if it might give her courage, she spoke the truth. "Neither, sir. I thought my family would wait until I was safely home and then we'd proceed as planned. I did not even know what a proxy bride was before my sister described it to me."

The minister's features stilled. "On what day did she so describe it?"

"New Year's Day 1789. I arrived at Auchengray at the dinner hour and discovered the wedding had already taken place."

A low murmuring moved through the room as the men conferred with one another, clearly agitated. Their voices grew more strident, their faces more grim. Finally Henry Murdoch raised his hand, and the men turned to her as one. "The crux of the matter is this: When you arrived at Auchengray, Miss McBride, were you surprised to find James and Leana were husband and wife?"

"More than surprised, sir." Rose bowed her head. "I was shocked." She squeezed her eyes shut. *Forgive me, Leana. But I was, and you ken it well.* Would they prod and query until she unveiled the rest? How Leana climbed into Jamie's bed and pretended to be her? How Leana stole her husband?

Reverend Gordon interrupted her thoughts with an entirely different question, one she'd hoped to avoid. "But, Rose, did you not in fact encourage your sister to marry James McKie?"

"Aye," Jock Bell chimed in. "I've had several witnesses round the parish testify to that fact."

Be fair, Rose. "When he first arrived, I did suggest he court my sister. She was most enamored of him, and…"

Henry Murdoch cut her short. "You were not in love with him at that point."

"I was not. Not at first."

"*When* then?" he persisted. "When did you decide you loved him?"

The truth, Rose. You promised the truth. "Not until after I left for Twyneholm."

The merchant's gray head tipped back as he rubbed his chin. "So when you left the parish, betrothed to be married, Mr. McKie was still not certain of your affections."

"Nae," she admitted, "but he was certain of my intentions." *Wasn't he?* She glanced at the empty chair again. "I wished to marry him."

"I'm afraid I don't understand." The dominie's thin brows rose high above his spectacles. "Why did Mr. McKie marry your sister?"

"Because he…because she…" *Tell them. Tell them about Leana.*

Rose tried, but the words would not come.

Instead she saw her sister's face filled with love for her every day of her life. Her sister's hands attending her sickbed. Her sister's voice singing to her. *Baloo, baloo, my wee, wee thing.* Her sister's words comforting her. *I love you like my own child, Rose.*

She collapsed onto the table and buried her face in her hands.

The elders did not wait long before Henry Murdoch insisted on an answer. "Forgive me, miss, but we must know the truth: Was Leana McBride the woman James McKie meant to marry on 31 December?"

Rose lifted her head, her gloves wet with tears. "'Tis a question I cannot answer. You must ask Mr. McKie."

The minister stood, shoving his chair behind him. "So we shall, Miss McBride. You can be verra sure of that."

Forty-One

Come, now again, thy woes impart,
Tell all thy sorrows, all thy sin.
GEORGE CRABBE

J amie!" Rose stumbled out of the dining room and fell into his arms.
"Cousin, are you ill?" He lowered her onto the hall bench, quickly
disengaging himself from her embrace. Leana pressed a hand to Rose's
cheek, for the girl's distraught face was as white as a floured board, then
hastened to the kitchen for a glass of water. Jamie stood over Rose, trying to keep his voice calm. "What happened in there?"

What did you tell them? That was what he needed to know. *What
exactly did you say?* She'd promised to speak the truth, but *whose* truth?
Her own? Lachlan's? The truth as it stood that night long ago…or the
truth as it stood now? Might she have seized the chance to turn the tables
in her favor? Even if it broke her sister's heart, even if it ruined his life?

He stared down at her as she sat in stunned silence. *Please God, you
didn't tell them the worst of it.*

The door to the dining room swung open. "Mr. McKie." Reverend
Gordon greeted him with a troubled look. " 'Tis your turn to speak to
the kirk session. I regret to say we have some difficult questions for you.
Questions that require an honest answer."

Jamie nodded, his mind reeling. *What questions? What have you done,
Rose?* He followed the minister into the room, warmed by the fire and
the heat of five men, one of whom wore a sheen of sweat on his brow.

Reverend Gordon pointed toward an empty chair. "Sit, please."

The scrape of his chair echoed through the silent room. Jamie took
a moment to arrange his coattails as he begged God for wisdom,
remembering the Almighty's promise to him, spoken in a dream the
night he left Glentrool and started for Auchengray. *I will never leave you.*
A word of assurance Jamie needed now more than ever.

He surveyed the men across from him, recognizing them by name or reputation. Millar, the new session clerk. Sproat, the schoolmaster. Murdoch, the merchant, a hardheaded sort. And Jock Bell, a neighbor and fellow sheep farmer, the friendliest of the lot. Jamie tipped his head at the man, though it did not erase Jock's worried look.

Reverend Gordon had no sooner sat down than the queries began.

Murdoch shot first. "Was it your intention to marry Rose McBride on 31 December?"

A loaded question. "At first I did intend to marry Rose," Jamie agreed, treading carefully. "But I chose to remain married to her sister instead."

"*Chose?*" Murdoch snorted. "Did Rose afford you this choice, or did you *choose* without asking her?"

Sproat leaned forward. "And *when* did you choose? In November? December? January?"

"And you say you chose to *remain* married." Millar's words bore the mark of censure. "That is not the same as choosing in advance, sir."

"Gentlemen!" Reverend Gordon banged his fist on the table. "One at a time, if you please. Have you forgotten your manners?" He turned to Jamie, while throats were cleared and collars loosened. "Jamie, your cousin Rose presented us with information that…ah, differed from your uncle's account. We are simply trying to sort out what took place." The minister looked round the room for a moment, settling them with his solemn gaze. "Mr. McKie, why don't you tell us what happened in your own words? In doing so, you may answer all our questions for us. If not, you can be sure we'll ask them. Go on, son."

Jamie bowed his head, desperately trying to collect his thoughts. *Speak the truth in love.* Aye, there it was. He would tell them the truth, that he loved Leana and did not love Rose. It was not the beginning of a story that mattered but the end of it. He looked up and met their gazes squarely. "I have been the husband of one woman, Leana McBride McKie, for one year and two months. I love her with all my heart and am grateful that she willingly married me on Hogmanay 1788. We have one son, my legal heir, Ian Lachlan McKie. We request the kirk record show that on 31 December 1788, Leana McBride married James McKie."

Two of the men looked relieved. Willing, even, to end the inquiry there. But three men did not. And Reverend Gordon was one of them.

"Jamie, why did you not tell me this at the bride stool? Why did Leana stand in for her sister as proxy if you both intended for Leana to be your bride?"

The worst possible question.

"Because then…" Jamie faltered. Any road he took ended in a peat bog. "Because the decision to marry Leana came after the banns had been read." *And after the wedding as well.* Jamie did his best to look embarrassed, as though the couple were naught but two impatient lovers. "I was eager to proceed with the wedding, Reverend. So was Leana." *'Twas true, but for different reasons.* "It seemed prudent to carry on with the ceremony as planned."

"Prudent, you say?" The session clerk wagged his pen like a scolding finger. "You assumed you'd simply fix the kirk records later. Was that it?"

Jamie bowed his head. He did not care what they thought of him or how foolish he appeared. He only wanted to save his marriage to Leana. "Aye, sir. We lost our heads."

The minister's voice was low and not unkind. "The penalty for what you've done is not quite that severe, James. All three of you will keep your heads on your shoulders. But there are still discrepancies between your story and Rose's that do not sit well with me. 'Tis a matter of the timing of things. Anyone in our parish can see that you cherish your wife and son. Rose's contentment with the situation is less apparent. She has refused an offer of marriage from a young man of the village, I understand."

Jamie nodded, relieved to shift the focus elsewhere for a moment. "Neil Elliot sought her hand in marriage, aye."

"Did you encourage her to pursue that match?"

A memorable scene floated before him. Rose and Neil standing in the shadows of Sweetheart Abbey. Kissing. "Indeed I did. My uncle was in favor of their marrying as well. But Rose was unwilling, and there was no reason to force her."

"You mean nothing improper had occurred between them."

Jamie felt certain of his answer. "Nae, sir. Nothing improper."

Reverend Gordon turned to the others. "I must confess, having known Rose McBride all her young life, she is a lass prone to exaggeration and vivid emotion, an ever changeable girl whose mind seldom lands on any one thing for very long."

Jamie managed a smile. "You ken her well, sir."

Shrugging, the minister added, " 'Twould not surprise me at all if she chose to marry you one minute and chose not to the next."

"Aye, you've captured her nature exactly." Jamie had to work to keep the elation from his voice. If they saw Rose as capricious, there was still cause for hope.

A soft knock at the door heralded Mistress Gordon with a heavy tea tray. "I waited for a quiet moment." She made quick work of distributing cups and pouring tea. "There's a plate of cakes, if you're a bit peckish, and milk for your tea." The reverend's wife slipped out as unobtrusively as she'd entered.

While the elders enjoyed their repast, Jamie sorted through all he'd said. And had not said. If no other questions were raised, perhaps the worst had come and gone. When saucers were pushed aside and crumbs brushed from waistcoats, Jamie tried to appear relaxed and confident, as though he had naught on his mind but ginger cake.

"Forgive me, Reverend Gordon." Walter Millar tapped on his book of minutes. "But we're neglecting one of Miss McBride's later comments. Mr. Murdoch asked her if she was surprised to return home from Twyneholm and find that James and Leana were husband and wife. Her answer was, 'More than surprised, sir. I was shocked.' "

Jamie's heart thudded to a stop. *Oh, Rose.* She'd told them the truth after all. *Too much truth.* Jamie was neither surprised nor shocked. But he was undone.

"Why was she shocked, Mr. McKie?" Sproat's voice bore a hint of accusation.

"I cannot say, sir." *The truth, Jamie. Leana expects no less.* "As Reverend Gordon attested, her emotions are unpredictable. I only ken that she left for Twyneholm having never once stated that she loved me."

"And her sister, Leana. Did she confess her affection for you, her desire to be your wife?"

Jamie, I love you still.

"Yes, sir, she did. Several times." Please God, he would not fail her. Not now, when every word meant the life or death of their marriage. "Leana McBride made it very clear she would be pleased to be my wife. And I am honored to be her husband."

"We asked your cousin a question in closing, Jamie," the minister explained, "one which she deferred to you. Mr. Millar, would you read it please?"

Beneath the table, Jamie pressed his heels into the floor, steeling himself. He'd promised Leana that he would allow the Almighty to guide his words. *O my God, I trust in thee: let me not be ashamed.*

The session clerk's head bobbed up and down on his too thin neck. "Mr. Murdoch asked, 'Was Leana McBride the woman James McKie meant to marry on 31 December?' And how would you answer that, sir?"

Meant to marry. Jamie stared at the flickering hearth, buying time, considering his response. If they were asking if he *intended* to marry Leana, the answer was no. But was Leana the woman he was *meant* to marry, by God's gracious provision? That he could answer honestly without hesitation.

"Aye. I was meant to marry Leana."

"Not Rose McBride."

"Nae, gentlemen," Jamie said firmly. "Not Rose."

"Do you have any reason to believe that Leana will not concur with all that you've told us?"

On this point, he could speak with confidence. "Leana and I are in complete agreement on these matters."

"Aye, I'm sure you are." Reverend Gordon stood to pace before the fire, his hands clasped behind his back. "Jamie, you'll forgive a question now of a more personal nature. But 'tis the duty of the kirk session to see that its parishioners abide by the Ten Commandments. In particular the seventh of those good laws."

Jamie counted through them. *Ah.*

"Your son was born rather soon after your wedding day."

"Nine months and four days, sir." Much as the question irked him, he remained calm. "If your question concerns Leana coming to our marriage bed a maid, you can be certain she was." *Verra certain.*

The clerk spoke again, pen poised. "The week that Lachlan McBride came to the kirk session meeting and testified on your behalf, none of us were present, save Reverend Gordon. And, as you ken, a written record does not exist. But I believe your uncle stated that your marriage was consummated the night of the wedding."

Jamie kept his voice even, though his jaw tightened. "It was."

"So it is possible your son, Ian, was conceived on that night."

" 'Twould seem my wife is blessed of God with a fertile womb, aye." Uneasy with the direction their questions were taking, Jamie tried a different tack. "Reverend Gordon will attest that a sufficient amount of silver was paid as a fine for our impetuous actions, and rightly so." He touched a hand to his purse, hidden beneath his waistcoat. "However, if an additional amount—"

"Mr. McKie!" The minister's voice rang through the room like Judgment Day itself. "You cannot buy righteousness."

"Forgive me, Reverend." Heat crawled up his neck. "I meant no disrespect to the kirk or to the Lord. I only meant—"

"Aye, aye." He waved away Jamie's apology. "The fault is mine. I'm a bit sensitive on the subject, as many a parishioner has tried to pay for his sins in silver rather than face the repentance stool."

Heat continued to rise toward Jamie's face. "I pray there's been nothing said this evening that requires such…ah, severe discipline."

Reverend Gordon's steady gaze was less than comforting. "The evening is not over, Jamie. Send in your wife."

Forty-Two

Only a sweet and virtuous soul,
Like seasoned timber, never gives.
GEORGE HERBERT

Leana, the men are waiting for you."

She looked up, and her heart overflowed like a stream in March. *Dearest Jamie.* He stood there in the hall of the manse, handsome as ever, and yet he looked wrung out, like a rag draped over Eliza's bucket. "Come and sit, dearie. Rose is out of doors, breathing some fresh air to revive her spirits. You'll have the hall to yourself for a bit."

"I'm glad of it." He joined her on the bench, his gaze intent, traveling over her from head to toe, as if committing her to memory. "Beloved wife." Grasping both her hands, he kissed her lips, then her cheek, before he whispered in her ear, "Be careful what you say."

She squeezed Jamie's hands once more, then rose at Reverend Gordon's urgent bidding from the dining room doorway.

"Come, lass. The hour is late, and we have many questions that beg answering."

Easing past the minister, she turned for a final glimpse of Jamie before the door closed between them. *Beloved husband.* If all went well, he would be hers alone before evening's end.

The room was far brighter than the hall. Leana blinked, letting her eyes adjust, then sat down, scooting the heavy chair toward the table with some difficulty, for her knees were shaking. *Preserve me, O God: for in thee do I put my trust.* She was nervous, aye, but she was eager as well. Eager to tell the truth and have any lingering stain on their marriage scrubbed clean.

Leana folded her hands at her waist, not touching the table, sitting as straight as she could. *Mother would be proud.* She looked down at her white silk gloves. The gloves Agness McBride had worn on her wedding day. The gloves Leana had worn when she spoke her vows to Jamie. *Mother's gloves.* Pure white silk, without spot or blemish, kept in a drawer and wrapped in linen, left untouched most of the time.

Except tonight.

Tonight she would hold out her heart for inspection and let them see that she loved the Lord God and that she loved Jamie. Both also loved her. And both had forgiven her. She was a sinner, aye, but she was washed clean by grace. *Who shall stand in his holy place? He that hath clean hands, and a pure heart.* Leana looked across the table at those who held her life in their grasp and prayed for mercy.

"Mistress McKie…ah, Miss McBride." The clerk splayed his fingers, clearly at a loss. "Until we finish these proceedings and a decision is made, how shall we address her, Reverend?"

"With her permission, we will call her Leana. Will that suit you, lass?"

"Aye," she said, bowing her head in respect. "My mother chose the name."

"Did she now?" Amid the minister's wrinkles a slight smile appeared. "And do you ken the meaning?"

Leana lifted her brows, curious. "I assumed she liked the sound of it."

"The name means, 'Serves Ian.' Perhaps Jamie knew that when he chose your son's name?"

"Except I chose it." Leana bit her tongue, wishing she'd kept that truth to herself. It made Jamie sound uninvolved. Disinterested. Perhaps it was not too late to mend her mistake. "Our son's name means 'gift from God,' and Ian certainly is that. A gift to both of us."

"Aye, he's a fine lad," Reverend Gordon agreed, shuffling his papers. "He greets rather loudly during services, but most bairns do."

"I try to keep him quiet." Leana noticed the other men growing impatient with their chatter. She was pleased to talk about Ian, though she must do so with care; two hours had passed since she'd nursed him. And she was happy to chat about Jamie. But naught would be accomplished until she spoke of Rose.

"Let us press on with more serious matters," the clerk said, his tone weary and a bit short. "Miss…ah, Leana. Your husband—that is to say, Mr. McKie—said, and I quote, 'Leana McBride made it very clear she would be pleased to be my wife.' Is that a true statement?"

She beamed across the table. "Aye, it certainly is true."

"When did you make that 'very clear' to him? In October when he arrived? In November when he proposed to marry your sister? In December at the bride stool? When exactly?"

So many questions. Leana pressed her lips together, trying to preserve whatever moisture remained before her mouth dried to cotton. "I was…" *Attracted? Enamored? Infatuated?* "That is, I liked my cousin from the first. My feelings for him grew rather quickly." She turned away, certain her cheeks were as red as hindberries. *Liked him?* She had loved Jamie from the moment she saw him walk across the lawn of Auchengray and heard him speak her name.

Andrew, the schoolmaster, took pity on her. "Were those feelings returned, lass?"

"Not at first." *Not until two months ago.* "But eventually, aye, they were."

Her conscience tugged at her. Nagged at her. *Speak the truth.* She would answer every question with complete honesty, of course. But must she speak the truths they did not ask to hear? How much truth would be enough?

"Tell us, Leana." Jock Bell's kind voice bore no challenge. "Did your sister, Rose, encourage you in your affection for Mr. McKie?"

"She did. She certainly did." Leana nodded, praying the movement might cool her cheeks. "Rose seemed eager to see Jamie and me wed."

At first. Not later. *Forgive me, Rose.*

Henry Murdoch, a man as short-tempered as her father, snorted with obvious disdain. "Your sister, the matchmaker. Is that the way of it?"

Leana hesitated, unsure of his intention. "So it appeared to me, sir."

"Well, *Miss* McBride, 'twas not the way it appeared to your sister." He used the title deliberately, his face suddenly hard as flint. "When she arrived home from Twyneholm on New Year's Day and found you married to her betrothed, Rose McBride was, in her words, 'More than surprised…I was shocked.'"

Oh, Rose. Leana tried to swallow, but her heart lodged in her throat. How much had her sister told them? All of it, every sordid detail? *Be careful what you say.* 'Twas too late for such precautions if her sins had already been confessed by another.

Mr. Murdoch either didn't notice her discomfort or didn't care, for he plowed forward in relentless pursuit of the truth. "Gentlemen, I believe our answer rests here." His mottled face, lit by the fire, threatened to ignite. "If it was Rose's desire that you marry Mr. McKie, then what did you do, Leana, that was so surprising? So...shocking?"

She bowed her head, pleading for the strength to go on.

I have chosen the way of truth.

"I took..."

Words failed her. It was one thing to make her confession to Jamie, to Rose, to Neda. Even Almighty God had not flinched when she poured out her sins before him like tears from a bottle. But in this room...with these men...

The clerk prompted her. "You took *what,* miss?"

"I took...what was not mine...to take."

Reverend Gordon leaned over her. "We need you to be more specific, Leana." His tone was gentle but firm. "Did you wear your sister's wedding gown; is that what you took?"

"Nae, her...*kell.*"

"Her bridal veil?"

"Aye," she murmured. "I wore my own gown, but I took Rose's kell to the kirk."

"I see." Mr. Millar tapped the silver nib of his pen on the inkstand. "This does not constitute a breach of moral law, unless we choose to see it as either stealing or coveting her sister's property."

"You've missed the point, sir." Jock Bell wagged his head like one of his tups. "However fine the embroidery work, the borrowing of a kell— you did give it back to her, didn't you, lass?—hardly constitutes a sin, not in any parish in Scotland. Nae, gentlemen, there's something else afoot, for I spy it in the lady's countenance."

Leana looked up in time to find Mr. Bell peering at her across the table. He saw too much. He saw the truth.

"Leana has not told us the lot of it. Confess, lass, for we'll not leave this room 'til the thing is settled."

The five of them trained their eyes on her and waited.

In the hearth, a pine log shifted, sending sparks flying into the air. In her heart, something shifted as well. *I will walk in thy truth: unite my heart to fear thy name.* It was God she feared, with a holy fear, not these men. She would speak the truth. All of it. Not because of what they knew, but because of what she knew. The whole truth. She would no longer be ashamed, for there was no shame in truth. Only in hiding it.

"I am ready," she said calmly. And she was.

Mr. Murdoch cleared his throat. "Answer this, then, for 'tis the question we've posed twice before on this night: Were you, Leana McBride, the woman James McKie meant to marry on 31 December?"

The truth. "Nae, I was not."

A furor rose, heating the air, filling the room. "Explain yourself, Miss McBride!"

"So I will." Fear and trembling fell away like scales, and strength poured through her like living water. *The truth.* "Mr. McKie thought he had married my sister. Instead I claimed him for myself."

"*Claimed* him?"

"Aye. I went into his room in the dark of night and presented myself to him as his bride."

Now 'twas the elders who were shocked. They threw words at her like rocks. *Hizzie. Tairt. Ill-deedie. Limmer.*

Reverend Gordon nearly shouted at her, "Are you saying when James McKie spoke his vows in my kirk, he spoke them to Rose? Not to you?"

"He did. Rose is his wife by the law of the kirk."

"Then what are *you?*" another roared.

"I am his wife by habit and repute." She spoke without shame. She spoke without fear. "I am the mother of his son."

Sharp-edged questions landed at her feet. "What did you tell him that night?" "Did you seduce him?" "How was he deceived?"

Leana felt the blows but not the sting. "Jamie did not realize I was the one by his side until morning. Until it was too late."

"Why would a woman do such a thing?" Jock bellowed.

"Because I loved Jamie completely. From the beginning." *Jamie, I love you still.* "And because I thought he loved me and kenned it was me that night. But he did not."

"Och! Enough, lass, for 'tis naught but lies."

"'Tis anything but lies, sir." *For my mouth shall speak truth.*

Above the din a voice of reason cried out, "Is no one else to blame, Leana? Your sister? Jamie? Your father?"

She shook her head. Let her father name his own sins. They were not hers to confess. "I alone am to blame. No one else."

"But, Leana—"

"Gentlemen!" Reverend Gordon thundered. "That's quite enough." He held his arms out over the table, his long, pale hands like the tablets of Moses. The elders grew silent, though their breathing sounded heavy and dark, like that of feral dogs run to ground. "Leana has told us more than we asked," the minister reminded them, his fury retreating. "We have all we need to make a just decision."

He turned to Leana. Though his brow was fiercely knit, something akin to respect shone from his eyes. "You were honest, lass, and courageous. God will surely reward you. But here on earth, your punishment will be swift, and your sentence painful, for much wrong has been done your sister."

Forgive me, Rose. "I do not deny it, sir, for I love her dearly."

"Come then, let me deliver you to your family while we deliberate over what's to be done." He clasped her elbow as though he expected her to faint, though she did not so much as stumble. They entered the shadowy hall, where Rose was nowhere to be seen and Jamie sat in abject misery. 'Twas clear he'd heard the shouting, for when he stood to join them, his posture was that of a broken man.

Distraught, the minister pulled her aside. "Why, lass?" he said, his voice hoarse with emotion. "Your husband willingly claimed you as his wife. Why did you not hide beneath his covering?"

Leana looked into his eyes. "Because someday, Reverend Gordon, I will stand, not before this kirk session, not before my husband, not before my father, but before Almighty God." His name gave her the strength to continue, even as her eyes filled with tears. "And when I stand before him, I will not be ashamed. For the LORD is my rock, and my fortress, and my deliverer; my God, my strength, in whom I will trust."

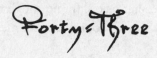

Forty-Three

Man's inhumanity to man
makes countless thousands mourn.
ROBERT BURNS

Reverend Gordon shook his head in disbelief. "My prayers are with
you both."

Jamie stood behind Leana as the minister returned to the meeting
room. His hands were poised to catch her if her knees gave way. Yet
she'd sounded anything but weak. Her voice was strong, her words sure.
The LORD is my rock. An extraordinary woman, his Leana. Perhaps her
meeting with the kirk session had gone better than he imagined.

When she turned toward him, her face awash with silent tears, his
hopes died a quick death.

"Oh, Jamie," she cried, falling against his chest, "I spoke the truth."

"Aye, I'm sure you did." *My brave lass.* Jamie smoothed a hand
across her hair. "For if you did not speak the truth, you would not be
the woman I love."

"But Rose told them...Rose said..."

"Now, now," he whispered, as gently as a father to his bairn. He
pressed a handkerchief into her palm. "Rose is not our concern." *Mine,
perhaps. But not yours, beloved.*

Leana wiped her tears, though they would not stop. "Reverend
Gordon said my punishment will be swift..."

Nae. His throat tightened, even as he tightened his embrace. *Not
my Leana.*

"And my sentence, he said, will be...will be...painful." She buried
her face in his chest, her voice muffled against his waistcoat. "I'm afraid,
Jamie."

He stifled a groan, shutting his eyes. The stool of repentance stood
like a gallows, stark and empty, waiting for his wife to mount it. It had

no sharp points to pierce her pale skin, no rough metal collars to chafe her slender neck. But it would wound her. Shame and humiliation cut deeper than a dirk.

Let me bear the shame. Oh, God, let me bear it for her!

"Jamie, what could he mean? What kind of pain?"

"Do not think of it, beloved. Think only of how much I love you." He kissed her then, stroking her hair, wanting to comfort her, wanting to ease her fears. Neither of them paid attention to the front door opening and closing behind them, until a familiar voice echoed through the hall.

"Is it…over?"

Rose.

Jamie straightened, brushing back Leana's hair that had fallen loose from its pins. He kept her close to him as if protecting her from impending harm.

Rose edged toward them, clearly wary. "Did it go…well for you, Leana?"

When Leana shifted as though to move away from him, Jamie held her in place. *Stay with me, lass. We will face her together.* "Never mind Leana's testimony, Cousin." His voice was as sharp as an archangel's sword and his aim as true. "What did you tell the elders?"

Rose flinched before she answered. "I told them the truth."

"I'm proud of you, Rose." Leana dabbed at her eyes.

"I did not tell the elders *all* of it though. I might have told them much more." Rose eased down onto the bench, folding her gloved hands. "I could have described what happened on my wedding night."

Jamie glared at her. "Except you were not there." Had he ever been so glad of anything in his life? " 'Twas not your story to tell. 'Twas mine, if I chose to reveal it. Instead I kept those details to myself."

"But I did not." Leana pressed the handkerchief to her mouth as if to stop the words from coming out. "I told the elders the truth."

Jamie froze. "All of it?" *Oh, lass.*

Leana hid her face, bright with shame. "I thought Rose… I was sure…"

" 'Tis not my fault!" Rose cried. "I told them almost nothing!"

"I told them everything." Leana turned to look at them both, her cheeks still red but her voice stronger. "I had to speak the truth, no matter what else was said in that room. 'Twas Almighty God I wanted to honor, not myself. But I did not mean to hurt you, dear Jamie." She touched his face with a shaking hand. "Please…please forgive me…"

"Nae, Leana." He held a finger to her lips. "You did what was right. There is nothing to forgive."

"What of me?" Rose's voice was taut. "Am I forgiven as well?"

Leana stepped closer, her hands held out in mute appeal. " 'Tis *your* forgiveness I must have, Rose. Yours above all, for you are the one I wronged most." She bent toward her sister's cloak, her delicate fingers fluttering over the green folds. "Will you forgive me, Rose? With all your heart, not just words. Please?"

Jamie's hands clenched as each second went by without a response. *Say something, Rose. After all you've done, do not punish her like this.*

"You have a right to be angry, Rose, to feel cheated." Leana knelt at her sister's feet, spreading her skirts across the floor. "The kirk session will take their pound of flesh, of that I have no doubt. What I ask of you is a greater sacrifice, Rose. 'Tis mercy." She rested her white silk gloves on Rose's cotton ones, covering the stain. "Have you any mercy to give me, dear Rose?"

"You may have your mercy, Leana." Rose looked up at him, her eyes pleading. "If I may have my Jamie."

"Och!" He nearly spit on the floor. "I am not a trinket in some packman's sack, bought for a penny. You will ne'er have my heart, even if you manage to claim the rest."

Leana's shoulders sagged. "The elders will decide who Jamie's wife will be. Perhaps they've already done so." She stood once more, less steady on her feet this time. "Rose, even though you cannot forgive me, I forgive you. For whatever you said in that room tonight, true or false. For all you've done since the wedding day. None of it matters now."

A sharp wind blew through the open front door.

Lachlan McBride's voice carried down the hall. "So we're done with things, are we?" He scowled at them as he crossed the threshold, then shut the door with a resounding bang. "Your bairn is greeting for his supper, Leana. 'Tis long past time you were home, all three of you. Surely you're finished here." Lachlan strode past them, then knocked on the dining room door before anyone could stop him.

The door swung open, and Reverend Gordon stepped out. He was taller than Lachlan McBride and at the moment more perturbed. Looming over the bonnet laird, the minister said curtly, "You were not summoned to this evening's proceedings, Mr. McBride. What business do you have here?"

"Merely collecting my family, Reverend, for the hour is late." He peered over the minister's shoulder, rising on his toes to do so. "Shouldn't your elders be about their rounds, making certain that all in the village are home where they belong and not loitering about the streets?"

Reverend Gordon consulted his pocket watch, though Jamie suspected it was more to curb his temper than to learn the time. "Shortly but not yet. Since you are here, and we have made our decision, I suppose you may join us." The minister pointed a finger between his uncle's gray eyes. "But you'll not speak unless spoken to, nor offer an opinion. Is that understood?"

"Aye," Lachlan said gruffly, stepping back from the menacing digit. "Follow me, Jamie, and bring your women. Pray you'll not lose one of them to the *cutty stool* before this night ends."

Please God, may it not be so. Jamie led Leana into the room, with Rose trailing along behind them. Seats were taken amid much scraping of chairs. The fire had died down, yet the air was warmer than ever. Seated between the sisters, Jamie prayed for strength. And aye, for mercy, though 'twas too late for that now, for the elders had set their course. Their hands were folded on top of their numerous papers. The session clerk had put down his pen, his finger resting on a particular entry, the last on the page. All eyes turned toward Reverend Gordon, who stood at the head of the table, his imposing form outlined by the light of the fire.

"We have been presented with a most difficult task this evening, yet one we are ever charged with as parish leaders: to uphold God's law." He nodded at his elders, and they responded in kind. "What began as a simple clerical error has grown to a moral issue of grave significance. In all my years in the pulpit, I've ne'er seen its match. When emotions are put aside, however, 'tis a clearer case than one might first imagine."

The minister glanced at his notes and then at Rose. "On behalf of the elders, for my vote counts no more than theirs, I will present to each one of you in turn our decisions. Rose, you are first."

Out of the corner of his eye, Jamie noticed her sitting up straighter, a look of expectation on her face. *Nae, Rose. Do not wish for this, for I cannot love you again.*

"We find that Rose McBride—or should I say, Mistress McKie—is innocent in every regard."

Rose gasped aloud, her eyes and mouth widening.

Jamie gripped the arms of the chair so hard he feared the wood might crack. *Not Rose. She cannot be my wife.*

Reverend Gordon continued as though reading a market list. "Though you've waited a long time to be pronounced Mistress McKie, you must wait a bit longer to claim your husband. However, by law, you already have a legal right to his name and his property. And soon, his person."

Jamie watched in despair as Leana slid her wedding ring off her finger and quietly placed the silver band before her sister, who stared at it for a moment, then slipped it on.

Nae. This cannot be right.

He grasped Leana's hand under the table, but it was limp, and she did not squeeze back. *Oh, Leana. 'Tis not over. Do not despair.*

"Mr. McKie, we have a decision for you as well."

He looked up but did not acknowledge the man. Hadn't his life already been decided for him? *Not for. Against.*

The minister's pronouncement was matter-of-fact. "Leana has attested that you meant to wed Rose and not her. Since you were deceived at the outset—entrapped, as it were, by your cousin Leana—we will not hold you accountable for your remarks to this kirk session regarding your relationship with her."

"They were not remarks," Jamie corrected him through clenched teeth. "They were the truth. I love her."

He held up his hand, stemming his words. "Aye, so we've heard. That you have come to cherish Leana is both admirable and regrettable but does not change the facts of the case. We have concluded that you were merely trying to protect her. An honorable effort and therefore not to be held against you."

Were they not listening? Did they not hear him? Jamie spoke more forcefully. " 'Twas not an effort, Reverend Gordon. Leana is my wife."

"*Was,* Jamie. Leana *was* your wife but is no more."

"But she—"

"The law of the kirk recognizes Rose as your wife *per verba de praesenti.* Leana's claim of habit and repute came after her sister's, and therefore is invalid." Reverend Gordon shrugged his shoulders. "You cannot be married to both women, Jamie. 'Tis against the law of God and society."

The room seemed to shift, as though nothing were nailed in place. Jamie heard the minister speaking, yet the man made no sense. *Per verba,* he'd said. By *whose* words? And *what* words? If he'd broken the law, then he would pay the price. Jamie looked up and prayed the ground beneath his feet would stop moving. "What is my punishment then?"

"You do your cousin Rose an injustice, sir." Henry Murdoch glared at him from across the table. "You once chose her, loved her, pursued her, and labored for her hand in marriage. Most men would not consider marriage to such a woman punishment."

Jamie sank in his chair. "I am not most men." *I am the least of men.* The room had stopped spinning, but his stomach had only begun.

Reverend Gordon leaned across the table, his voice lower. "Understand this, Jamie: Had the circumstances been different, we would have charged you with adultery. Had you told us that you chose Leana for your wife on your wedding night, having spoken the vows to Rose, our only recourse would have been to punish you both. But…"—he straightened, holding his hands out—"as you were deceived, our decision of innocence stands."

Innocent? Jamie knew he was guilty in every regard. For hurting Leana and loving Rose. For loving Leana and now hurting her again.

For whosoever shall keep the whole law, and yet offend in one point, he is guilty of all.

"I am not innocent," he declared, standing to his feet. "I am guilty." He said it again, with more force. "I am *guilty*. Leana is not the deceiver here…*I* am. I deceived my father. I deceived my brother. Worse of all, I deceived myself into thinking I loved a bonny lass who loves no one but herself."

"Jamie!" Rose cried.

He did not look at her. He looked only at Leana. "Please…please forgive me."

Her eyes held no judgment. "You are already forgiven, Jamie."

Henry Murdoch pounded on his notes. "If there is forgiveness and mercy to be extended in this room, it must come from this side of the table."

"Nae, sir." Jamie looked at Henry but did not quite see him for the tears that stung his eyes. "'Twas not your mercy I required, gentlemen, but Leana's." He gazed down at her, speaking to her with his eyes, knowing she would hear him. *I will never leave you.*

Her pale blue eyes spoke in return. *I will always love you.*

"Well then." Millar, the clerk, tapped at his record book. "Since Leana seems to have forgiven you, you are a free man, James McKie."

He looked away as Rose reached for his hand. "I am anything but free, sir."

Forty-Four

Misfortune had conquered her,
how true it is.

MADAME DE STAËL

The truth had made her free, but it was the one freedom Leana did not want: a life without Jamie. Leana knew the elders would find her guilty. Guilty of loving Jamie. And guilty of being a woman who deceived men. *Cursed be the deceiver.*

"Leana?" Reverend Gordon's voice. Gentle, not harsh, yet firm. " 'Tis time we addressed you."

She lifted her head. The room grew very still. Even the hearth seemed to hold its fiery breath.

"Leana McBride, on behalf of the kirk session of Newabbey parish, it is my unfortunate duty to pronounce judgment on your sin. Are you prepared to receive our word on the matter?"

"Aye, for the word of the Lord is right." She drew herself up, as if she were about to be lashed to a stake. "I am ready."

"Let us begin by clearly stating the nature of your transgression." The minister held his notes close to his spectacles, reading them aloud as though they were someone else's words and not his. "On the night of 31 December 1788, did you willfully take this man, James McKie, as your husband by a deliberate act of deception?"

Willfully. Deliberately. Deceptively. Was that the way of it? *Nae, but it was the look of it.* "I did not identify myself by name when I went to Jamie. And so, aye…he was deceived."

Reverend Gordon continued, "Having then deceived Mr. McKie, you forced him to commit adultery without either his knowledge or his consent."

Adultery? "But I thought Jamie was not—"

"He is not being charged, Leana." The minister's stern brow appeared above his handful of papers. "We've already determined that."

"Good, good." She was ever aware of Jamie's presence beside her. "I could not bear for him to suffer on my account."

Jamie's hand reached for hers beneath the table. She could not look at him, or she would be undone. *Thou art my strength.*

Reverend Gordon shook his paper, calling her attention back to the matter at hand. "Though you did not intentionally impersonate your sister, that was the upshot of things. Is that correct, Leana?"

"Aye. In the dark Jamie thought I was Rose."

"But you knew that you were not married to this man."

"I knew," she whispered.

"And yet, knowing Jamie was not your husband, you...you engaged in..."

"Aye." She hung her head. "I did."

"You are therefore charged by this kirk session with *hochmagandy*—"

"Nae!" Jamie shot to his feet, even as Leana's heart gave way, like a sand dune crushed beneath a great wave.

"Sit down, Mr. McKie, or leave the room."

" 'Tis not right." Jamie threw himself into his chair, shaking with anger, muttering under his breath. " 'Tis not fair."

Reverend Gordon, ignoring him, continued. "Paul's letter to the church at Corinth speaks against this detestable sin: 'Now the body is not for fornication, but for the Lord.' Do you agree, Leana, and commit your body to the Lord and his care alone?"

She nodded. *In him will I trust.*

"I'm sorry, lass, but you must respond verbally. Do you repent of your sin?"

Leana lowered her eyes, though her voice did not falter. "I do repent. I am truly sorry." *For godly sorrow worketh repentance.*

She looked up, not at Reverend Gordon, but at her beloved Jamie. He must understand, he must know without a doubt what she was saying and what she was thinking. *I am sorry I deceived you. But I am not sorry I love you.*

The words in his eyes were a mirror of her own. *I love you still.* They kept their gazes locked as her sentence was read.

"Leana McBride, you are hereby required to *compear* on the stool of repentance in sackcloth, barefoot and bareheaded, for three consecutive Sundays beginning this coming Sabbath, as befits your grievous sin."

Stunned, she clung to Jamie's hand. *The cutty stool.* Not even as a child, playing between services, did she go near the hated stool. 'Twas for wicked people. *Reprobates* her father called them. Sinners.

Now the stool was for her.

My punishment is greater than I can bear. The words of Cain. *My words.*

Jamie's hand squeezed hers so tightly she feared he might crush her bones.

The minister spoke again. "Any conjugal rights and privileges between James McKie and Leana McBride are now severed."

Nae. She could no longer look at him, for the pain was too great. *Oh, Jamie. Never to hold you. Never to touch you. Never to kiss you.* 'Twas the harshest punishment of all, the very worst.

Reverend Gordon pressed on, as though he were reading an announcement at the start of services. "Lachlan, you are to see they reside in separate rooms from henceforth. James, your marriage is to be consummated on Saturday, 27 March, following a second reading of your marriage banns each Sunday that Leana appears on the stool."

Rose spoke up. "If Jamie and I are already wed, what use can the banns be?"

Mr. Millar hastened to reply. "The banns allow persons to come forth who would dispute a claim of marriage. Considering all that has transpired in this case, we thought the idea prudent." The session clerk consulted his book, then turned to Lachlan, who'd sat through the proceedings sullen and silent. "There is also a fine of thirty shillings of silver to be paid without delay. That responsibility falls on the one who is legally responsible for the party. As Leana McBride is unwed and living under your roof, sir, the debt falls to you."

Lachlan reached into his waistcoat and produced a calfskin bag, heavy with coin. When he tossed it on the table, the bag landed with a mighty crash, startling the poor schoolmaster. Lachlan's voice was as cold as his silver. " 'Tis always a costly thing to sit before the session."

Reverend Gordon ignored the purse, but not the man. "Mr. McBride, as the only witness in this room who heard your testimony on 5 January 1789, I must confess that the truth revealed this night has little resemblance to the story I heard you tell last year. However, as no written record exists of your testimony, such discrepancies cannot be counted against you, nor may any punishment be levied."

" 'Tis just as well, Reverend." Lachlan pinned his hard gaze on Leana, disgust written across his features. "I have a *howre* for a daughter. That is punishment enough."

She bowed her head and bowed her heart. *Deliver me, O my God, out of the hand of the wicked, out of the hand of the unrighteous and cruel man.* The thought of living beneath her father's roof, suffering beneath his judgment for the rest of her life was beyond bearing. *Deliver me, O my God.*

The minister gestured in her direction with his papers. "Now to the matter of Ian."

Ian. Leana's heart stopped.

" 'Tis Mr. McKie's decision whether or not the lad is to be recognized as his rightful heir or considered a bystart."

Jamie's voice rang out like a bell. "Ian Lachlan McKie is my legal son and my only heir." He shot a pointed look at the session clerk. "See that my claim is duly recorded."

Leana smiled at him through her tears. *Such a good father.* Jamie's claim on their son meant she would always be a small part of Jamie's life as well.

"On the subject of Ian," Lachlan said, "I will *not* claim him as my grandson nor name him as heir to Auchengray." His manner was indifferent, as though the child was of little consequence and only the property mattered. "As I have no sons, 'tis my legal right to choose my heir." He pointed a thick finger at the clerk. "You will record *that* in the minutes of this kirk session meeting as well."

Leana was almost relieved. The less her father had to do with Ian, the better. She would raise him herself, in their own corner of the house, knowing Jamie was not far away. *My sweet boy, my dear Ian.*

"Very well," Reverend Gordon agreed, though 'twas plain Lachlan's callous decision did not sit well with him. "Our greater concern for the child is not his future inheritance but his present moral upbringing."

"Aye," Leana sighed. She could not agree more.

"It is our wish to see Ian McKie reared in a devout and pious home, free from...ah, improper influences."

A sharp intake of breath. *He means me. I am improper.*

"Therefore, the sole responsibility of caring for the boy will fall to his father, James McKie, and to his stepmother, Rose McKie."

Nae!

Leana nearly fainted before Jamie grasped her arm. "Gentlemen, Leana is the child's *mother.* You cannot do this to her."

She tried to breathe. *"Please..."* It came out on a sob. "Please... don't take...my son..."

"I am sorry," the clerk said, sounding as though he meant it.

"Please," she moaned, "you cannot do this. Ian is...my only... Ian is..."

"Look at her!" Jamie lunged to his feet, pulling her up with him. "Can't you see what you are doing to my...to this good woman? Isn't the cutty stool punishment enough? How much must she endure for the sin of loving me?"

Oh, Jamie. She struggled like one climbing out of a deep well, clinging to Jamie's arm, as if 'twere a rope thrown down into the darkness to save her. Without Jamie, she would drown. Without Ian, she would not fight the water's pull.

Reverend Gordon called the room to order, for in every corner were murmurings and anxious faces. He stretched a calming hand toward Jamie. "Come now, Mr. McKie, there is no need for this outburst. You will all live under the same roof, at least for the moment." The minister nodded at his elders. "No one here is without sympathy for your situation. We are merely concerned with your son's welfare, as you should be."

"I am the child's father," Jamie said in a voice that demanded to be heard. "And Leana is his mother. No one is more concerned with Ian's welfare than we are."

Reverend Gordon waved his hand in acknowledgment. "Aye, aye, we can see that you are." Checking his notes once more, then folding them in half, the minister explained, "Leana may continue to serve as the child's wet nurse."

"*What?*" Jamie spoke on her behalf, for Leana could not speak at all.

"However," the reverend amended, "come the twenty-seventh of March the child must be weaned from his mother and released to the McKies."

"You cannot mean that!" Jamie roared, leaning halfway across the table. "Is there some purpose for this cruelty? I thought you were concerned for the health of my son. Would you deprive him of what he needs most?"

"Now who is being unkind?" Reverend Gordon countered. "To ask Leana to continue to nurse a child that is no longer her own would be merciless. Nae, 'tis best to be finished on the twenty-seventh." He waved his hand about. "There are wet nurses to be found throughout our parish, Jamie. You and Rose will have no difficulty there. But 'twould be unreasonable to expect Leana to serve in so menial a role."

Instead I will have no role at all. Leana drew her arms about her bodice, praying her milk would wait until Ian was in her arms. "The hour grows late. Are you...finished with me?"

Reverend Gordon exchanged glances with the other elders. "Aye. Though the kirk session will continue for a few moments longer, you are free to go." His gaze, now directed toward her alone, grew stern. "I will meet you on the Sabbath at the kirk door. Before the first bell."

"I will not forget." Leana rose and fled from the room.

Forty-Five

Both man and womankind belie their nature
When they are not kind.
PHILIP JAMES BAILEY

Rose tarried outside the nursery door, listening for Leana's soft voice or Ian's high-pitched cooing. All was quiet within. The door was already ajar; one slight push allowed Rose to slip past with no one the wiser. She eased the door back in place, then discovered the room was not empty after all. Leana and Ian were catching a late-morning nap.

The wheeled *hurlie* bed had been moved from the servants' floor into Ian's cramped room yestreen after the family arrived home from the kirk session meeting. Father was not being unkind to Leana; he was simply fulfilling his promise to provide separate rooms for Jamie and her sister. Rose was relieved, of course. Yet seeing her sister here, curled up on the blue-and-white embroidered coverlet, sent a fresh wave of guilt washing over her. Could her father not have done better than this? The hurlie bed was too narrow for a grown woman. Low to the floor, it usually remained hidden beneath a larger bed, to be rolled out on the odd occasion when a visitor required bedding.

The room was too small as well. A single, small window facing north toward the gardens and Auchengray Hill afforded the only light. Rose lifted her skirts and moved soundlessly across the floor, then turned her back on the window for a better look at things. She'd only meant to investigate Ian's room, preparing for the day when she would need to know what it contained, and instead had chanced upon a still life worthy of a painter's brush.

Leana had not braided her hair that morning, so it fanned across the coverlet like a golden cloud. Her expression was serene, her skin as pale as Ian's, both of them lit by the slanted rays of the forenoon sun falling across the room. The boy lay curled on his side with his chubby fists tucked under his chin, his wispy brown hair still damp from his bath. Leana circled round the child, making a C with her body, as if protecting him.

From me.

Rose bowed her head, tears stinging her eyes. *I would never hurt your son, Leana.*

How had it come to this? Aye, Rose wanted Jamie and was grateful the kirk session had seen fit to honor the wedding vows spoken on her behalf. But much as she adored the child, she'd never meant to have Ian.

Ye're aboot tae become a mither. And a wife. Was this what the wutch had meant? Both at once? Rose longed for a son, aye, but her *own* son. Jamie's son, from her own body. Though in truth, she had no notion of how to care for a child alone. Would Leana show her how to change and bathe the boy? Would Neda tell her Ian's favorite foods? Or would they watch her frantic attempts to handle him with smug satisfaction?

Nae. Leana could never look smug.

Her sister was a finer mother asleep than many women were awake. All of Leana's admirable qualities—patience, gentleness, contentment— served her well in motherhood. Rose knew she had none of those attributes. She was impatient, restless, always wanting more. Jamie had assured her he liked those things about her when they had first met, praising her speeritie ways. *Your joy captured my heart.* Aye, that's what he'd said.

Now he wanted quiet, peaceful Leana. The mother of his son.

Rose bit her lip, looking away from the tender scene. *Please want me instead, Jamie. Please want me at all.*

"Rose?"

Jamie.

He stood in the doorway, the man who was her husband, yet not her husband. "What brings you here?" she said, keeping her voice down. "Have the ewes tired of your company?"

"The better question is, what brings *you* here?" Jamie walked softly across the room, casting a warm gaze at mother and child as he passed by. Without another word he grasped Rose's sleeve and led her back the way he'd come and out into the hall, releasing her at once. His gaze was no longer warm nor his voice low. "You have no business in that room while my...while Leana is caring for Ian. You are not his stepmother yet, Rose."

"Nae, but I *am* your wife, if only in name." She lowered her eyes, wondering how she might endear herself to Jamie. "I thought I'd learn something about your son. About his care and how I might tend to his needs."

"Look at me, Rose."

She did so at once, startled by the request, and gazed into his handsome face.

He scrutinized her for a moment. "I merely wanted to see if you meant what you said." Jamie folded his arms over his linen shirt, already stained from his morning labors. "To see if your eyes matched your words. You are quite the dissembler, Rose. If anyone could deceive a man in the dark, it would be you."

Her spirits sank. "Jamie, I ken you're...angry."

"Angry?" He snorted. "That isn't the half of it."

"You have every right to be furious. But not with me, Jamie. Please, not with me. The clerical error was no one's fault. As to my testimony yestreen, I didn't give them a single detail about our...that is, your wedding night."

His jaw tightened as she spoke, and then he mimicked her. "'More than surprised, sir. I was shocked.' You gave them all the evidence they needed, Rose. 'Twas very clever on your part. Naught weighing on your conscience, yet you got everything you wanted."

"Not quite everything," she said meekly, with no artifice at all. "For I do not have your heart."

"'Tis true; you do not." He stood back, unfolding his arms. "It belongs to the woman in that room and always will, as long as we two shall live. You've made a sorry bargain, Rose. Ask Leana what it is like to be married to a man who did not choose you and does not love you."

Her spirits rallied, for on this point she had the upper hand over her sister. "You did choose me once, Jamie. You favored me above Leana. And you did love me. I ken that you did, for you told me so. Often."

He shook his head. "You're talking about the past, Rose. Did I love you once? I did…or thought I did. But you are not the same girl I met when I came to Auchengray. You are more secretive and prone to self-ishness." He looked troubled, as if he did not enjoy hurting her. "Your heart has grown hard, Rose. Perhaps 'twas always thus, and I did not see it."

She looked away, ashamed of what he might find in her eyes. Guilt. Pain. And the sad realization that he spoke the truth. "If my heart is hard, 'tis because of so many repairs." Drawing a handkerchief from inside her sleeve, she touched the linen to her nose with a dainty sniff. "All of what you say is true, Jamie. But I want to change. I want to be the blithe and carefree Rose you once knew. And loved."

"You cannot change all that has happened, Rose."

"Nae," she agreed, stepping back as well. "But I can change me."

And she could. She *would*. Beginning this very instant.

Rose spun about and hastened down the stair, strengthening her resolve with each step. Now that the kirk session had set things aright, she would work to deserve Jamie, to make him glad things had turned out this way. She would become Neda's shadow in the kitchen, discovering what Jamie preferred at table. She would unearth her hatesome sewing needle and make Jamie a cambric sark—on her own this time, without Leana's skilled hands doing most of the work. Perhaps a day in the stillroom would be well spent. And she'd learn about birthing and caring for bairns from someone other than her sister, for 'twould be most unfair to ask Leana to teach her.

Rose no sooner reached the front hall than a name came to mind. *Jessie Newall.* Happily married, Jessie was twice a mother, with a babe weeks old. Who better than Mistress Newall to show her what was to be done to keep a child content? Rose would go at once and never mind dinner. The meal would be every bit as awkward as breakfast had been earlier with Jamie so sullen and Leana fighting tears. In another day or two, things might improve. But today the kindest thing she could do was disappear.

Tossing her cloak over her shoulders, Rose was soon off to Troston

Hill farm, grateful to breathe the freshening air that bore the scent of spring. New grass poked through the spongy ground beneath her feet, and bright green buds covered the branches of the stately oaks along March Burn. Like woolly white cairns scattered across the hills, the ewes, heavy with lambs, bleated for their shepherds. *Och!* How she'd missed being out on the braes. No wonder Jamie loved it, just as she once had—and would again, if it might win his heart.

Though 'twas newly March and chilly, the sun warmed her face and pointed the way over Auchengray Hill, down the other side, then halfway up steep Troston Hill. She'd forgotten how rough the pastureland was, thick with rocks and gorse, which plucked at her stockings. Her sturdy boots kept her feet dry at least, and her bonnet shaded her skin. Since it seemed Jamie preferred pale skin, she would not let the sun ruin her complexion.

The Newalls' farm came into view, with its tidy mains and steading and a small flock of blackface sheep. At the heart of the property was a one-story house built of whitewashed stone, overlooking both Lowtis Hill and Criffell. Buoyed by the splendid weather and the prospect of an afternoon spent with Annie and her newborn brother, Rose knocked at the door and sang out a greeting.

A bleary-eyed maidservant ushered her withindoors, offering a timid curtsy. "I'll tell Mistress Newall ye're here. She'll be along *suin.*" The maid faded off to the kitchen while Rose tried not to gawk at her surroundings. Her memory of Troston Hill—for two years had passed since she'd called on the Newalls—was a neatly furnished cottage where all was in order and scrubbed clean as new linen. Now there was barely anywhere to stand, let alone sit, for the stacks of laundry. The remains of breakfast were still strewn across the table, and the hearth had not been tended for some time. Surely two children didn't throw a household into such chaos.

"Jessie?" she called out tentatively, beginning to wonder if she'd come to the wrong house. Clearly she'd come on the wrong day.

"Rose McBride, is it?" Jessie strolled into the room, a bairn in her arms, Annie clinging to her apron, both fussing. Her expression was anything but friendly, her tone barely civil. "Or should I say Mistress McKie?"

Rose's mouth fell open before she recovered her wits enough to ask, "However did you... I mean, 'twas only last night..."

"*Och!* Did you think so scandalous a tale could be kept between Auchengray's walls? Every man present yestreen told twenty others in the parish afore breakfast, and they've told another dozen afore noontide. My orraman, just back from Newabbey, says 'tis all the villagers can talk about, hanging over their gates and blethering 'til they're blue about James McKie and his women."

Rose wilted beneath her harsh spray of words. "I had no idea news would travel so quickly."

"If 'twere any other parish *clack*, 'twould take a day or twa longer." Jessie brushed past her, inclining her head as an invitation to follow. "But one bride being traded for another? Really, Rose! Newabbey has ne'er fixed its teeth into so *michtie* a cut of meat as this one."

Rose sank into a chair at the kitchen table, and her hopes sank with her. "Now I'm ashamed to tell you why I'm here, Jessie."

"Better get used to the feeling, lass." Jessie eased into a seat, pulling out a chair for Annie to join them. "For you'll be wearing shame thick as your green cloak all through the spring. In truth, Rose, you'll find nary a welcome at most doors."

"But Jessie..." Rose looked at her aghast. " 'Tis not my fault..."

Jessie's sharp gaze put a stopper in her mouth. "Do you have any idea the high regard this parish bestows on your sister? *Do* you? Leana is her mother's daughter, gentle and meek. You'll forgive me for saying so, Rose, but you favor your father."

Rose said nothing. There was no point in arguing when 'twas so painfully true.

"None of us will e'er ken the truth of what happened that Hogmanay night. But I was at the wedding, and so was most of Newabbey. And we saw a blithe bride and a handsome groom look verra pleased to be in each other's company, straight through 'til the first foot crossed the door at midnight."

Rose stared at the table as tea was placed before her. Although her mouth was dry as toast, she had no strength to reach for the cup.

"While I'm telling you the truth, Rose, I'll tell you the rest of it." Jessie poured a saucer of tea for herself and milk for Annie, whose blue eyes were fixed on a plate of oatcakes. "I'm not the only one at the bridal who encouraged Leana to claim Jamie for herself. And I'm not sorry I did so. I'm just sorry you've undone my good efforts."

Rose stood, too upset to listen further. "I've told you, Jessie. None of this is my fault. The session clerk was meant to change the bride's name in the records, and he didn't."

"Such as that may be, lass. But the story going round names you as the one who pointed the cutty stool in Leana's direction." Jessie blew across her saucer of tea to cool it. "You'll want to remember that come the Sabbath, when Leana mounts the stool and every eye in the kirk is on you."

Forty-Six

O, white innocence,
That thou shouldst wear the mask of guilt to hide
Thine awful and serenest countenance
From those who know thee not!
PERCY BYSSHE SHELLEY

Leana bowed her head and slipped the *harn goun* over her tightly braided hair. Her hands did not tremble, nor did her knees give way. *For I am now ready to be offered.* The Sabbath had come at last and with it an end to the agony of waiting.

Ian lay in the crib at her feet, sound asleep after his early breakfast. The room was lit by a single candle and the pale gray light of morning. A silvery mist illuminated the small window, and beyond it, birdsong filled the air. Leana had no need for more light or for a mirror; her gown was not meant to make her look appealing. She arranged the loose folds about her waist and shook out the sleeves, absent of cuff or button. Plain and white, it was meant not to adorn, but to disgrace.

For three days counting she'd run her needle through the bleached linen, fashioning her robe of shame. *I have sewed sackcloth upon my skin.* The shapeless gown felt rough against her neck, chafing the sensitive flesh along her collarbone. Such coarse fabric was meant for a servant's bedding, not for wearing on Sunday or any other day. But wear it she would, and bear it she must.

Jamie was innocent, yet he too would be forced to pay a terrible price. Ian, more innocent still, would grow up ashamed of his own mother. *And raised by another.*

"Nae!" Leana moaned, her courage gone. She leaned over the crib, taking the sleeping babe into her arms. *Forgive me, dear one!* He molded himself to her, burrowing his head beneath her chin. *Ian, sweet Ian.* She tried to sing to him but could not. She tried to speak, but no words came. Instead, she bent her head and soaked his cotton gown with her tears.

Minutes passed before she heard a soft tapping at the nursery door. "Leana?"

Jamie pushed the door open, not waiting for a response. Had he heard her weeping? His eyes, rimmed in red as though he'd suffered a sleepless night, widened in dismay at the sight of her sackcloth gown. "Och, poor lass! Must you wear that wretched thing now? Can it not wait 'til we reach the kirk?"

" 'Tis best I dress here, for I dare not approach the kirk without it."

"Aye," he said, the weight of his sigh heavy in the morning stillness. "You'll not face this alone, Leana. When do we leave for Newabbey?"

Oh, Jamie. Did he not understand? "You cannot go with me, love. 'Twould ne'er be permitted."

"I'll disappear into the pine woods when we reach the bridge," he insisted, his voice brimming with conviction. "No one will be the wiser."

"And what of my father? And Rose? And the neighbors we might pass along the way? What would they think if they saw us together, today of all days?" She stretched out her hand to cup Jamie's rough cheek. "Nae, Jamie. I must walk to the kirk alone. 'Tis right that I do so."

"None of this is right." He pressed her hand against his face, then kissed her palm. "I wish I could do this for you. Stand there on your behalf."

" 'Tis my sin that must be atoned for, not yours," she gently reminded him. " 'Twould be worse for me to watch you mount the repentance stool."

His eyes, unblinking, shone with pain. "Instead I must watch you."

Dear Jamie. She stepped into his embrace, their child cradled between them. They stood just so for many minutes, shutting out the world and all its sorrows.

When Jamie spoke at last, he stepped back only enough to see her face. "We will follow not far behind you. Duncan and Neda and me."

"And Rose?"

His jaw tightened. "I care not how or when she arrives at the kirk."

Rose. Her sister had barely spoken to her all week, yet she'd studied

Ian with eager curiosity. 'Twas unthinkable, Rose caring for her son, though Leana knew her sister loved him. Leana told herself it was Jamie who would raise him, Jamie who would see to his son's welfare. Beginning this morning. Beginning now.

Leana looked down at their son. "You will…care for Ian?"

"You ken that I will, lass."

She eased the slumbering child into Jamie's arms, kissing his downy head as she did, then stepped back and smoothed the wrinkles from her sackcloth gown. Her hands were shaking again. "Jamie, I must leave at once, or I fear I'll not have the strength to leave at all."

He did not speak, only planted a fervent kiss on her forehead, then drew Ian tighter against his chest so Leana could slip past them. She could not tarry. She could not look back. Easing down the stair with careful steps, she prayed no one would see her slipping out the door at that early hour. She would face them all soon enough. Though she heard voices in the kitchen, not a soul was in the hall when she opened the heavy door and walked out into the Sabbath morning.

A thick mist enveloped her, curling her hair in wisps about her face. How strange it felt to wear no bonnet and stranger still, no shoes. The ground was cold beneath her feet and the grass wet. By the time she passed the orchard, the hem of her harn goun was drenched. Yet when she took to the gravel path, its sharp stones pierced her skin and slowed her steps. No matter the pain, she must arrive by the first bell. *Must, must.*

When she reached the road that led to Newabbey, Leana looked neither left nor right but fixed her gaze on the hard-packed dirt and started toward the village, avoiding the rocks strewn across her path. Even the rounded ones, polished by water and wear, bruised the tender soles of her feet. Unlike shepherds and farm laborers, who went barefoot year round, Leana seldom ventured out of doors without shoes or boots. Cringing with each step, she forced one foot in front of the other, pleading for the strength to go on. *I am thine. Save me.*

The rolling landscape remained shrouded in fog, rendering boulders and trees into gray, shapeless mounds. Gone were familiar landmarks to guide her steps or mark her progress. Criffell? The snuff mill? Nowhere in sight. Marriage? Motherhood? Nae longer in view. Naught stretched before her but a bleak and colorless future. Three Sabbaths on the repentance stool, then nothing.

Nae, Leana. 'Twas not true. On the very Sabbath that Ian was born, she'd discovered a truth, oft neglected in the happy days that followed: God's love was enough. His faithfulness was sufficient. *I will never leave you.* Aye, the Almighty had said that to Jamie in a dream. And she sensed him repeating it now, a silent whisper in the recesses of her heart. *I will never leave you.*

"Please don't," she said softly.

Leana had just crossed the village bridge when a voice called out from the mist.

"If it isna Miss McBride, come tae warm the cutty stool."

The miller. She spun toward the sound, wincing as a stone gouged her foot. "Sir?"

Brodie Selkirk swaggered toward her, his arms folded across his chest. "I niver thocht tae see the day! Lachlan's guid dochter brought doon tae shame." His narrow eyes were filled with reproach. "Make haste, for the kirk bell's about tae clang, and the line o' folk gatherin' tae *walcome* ye grows lang."

Leana shuddered, picturing the scene that awaited her. The neighborhood gossips, like osprey with freshly caught fish in their talons, would feast upon her disgrace. She bowed her bare head toward Mr. Selkirk and pressed on, grimacing with each painful step. When the kirk came into view, her heart sank. The miller had not exaggerated. Three dozen or more villagers were crowded round the kirk door, Reverend Gordon among them.

"Come, Miss McBride," he called out, waving her forward. "'Tis time."

She did not meet their curious stares, yet could not avoid hearing their remarks as she walked past. "A braisant lass." "Och! Sae michtie, that Leana." "Ill-deedie, like her faither." "And she, the *halie* one!"

Not all spoke unkindly nor looked at her askance. Maggie Hamilton nodded as she passed. So did Jock Bell's wife, dipping her black bonnet in sympathy. "Puir lass," Leana heard another say. "'Tis her sister wha's tae blame."

Nae. Rose was the innocent one. Even their father had said so.

Above her the kirk bell rang the first of three times that morning. "You will stand here, Leana." Reverend Gordon stepped aside, revealing a flat, raised stone by the doorway.

She'd paid little attention to the spot before, even less to the jougs protruding from the wall. Now Leana stared at the iron collar, horrified. "Am I to…that is…"

"Nae, Leana. We've no need to clap the jougs round your neck. Stand here, please." The minister guided her into place. "A question from the Buik now." Though his voice was gruff, his wrinkled face reflected a compassion he seldom revealed. "Can thine heart endure?"

"Aye," she whispered, answering him in kind. "What time I am afraid, I will trust in thee."

"Well said, Miss McBride." He stepped back to give her room, motioning for the others to do the same. "You must remain here 'til the third bell and face your neighbors. Though you've damaged their trust, you've not hurt their property. There's no call for them to strike you." He glared at the assembly. "If any do, they'll explain themselves to the session."

His warning delivered, Reverend Gordon marched into the kirk, leaving her to weather whate'er might come. Leana took a deep breath, straightening her shoulders, and prepared herself for the scorn and ridicule sure to follow.

She did not have long to wait.

Thomas Clacharty spat at her, marking her harn goun with a dark circle of saliva.

Nicholas Boyle gave her a wide berth as he stepped through the doorway into the kirk, muttering insults as he passed.

David McMiken shook the Buik in her direction as he stamped by, refusing to look at her.

Mary McCheyne pulled her children behind her skirts, then thrust words at Leana's heart, as sharp as any sword. "Ye're a filthy limmer!" she hissed. "A hizzie o' the worst sort, stealin' yer sister's husband."

Lydia Taggart brandished verses instead: "The works of the flesh are manifest, which are these: adultery, fornication, uncleanness, lasciviousness." Lydia seemed to delight in pronouncing each sin, her green eyes blazing.

Leana denied none of her accusations, letting the truth of them cleanse her. *Wash me thoroughly from mine iniquity.*

Others hurried past without acknowledging her at all, as though ashamed on her behalf. Many looked but did not comment. Leana forced herself to gaze at each one of them, letting them see the truth that burned inside her. Aye, she was a sinner. But her confession had set her free. Though her neighbors might sully her gown, they could not besmirch her soul, for it was washed clean, white as snow, pure as lamb's wool. She was not innocent, but she was forgiven.

A chaise pulled to a stop not far from the door. *Rose. And Father.* Leana did not know where to look or what to say as they approached her. If only she might run and hide among the abbey ruins! Her father did not look at her as he swept past, though his expression said enough: He was ashamed to claim her as his daughter. Rose hung behind, clearly wanting to speak, but the words would not come. At last she, too, disappeared into the kirk.

Reeling from their silent rebuke, Leana pressed a hand to her stomach, fearing she might be ill, though she'd eaten nothing for a day or more. When she looked up moments later she noticed a small circle of parishioners inching toward her, as if they'd waited for the crowd to dwindle.

From among them stepped Alexander Lindsay, an auld man bent with years. "Yer mither would be proud, seein' ye tak what others gie ye wi'oot turnin' awa."

Mother. Leana swallowed hard, picturing Agness McBride standing before her now. Would her mother truly be proud? "Thank you," she murmured as Mr. Lindsay tottered into the kirk.

Isabella Callender grasped Leana's hand, squeezing it. "Ye're a fine girl with a guid heart. Whate'er betides ye, may this day be the worst."

"Aye," Leana agreed, as tears began to well in her eyes. One by one, Janet Sloan, then Maggie Hamilton, then James Glover offered her words of comfort. It wasn't until after Peter Drummond passed by that

Leana noticed the red-haired lass standing a few paces away, her arms outstretched.

"Jessie!" Leana cried. The two fell together in a fierce embrace. "Dear friend, I am so grateful you came."

"And where else would I be on the Sabbath?" Jessie Newall teased her, stepping back to dab at her eyes. After they spoke for a moment, Jessie said, "You've others waiting their turn." She motioned toward the arched gateway to the kirkyard, where a knot of people stood in silent support. Jamie, holding Ian. Neda. Duncan. Eliza. Annabel. "Many folk love you, Leana. Remember that as you mount the stool. You are not alone."

"Nae, I am not." She took a deep breath for the first time that morning and gazed toward the gateway, blinking away tears. "The LORD is the strength of my life." *And you, Jamie, are the only man I will ever love.*

Forty-Seven

For my heart
Is true as steel.
WILLIAM SHAKESPEARE

He loved her. Could he tell her so, standing in that terrible place of judgment? He could and he would, for she deserved to hear it. And he needed to say the words aloud, even knowing 'twould not ease the guilt that twisted his gut.

"Jamie, ye maun go first." Duncan nudged him. " 'Tis yer comfort the lass needs most, not ours."

"Then she shall have it." Holding Ian against his chest, Jamie walked resolutely toward Leana. Her gaze had not left his from the moment she saw him. As the kirk bell rang a second time, muted by the misty air, the boy in his arms patted Jamie's cheeks—jubilant, it seemed, to have his father all to himself. "Da-da-da-da!"

"Aye, lad." He brushed a kiss across the child's hair, all the while looking at the woman he loved. "I am indeed your father. And there is your brave mother."

Leana stood alone now, for the second bell had summoned the parishioners to worship. Tuneless voices floated through the open kirk door. The precentor chanted each verse of the psalm, then the congregation sang it back to him, in *run-line* fashion. "O LORD my God, in thee do I put my trust." Jamie had never been so thankful for a lengthy gathering psalm as he was this day.

"Jamie." When Leana spoke his name, it sounded like music. "Bless you for being here," she whispered, ducking her head to hide her tears.

He did not lower his voice, as she had, but spoke boldly, drowning out the singing. "I love you, Leana. I will always love you."

When she looked up, her face infused with hope, Ian could wait no longer. He dove for his mother, landing in her arms.

"Och, lad!" She held him close, covering his face with kisses. "You know not where we are."

"Ian does not care where you're standing." Jamie brushed back the damp tendrils from her face. "Nor do I."

Leana's response was a balm to his soul. "Whate'er would I do without my two braw lads?"

He tucked a loose strand of hair behind her ear, even as he reached for a phrase that might encourage her. "Please God, that time will ne'er come."

"But will you not leave for Glentrool after the lambing?" Leana draped Ian over her shoulder, as if to shield him from the awful truth. "With your...with...Rose?"

Jamie did not hesitate to answer, for he'd given the situation a great deal of thought. "Nae," he answered. "We will not move to Glentrool. Not unless you come with us."

Her pale eyes widened. "Jamie, I could never do such a thing!"

"Then we'll remain at Auchengray." For her sake, he would do anything. Give up his claim to Glentrool. Live under Lachlan McBride's roof. Anything. "I will not see my son separated from his mother. Nor will I leave the woman I love in the hands of so hatesome a father."

"But Rose..." The clang of the bell cut her short with a gasp. "Jamie, you must go inside at once! Quickly, before the beadle comes for me."

He did not argue but disengaged Ian from his mother's arms, despite the lad's protests, and ducked inside the kirk as the bell rang above. Jamie felt like a coward, abandoning her at the kirk door. Yet it had to be done, or she might be assigned another Sabbath on the stool for speaking to him after the start of services. A dozen curious gazes followed him as he made his way forward with Duncan and the others close on his heels. Jamie prayed the servants had said a brief word to Leana as well, for she would need their warm sentiments to carry her through this most difficult morning.

Nae, not difficult. Impossible. Unimaginable.

Reverend Gordon reached the pulpit as the bell grew silent. He bowed to the Stewarts seated in the laird's loft, who rose in turn to bow, as was customary for the heritors of the parish. The minister then signaled to the precentor to cease his singing by leaning forward and tapping the man on the head with his psalm book. Jamie, meanwhile, slipped into his uncle's narrow pew, sitting as far away from Rose and her father as he could without inviting their censure. The congregants had enough gossip on their palates without adding another savory tidbit.

"Before our first prayer of the morning, I would call forth Mr. Millar for the crying of the banns."

Jamie's heart stopped cold. Consumed with Leana's ordeal, he had forgotten the other matter on the kirk session's docket: the banns. *Mine. And Rose's.* 'Twas ill luck to be present for the reading of one's own banns. Jamie did not care. Neither, it seemed, did Rose, who leaned forward as though to hear better, no doubt relishing the moment. He turned to see if Leana had already been ushered through the door. *Bethankit!* She had not. The morning carried enough heartache for her without adding this one.

Mr. Millar, the session clerk, rose from his pew near the pulpit, then faced the parishioners, who held their breaths in avid expectation. "I hereby proclaim the names of those seeking to have their marriage recognized in Newabbey parish. James McKie of Auchengray will publicly acknowledge Rose McBride McKie as his lawful wife on 27 March. Are there any present who claim some impediment to this union, which stands in the kirk session records as of 31 December 1788?"

The crowd gasped as one.

Jamie stared down at the floor to keep from losing his breakfast. Few present were hearing this news for the first time; little else had been discussed in the parish since Monday. But to hear it spoken by the clerk during services gave the sordid story the ring of authority. When he looked up, prepared to confront his neighbors, Jamie discovered they were staring not at him, but at Rose.

She was smiling, a hopeful expression on her face, as though seeking their approval. Not many smiled back. Some appeared cross and others appalled. Might the parish's sympathies lie with Leana rather than Rose? He would find out soon enough. Only the first prayer of the morning stood between Leana and the dreaded stool.

Reverend Gordon lifted his hands, and the congregation rose to their feet, the men pulling off their hats as they stood. Jamie left his tricorne on the pew so he might have both hands free to attend to Ian, who often fussed when it was least appropriate. As the prayer began, Rose edged closer to him, her gaze directed toward the lad, as if offering to help. Jamie shook his head ever so slightly, not wanting to draw anyone's attention, yet determined to stop Rose from reaching for his son. As if she had the right. As if he would ever let so selfish a creature as Rose care for Leana's child.

A handful of words—*More than surprised, sir. I was shocked.*—and Rose had ruined his life. More so, Leana's. How could he hope to love a woman he could not forgive?

The answer came too quickly. *For if ye forgive men their trespasses, your heavenly Father will also forgive you.* But this was more than a trespass; it was a travesty.

Jamie was relieved when the minister's prayer, usually long winded, was blessedly short, since every minute Leana spent waiting out of doors would no doubt be torturous for her. At Reverend Gordon's thunderous "So be it," Jamie sat with the congregation, yet turned at an angle so he might watch her enter.

"And now, if Mr. Hunter would bring forth Leana McBride to compear before this congregation on the repentance stool. For as the Buik commands us, 'Them that sin rebuke before all, that others also may fear.'"

Jamie's heart was in his throat as the beadle shuffled toward the door while the worshipers seated round him blethered none too quietly. "I heard she swicked him at his ain wedding!" "Aye, and *clecked* her babe that verra nicht!" There was no point glaring at them; 'twould only make things worse for Leana.

William Hunter, an older man with a sideways gait and more gums than teeth, served as beadle to the kirk, performing whatever menial tasks the elders required. This morning 'twas his duty to bring forth the penitent for all to see and for many to mock. The beadle escorted her to the center of the kirk as the talk in the pews rose to an ugly pitch.

Leana approached the repentance stool, conspicuously placed in front of the pulpit. The wooden stool had not been occupied for many months, the kirk session handling minor offenses without the need for public rebuke. But marriage vows were not lightly put aside, not in any parish. There were two rectangular seats on the six-legged stool—one lower, one much higher. Small offenses warranted the lower seat. Leana would climb onto the higher one, where all might see her without straining their necks.

Jamie held his breath as she stepped onto the lower stool, for 'twas not a graceful thing to mount and likely to tip over unless she had a steady hand to help her and a ferlie sense of balance. It seemed she had both. In a moment Leana was seated more than one Scots *ell* above the flagstone floor, her sackcloth modestly tucked about her. She tipped her head toward Reverend Gordon in obeisance, then sat with her hands folded before her, as befitted a gentlewoman. *God is in the midst of her; she shall not be moved.*

At the sight of his mother, Ian squirmed in Jamie's arms. "Easy now, lad," Jamie said softly, pulling the child close. "See how still your mother sits? We must do the same." The congregation seemed to sense her mood as well, for they soon fell silent.

The beadle turned the sandglass, marking the start of the minister's sermon. Leana would be forced to sit through the hour-long discourse, awaiting the rebuke to come at the close of the service. Sermons were to be delivered without notes, yet Reverend Gordon glanced at his papers more than once, his sonorous voice pounding away at his parishioners like a velvet hammer. Jamie paid him little mind. Instead his gaze focused on Leana, who did not flinch at the minister's verbal blows, nor did she blush when the message appeared to be directed toward her. That would come soon enough.

The sand in the glass seemed to stop as the hour dragged on. Stomachs growled and children grew fidgety. When Ian drifted off to sleep, Jamie passed the child to Neda, then resumed his vigil. Watching his wife. Loving her from a distance. Suffering with her. Wishing he might take her place.

At last the upper half of the sandglass stood empty, and the minister brought his sermon to an end. "And now 'tis my responsibility to call your attention to Leana McBride, who sits before you."

Jamie grimaced. Not a soul present had paid attention to anything else.

"Miss McBride begins her course of repentance this Sabbath day and will compear before this assembly again on the fourteenth and twenty-first of March. As she is charged with hochmagandy, so shall this morning's rebuke address her heinous sin, duly described in the book of Proverbs."

Jamie cringed as the first line was delivered.

" 'Such is the way of an adulterous woman; she eateth, and wipeth her mouth, and saith, I have done no wickedness.' Yet is that not what we have seated before us? A wicked temptress, who has supped at our tables and wiped her mouth on our linens and walked among us as a *gracie* woman? And all the while she was engaging in deceit, pretending to be a wife when she was in fact a harlot."

Nae!

The congregation fell back against their pews. Jamie's skin grew hot. How dare the minister demean Leana so! Aye, the word appeared in the Buik, but 'twas rare to hear it used so harshly from the pulpit. No doubt the reverend was determined to make an example of Leana. But had the man no mercy?

"And what is it that disquiets the earth?" the reverend continued, not waiting for a response. "The Buik tells us 'tis 'an odious woman when she is married.' And I tell you, *this* odious woman is far from married, though she fooled us all, including her sister's husband."

Nae! Jamie ground his teeth, wanting to argue, wanting to shout back at the man. *She did not fool me. She loved me.*

"A virtuous woman," the minister intoned, "is a crown to her husband: but she that maketh ashamed is as rottenness in his bones." Reverend Gordon swung about to face him. Though the man did not point an accusing finger, Jamie nonetheless felt it poking into his chest. "I see no crown upon your head, Mr. McKie. You are no prince of Scotland, nor is your son heir to a throne. For Ian was conceived in sin and born of a harlot—"

"That's enough!" Jamie bolted to his feet. "I'll not hear my son's name sullied, for he is innocent." *And so is his mother.*

"We are none of us innocent, Mr. McKie. 'For all have sinned, and come short of the glory of God.' Your own bones are rotten, sir, spared only by the mercy of Almighty God and this kirk session." He leaned forward, his thick eyebrows drawn into a terrible knot. "Are you not grateful, sir? At month's end will you not claim your proper wife, the chaste and fair Rose McKie?"

Jamie gripped the back of the wooden pew before him, shaking with anger and frustration, biting back the words he longed to say. *I am not grateful. I do not wish to claim her.*

"Speak, man! For it is clear something gnaws at you." He gestured toward Leana, who sat in silence, her face as white as her gown. "Is it this woman's swickerie? Is that what you wish to decry? Would you rebuke Leana now, as is proper?"

Jamie looked up, higher than the minister's lofty pulpit. *Gird me with strength unto the battle.* He matched his voice to the reverend's, that all might hear. "I will not rebuke her."

"Then you do not love her," the minister declared, "for the Buik says, 'As many as I love, I rebuke and chasten.' "

"*Nae!*" Jamie shouted, pointing at the cutty stool. "*That*, sir, is not love." He vaulted over the empty pew in front of him and advanced toward the pulpit as though a mighty army followed in his wake. "Tell me, Reverend. Is this how you love your flock? By degrading them? Humiliating them?"

The minister held up his hands like a shield. "That is far enough, Mr. McKie."

Jamie stopped at the foot of the stool and reached up to clasp Leana's hand. "Rebuke her sin if you must, but do not debase the woman I love. For I do love her. Let there be nae misunderstanding on that point. Read all the marriage banns you wish. 'Tis Leana McBride whom I love and nae other."

Forty-Eight

Sooner or later the most rebellious
must bow beneath the same yoke.
MADAME DE STAEL

Rose slumped back against the pew. *Oh, Jamie.* He would never say so scandalous a thing standing before the pulpit unless 'twere true.

No one marked her suffering, so absorbed were they with the drama at hand, not even bothering to lower their voices as they commented to one another. Reverend Gordon stretched out his hands and bade the congregation be quiet. Though his features remained stern, his voice no longer thundered. "In this one instance, Mr. McKie, I will overlook your zealous behavior. No matter the extent of your regard for Leana McBride, your cousin's sin demands a sound rebuke. It is the duty of this parish to hold her accountable."

Jamie's words carried above the din. "And it is my duty to love her, sir."

And nae other. Not even me. Rose cringed, watching the two of them gaze at each other as if no one else were in the sanctuary. Jamie was *hers,* was he not? Even the kirk said so. But his eyes did not say so. Nor his words. Nor his hand, gripping her sister's.

"Reclaim your pew now, Mr. McKie. 'Tis time Miss McBride made her confession, with proper humility, upon her knees."

Rose straightened with a jolt, until she remembered it was *Leana* who was Miss McBride now, not her. *Thanks be to God.* She could hardly do what Leana was about to do.

Her sister eased down from the high stool, then turned and knelt on the lower one, bowing her head for so long that the congregation fell silent. Rose craned her neck to see. Was Leana weeping? Praying? Begging for mercy?

At last Leana lifted her head and addressed Reverend Gordon in a clear, unwavering voice. "I am guilty of the sin you have named. Though 'twas not my intent to break the seventh commandment, 'twas indeed the result." With each phrase, her face grew more radiant, as though a cloud had moved aside to reveal the sun. "I blame no one but myself. All are innocent except me."

Oh, my sister. How could she be so brave?

When Leana looked at her, Rose turned away, chastened. 'Twas innocence she saw in her sister's eyes. And guilt she felt in her own heart. Had her sister wronged her? Or had she wronged her sister? Envy and mercy fought for the upper hand until Reverend Gordon's strong words demanded an answer.

"Are you truly sorry, Miss McBride?"

The question pierced her through like the sharpest of knives. *Are you sorry, Rose?* In the privacy of her pew she bowed her head. "Aye," Rose whispered. "And nae," for that was the truth as well. *Forgive me.*

Leana's response floated across the hushed assembly. "I am more sorry than I could possibly say. I have hurt my family and sinned against the Almighty."

"And do you repent? That is, before so great a cloud of witnesses, do you pledge to sin no more?"

"Before God and this assembly, I repent with all my heart." Leana rose from her knees but only for a moment. Turning toward the congregation, she lowered herself onto the stone floor. Her knees touched, then her shoulders, until she lay prostrate before them, her cheek pressed against the cold flagstone, her arms outstretched. Below the blond coil of her braids, her stiff linen gown fanned about her like wings.

Her voice was soft, yet certain; strained, but not broken. "For the LORD is good; his mercy is everlasting; and his truth endureth to all generations."

Silence reigned from floor to loft. Women pressed their fingers to their lips. Men slipped off their hats. Even the bairns sat still, eyes wide with awe.

Rose was in agony. Leana's sins were confessed and forgiven; hers were neither. Her sister was washed clean, while she sat in the filth of her selfish desires, afraid to pray, wishing the flagstone floor beneath her pew would yawn and swallow her whole. Reverend Gordon's prayer, then a psalm, then his benediction were yet to follow. The kirk door, locked at the start of the sermon, would not be unlocked until the minister's final "So be it." Could she wait that long? Could she endure it?

As the assembly sang from the book of *Paraphrases,* Rose could barely make out the words swimming before her on the page.

> Lord, we confess our num'rous Faults,
>   how great our Guilt has been!
> Foolish and vain were all our Thoughts
>   and all our Lives were Sin.

'Twas true, every word of it. *Faults. Guilt. Foolish. Sin.* She had sung the words before. Why had they never affected her so?

Rose fled from the kirk the moment the beadle fitted the key into the lock, almost knocking him down in her haste to escape. She would walk home. Nae, she would *run.*

Out of breath by the time she reached the mill, Rose slowed her steps across the bridge, brushing hot tears from her cheeks. No one had spoken a word to her all morning. Not one. Reverend Gordon had called her "fair," yet 'twas her fair-haired sister who'd won their sympathy, just as Jessie Newall had warned her might happen.

Several neighbors passed by on foot or on horseback, traveling home for a brief Sabbath meal before returning to the kirk for the second service. They were polite but not friendly, tipping their hats rather than speaking to her. Discouraged by their cold greetings, Rose plunged into the piney forest near Barlae. Undoing her sash, she kilted her full skirts out of harm's way and ventured deeper into the woods, plunging her shoes into the thick carpet of dry, brown needles and leafy bracken. Without the sun's warmth, the air grew cool. She would follow the burn, circle round behind their neighbor's property, and approach Auchengray from the hill. Let the rest of the household remain for another sermon; her heart could bear no more.

The pines began to thin as she skirted along the base of Barlae Hill, careful to keep her shoes and skirt hem from dipping into the burn that pointed toward home. Far on the other side of the hill another stream ran parallel with this one. How long had it been since she'd risked life and limb to pick hazelnuts there?

" 'Tis four months and counting since ye visited March Burn."

Startled out of her wits, Rose spun round. "Lillias," she breathed, seeing the wutch emerge from a copse of wild crab apple trees. "Whatever are you doing abroad on the Sabbath?"

The wise woman laughed, tossing back her head, putting her mouthful of crooked teeth on display. " 'Tis me favorite day tae roam the land. A' the halie fowk are in the kirk, and I've the parish tae meself." She peered at the ribbon round Rose's neck. "I see ye're wearin' the necklace I gie ye."

Rose touched the stone, well hidden beneath her bodice. She was ashamed to wear it, yet desperate for a babe the moment Jamie was truly her husband.

"Have ye worn it every day syne ye came tae Nethermuir?"

"Aye," Rose lied, forcing herself not to look away. "Dr. Gilchrist told me—"

"Bah!" The old woman swatted at the air. "Me magic is stronger than his."

"Your spells are powerful, Lillias," Rose agreed. Though the woman made her ill at ease, the wutch's skills were undeniable. Jamie was almost hers, wasn't he? "If there is something else I might do…"

Lillias Brown rubbed her wizened mouth, drawn tight as a leather pouch. "There be mony things," she said at last. " 'Tis cleckin' a bairn on yer *waddin* nicht ye're wantin', aye? The moon will be nigh tae fu', though not quite. Ye had a fu' moon the nicht of yer meetin' at the manse, and ye see how weel that turned oot."

Rose could barely swallow, so dry was her mouth. How did Lillias know these things? "On my…my wedding night," she stammered. "What must I do to be sure…that is, to…"

"Have ye a green goun tae wear for yer vows?"

Rose nodded, relieved. Her prettiest dress and a favorite of Jamie's.

"See yer cook serves ye hare soup the nicht ye join wi' yer husband."

Hare soup? Rose wrinkled her nose. "Neda can certainly prepare it, but—"

"Guid. Ye'll remember I draped ivy round yer neck. Cut some fresh vines that morn and style them in a bowl nigh yer bed."

Aye, she could do that, for ivy grew along their hedgerow.

"'Tis the wrong season for findin' cones and nuts, though if ye've almonds in yer cellar, add them to yer mornin' parritch." Lillias tipped her head, regarding her. "'Tis a shame 'twill not be a guid time o' the month for ye."

"Nae," Rose sighed. She knew very little of such things, though now her fears were confirmed. "Is there naught can be done?"

"Oo aye, lassie." She chuckled, clearing a grassy spot. "There's meikle can be done. Sit doon, if ye will, wi' yer face tae the village."

Rose hesitated but not for long. If the auld wutch could help her, would that be so terrible? She did a half-turn, then eased down onto the ground, her arms covered with dappled sunlight. "Why toward the village?"

"Newabbey sits tae the east." Lillias knelt behind her, placing her hands on her shoulders. "We'll draw the power from the sun tae warm yer wame. And gather the strength o' the earth tae make ye fertile as the soil in spring. Bide a wee while and dinna speak."

Rose closed her eyes, aware only of the cool grass beneath her and the gentle weight of Lillias' sun-browned hands on her shoulders. How much more pleasant this was than sitting in the kirk and feeling guilty! Birdsong filled the air, and a light breeze lifted the tiny hairs that framed her face. Rose smiled, relaxing her spine, succumbing to the pleasant sensation of sinking into the ground like a plant sending forth roots.

Naught was said. Naught was done. Minutes were left uncounted.

When she felt compelled to open her eyes, Rose found her shoulders no longer bore the wutch's hands. "Lillias?" she whispered, looking to either side.

A chuckle came from behind her. "I'd niver leave ye in sic a state. D'ye feel stronger, lassie?"

"Aye." Rose said, amazed to discover it was true. She scrambled to her feet without assistance and brushed the woodland debris from her skirts, invigorated, as if she'd taken a brisk walk in fine weather. "I've not felt this healthy since—"

"Since afore ye had croup." Lillias frowned, digging in her pocket. "If yer friend had breathed the feverfew, she might be wi' us still."

Rose sensed the hairs on her neck rising. "You mean Jane Grierson?"

Lillias shrugged. "I couldna deliver a sack o' herbs tae Dunscore." Her gaze met Rose's. "But I ken ye found yers on yer doorstep."

"Reverend Gordon was the one who found it."

Lillias shuddered visibly. "But he didna touch it?"

"Nae."

"Guid, for his power is borrowed and not from the truest source."

Rose stepped back, her uneasiness returning, knowing what Reverend Gordon would say. *Woe unto them that call evil good, and good evil.* "I...I must go, Lillias. I'm...expected. At home."

"Ye'll not leave afore I gie ye a praisent." Lillias produced a thick green cord tied with knots. " 'Twill make ye mair than fertile, Mistress McKie. 'Tis the most powerful spell o' the lot."

Rose stared at it, her eyes widening. "My...my father has such a cord."

"Aye." The gray head bobbed up and down. "Mr. McBride has it hidin' in his thrifite, does he not?"

"He does." Rose swallowed the sickening taste that rose in her throat. "Leana described it to me. Except for the color, I believe 'tis like that one."

"I made them both." Lillias fingered the cord with obvious pride. " 'Tis a seven-knot charm, each knot tied as the power rose inside me, then I waved the cord through smoke doused wi' herbs. Yers is green tae make ye fertile." She held the cord out to Rose once more, bidding her take it. "Yer faither's is *goud* tae grow his riches."

"When..." Rose eyed the green cord, not touching it. "When did my father...come to you?"

"I came tae him, same as I did tae ye in the hazel grove. Headin' hame from a meetin', he was. Walkin' up the road from Newabbey, bauld as ye please." The wutch twirled the green cord round, as if 'twere a snake and she its handler. "We chatted a bit, yer faither and I. Same as ye and I did, Rose. Then he knocked on me door at Nethermuir just afore yer cousin came tae stay. And took hame seven knots." Her laugh made Rose cringe. "This verra cord will be yer salvation."

I am thy salvation.

"My…salvation?" Rose echoed, confused. 'Twas as if two voices spoke inside her at once. One low and sure. The other louder but less certain.

"'Twill save ye from barrenness and bring ye twa bairns."

"Two?" Her breath caught. "Are you certain?"

The woman's smile was neither kind nor comforting. "Will ye tak the cord or not?"

"N-not!" Rose exclaimed, the word sharpened by fear. Whatever was she doing, conversing with such a woman? Lillias Brown knew things mere mortals were not privy to. Even Jane—*oh, my poor, lost friend!*—had called Lillias "the devil's midwife." *You were right, Jane.*

"I am not o' the de'il," Lillias said, gathering her skirts about her. "Nor am I o' yer Lord."

Rose stared at her in horror. "What are you then?"

"I'm yer friend, Rose McKie. And Jamie is yer husband now, aye? Just as I promised ye?" Her smile was a hideous thing. "Do as I've told ye, and a bairn will be yers as weel."

"Nae." Rose backed away from her, glancing at the path she'd taken through the pine forest behind her. "I have a son already. Ian will be my stepson."

"Och!" Lillias shook the cord at her. "D'ye think anither woman's bairn will bind Jamie tae yer side? Nae, lassie. Ye must have twa sons— mair than yer sister—tae win Jamie's heart. 'Tis the only way, Rose. Ye ken I speak the truth."

His truth endureth. Leana's words that morning taken from the Buik.

"Nae," Rose said with conviction. "You speak nae truth at all, Lillias." She yanked the ribbon from her neck and threw the stone neck-lace at the wutch's feet. "Keep away from me. And from my family."

Rose did not wait for a reply but turned and ran like the wind through the trees, her heart pounding. *Depart from evil.* 'Twas all she could think of, crashing past the pine branches that tore at the pins in her hair, leaping over fallen limbs with her skirts held high. *Keep thee from every wicked thing.* Lillias Brown was wickedness itself. And to think, she had trusted her! *Forgive me, Lord. Forgive me.*

When she burst into the sunlight at the edge of the forest, Rose stopped only long enough to catch her breath and wipe away the last of her tears, grateful to be free from the woman's grasp and back on the road toward home.

Forty-Nine

A baby was sleeping,
Its mother was weeping.
SAMUEL LOVER

H ush-a-ba, birdie, and hush-a-ba, lamb," Leana sang softly, skimming her fingers through Ian's silky hair as he dozed in her arms.
Neda had spread a thick tartan in front of the hearth in Jamie's bedroom, where mother and child could nurse and then nap in private,
while the rest of the household went about their Wednesday afternoon
tasks. As for Jamie, he was spending the day in the far pastures with
Duncan, seeing after the ewes.

"In two weeks, your father tells me, he'll have his first lambs." Leana
smiled to herself, lowering Ian to the blanket with great care. "But I
already have mine." She covered him with a cotton blanket and wrapped
him in a lullaby. "And hush-a-ba, birdie, my bonny wee lamb."

The child was growing before her eyes. He could reach for things
and grasp them tightly now. Not waving his arms about but aiming his
hand straight toward a carved block or his doeskin ball with a determined look on his face quite like his father's. She wore a string of colorful wooden beads about her neck whenever she held him in her lap
for long periods. He played with the beads, utterly fascinated, while she
chatted with a visitor or listened to Jamie read aloud in the evenings.
Jessie Newall had taught her that. Jessie, the blithe mother of twa bairns.

And I am the mother of one. "But not for much longer, lad."

Leana drew the front laces of her gown together, tying them tight,
biting her lip as she did. *No tears, Leana.* Hadn't she wept enough? Her
eyes flooded nonetheless, spilling tears over their banks. By evening her
breasts would be full again, a tender ache which only a hungry babe
could relieve. How would she bear it when the dreaded day came?

When she handed Rose her son? When she watched a stranger nurse Ian? When she saw another woman tuck him into his crib at night?

"Haste thee to help me." She patted her cheeks dry, only to find them wet again moments later. Enduring the cutty stool was naught compared to this. Shame, reproach, rebuke—those burdens came and went in mere hours. She had poured them out before the Almighty, and he'd kindly borne the weight of them on her behalf. But this sacrifice was too great.

"Help me!" she whispered and buried her face in her hands.

A sharp knock announced Neda's appearance in the doorway. "Leana? Is something wrong?" The concern in Neda's eyes turned to sympathy. "Och, lass." She slipped into the room, latching the door. " 'Tis a heartless deed they've done, the kirk session. Not a mither among them, or they'd niver have thocht of sae *ill-kindit* a thing."

" 'Tis for Ian's sake." Leana tucked the blanket closer about his neck. "They say I'm not fit to be his mother."

"Wheesht!" Neda shook her apron as if their words were crumbs easily discarded. "Ye're a woman wha made ane mistake and that only by chasin' yer heart. Yer sin has been lang atoned for, and the whole parish kens it. Did ye not see them flockin' aboot ye after the first service?"

"Not everyone flocked," Leana reminded her. "Thomas Clacharty spat at me, and Mary McCheyne called me a 'filthy limmer.' "

Neda's eyes narrowed. "Let Mary McCheyne say that again Sabbath next, and she'll answer tae me. For I ken a thing or twa aboot her. News that wouldna sit weel wi' the kirk session."

"Now, Neda. There are secrets behind every neighbor's door."

"Aye, 'tis true enough." With a thoughtful nod, Neda was her jovial self again. "As it happens, I have mony a saicret hidin' behind the still-room door. See that ye dinna go pokin' aboot whaur ye're not walcome."

Leana smiled, this time with her whole face. "Can't we pretend I don't have a birthday in the morn? Twenty-two seems very old."

"Nae, *fifty*-two feels auld," Neda corrected her, tugging at the silver hairs woven among her coppery ones. "Ye've meikle years ahead o' ye. Guid years, I'll warrant." She turned toward the door, leaving a hopeful word in her wake. "God has not lifted his hand from yer life, Leana. Wait and see."

When Leana awakened on Thursday morning, she heard the sound of maids tittering on the other side of the nursery door. 'Twas simple to name them: Annabel's upbringing in Aberdeen transformed the girl's speech into a Scottish air, and Eliza chattered like a jackdaw when she was with the other maids, then pinched her beak shut round the laird of Auchengray. *Wise lass.*

Since Ian had already begun to stir, Leana could not resist tiptoeing to the door and sweeping it open. "Good morning!" she sang out.

The girls nearly tumbled into the room before they caught themselves, blushing and stammering as they curtsied. "Mornin', mem."

Leana tightened her wrapper, then stretched out her arms. "Do I look older?"

"Nae, mem," Eliza assured her, "but yer son grew another inch since yestreen."

Leana turned to find Ian sitting up, preparing to crow for his breakfast. "So he has." She scooped him out of his crib and waved the maidservants down the stair. "Back to work with you, for I've a starving child to feed."

Annabel's freckles made room for a toothy smile. "And whan will ye be joinin' the family at table?"

Leana told them to expect her at eight, then closed the door on their giggling and scheming. Och, to be fifteen years old again! Innocent as lambs, spared of life's heartaches. *Except Rose was not spared.* Leana was chagrined at the realization. Rose had been fifteen when her life had fallen apart. It was hard to be angry with Rose when Leana knew she'd wronged her so. Yet it was hard to be charitable when the price for her sister's happiness was so dear.

"You, lad. You are what Rose wants most: a babe of her own." Leana changed his soiled linens, then promptly put him to her breast. "And 'tis easy to see why, for you are a joy." She kissed the tip of her finger and touched his tiny nose. "Your father says he'll remain at Auchengray just so I can watch you grow." *Bless you, Jamie.* She could only hope and pray 'twould come to be; such choices in her life were made by others now.

"Come, let's think of something more cheerful for your mother's birthday. A cradle song I've not taught you yet, aye?" She leaned back in the chair, tucking a pillow beneath her arm to support them both. "O can ye sew cushions and can ye sew sheets? And can ye sing bal-la-loo when the bairnie greets?" She rubbed her thumb across the soles of his bare feet, treasuring the feel of them. "Lad, before this day is done, I'll no doubt sew, and you'll surely greet, and so our song will come true."

They spent a quiet hour together, then it was time to make use of her water pitcher. While she bathed, Ian sat near her feet, entertaining himself with horn spoons, which made a genial clatter when banged together. Eliza arrived at her door before eight to help her finish dressing and see to Ian's linens, then the servant guided mother and son down the stair at a spirited pace.

" 'Tis only breakfast," Leana teased her. "Will the porridge cool so soon?"

Her porridge cup was steaming, and her tea still hot, though what caught her eye first were the gaily wrapped presents sitting by her plate. Not one or two, as was customary, but a dozen or more spilling about her place at table.

Her father pointed his butter knife at them. "See to those first, for there won't be a bittie of work done in this house 'til you do."

Leana numbered more than half the household loitering about the dining room, holding a single plate or cup, trying to look useful. "Suppose I open these packages first," she said lightly. They surrounded her at once, elbowing one another and laughing behind their plates. "Who might this one be from?" Leana wondered.

"Willie! Willie!" Eliza waved him closer.

Two pale blue ribbons lay inside the plain paper. "Won't these look lovely?"

"They're meant tae match yer eyes," Willie confessed, his face reddening.

Each present was more thoughtful than the last. Sewing needles from Birmingham. Freshly dipped beeswax candles. Lavender water. French writing paper. Pressed flowers. Even her father had a gift waiting for her. Yet the servants, who earned no more than seven pounds a year, were the most charitable of all. "However can I begin to thank you?" she wondered aloud when all the gifts were opened and all the faces round the room were shining. "You are all too kind."

Neda, who had the look of an instigator, smiled broadly. "Will ane o' ye be guid enough tae bring yer mistress anither cup o' oats? Hers is lang gone cold." Eliza and Annabel both took off for the kitchen with the others trailing behind.

"Such a vulgar display of affection," her father grunted, plunging his spoon into his porridge. "Have these people forgotten their place?"

"Their place is near our hearts," Leana murmured, then held up his gift. "Thank you for the new pen, Father. 'Twill make my letters look more elegant, to be sure. And the French writing paper is lovely, Rose."

"Joyeux anniversaire," her sister said, a timid smile on her face. "You might want to look through it…later." She shifted her gaze, fidgeting with her napkin.

"I will, dearie," Leana promised, taking a long look at her sister. Rose had been so quiet the past few days. Pensive and subdued. Leana prayed that her sister was not still suffering the last vestiges of her croup. Not only her womb might be affected but also her heart, Dr. Gilchrist had said.

Jamie caught her eye next. "I, too, hope your birthday is a happy one, Leana." His warm gaze said what he could not. *I love you.* "Is the sash the right color for your blue gown?"

"Aye, 'tis perfect." She prayed her smile would convey her thoughts. *I miss you.*

Annabel arrived with a fresh cup of porridge and a small pot of wild daisies. "Time ye were back in yer *gairden,* mem. I picked these from the lawn, but they canna compare tae the flooers ye grow."

"On the lawn, you say?" Leana touched their tiny white petals. "Could you place your foot over seven at once?"

"Oo aye!" The red-haired maid clasped her hands. " 'Tis spring, or nigh tae it."

"Ten days, by my count. Come the first day of spring, the women of Troquire parish will be sneaking off to Saint Queran's Well."

"Not if the kirk session hears of it," Lachlan muttered, putting his butter knife aside with a dull clang against the wood.

Rose's eyes shone with a curious light. "What sorts of women go there?"

"Barren ones," Leana answered without thinking, then froze. *Oh, my poor sister.* But it was too late.

The color seeped from Rose's cheeks. "You say the waters from this well heal…barrenness?"

"So they say." Leana hastened to make amends. " 'Tis centuries old, a crumbling heap of stones. And anyway, May is the better month." She shrugged, hoping she might change the subject. "Father is right. 'Tis not seemly for a Christian woman to visit a saint's well on the Sabbath."

Rose wrinkled her brow. "But do they not call them '*holy* wells'?"

"Aye." Lachlan's unshaven beard bristled. "Holy *papist* wells."

Leana cringed at his callous tone. There were but six Roman Catholic families in the parish, including Lord and Lady Maxwell. Lachlan knew them all by name and belittled them at every turn. Except the Maxwells, of course. Intolerant as he was, Lachlan still deferred to wealthy neighbors who might be of some benefit.

Leana ate her porridge in silence, aware of Jamie watching her. She longed to know what he was thinking, what he was planning. Yet to slip off together for a quiet discussion would be to invite disaster on their heads. She tried to be content with snatches of conversation in the hall, glances exchanged over meals, a brief touch in passing. They were hardly enough to satisfy her woman's heart, for she missed his tender kisses and the heat of his hands. *Jamie, Jamie.* To think of never sharing his bed again was to die a slow death, hour by hour. To think of Rose's loving him instead was beyond imagining.

Too soon the week ended. Too soon the sun rose on another misty Sabbath morn.

Leana dressed quietly, preparing her heart, quelling her nerves. Neda came looking for her, offering a bannock for Leana's long walk since she'd not appeared at table for breakfast. "I have no appetite for food or drink," Leana admitted. "An empty stomach is best."

"Perhaps." Neda slid the bannock in her apron pocket. "Duncan and I would be honored tae walk ye tae the kirk this morn. Seems a shame for ye tae travel alone. I ken Jamie canna take ye, but surely we can."

"Bless you." Leana bowed her head. "I'm not sure my own mother would have been so generous."

"Och! Ye didna ken yer mither as weel as I did, sorry tae say. She'd stand by ye at the kirk door and help ye mount the stool as lang as she kenned yer heart was *richt* afore God. Niver was a woman mair attuned tae mercy than Agness McBride."

"However did she countenance my father?" Leana said, then pressed her hand to her mouth. "Forgive me for speaking ill of him on the Sabbath."

"Wheesht! I'll not tell a soul, for 'tis the fifth commandment ye've broken." Neda winked at her. " 'Tis a guid question ye've asked, wi' an easy reply: For a' his mony faults, yer mother luved the man and earned the respect of a' wha kenned her. And speakin' o' respect..." Neda opened the door behind her. "I've a guid man standin' beyond yer nursery door, hopin' tae wish ye weel this sorry day. Ye'll see him, aye?"

Jamie. Leana smoothed back her hair and pinched her cheeks. "Aye."

"Duncan and I will be waitin' in the hall." The last she saw of Neda was her kindhearted smile.

Jamie's expression was more tentative as he entered the room, as if testing her mood. "I see you're ready, Leana." He stepped closer, resting his fingers on the sleeve of her harn goun. "My prayers go with you, and my feet will soon follow."

His scent, his warmth, filled the air around her. Overcome at the nearness of him, she lowered her gaze. "I wish you did not have to see me like this."

"I would see you any way I could."

She heard the rough tenderness in his voice, the banked desire. *My husband. My love.* "Jamie, I dare not ask you to kiss me."

"Then do not ask." He pulled her against him, crushing the sackcloth against her body and his mouth against hers.

They say sin touches not a man so near
As shame a woman; yet he too should be
Part of the penance; being more deep than she
Set in the sin.

ALGERNON CHARLES SWINBURNE

Jamie tasted her kiss all morning. He was proud of himself for stealing no more than that. And ashamed of taking what was no longer
his. *Forgive me, lass.*

She stood by the kirk door in the bright March sunshine. More
parishioners were kind than cruel this time, but meanspirited ones still
walked among them. Jamie tarried mere steps away, silently daring anyone to hurt her, while Neda and Duncan stood on the other side of the
door, distracting folk with a blithe welcome.

I should be standing by the jougs.

Hochmagandy was not a sin one committed alone. It required two
willing parties. He may not have been sober on his wedding night or
fully awake when she climbed into his bed, but he had been willing.
Aye, he had been that. If he'd spoken Rose's name, even once, Leana
would have confessed the truth at once and fled from his box bed. Was
it not his fault as much as hers then? If not more? He kicked at a clump
of mud, shame heating his cheeks.

I should be wearing sackcloth.

When he settled into the pew at the second bell, Ian nestled in the
crook of his arm, Jamie realized his fine cambric shirt felt uncomfort-
ably tight about the neck. Sinners belonged in a harn goun. He should
have asked Leana to make a second one, with longer sleeves and a fuller
cut across the shoulders. The clerk's reading of the marriage banns only
made things worse.

I should be climbing onto the stool.

The beadle delivered Leana to the repentance stool after the first prayer. No one gasped aloud this week when she climbed onto the narrow seat, though the murmuring swelled, as if a conductor had raised his baton. At the turn of the sandglass, Reverend Gordon began his sermon from Isaiah. Jamie listened, his heart perched on a high stool, beating in time with Leana's, begging her forgiveness.

I should be with you, beloved.

On the Sabbath last he had defended her. Supported her. Refused to rebuke her. Proclaimed, at some risk, his feelings for her before the congregation. *'Tis Leana McBride whom I love and nae other.* Then why did he still feel guilty? Why did his insides grind like Brodie Selkirk's millstone?

Because Leana is paying the price for her sin. And you are not.

The sermon ended, and Jamie's agony began in earnest. Now Reverend Gordon would offer a second rebuke and invite his parishioners to do the same.

"Flee fornication," the minister stated boldly. "The Buik tells us, 'Every sin that a man doeth is without the body; but he that committeth fornication sinneth against his own body.' Leana McBride compears before this assembly a second time that she might be reminded to flee sin rather than to follow it, for her body's sake."

Jamie rested his chin on his son's head. *But her precious body produced Ian.* Good had come from bad, blessing from sin. Was that the grace of the Almighty at work? Did God's mercy stretch that far, that wide?

"Know ye not that your body is the temple of the Holy Ghost which is in you, which ye have of God, and ye are not your own?" Reverend Gordon peered over his glasses at Leana. "To whom do you belong, Leana McBride? Speak, and let us hear you."

Her voice rang like the kirk bell. "My body, my soul, and my mind belong to the Lord."

"Aye, and the Buik tells us, 'To avoid fornication, let every man have his own wife, and let every woman have her own husband.' Do you have a husband, Leana? Is there a man who will claim you?"

I will gladly claim her. Jamie slid forward on the pew, as if waiting for a cue to stand. *Say the word, Leana.*

She sat up straighter, smiling as though she could not wait to give her answer. "I do indeed have a husband. 'For thy Maker is thine husband; the LORD of hosts is his name.'"

Jamie sank back, ashamed of his disappointment. *Forgive me, Lord. For I ken she is yours.*

Reverend Gordon nodded at her, trying not to look pleased and failing. "So then. You will state again your wish to repent."

She slid gracefully to the lower stool and then to the floor, presenting herself to the congregation, her soul bared before them as plainly as her head and feet. "I do repent and plead for your forgiveness."

"Only God has the power to forgive our sins," the minister reminded her. "Though 'tis our Christian duty to show you mercy. And so we shall."

After the benediction Jamie found her in a sunny corner of the kirkyard, where parish members convened for a bit of gossip and a bite of cold meat between services. Duncan and Neda stood guard a few feet away, giving Jamie and Leana a moment's privacy before the rest of the household appeared.

He turned Ian around so he could see her. "Look who is waiting for you, lad. Your fine mother."

Leana held out her arms to collect their wriggling son, not quite meeting Jamie's gaze. "Jamie, I must ask a favor. A difficult one for me." She bent over Ian, as if hiding her shame. "You cannot…kiss me again. This morning…"

"Aye, lass." His heart fell to his knees. "I had no right."

"Nae." She dropped her voice to the faintest of whispers. "You had every right, for I welcomed it. But your kisses are too tender, Jamie. And my love for you is too great. 'Twill only make what is to come more… difficult."

He reached out to comfort her, then drew his hand back. "I ken you speak the truth, though I do not like to hear it."

"Nor I, Jamie." She glanced toward the kirk. "I sensed you sitting up there with me this morning."

"You did?" Guilt, like the tidal bores of the Solway, washed over him without warning. "I belonged up there, Leana. Right beside you."

"Nae." Her blue eyes watered, if only from the sun. "Were you to mount the repentance stool, we'd both be marked as ill-deedie parents. And whom do you suppose would be given Ian to raise?"

He hadn't given the awful possibility a moment's thought. "Rose? Your Aunt Margaret?"

She slowly shook her head. "My father."

God help us. "Leana, that cannot happen. Must not happen."

Lachlan McBride's booming voice carried across a dozen headstones. "What are you two blethering about?"

Jamie spun on his heel to face him. Leana wouldn't lie, not even to protect herself. He, on the other hand, still had enough swickerie left to fool his uncle. "Leana cannot—nae, *must* not fall off the repentance stool. The flagstone would break her neck."

Lachlan looked at him askance, absently pulling out his pocket watch, then slipping it back inside his waistcoat. " 'Tis an odd thing to concern yourself with, Jamie."

Neda appeared, brandishing a willow basket. "Suppose we concern ourselves with dinner. I've pigeon pies for everyone. Mr. McKie, might you find us somewhere dry to roost?"

Jamie guided the family toward a pair of unclaimed stone benches near the abbey ruins, surprised that Rose hadn't found someone her own age to share dinner with, as she often did. It seemed she'd lost whatever parish friends she'd once had. A fleeting wave of sympathy passed through him.

Neda saw the family settled, fresh pies in hand, then attended to the servants who'd found a patch of new grass to sit upon. Leana had her hands full, spooning cold porridge into Ian's mouth, while Rose arranged her skirts and nibbled at her pie briefly before putting it aside and clearing her throat.

"Since we're all here, might we discuss the twenty-seventh?" When she received naught but blank looks, Rose was crestfallen. " 'Tis my… my wedding day."

And mine. Jamie put aside his pigeon pie as well, for his appetite had vanished.

"Father has asked that we have no bridal party afterward." She bent her head toward Lachlan without looking at him. "Too costly. Nor will we invite guests to the kirk."

"The *kirk?*" This was the first time Jamie had heard that detail. "Can we not repeat the vows at Auchengray? 'Twill require but a few minutes with the minister."

Her plaintive reply took him aback. "Please, Jamie? It would mean so much to me."

When Leana nodded slightly, he knew he could not fight them both. "Aye, if you wish."

"We only need two witnesses," Rose added, staring at her hands clasped in her lap. "Reverend Gordon said they should be family members. Father, of course, will be one. And the other...if you will, Leana..."

"*What?*" Disgusted, Jamie stood to pace the ground rather than look at his future wife. "You cannot ask your sister to serve as a witness for...for..."

"Jamie," Leana interrupted, "I can manage."

" 'Twas not my suggestion," Rose explained, splaying her hands. "Ask the minister, if you like."

Jamie stopped in front of her. "You can be verra sure I will."

The notion nagged at him all through the second service: Leana suffering yet another humiliation. *Because of me.* Since she was not required to mount the stool in the afternoon, she sat at the end of the pew, quietly tending Ian. However did Leana remain so calm? When Rose asked her sister to serve as witness, Leana had not even blinked.

Jamie folded his arms across his chest, determined to be angry on Leana's behalf. What sort of sister would ask such a thing? *A heartless one. A spiteful one. A jealous one.*

Yet even as those words rang inside his head, certain truths about Rose demanded his attention as well. Rose was not yet seventeen, a full five years younger than Leana. She'd missed having a mother and had a *scoonrel* for a father. Her only sister had claimed the husband meant to be hers. Rose had also lost two dear friends: Susanne from Rose's own foolishness and Jane from an untimely death. And hadn't Rose been seriously ill herself for a long winter's month?

'Tis not the worst of it, man. Rose had waited more than a year to be his wife, convinced that he still might love her. *And whose fault is that?*

Walking home from services, Jamie fell well behind Lachlan and Rose, who were chatting amiably about the fine weather and the lambing to come. How the girl did favor his mother, Rowena! The same dark hair and eyes, the same trim waist. *Aye, and the same heidie nature.* In a fortnight Rose would be his wife. In a twelvemonth he would understand more fully the life his father led, married to a headstrong lass.

Until then his heart, if naught else, belonged to Leana. It grieved him that he couldn't walk side by side with her, lest a passing neighbor jalouse they were still behaving as husband and wife. *I would if I could.* That was what he'd said to her on their wedding night, standing on the stair outside her bedroom, never imagining what was to come. *I would if I could.*

Might she remember those words and grasp his meaning if he repeated them in her ear? Would they capture all else he longed to say? *I love you still. I want you only. I know 'tis impossible.*

He drew near to her on the pretense of seeing after Ian's blanket, which was gradually unwrapping itself from his feet. "Leana," he said softly and waited until she angled her head toward him. "I would if I could."

Her smile was tinged with sadness. *She remembers.*

"I would too, Jamie." She bowed her head. "Even if I should not."

"We are still married," he reminded her, trying to convince them both.

"Nae. We were never married." When she looked up, her eyes glistened with tears. "Nor shall I speak those vows again, for no man would have a woman whose name is so besmirched."

Jamie clasped his hands behind his back lest he follow his heart's leading and brush the tears from her cheeks. "Any man would be proud to have you as his wife." When she only sniffed in response, he searched his mind for something else that might lift her spirits.

"Leana McBride," he said at last, using his most ministerial voice, "I ken not what passages Reverend Gordon has selected for your final morning on the repentance stool Sunday next, but I've chosen a few verses that suit your…ah, behavior."

"Aye?" She glanced at him sideways. "Do these verses have the word 'hochmagandy' in them?"

"Nae, they do not. Though I do have suitable commentary for each one, just as the reverend does." He fell in step behind her, for propriety's sake, then began his impromptu lecture. "Who can find a virtuous woman?"

"Och! Now there's a fairy tale." She shook her head, though he heard the smile in her voice. "I am far from virtuous."

"Beg to differ, lass. When you discovered what a liar and thief I was, you still treated me like a prince." He tapped her on the shoulder. "And may I remind you, the accused is to listen and not to interrupt."

"My apologies, sir," she said demurely.

" 'For her price is far above rubies.' Would that a price could be put on your fair head, Leana, for I would sell all of Glentrool to have you for my own."

Her sigh was softer than any spring breeze. "Oh, Jamie."

"Silence, Miss McBride, or I'll sentence you to another kiss in the nursery."

Her low voice floated over her shoulder. "Pray, do continue then, for 'tis a punishment too sweet to bear."

" 'Strength and honour are her clothing.' Aye, and well dressed you are, Leana."

She paused to look at him. "I would hardly call sackcloth honorable."

Jamie placed his hands on Ian's head and feet and prayed she would feel them resting on her as well. "You are wrong, beloved. Only a very strong woman can stand before her neighbors and confess her sins. Would that I had your strength."

"You do, Jamie. And you will impart that courage to our son." She leaned closer as the servants passing them kindly averted their eyes. "I ken the rest of that verse, beloved, but cannot see my way through it: 'She shall rejoice in time to come.' When, Jamie? When shall I rejoice?

When I hear you speak your vows to Rose? When I watch her raise our son?" Her eyes filled with fresh tears and her face with sorrow anew. "I love my sister dearly. But to think of her loving you and bearing your children... Oh, Jamie, how shall I ever rejoice over that?"

Fifty-One

I must become a borrower of the night
For a dark hour or twain.
WILLIAM SHAKESPEARE

'Twas midnight at Auchengray, the first hour of the Sabbath. Rose
pulled the covers round her neck and tried to sleep, if only for a
short time. She would leave long before daybreak for Saint Queran's
Well. Earlier in the week she'd sought out her old friend Rab Murray,
shepherding on the nearby hills, to see if he might direct her to Saint
Queran's, since the herds knew the land better than anyone. In exchange
for a pocketful of rich shortbread, the canny lad had divulged the
whereabouts of the sacred well.

"'Tis naught but a circle o' stones," Rab had explained between
mouthfuls, "built round a shaft o' water that o'erflows into Crooks Pow.
At the sharp bend in the road at Cargen—afore the bridge, aye?—turn
left o'er the moss. A *clootie* tree stands nigh the well, a silver birch wi'
the rags of mony a pilgrim danglin' from its branches. Ye'll have nae
trouble findin' the place. Six and a bit miles on horseback by the
Newabbey road tae Dumfries, less on foot o'er the hills." He'd squinted
at her then, his curiosity aroused. "Ye'll not be thinkin' o' walkin' across
that wild *kintra-side* in the dark o' morn come the first o' May, will ye,
Rosie?"

"Nae!" she'd told him, laughing brightly, pretending not to mind
being called by her childhood nickname, though she minded very
much. "I would ne'er do so unchancie a thing as to visit a well in May."

Indeed she would not wait until May; she'd go this morning, the
first day of spring. And she would not walk; she'd ride Walloch, Jamie's
handsome gelding. If the holy waters of Saint Queran healed a barren
woman's womb, then she would drink them, wash her hands in them,

soak her feet in them, whatsomever was required. Her wedding was six days hence, and she was running out of time.

She awakened while it was still night. The slow-burning taper, marked for each hour, showed the time near four. *Two hours until sunrise.* If she dressed in a twinkling and saddled Walloch without delay, she could be on her way to Saint Queran's before Neda rose to start the porridge cooking.

Rose donned her oldest gown—the hemline torn by brambles and gorse, the blue drugget faded to gray—and slipped down the stair, holding her breath to listen for a latch to click or a sleepy voice to call out. She reached the hall and opened the front door with exceeding care, then pulled it closed behind her with a measure of relief. *Now to Walloch.*

The first quarter moon had long since set, blanketing the mains in utter darkness. In the farm steading, the seasonal workers grunted in their sleep as she passed their bothies. Walloch heard her approach the stables and neighed in greeting. "Guid lad," she crooned, smoothing a hand over his sleek hide, calming him. "You'll not mind my sidesaddle, will you?" Heavy as it was, she managed to hoist the leather saddle on her own, tighten the girth, then use the lowpin-on-stane to mount the spirited gelding. "Steady now, for I've no wish for a broken neck."

Not a candle was seen in a window nor a shout heard at the door as horse and rider took off at a gentle pace. 'Twas not until they were halfway to Newabbey that Rose realized what a mistake she'd made not leaving a note at the stables. Annabel would not come looking for her until eight o' the clock; she'd be safely home by then. But Willie would rise to feed Walloch long before that and think the horse stolen. "Only borrowed," she whispered into the dank, chilly air, running a gloved hand down Walloch's neck. "I'll have you back for your morning oats soon enough. Won't I, lad?"

The two fell into a comfortable trot and soon turned north toward Dumfries rather than crossing the bridge into the village. A thick forest of Scots pines crowded the road on both sides. Uneasy at the thought of a highwayman bounding from behind the cover of trees, she gave Walloch a nudge with her heel. He needed no further direction and increased his stride to a gallop as she shifted her weight forward. *Och, such a fine beast!* They would arrive at the holy well long before sunrise.

Without moonlight to guide her, Rose depended on Walloch's keen eyes and ears to keep them on the road as they passed Whinny Hill, then Gillfoot. At Cargen she guided the horse down a narrow track not much wider than a footpath. The moss had been well trampled. She was not the first to seek out Saint Queran's healing waters.

Though 'twas some time before sunrise, the air seemed lighter, the darkness thinner. Rose saw the clootie tree first and then the well, surrounded by flat, rough boulders. A woman was there. Alone, weeping. *Poor lass!* Rose felt her throat tighten in sympathy. She had only the *fear* of being barren, the dreadful expectation; this woman clearly had nae doubt of her condition. Rose quietly dismounted and tied Walloch's reins to a small tree near the flowing burn, then walked toward the circle of stones, staying far enough away that the woman might seek relief in privacy.

Rose pretended not to watch or to listen as the stranger removed her boots and hose, cold as the night was, then circled the well three times in silence. She walked *deasil,* circling it like a clock, then tossed a coin into the well. Silvering the water, Rab Murray had called it. Rose patted her hanging pocket, relieved to feel the coins beneath her fingers. When the woman began to mumble her entreaty, Rose could not make out the words, but she heard the sentiment of her prayer well enough and nodded in sympathy. *I ken, lass. I do.*

Her prayer finished, the woman lifted a cup of the well water to her mouth and drank greedily. Refilling the cup, she produced a clootie, plunged it into the water, then raised her skirts to her waist, baring herself to the night. Rose turned her head, for 'twas painfully clear what came next. The wet cloth was dragged across the afflicted part that required healing—her exposed belly—then the rag was tied to the clootie tree and left to rot, in hopes that whatever caused her barrenness would wither away as well.

Rose had neither the cloth nor the nerve for such a humiliating task. Could she not simply silver the water and drink her cup dry?

Oh, Jamie. She wanted his son, and she wanted him soon. If 'twould help, she would endure whatever abasement was necessary to secure a healthy bairn. The well was not a wutch's cantrip; it was a holy place. Rose took a deep breath for courage, then turned to see if the woman had ended her strange ablutions.

She was gone. The circle was empty. No other pilgrims were in sight.

Rose hurried to the well, shaking all over from cold, from nerves, from embarrassment. Even the moon would not see her, yet she felt as though the eyes of the earth were watching. Except for her prayer, the woman had remained silent; Rose vowed to do the same.

Bonnet, boots, gloves, and hose were put aside. She clenched her teeth to keep them from chattering and circled the well. It was all she could do to pluck out one coin without spilling the rest on the ground, so violently did her hands shake. Down the well went her silver, making a tiny splash as it landed. Uncertain of what words she should pray or to whom—the Almighty? Saint Queran? the guardian fairy of the well?—Rose simply whispered the truth: "I love my husband, and I want his child." *I do. Truly I do.* "Heal my womb. Make it healthy and whole, ready for his seed. Please, I beg of you. Please." *Please.* She choked on the word and could pray no more.

Rose wiped away her tears, hot against her icy fingers, and noticed the woman had left the drinking cup. Or perhaps it had been there for years. Apprehensive, Rose rinsed it first, then drew a cupful from the well, sipping at it tentatively. The water was fresh enough, though the peaty soil added its own peculiar flavor. She drank it down, then filled the cup again, perching it on the edge of the circular shaft. Tearing off a strip of her petticoat, she soaked it in well water, then held it out, dripping wet, knowing what she must do next.

'Twas now or not at all. *For your son, Jamie. For you.*

Glancing about the deserted field, convincing herself that no one would see her, Rose inched her skirts up past her calves, then her knees, then her thighs, finally baring herself to the waist, struggling to keep her full skirt and petticoats pulled aside with one hand while she hastily wiped her belly. She nearly cried out from the cold as the water sluiced down her legs. At last she dropped her skirts in place, the drugget fabric covered in watery stains. However would she explain herself when she arrived at Auchengray? *Rose, Rose. Do you never think things through?*

The dawn was coming sooner than she'd imagined. She hastily tied the clootie to the nearby birch tree, its silvery white trunk easily seen now. "Please, please," she murmured again. Her ordeal was almost over; if it healed her womb, 'twas worth everything. When she turned to collect her discarded stockings, the sky was no longer black but a deep blue. *Hurry, hurry.* According to the blether she'd heard from Rab Murray, it was vital to depart the well before daybreak, or all her efforts would be for naught. She pulled her hose on with such haste she tore them, then yanked on her boots and laced them only halfway. Wasting no time mounting Walloch, she took off at a trot, with her back to the well and Walloch's nose aimed due east.

Morning broke across Galloway as they reached the road south to Newabbey. With the reins well in hand and her knee hooked firmly round the pommel, she gave Walloch his head and tugged her bonnet low across her brow. Should one of the elders learn of her pilgrimage to the well—and their informers were everywhere—she'd be called before the kirk session and charged with profaning the Sabbath and honoring papist ways. Yet another McBride sister would warm the cutty stool. *Nae!* She could not bear it.

Her only hope was to take a roundabout way, approaching Troston Hill from the north, then passing Glensone, and finally taking the road to Auchengray. 'Twould add time to her journey and require passing the farms of friends who might look at her askance in her torn hose and splattered dress. But to ride through the outskirts of the village was to risk being seen by any number of folk who might delight in mentioning her name to an elder. *Nae.* She would take the longer route and pray no one noticed her.

Walloch gamely started down the rough and unfamiliar road, but the gravel soon gave way to mud and rocks, slowing them further. She studied the sun's arc. Was it seven already? Later than that? She must get to the kirk on time, for her marriage banns would be read once more. When Jessie Newall's house came into view, Rose nearly cried out with relief. "Almost home!" she promised Walloch, trotting past the white-washed mains and down the steep hill, grateful to be back on more sound footing.

Her mount, eager for his morning oats, took off on the straight road at a gallop. "Slow down, lad!" she cautioned, though 'twas no use. Bent over the pommel, Rose paid little attention to the figure in the distance standing at Auchengray's gate. Not until she was almost on top of him.

"Jamie!" She brought Walloch to an abrupt halt, though the horse shook its head in protest.

Jamie glared at her, arms folded across his chest. Dressed for kirk, his chin scraped clean and his boots polished, he made an imposing sight. All at once she felt like a milkmaid bound for the byre.

"I see you are up early as well." Rose dismounted, keeping her eyes well hidden beneath the brim of her bonnet. When she turned to lead the horse toward the stables, Jamie snagged her by the elbow none too gently.

"Where did you take Walloch and why?"

"The horse belongs to my father," she reminded him, then wished she hadn't, for his frown grew more pronounced. "And until you are my husband, my time is my own, is it not?"

Jamie's eyes sparked. "Need I mention I am already your husband?" He released his hold on her but not his hard gaze. "According to Willie, you left well before sunrise. Where does a woman go at that hour of the morning on horseback?"

Please, Jamie. She could not bear to tell him the truth. To see the look of disbelief on his face. Would he mock her? Scold her? Be ashamed to call her his wife? But she *was* his wife. He deserved to know.

"I went to a...well."

"Och! We have a suitable well less than a furlong from Auchengray's door."

"But I went to Saint Queran's Well."

He gaped at her. "Whatever for, Rose?"

"To heal my womb." Her cheeks burned. "To...to make certain I can give you...sons."

"Lass, you cannot be serious!" His anger lifted like a morning mist;

FAIR IS THE ROSE

'twas there one moment, then gone completely. "Of course you will bear my sons, if it pleases God." He stepped before her, taking her hands lightly in his. Only then did she begin to tremble from the cool morning and her wet clothes. And from Jamie standing so near.

Rose hastened to explain herself, rushing over her words. "Leana told us about…about the well. Remember? The morning of her…her birthday."

"I confess I don't recall the details. Something about barren women, wasn't it?"

"Aye." She forced herself to meet his gaze. "Jamie, I…that is, when I was recovering from croup, Dr. Gilchrist gave me some…very bad news."

Jamie gripped her hands. "What is it, Rose?"

But he already knew. She could see it in his eyes. "We cannot be certain that I am…am unable to have children. But if the waters of Saint Queran have the power to heal me, I had to try. Don't you see, Jamie?" Her eyes began to swim. "I will do anything…anything I can to give you children. To…to make you …to make you…"

Jamie nodded as though he understood. "To make me a father again."

"Nae." Rose hung her head, letting her tears drop onto the gravel at her feet. "To make you love me again."

Fifty-Two

'Tis time to run, 'tis time to ride,
For Spring is with us now.

CHARLES LELAND

Leana watched the two of them from the window at the top of the stair. Walking toward the stable. Shoulders almost touching. Jamie offering Rose a handkerchief. Rose dabbing at her eyes.

Leana loved them both. But not like this.

Lord, how am I to bear it?

She backed away from the window, feeling sick, wanting to run, wanting to hide before they came through the door and found her there. In six brief days she would release Jamie into her sister's waiting arms. How tempting it would be to let the thread of life slip through her fingers as well. Her stillroom shelves contained all she needed to put an end to her misery. *Henbane. Herb Paris. Hemlock.*

Nae. Leana shook her head, dislodging the wicked thought before it took root. She would do what she must. Life would go on, if only for Ian's sake.

At the sound of their voices in the hall below, she pressed her damp hands against her sackcloth gown and hastened toward her sewing room, seeking sanctuary. The small room where she and Rose had spent so many peaceful hours brightened considerably when Leana tied back the curtains, letting in the morning light. She eyed her spinning wheel, which cast an intricate pattern on the hardwood floor, and the carding paddles, cleaned and neatly stacked where Rose had left them. Would the two sisters meet here each Monday as usual? After Jamie and Rose were husband and wife, would life at Auchengray continue, with naught changed but their sleeping arrangements?

Heaven help me! She sank onto the three-legged stool, her harn goun wrapped about her bare legs, her face buried in her hands. How could she possibly live beneath the same roof? Where would she find the strength to watch them sit together at table and at kirk, her husband and her sister? How could she lie in bed at night and imagine the two of them…

Nae! I cannot!

When a footstep sounded at the doorway, she pretended not to notice, praying whoever it was might leave her in peace.

"Leana." Jamie's voice. "May I…walk you to the kirk?"

She shook her head, not letting herself look up at him, for it hurt too much, like the summer sun piercing her eyes. "You know 'tis not wise, Jamie. Neda will keep me company."

He was quiet for a long time. "How might I make this easier for you, lass?"

Love me, Jamie. She could never speak such a braisant invitation aloud.

"Please, Leana, tell me what I might do." He crossed the room and rested his hand on her head. She felt the warmth of him beneath her circle of braids. "I cannot bear to see you suffer, not only today on the cutty stool, but every day we are together…yet apart."

The longing in his voice consoled her a little. To know that he missed her touch as much as she missed his. Wiping her cheeks with her sleeve, she straightened, grateful he did not move his hand, even when she tipped back her head to gaze at him. "Forgive me, for I ken my face is—"

"Bonny as any in Galloway. Especially to me." He bent down and kissed her forehead, edging lower as if he intended to kiss her mouth as well, then thought better of it. "Ne'er forget that, Leana."

An hour later the word still decorated her thoughts like ribbon on a dress. *Bonny.* She'd not been called that many times in her life. Her sister, aye. But not her. *Bless you, Jamie.*

"Whatever ye're smilin' aboot, I'm glad tae see it." Neda walked beside her on the road to Newabbey, matching her slower, barefoot pace. The rest of the household would find their way to kirk soon enough; Leana was grateful for the time alone with Neda and sweet Ian.

He was awake but blessedly content, babbling away at the changing scenery as he bounced on her hip. " 'Tis spring, Ian. Your first." Evidence of the new season greeted them at each bend in the road. Catkins covered the willow trees, soft as gray kittens, and yellow coltsfoot bloomed in the fields. Beside the meandering stream grew pale pink clusters of butterbur. To the north stood a grove of larch trees dotted with rose-tinted buds and vivid green needles.

"I've always loved the first day of spring," Leana said wistfully, thinking of her garden. "I plan to spend the week digging and planting." *And weaning Ian. And letting go of Jamie.* "You will help Rose, won't you, Neda? When 'tis time?"

"Ye ken I will, Leana, for I luve yer lad like me ain granbairn." The woman's sigh was long, laden with sorrow. "Yer sister's been plyin' me wi' questions whan ye're not aboot. Wonderin' if the wet nurse she found will suit. Beggin' to learn Ian's favorite games. Askin' what foods please the boy."

"You must teach her such things, Neda." Leana brushed a kiss across her son's head, kept warm beneath a cotton bonnet. "For Ian's sake. And for mine."

Neda wrapped an arm round Leana's waist as they walked. "Oniething to help, lass. Ye ken there's naught I willna do for ye and yer son."

Dear Neda. Leana knew she could never have endured the last month without her kind presence. "This morning you can help me most by standing where I might see you and Ian as I compear beside the kirk door. 'Tis a lonely time, that."

Neda glanced over her shoulder. "Ye can be sure me husband and yer Jamie are not far behind, Leana. They'll tarry nigh the door as weel. We'll see ye through."

Neda Hastings seldom made a promise she did not keep. At the first bell she and Duncan and Jamie stood like three sentinels by the gateway, taking turns holding Ian, glaring at any who spoke sharply to

Leana, smiling in agreement when a kind word was offered. Her father barely acknowledged Leana in passing. Rose hung back, as though she wanted to say something.

"Leana?" The fragile skin beneath her sister's eyes looked almost bruised, as if Rose had wept through a long night without sleep. "May we speak later?"

Leana merely nodded, for their father was staring at Rose and demanding she follow him at once. Any number of things might be on Rose's mind. Jamie had mentioned Rose's trip to Saint Queran's Well. Perhaps that was what troubled the lass. "Aye, later," Leana whispered before her sister hastened for the door.

After the second bell called the parishioners to worship, Leana waited alone for the beadle to collect her. Instead, Reverend Gordon stepped out into the cool March sunshine and shook out the sleeves of his black robe. The fine fabric presented a stark contrast to her rough sackcloth with its soiled hem. "Leana, your conduct the last two Sabbaths has...ah, surprised me."

Her breath caught. "For good or for ill?"

"You ken the answer to that. I've ne'er seen a woman manage the stool with such grace. Even when no mercy was given you, you extended it to others." His bushy brows rose as he appraised her. "Though I've done what's expected of me, I've taken no joy in your rebuke, Miss McBride."

She bowed her head, uncertain how to respond. His words had been harsh the first Sunday, a bit less so the last. Might he be merciful this morning?

"The elders have requested that you subscribe a band—a pledge to proper behavior in the future—to be written in the session records, with your signature. I felt certain, with all that has transpired, you would be more than willing to do so."

"Aye." 'Twas a simple request to honor. The circumstances of her sin would not be repeated in a lifetime. "When shall I subscribe this in the record book?"

"Saturday, before the exchange of vows, come to the manse. 'Twill not take long, though you might give some thought in advance to what you will write, as 'tis a legal and binding statement and not to be taken lightly."

"I would ne'er take repentance lightly."

"Nor should any of us." He nodded his farewell, then departed for the pulpit and his first prayer of the Sabbath.

When the beadle escorted her withindoors moments later, she mounted the stool without mishap and settled onto the hard, narrow seat. The minister's sermon covered the same passage from Isaiah as the previous week, a handful of verses ground down until only dry dust remained. Leana fixed her gaze on Jamie and Ian, drawing strength from them, preparing for her final humiliation.

When the sandglass was turned over, Reverend Gordon put aside his notes. " 'Tis our last week to rebuke Miss McBride, who compears before us. Will any speak against her? Come forth, or *haud yer wheesht*."

No one stood. Not a voice was raised. Every eye was trained on her, but none bore the glint of reproof.

"Verra well." Reverend Gordon leaned on his forearms and peered over the pulpit. "Then hear my closing words for you, Miss McBride, taken from the Gospel accounts." He did not consult either Buik or notes but proclaimed his chosen verses loudly through the sanctuary. " 'They that are whole have no need of the physician, but they that are sick.' Has the Great Physician come to your aid, Leana? Has he healed your soul?"

She looked him in the eye, unafraid of her confession. "He has, sir."

Reverend Gordon's voice remained stern, but his expression softened. "Our Lord came to this earth, not to call the righteous, but sinners to repentance. Has he called you to repent of your sins?"

"Aye, he has called me, and I have repented." *And he has forgiven me. Thanks be to God.*

"The people of Galilee sought out John in the wilderness, who baptized them for the remission of their sins." Reverend Gordon covered his thumb with spittle and held it out, startling the congregation. A hush fell across the room. "As I baptized your son, newborn into the world, so do I baptize you with these words, Leana McBride: 'Daughter, be of good comfort: thy faith hath made thee whole; go in peace.' "

My peace I give unto you. She stood on shaking legs and climbed down from the high stool, then the lower one, her gaze fixed on the pulpit. Whatever had happened to Reverend Gordon, the man was not the same. Nor was his flock. Nor was she. By the time Leana reached the flagstone floor, the whispering in the sanctuary had swelled to an unsung chorus. A hymn without words. Nae, with one word: *Mercy.*

The beadle led her toward the door. Hands reached out to clasp hers as she passed. Some eyes were dry, and others were not, as a great sigh of relief swept through the room like the spring wind, carrying Leana in its wake. Their mercy made her long to be merciful. She inclined her head toward David McMiken and Mary McCheyne and Lydia Taggart, each one in turn. *As you have forgiven me, so I forgive you.*

Only one pair of eyes that met hers shone not with peace but with sorrow.

Rose.

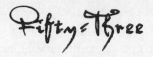

Fifty-Three

One common fate we both must prove;
You die with envy, I with love.

JOHN GAY

F *ive days.* That was all that remained before Jamie and Ian were lost
to her. The Almighty had comforted Leana each Sabbath on the
cutty stool, and Reverend Gordon had blessed her with forgiveness. But
nothing could stem the tide of time, nor undo what was done.

Monday brought clouds and a threat of rain as Leana worked in the
garden, turning over the soil with her fork, keeping her hands busy
until Ian woke from his nap. Her physic garden was the first to show
signs of life. Wild arum, with its glossy, arrow-shaped leaves, unfurled
above the soil. The downy stalk of cowslip promised a yellow head of
flowers in another month. She worked a handful of sand into the soil
round the neat spears of shepherd's-purse, thinking of her beloved shepherd on the hills.

While she gardened this week, Jamie would spend every waking
hour with the ewes, examining them, preparing them. As the lambs
dropped lower in their wombs, the ewes grew swaybacked and restless,
bleating for attention, their udders swollen with milk. Leana felt every
bit as unsettled and ill at ease, desperate to hear Jamie's calming voice,
her breasts full as she tried to wean Ian. *Five days. And then no more.*

Tuesday afternoon she found the note Rose had hidden among
the leaves of her French writing paper before she'd presented the gift
to her on her birthday. One sentence, unsigned: *Leana, can you ever
forgive me?*

She held the note with both hands, staring at the familiar swirl of
letters. If Rose was referring to her testimony before the kirk session,
there was nothing to forgive. Her sister had merely told the elders the
truth, though Jamie insisted otherwise. Leana gripped the note harder.

Perhaps there was one thing, one unforgivable thing. *Ian.* She crumpled the paper in her hands. *Four days left.*

On Wednesday Rose knocked on the nursery door while mother and child were stacking wooden blocks. Leana was not surprised; Rose had been shadowing her since Sunday, observing her with Ian, her eyes full of questions. *May we speak later?* Perhaps that hour had come. Leana looked up from the floor where she sat with Ian in her lap. "What is it, dearie?"

Rose took a tentative step inside the nursery. "I hoped you might teach me..." She looked about the room, avoiding her gaze. "That is, I need to learn how to care for Ian."

"Aye, you do." Leana rubbed her cheek on Ian's downy head, willing her tears to stop before they began. *I must do this. I must.* "Sit you down, Rose. Here on the rug."

Rose did as she was told, tucking her skirts round her, their knees almost touching. Ian sat between them, banging blocks together with glee. Rose could not take her eyes off the child, smiling at his antics. She adored Ian; Leana had known that from the first. But would she love him enough to tend to him when he was sick, to discipline him when he was naughty, to hold him when he cried for no reason? *Will she love him as I love him?*

Leana took a steadying breath and circled her hands round Ian's chest, holding him long enough to place him in her sister's lap. Letting go of him, even for a moment, took all the strength she possessed. "I will teach you what I can, Rose. Many things Ian will show you himself, over time. Won't you, lad?"

Now that he faced his mother, Ian became even more animated, tipping toward her, trying to reach her nose with his fingers when she bent down, squealing with delight when she pulled away just in time.

Rose looked at her in surprise. "Do you play with him like this often?"

"Every moment I can." Leana pulled her apron up to hide her face, then peeped over the edge of it as his eyes widened, watching her, before his face bloomed into a smile. "Include him in your daily tasks, Rose. If you are carding wool, keep him away from the sharp teeth and let him sit at your feet with a handful of wool. If you are helping in the kitchen, be certain he is safe from the fire while he bangs at a pan with a horn spoon."

Rose laughed, leaning round to look at Ian. "You like to make noise, don't you, young man?"

"Children *are* roarie," Leana agreed. "When he starts to greet and carry on, think through a list of possibilities. Has he wet his linens? Is he hungry? Is he tired? Is something poking him? Does he need to be held?"

Her sister's mouth fell open. "But which one should I do?"

"All of them, in the most sensible order, 'til the lad is content." Leana leaned forward and kissed his button nose. "Make no mistake, 'tis a great deal of work, mothering. Annabel will help you. And Neda."

"And *you* will be here," Rose was quick to add.

"Aye." Leana ran her thumb across his bare toes, counting each one. "I will be here."

The sisters took turns entertaining Ian until he began to fuss and swat at them, as if two mothers at once were too many to please. Leana stood and gathered the babe into her arms, then helped Rose to her feet as well. "Time for your first lesson, Rose. Do you remember our list?"

Rose's hands shook as she unwrapped the child's soiled linens. She made a face, then quickly recovered. Her movements as she changed him were clumsy, but her attention was fixed on the task. Even Leana could not deny that Rose was trying her best, much as it grieved her to admit it. What had she expected? That Rose, who loved children, would not love Ian? That she would fail miserably and refuse to care for him? That she would beg Leana to continue as Ian's mother, dismiss the wet nurse, and all would be as it was before?

Nae, Leana. Nothing would ever be as it was before.

Mother, stepmother, and child spent most of the rain-soaked day together. There were moments—few, but dear—when both sisters laughed at Ian and exchanged a warm glance or when their hands touched and neither of them pulled away. Leana kept one thought uppermost in her mind: *Ian's happiness.* His welfare was all that mattered. If Rose was to nurture him, then Leana would see that she was well prepared.

When Ian settled down for his afternoon nap, the sisters tiptoed down the stair in search of a bracing cup of tea. Annabel served them in the front parlor with a wary gaze, treating them more like guests than family. "If ye need oniething else, ladies, ye ken whaur tae find me." She curtsied and left them to their treacle scones as a steady rain pelted the window sill.

Without Ian to cushion the tension between them, Leana realized they were behaving like polite strangers, chatting about the weather, the lambing season, safe things. No mention was made of the wedding to come or the wet nurse. Or Jamie. Or Ian. When their conversation dwindled into an awkward silence, Rose stood long enough to add another brick of peat to the fire, for the room had grown cool. She reclaimed her chair, drawing it closer, then pinned Leana with a troubled gaze.

"Did you…find my note? In the writing paper?"

Finally it had come. The question she could not answer. "I read it yesterday." Leana spread a thin coat of butter on the last bite of her scone, waiting.

"What say you then?" Her sister's hand rested on hers, stilling her butter knife. "Can you ever forgive me?"

Leana searched her heart for an honest answer. "I love you, Rose—"

"Nae!" Rose fell back on her chair, her hands falling limp to her sides. "You always say that, but 'tis *not* what I asked you. I need to know if I'm forgiven. For Jamie. For Ian. For all of it."

Leana pushed aside her plate, ashamed to find her hands shaking. "I cannot say that I love you and *not* forgive you. They are twinborn, Rose. Love and mercy."

Rose turned away, pressing her cheek against the upholstery. "You say the words, Leana. I wonder if you mean them."

Leana stared out the window as if the rain held some answer she could not find inside her. "I *want* to mean them, Rose," she said at last. "How can I fault you for speaking the truth? Or for wanting a man who was meant to be yours?"

"But the truth that I spoke cost you everything."

"Not quite," Leana reminded her. "You are still my sister."

"Och!" Rose's voice tightened on the word. "Small comfort, that. A sister who is selfish and hatesome like Father. Aye, and spiteful and envious and willful. Everything you are not."

"That's not so, Rose. I have my own ledger of sins to account for." Her sister wiped her eyes with the back of her hand. "Name one."

Did she dare speak the truth? "I will tell you the most shameful one, Rose: I will never stop loving Jamie."

Her sister stared at her in disbelief. "But you cannot have him."

"Nae." Leana stood, brushing the crumbs from her skirt. "I cannot."

Fifty-Four

Ah! what avails it me the flocks to keep,
Who lost my heart while I preserv'd my sheep.
ALEXANDER POPE

The first lambs arrived early Thursday, born to a mature ewe who wasted no time delivering her twins onto the dewy grass. She licked them clean while Jamie watched with a shepherd's pride, having cut the cords with a dull knife to reduce the chance of bleeding. The twins were up on their tottery legs within the hour with the ewe nudging them toward her udder. Jamie eyed each lamb's tiny tail; if it ticked back and forth like the pendulum of a clock, the lamb was getting milk. He watched their small bodies fill out and their stomachs grow tighter.

"She's a good mother," he commented, nodding at Duncan, who'd joined him. " 'Twill be a long day. I've heard ewes grunting hither and yonder."

"Aye, there are shepherds stationed a' o'er the braes. Yer lambs are the first of mony. And twins at that." Duncan slapped Jamie on the back. " 'Tis a good sign, lad. Usually wi' blackface, half gies ye twins, and the *ither* half drops ane. We'll see how yer luck holds."

As he made his rounds across the hills and pastures, Jamie found a dozen or more ewes hard at labor, noses pointed up, straining to bring their lambs into the world. A second ewe of the morning bore twins, then a third. He'd chosen the tups with care, making sure all were twin-born as well, but the odds were against so many ewes birthing two lambs. Even so, as the day progressed, the lambs continued to come in pairs. One ewe laboring on Auchengray Hill tried to push both out at the same time. Without a shepherd's guiding hand, the ewe would die and the lambs as well. Jamie reached inside her to tie a string betwixt the two front legs of one lamb, then positioned its head before pulling it out. The second lamb quickly followed.

He paused, thinking of the McKie brothers: *Evan. Then James.* Had he been born first instead of his brother, his past, present, and future might have looked verra different. No fleeing to Auchengray to escape his brother's wrath. No Leana. No Ian. *And no Rose.* In two days he would claim her as his rightful wife. *God help me.* Until then he would deliver lambs and pray for his own deliverance from an impossible situation.

When he came upon a newborn lamb struggling to breathe, Jamie grasped it firmly by the hind legs and swung it round him in an arc, expelling the phlegm in its throat by sheer force. The startled lamb wobbled about for a moment before finding its balance and tottering after its mother. "Well done, lad!" Duncan crowed, watching from an adjoining pasture. Jamie waved at him, relieved to have control over something, however fleeting.

Neda dispatched a basket of venison pasties for the hard-working shepherds by way of one of the servant lads, for there was no time for dinner at the mains. 'Twas the gloaming before Jamie staggered back home, exhausted but satisfied. He would sleep with his window open, listening for anguished bleating overnight, the sure sign of a ewe in distress. 'Twould be a shame to lose any lambs after such a remarkable day of twin births, all healthy.

Leana greeted him at the kitchen door, bearing Ian on her hip. "Neda tells me Auchengray's hills are covered with lambs."

"Aye." Jamie grinned in spite of his weariness. "We've had more than our share of good fortune today." Moving toward the stair, he extended a familiar invitation. "Come, Leana. Keep me company while I dress for supper."

A soft gasp sounded behind him. "Jamie, I cannot…"

Och, man! Could he not think before he opened his mouth? "Forgive me." He turned back to find a wounded look in her pale eyes. "My fault entirely. Habit, I'm afraid." A habit he'd enjoyed. Having her near. Seeing her blush as he dressed. Stealing a kiss whenever Hugh looked the other way. How could such simple pleasures be gone forever?

He could not even touch her cheek now to comfort her or brush the hair from her brow. Instead he bent and kissed their son, hovering over the child's head nestled against his mother's heart. For longer than he should, Jamie reveled in Leana's warmth and the sweet scent of lavender that wafted from her gown.

"Jamie," she murmured.

How he loved hearing her speak his name. "Aye, lass?"

"You must change your shirt before supper," Leana reminded him, though she did not move. "And I must feed your son."

"So we must, on both counts." Jamie reluctantly lifted his head, glad to see her faint smile. "Will you walk with me up the stair at least?"

They mounted the stone staircase side by side, shoulders barely brushing, as Jamie told her more about the lambing. No sooner had they reached the top than Rose came sailing out of her room, almost knocking them over.

"Oh!" Rose stepped back, palms up. "Goodness, I did not expect…" She lowered her hands and her eyes as well. "That is, I was…looking for you, Jamie."

"I'm escorting my…my son's mother up the stair," he explained, as Leana disappeared into the nursery with Ian. Whatever was he going to call her if not his wife? He could not call her his *beloved*, though she was. Nor his *lover*, for that she was no more. Nor his *friend*, for the word hardly suited. Nor his *cousin*, for he had two of those: one whom he loved and one whom he was about to marry. Again.

The second of the two eyed him now, waiting to have a word with him. "After I'm properly attired, Rose, I'll meet you in the front parlor before your father rings the supper bell at seven."

Her features brightened. "I'll go at once."

Jamie dressed, though he was in no hurry to join her. Whatever did the lass have on her mind? *A fool's question.* They had spoken very little of the wedding. Now it loomed before them. It was not the brief ceremony that concerned him but all that would come after.

He found her standing by the front window of the parlor, her thick braid trailing down the back of her embroidered gown. She turned slowly—for effect, perhaps—as candlelight illumined each feature. Rose was altogether lovely; he could not deny it.

"Jamie." Her soft voice seemed an affectation as well. "Have you thought about our wedding night?"

As little as possible. But he could not say that. "Only that it will be...difficult. For both of us."

Her smile faded. "But I love you, Jamie. 'Twill not be difficult for me." When he said nothing, she hastened to fill the silence. "You learned to love Leana. Perhaps you will learn to love me once more."

"Perhaps." *Och! What are you saying, man?*

As if that single word were an invitation, Rose glided across the room until she stood before him, her forehead almost brushing his chin, so near that he could no longer look into her eyes. Her heathery scent assaulted him instead, and her breath tickled his neck. "Since you are aware that I...I may be barren..."

He stepped back, seeking an escape. "We dinna ken that for certain, lass."

"But the only way to be certain is..." She had the decency to blush. "The only way is for us to...try."

'Twas clear she had no inkling of what *trying* entailed. "If it is a child you want, we already have Ian to raise."

"And I *love* your son," she was quick to say. "I *do.*"

"I'm glad to hear it." He had no reason to doubt her; Leana had said the same.

"But I want children of my own, Jamie. Your children." She rested her hand on his coat sleeve, her fingers plucking at a loose thread. "When we come home from the kirk on the Sabbath eve, might we retire to...to my room rather than yours? 'Tis awkward to think of sharing the same bed where you...where my sister..."

"Fine." He would not defile so sacred a place.

Her tone grew more uncertain. "You will...do your duty by me, won't you, Jamie?"

"Aye." Heat crawled up his neck. "As long as you understand 'twill be duty, not pleasure."

She gave a small shrug. "Call it what you like, as long as it might... as long as I..."

"Wheesht." He wrapped his hand round her forearm, making very sure she was listening. "If you do not bear children, Rose, 'twill not be because I fail you as a husband, but because God chooses not to bless your womb." The supper bell punctuated his sharp words as Jamie released her and strode out the door. Was it a husband she wanted or naught but a tup to give her children?

When they entered the dining room in tandem, both bristling, Lachlan ignored them, while Leana aimed her gaze at her empty pewter plate. Ashamed at his outburst, Jamie could not look at Rose. Nor could he look at Leana, who seemed embarrassed for him. He bowed his head instead and begged for mercy. *Two more days.*

Lachlan spoke a brief grace over the table, then ordered the meal served. Annabel and Eliza swept into the room with steaming dishes of barley broth thickened with peas, carrots, and turnips. "Barley bannocks, too?" Lachlan muttered. "Have we naught in our cupboards but barley?"

Neda stood by the door as usual, directing the servants. "Beggin' yer pardon, sir. I'll see we have mair variety at table supper next."

Rose sat up straighter, as if she'd just thought of something. "Neda…" Her tone was sweeter than syllabub. "Might you serve hare soup on our wedding night?"

Neda looked at her askance. "Aye, if that's what ye're wantin', lass. I'll send ane o' the lads tae hunt doon a brown hare by the light o' the moon. 'Tis the best time tae catch them."

Hare soup? Whatever was the lass up to now? Jamie looked up from his plate to find Lachlan staring at him.

"Nephew, I trust things are in place for Saturday."

Jamie held his frustration in check "There's little to be done. Our vows will be repeated at the kirk door, our union blessed by Reverend Gordon, and the session record book signed by our witnesses."

"Have you no plans beyond that?" Lachlan tossed his napkin aside. "A bridal week perhaps?"

Is the man daft? " 'Tis lambing season, Uncle. I can barely take time for the trip to the village." Jamie stared hard at Rose. "There'll be no bridal week. None whatsoever. Any moments I can spare the next few days will be spent in the pastures."

Rose pulled her braid over her shoulder, smoothing her fingers over the ribbon that held the plaits tight, her eyes downcast. "I intend to spend Friday getting ready for our wedding."

"And I will spend the day with Ian." Leana gazed across the table at Jamie. "Working in the garden."

Jamie nodded ever so slightly. *I will come, Leana.* His ewes needed him. But Leana needed him more. *God help us both.*

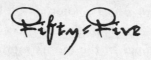

For every rose a thorn doth bear.

RICHARD WATSON GILDER

O *ne day.* 'Twas all that remained before Jamie was hers.

Rose perched on the edge of her box bed, staring at the neatly pressed gown hanging before her. 'Twas one of the dresses she'd hoped to take to Carlyle School in the spring. Her month in Dumfries seemed a distant memory, clouded by the saddest of endings. And now this, a wedding that was anything but proper. Though her gown was a lovely jade green, she'd worn it many times before. The wedding ring on her finger had graced Leana's hand for more than a year. Since their vows had been spoken before, the couple would not be permitted to stand inside the kirk. And she would have no bridal week; Jamie had made that verra clear. *None whatsoever.*

A coil of fear tightened in her stomach. He had promised to do his duty by her; indeed, the Buik required it. *Let the husband render unto the wife due benevolence.* Whatever that meant. The words did not sound painful, yet that was all she'd heard: *'Twill hurt.* Jane had shared a few sordid details in the confines of their sleeping room at school, leaving Rose more uncertain than ever. What might Jamie expect of her? Or she of him?

"Jamie would ne'er hurt me," she consoled herself. She'd seen how gently he handled the lambs, how carefully he shepherded the ewes. Surely he would treat her more tenderly still. Please God, in time she would have what she desired: a child of her own. She'd seen the way Ian looked at his mother. Pure adoration. Nigh to worship. And a bond that could not be broken. Whether 'twas selfishness or simple honesty, Rose could not say; she only knew she wanted a child who would love her completely, for it seemed of late that Jamie might never do so.

Tears stung her eyes. Was it so wrong to want to be loved?

Moments later when Annabel knocked on her door, Rose stood, suddenly at loose ends. Where might she go while the maid gave the room a thorough cleaning? In the morn's morn she'd have much to accomplish: new linen sheets scattered with rose petals, her best cambric nightgown hung out to air, and candles placed about the room to banish the shadows. But now, with Jamie busy on the hills, Rose had nothing to do but wait. And worry.

"Yer sister's in the gairden wi' Ian," Annabel said. "She'll nae *dout* walcome yer company."

Aye, and she might not.

Hugh, a basket of clean laundry in his hands, stood at the foot of the stair as she hurried down. "Whaur are ye bound, miss?"

"Off to the garden to visit Leana and pick some flowers for my room."

"Too early in the season for flooers, mem," he said as she slipped past him. "The trees in the orchard are fu' o' blossoms, but ye'll not find meikle bloomin' in yer sister's gairden."

There must be *one* flower. Wasn't spring nigh to a week old? Yet when she stepped out the kitchen door and into Leana's domain, Rose realized she'd paid little attention to pernickitie notions like growing seasons. Row after row of freshly turned soil and tiny green shoots were all the eye could see. Even her mother's beloved roses were little more than brown sticks covered with buds. 'Twas lovely out of doors though. A light breeze from the southwest heated the air, as did the late afternoon sun pouring across the land, painting the fields and pastures a vivid shade, greener than her wedding gown.

She spied Leana kneeling at the far end of her physic garden, her unbound hair falling to her shoulders, the mark of an unmarried woman. Ian sat by his mother's side on a thick plaid, gleefully slapping a porridge spoon against the wool. Rose called out to them, then lifted her skirts and made her way down the grassy expanse between the rectangular gardens. "Are there no flowers to be found on such a fine day?"

When Leana looked up, her smile was strained. "Naught but wildflowers. Field pansies and forget-me-nots sprouting along the lanes. I've been planting seeds this morning though. You'll have flowers in your garden before long."

"*Your* garden," Rose corrected her. "You ken verra well I have nae interest in plunging my hands in the dirt." She looked about the tidy grounds. "If you ever left Auchengray, these plots would go to ruin, I'm afraid."

Without warning, Ian tipped forward beyond the edge of the plaid, plunging his fists into the loamy soil. "Careful, lad," Leana said, putting aside her spade. "You'll uproot my valerian."

Her sister's warning came too late. The child grabbed the herb by its hairy stem and yanked hard as he fell back on his bottom, pulling up the plant by its roots. "Oooh!" he cried, waving the mass of thick, ivory-colored shoots about like a rattle.

Rose wrinkled her nose. "Whatever is that ugsome smell?"

"Valerian root." Leana reached for the plant, but Ian was too quick for her. He twisted away from her grasp, then toppled over on his blanket, shrieking with joy. Leana sighed, shaking her head. "I suppose it can't hurt the lad. If he pokes it in his mouth, which is what he does with most things, he will find the taste very disagreeable."

Rose gaped at her. "What if 'tis poisonous?"

"Valerian? Few plants have more to recommend them." Leana kept a watchful eye on Ian as she resumed her digging. " 'Tis so useful some call it All Heal. Haven't you noticed it in past summers here at the end of the garden? It grows quite tall in our rich soil, with pale pink flowers come June."

Rose nodded, unwilling to admit how little she understood about growing things. "So what malady is this miracle plant supposed to cure?"

Leana looked up, her blue eyes assessing Rose from beneath her wide-brimmed bonnet. "It calms the womb."

Calms the womb. Rose tried not to let her keen interest show. "What do you mean it 'calms' it?"

"Rose, I thought you knew." Leana brushed the soil from her fingers. "Valerian root has been used to heal barren women since the Romans came to Scotland."

"Truly?" Hope bloomed inside her. Could it be she'd found a cure in Auchengray's own garden?

Leana raised a cautionary hand. "Of course, one can ne'er be certain—"

"Please, dearie!" Rose dropped to her knees, not caring if she soiled her gown. "You were there when Dr. Gilchrist told me the news. You heard him say I might never have children."

"I did." Leana tipped her bonnet down, concealing her face. "And I'm sorry, Rose."

Was Leana genuinely sorry? Sorry enough to help her? Rose reached out, taking Leana's hands in hers. "What must be done with this valerian? Do you grind the root? Are the leaves brewed in a tea? Is it meant to be rubbed into the skin or swallowed in a syrup?"

Leana's straw brim did not move. Nor did she answer.

"*Please,* dearie. If valerian can heal my womb, won't you prepare some for me? You ken how much I long for children of my own. I…I only want what…what you have."

"Indeed, you want *all* that I have." Leana withdrew her hands, refusing to look up, though Rose heard the tears in her voice. "Aren't my husband and my son enough for you, Rose?"

"Oh, Leana. I didn't mean… I shouldn't have…"

"Nae," she said, the word laced with pain. "You should not have. You want all that is mine, Rose. And yet you offer me nothing in return. *Nothing.*"

"But, Leana…whatever would I have that you might want?"

Fifty-Six

On me, on me
Time and change can heap no more!
RICHARD HENGIST HORNE

Jamie. That is what I want.

She could never tell Rose that. She could never tell Jamie. But Leana could not lie to herself. An hour alone with the man she loved—that was what she wanted. Wanted but could not have. To even imagine it was a sin.

Leana found a corner of her sleeve that wasn't caked with dirt and wiped it across her cheeks. "There is nothing you can offer me, Rose. Nor should you need to, for I am your sister. I wronged you, without meaning to, as you wronged me. Let us speak no more of this."

"Aye." Rose looked relieved. "So…will you prepare the valerian for me?"

"I shall, Rose, but not this one." Leana plucked the valerian from Ian's grasp and replanted the uprooted stalk, patting the soil round it with her spade. "The dried valerian root I harvested last autumn is far more potent." Standing to her feet, she tucked her basket of garden tools beneath one arm and gathered Ian onto her hip with the other. "Come with me to the stillroom."

Neither sister spoke as they crossed the grass together and entered the house, though Rose's eagerness hung about her like a perfume. Did the lass think of no one but herself? *And who were you thinking of a moment ago, Leana?* Perhaps the tension between them would ease once the wedding was over. *Or perhaps 'twill be much worse.* Leana was grateful when Eliza met them at the door, for a stillroom was no place for a curious bairn. "Take Ian for a few minutes, will you, while I prepare a tincture for Rose?"

"Aye, mem." Eliza dipped her cap at Ian, who promptly yanked it off, releasing a wave of sandy curls. "Och! And tae think I'd planned tae gie ye a sweetie, ye naughty boy." The two went off in search of the hairpins that had gone flying, while Leana and Rose continued through the kitchen.

Leana stopped at the hearth long enough to light a taper, then led the way into the stillroom, where she'd spent many an autumn day processing her harvest from the physic garden. She settled onto a tall stool in front of her cabinet of tinctures, comforted by the familiar sight. Agrimony, lady's mantle, plantain, wood betony, and two dozen more tinctures stood at attention. 'Twas a long process to make them, steeping the dried herbs in rum and water for a fortnight, then straining the liquid through cheesecloth, then a wine press, before storing the concoctions in slender brown bottles. Potent medicines, though none of them strong enough to heal her ravaged heart.

To work, Leana. She soon located the valerian and added several drops of the tincture to a spoonful of water fresh from Auchengray's well. "Swallow this without letting it sit on your tongue," Leana instructed her sister. "The smell is most unpleasant." Rose did as she was told, making a terrible face. "Now you see why the Greeks called valerian *phu.*"

"Aye." Rose licked her lips, wrinkling her nose again. "Will I notice anything?"

" 'Twill make you relax, even feel a bit sleepy. Why not stretch out on your bed for a quiet hour before dinner?"

"But Jamie—"

"Will be tending his ewes until well past the gloaming. You'll not be missed, Rose."

"If you're certain." Her sister started for the kitchen, then turned back. Her cheeks were the very color of her rosy pink gown. "Leana, I am sorry to ask you this, but I...I have no mother and would be ashamed to ask Neda. 'Tis about...Jamie."

Leana began straightening the bottles in her cabinet as if she had not heard her, though her hands shook with the effort.

"Might you tell me...what to expect, Leana? What to...do...with Jamie? I ken verra little of...such things."

Leana shut the cabinet door so firmly the bottles tinkled against one another. "Are you asking me how to please my husband?"

"Nae," Rose whispered, "I'm asking you how to please mine."

The wooden stool wobbled behind her as Leana stood, gripping the table for support. "I taught you how to care for Ian. But I will not…" The words stuck in her throat. "I will not teach you…how to care for Jamie."

"But how am I to learn?" Rose wailed.

"Oh, *Rose!*" Leana brushed past her, bound for the door. "How can you ask such a thing?"

"Wait!" Rose snagged her sleeve. "Please, Leana."

She stopped but only because she feared where her legs might carry her. *To the hills. To Jamie.* Leana could not look at her sister as she spoke. "Let…me…go." Each word was torn from her heart, like pages from a book. "Please. Do not ask this of me."

"I'm sorry, Leana. I am just so…so *confused.* I ken not what to expect nor how to…prepare myself…"

"*Please,* Rose!" Freeing herself from her sister's grasp, Leana took off through the kitchen, tears blinding her eyes. She had to get away, to get out of doors where she could breathe, where she could think. Away from Auchengray. Away from Rose. She flew across the threshold into the fading light of early evening. In the gloaming the cooling earth released its heat, creating a mist that swirled along the ground, invisible yet visible.

Disoriented, she ran headlong into Neda, almost sending them both sprawling across the lawn.

"Och, lass! Whaur are ye bound wi' supper not an hour awa?"

Leana could hardly catch her breath. "Not hungry," she managed to say, then stumbled forward into the mist. Where *was* she bound? *Jamie.* Aye, she must find him, for he alone would understand. *Please, Lord. Just to see his face. Just to hear his voice.*

"Jamie!" she cried out as the thickening mist enveloped her. Skirting the farm steading, Leana hastened toward Auchengray Hill, calling the name of the man she loved. By the time she reached the crest, she could barely stand, so violently were her legs shaking. The gloaming and the mist conspired against her, for she could no longer see across the other hills nor down to the glens below.

"Jamieee!" She listened, breathing hard.

A voice floated up from the murk. "Leana?"

"Aye!" she cried out, plunging down the steep hillside, clutching her skirts with both hands as she made her frantic descent. *I'm coming, Jamie!* she wanted to shout, but her ragged breathing would not allow it. Surely he could hear her crashing past the gorse that tore at her petticoats. "Jamie!" she managed once more, and then she saw him emerging from the mist, climbing toward her, his eyes wide with concern.

"Leana, what is it? What's wrong?"

"Everything!" She threw herself into his embrace, stifling her sobs against his chest.

Love is the tyrant of the heart; it darkens
Reason, confounds discretion; deaf to Counsel
It runs a headlong course to desperate madness.

JOHN FORD

O ch, my love." His arms tightened round her, pulling her closer
still. "I am so sorry. So verra sorry."

Her hands clutched the back of his shirt. "Forgive me, Jamie. I…I
should not…be here."

"Wheesht," he whispered, rubbing his beard against her hair,
breathing in the heady scent of her. " 'Tis the one place you should be,
Leana." He did not need to know what had brought her running down
Auchengray Hill. She was where she belonged. *Here. With me.*

Jamie leaned toward the slope of the hill, jamming his boot heels
harder into the soggy ground so they would not fall. He dared not move
or let her go, for he knew Leana too well. Overcome with remorse, she
would run from his side. He would lose her soon enough; he would not
lose her now.

Though she tried to speak, her words were disjointed, nonsensical.
She gasped for air between phrases. "In the garden…with Ian…nae, in
the stillroom…Rose asked…"

Always Rose. "We've no need to speak of your sister."

"She wanted…" Leana pressed harder into his chest. "She wanted
to know how to…how to…please you."

Jamie bit back an oath. *The nerve of the girl!* " 'Tis advice your
sister will have no use for." He thrust his hands through her hair and
lifted her face to his. "You are the one who pleases me, Leana." He
brushed his lips across her forehead, feeling the heat from her skin.
When her eyes drifted closed, he kissed each one in turn. Then her
cheeks, wet with tears. And her chin with its faint cleft.

His mouth hesitated over hers. *You cannot kiss me again.* So she had begged him, and so he'd agreed. *'Tis a punishment too sweet to bear.*

"Can you bear it now, lass? May I kiss you?"

When she nodded ever so slightly, he had all the sanction he needed. The mist thickened, and the air grew darker as the gloaming faded into night. And still his mouth was fixed on hers, staking his claim. *You are mine, beloved. And I am yours.*

"Jamie." She nuzzled her cheek against his neck, a bit unstable on her feet. "Jamie, please…"

"Come," he murmured, "the bothy is not far down the hill." He gripped her hand, lest she pull away, lest she try to run. "This way, Leana. Mind your step." He led her toward the stone shelter, a mean refuge from ill weather, little more. There were no chairs, only a table and a stone bed built against the wall, where they sat down, both shivering though it was not especially cold.

" 'Tis clean at least," he said, wrapping his arm round her shoulders to draw her closer. "Alan Newall and I repaired the walls and straightened up the place last week. 'Twas a meikle mess." Why was he mentioning such things? They hardly mattered now. All that mattered was Leana.

Jamie pulled her onto his lap, steadying his legs to balance her. "Come, my love. Let me kiss you again."

Her mouth welcomed his as he slowly ran his hands over her hair, along her shoulders, down her back. "You are the woman I love," he murmured between kisses. *My wife. My Leana.* "Never forget that. Only you."

He held his breath, waiting for the words he longed to hear: *Love me, Jamie.* Her sweet invitation. Her gentle consent.

But those were not the words she spoke.

"Forgive me, Jamie." Leana slowly straightened, leaning away from him. Even in the darkness of the bothy he could see the sorrow in her eyes. "This is not right. Nor is it fair to Rose. And we both ken it well."

He groaned as his chin sank to his chest. *Too well.*

" 'Tis my fault." She slid to her feet, smoothing her skirts. "I should never have come looking for you."

"But I was glad to see you." *More than glad.* He stood, longing to embrace her, loath to let her go. "Do not punish yourself, beloved. It was only a kiss."

"Nae, Jamie." She stepped back, beyond his reach. " 'Twas a temptation. Forgive me, my love." Leana fled from the bothy, her blue gown disappearing into the mist.

His heart was still pounding hard against his chest as he walked toward the stables some minutes later. *Only a kiss.* Nae, Leana was right; 'twas more than that. A word from her, and he would have ruined everything. *Love me, Jamie.* Thanks be to God, she'd found the strength not to say it.

Only now did the repercussions of their meeting—however brief, however chaste—rise up to greet him like the mist. Did Rose know where her sister was headed? Might someone have seen them? He cared nothing for his own reputation; Leana's name alone mattered. She had paid dearly for this sin once. He would not watch her mount the repentance stool again, not for a kiss he never should have asked for.

The muffled sound of the front door opening and closing carried across the lawn as he drew near the steading. *Leana. Safely home.* Above him the doves cooed in their doocot, settling down for the night. *Forgive me, Lord. Forgive us both.* Slipping in the back door, he found the kitchen in its usual uproar, with pots clanging and Neda ordering the maids about. They curtsied politely, but no one looked at him twice as he passed through the room and into the hall. *Guid.* The sooner up the stair the better, before anyone asked too many questions.

"Nephew!"

Jamie froze in midstep. *Lachlan.* He turned and felt his stomach drop to his boots. Lachlan and Duncan both stood at the spence door, waving him in.

"Come, lad, for I've been braggin' tae yer uncle aboot the lambin'." Duncan clamped a hand on Jamie's shoulder and steered him into Lachlan's chambers. " 'Tis a blissin o' God and naught else."

"Twins, Duncan tells me." His uncle pointed toward the second best chair, pulled close to the hearth.

Jamie eyed the upholstery. "I'm filthy, Uncle. No use soiling your good chair." He needed some excuse to keep his visit short, for his clothes chafed him, as did his conscience. Had Leana slipped up the stair without mishap?

"All of them twins?" his uncle prompted him.

Jamie nodded, rubbing his beard to hide his discomfort. "So far every ewe has delivered a healthy pair of lambs. Of course, that could change come the morn. We've another fortnight before the lambing ends."

"Aye, aye," Lachlan grunted, pouring himself a dram. "Still, you've meikle to be proud of, James. I intend to write your mother and father and inform them what a good sheep breeder they've raised."

Jamie studied the man closely. Though he heard no trace of guile in his uncle's smooth words, Jamie sensed some ruse afoot. Lachlan McBride seldom offered praise without a purpose. "Is there anything else, Uncle? I'm eager for my bed, for the day has been long, and the morn will be longer still."

His uncle paused, the dram of whisky halfway to his puckered mouth. "Have you given any thought to the future?" He took a long sip, then licked his lips rather than miss a single drop. "Come the Sabbath, say, when you have an old wife and a new wife living under the same roof?"

Jamie's jaw tightened and with it his resolve to depart Auchengray in May. With both of Lachlan's daughters. "I've thought of little else, Uncle. Though I have nae solution to offer 'til the lambing is done, you can be sure of this: I will leave this parish, and I will not leave empty handed." Jamie flung himself out the door before Lachlan could respond, Duncan close on his heels.

"Jamie!" The overseer snagged his sleeve as they reached the stair. "Yer uncle was merely sayin' ye'd done a fine job wi' his flocks—"

"Aye. *His* flocks. Not mine," Jamie fumed. "You ken better than most the ill-kindit manner in which Lachlan McBride treats his family. Worse than if we were strangers."

"Listen tae me, lad." Duncan pulled him aside with a firm grip on his arm. "I've a scheme I've been workin' on. A plan tae see ye get half o' the lambs, seein' as they're all twins. But ye'll have tae mind yer temper wi' yer uncle. Through the lambin' *oniewise*. Will ye do that? For the sake o' yer auld overseer?"

"Och, you ken that I will." Jamie exhaled, glancing about the hall. "Forgive me, Duncan, if I spoke too sharply. I've got meikle on my mind."

"Now, now." Duncan gently shoved him up the stair. "Ye're wound tighter than a watch spring. I ken not the reason, though twa days o' lambin' will wear oot any man. See tae yer washbowl and a clean shirt. Ye've earned a guid nicht's sleep."

Rose might not think so.

Jamie slowed as he reached the top stair, his feet heavy with regret—not for loving Leana, but for disregarding her sister. Her bedroom door was closed. Perhaps she'd already retired for the evening. A few steps down the hall the nursery door was shut tight too. Was Leana within, nursing Ian? He paused beside the door, waiting, listening.

Guilt sliced through his heart at the unmistakable sound of a woman weeping.

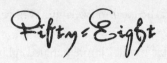

Fifty-Eight

But with the morning cool repentance came.

SIR WALTER SCOTT

In the hour before dawn, in the chilly confines of her hurlie bed, Leana awakened, having not truly slept. She had wept the night through, but only now did she see—truly see, as if waking from a dream—what had to be done.

She must leave Auchengray for good.

That Hogmanay night long ago when she'd sought comfort in Jamie's arms, she was innocent of all but her blinding love for him. But yestreen—oh, yestreen, she had been anything but innocent, anything but blind. She had run into the gloaming seeking his embrace, welcoming his kisses, nearly throwing aside all that she knew to be holy, all she believed to be true.

Leana touched her fingers to her lips, remembering the sweetness of his mouth, the warmth of his body. 'Twould never happen again. She would make sure of that. For Jamie's sake. For Rose's sake. Even for Ian's sake—*oh, my precious Ian!* So he might grow up in a home where harmony reigned and not discord, she must slip away.

But she could never manage it alone. After brazenly seeking Jamie's embrace, dare she ask the Almighty for help? *For thou, Lord, art good, and ready to forgive.* She pulled one trembling hand from beneath her bedcovers, then the other, and reached into the darkness of the nursery. *I stretch forth my hands unto thee.* Praying she would not wake Ian, Leana whispered, "Forgive me, Lord." She held her breath, waiting for assurance. At first, only Ian's soft breathing filled the emptiness round her. Then the words she most needed, the words she'd sung in the kirk, now sang in her heart. *The mercy of the Lord is from everlasting to everlasting.*

Leana sat up, taking a deep breath, as though a window had opened and freshened the air. She knew how this day must unfold. 'Twould require more courage than she possessed, more fortitude than she might ever muster. *Thou art the God of my strength.* Aye, the strength would come from above, for she had little of her own, not for this.

Leana slipped down the hall to her sister's room, then knelt by the door, bowing her head, one hand resting on the latch. *Forgive me, dearie.* If she thought her discarded harn goun would help, she would drag the sackcloth over her shoulders once more and scatter ashes on her head. Instead she prayed in silence, confessing her sins. *Forgive me, Rose.*

After easing to her feet, she made her way down the hall to Jamie's door and knelt there as well. Though the door to his room was slightly open, she dared not enter. *Forgive me, Jamie.* Pressing a kiss to her fingertips, she touched the latch. *Never again, my love.*

By the time Leana returned to the nursery, she was shaking all over. From nerves. From the cold. From fear. Fear that she could not do what else must be done.

Ian lay sleeping in his crib, his little limbs pointing in all directions. *Just like your father.* Bending over his bed, she gathered the child in her arms and cradled him against her shoulder as she stood. "There, there," she crooned, as he snuggled closer, still fast asleep. She eased into the upholstered chair where they'd spent many a peaceful hour together and covered his face with kisses. "Oh, dearest boy. My precious lamb."

A keening rose inside her as she rocked him in her arms, murmuring in his tiny ear. "Your mother loves you, Ian. Never forget that. Never, sweet boy." She bent over him, muffling her sobs in his blanket. Though she tried to sing, her voice broke and, with it, her heart. "Baloo, baloo, my wee, wee thing."

In a matter of hours Ian would nestle in the arms of a servant lass from Glensone with a babe of her own and enough milk for two. "But 'twill not be my milk." Leana moaned, pulling open her nightgown. "Please, Ian. 'Tis our last day together. Please."

He stirred at the scent of her, not quite waking as his small mouth found her breast. She sank back against the chair, ashamed of her neediness, yet grateful she could offer him something of herself, if only for a moment. "Thank you, Lord," she said softly. "For I ken your Buik says,

'I have behaved and quieted myself, as a child that is weaned of his mother.' Truly, I have all but weaned my child from my breast. But, Lord…" A fresh spate of tears gathered in her eyes. "I cannot wean him from my heart."

As if sensing her pain, Ian's eyes opened. And seeing her, he offered her a toothless smile, falling away from her breast as he did. "Och, Ian," she scolded him gently, blinking back tears as she moved him to the other side. "You're not making this easy for your mother." Though nursing soothed them both, of late it meant little sustenance for him. "Forgive me, lad, for there's not much there." Using her nightgown, she patted her cheeks dry with the Scottish bluebells that bloomed on her sleeve. "Another young woman will come to Auchengray twice a day to fill your belly. A lucky lass indeed, to hold you like this."

She could not be in the same room when dark-haired Jenny Cullen came to nurse her son. Nae, she could not be in the same house. Leana leaned over to kiss his forehead. "Jenny may feed you, Ian, but she'll ne'er love you as I do." She was glad he would not need a mother's milk much longer. A few more weeks and he'd be weaned altogether. Still, even one time with Jenny was too awful to imagine. Perhaps he would not take to her breast. The thought of it lifted Leana's spirits but only for a moment. Nae, he *must* take it willingly, easily, for he would need Jenny's milk to grow. Already a tiny pearl of a tooth had appeared in his lower gum. The maidservant's milk would be a blessing, not a curse.

"Though I wish it were my milk," Leana confessed as Ian drifted back to sleep from the sheer comfort of suckling. She pulled the neckline of her nightgown closed, careful not to jostle him. The first light of morning, spilling through the window behind her, filtered across the room. Familiar voices drifted up the stair, and the scent of bacon sizzling on the hearth slipped under the nursery door. Life went on, it seemed, as if this were the most ordinary of Saturdays. Yet, before the sun sank below the horizon, she would release her beloved son to a wet nurse and her beloved Jamie to Rose.

Help me, Lord. Help me bear it.

She lifted her head at a light knock on the door. Eliza, her white cap fringed with sandy wisps, appeared with a steaming pitcher of water in hand. "Mem? Will ye be needin' help wi' the lad this mornin'?" Her eyes said the rest of it: *Or would ye rather have him to yerself?*

"Nae, Eliza. We'll manage. Though if you'll meet me here at noon-tide, I'll need help dressing for…for…"

"Aye, mem." She placed the pitcher on the washstand with a fresh linen towel. "I'll have yer gown ready and yer ridin' boots polished."

"Is the rest of the household awake?"

"Mr. McKie has been oot wi' the sheep for some time."

"I see." No wonder his door was unlatched. He'd already left for the hills.

"Yer sister's still sleepin' though. I tapped on her door." Eliza shrugged artlessly, turning to go. "Ye'd think on sic a ferlie day, she'd be up afore the cock crows."

"Aye." Leana waved her maidservant out the door, then let her hand sag into her lap. *I will miss you as well, lass.*

Ian stirred again a few minutes later, awake for good this time. His eyes were bright, and his tummy clamored for porridge, for he stuffed his fist into his mouth and squealed, the surest sign he was hungry.

"I'll see to your breakfast, lad, and then to your bath." *The last time. The very last.*

She pressed him tight against her chest as if to stem the pain. *How will I do this, Lord? How will I say good-bye?*

Fifty-Nine

Love sacrifices all things
To bless the thing it loves.
EDWARD BULWER-LYTTON

A fter breakfast Leana sought refuge in her garden. Weak as she was, she knew if she stayed in the house she'd be listening for Jamie's footsteps on the stair or his voice in the hall. Instead she planted Ian on his plaid, plunged her hands deep into the soil, and begged for a strength she knew she did not own. *Be thou my strong rock.*

She had to leave Auchengray, of that there could be no doubt. The minute the vows were spoken she would flee. *But how, Lord? And where?*

She had no coins to pay an innkeeper, nor silver for meals, nor the means to hire a carriage. Though the Newalls might take her in, they lived too close to Auchengray. Though the McKies would gladly open their door to Jamie, they might not welcome their niece to Glentrool. Was there nowhere she might stay for a season? Was there no one willing to take her in?

Help me, Lord. Show me the path.

A quiet hour of praying and listening slipped past as her bleak future took shape in her mind and in her heart. Bent over her seedlings, singing cradlesongs to Ian, who'd curled up for a nap beside her, Leana suddenly felt a presence behind her, blocking the sun, cooling her shoulders. 'Twas plain whose bold shadow hovered over her. *Jamie.*

"Please, Leana. Don't look round."

His voice was so strained she feared he had taken ill. Concerned, she turned her head toward one shoulder. "Jamie?"

"Nae, lass." This time she heard the tears in his voice. "I beg of you, do not look at me, for I cannot bear it."

"Oh, Jamie." Now there were tears in hers as well. *Not like this, Lord. Please, not like this!* "I can never hold you again, nor taste your kisses, nor stand close enough to smell the heather on your skin. And now I cannot look at you. Oh, my love." She bent in two, her face nearly reaching the ground. "Is this how we must part? Sense by sense until we are numb to each other?"

Jamie bent down. Though he did not touch her, he was so close she could feel the warmth of his breath on her neck. His voice was gentle and low, like the summer wind. "I will always love you. God forgive me for speaking the truth."

She nodded but could not speak. *And I will love you. Always.*

"You and I both ken that what happened yestreen must ne'er happen again. I have begged for God's mercy and have received it. But I will ne'er repent of loving you. Do you hear me, Leana? I will always love you."

"Always," she whispered, her eyes flooded with tears. *Good-bye, beloved.* By the time she'd dried her cheeks with her apron, the shadow was gone.

Strengthen thou me.

Her time with Ian in the garden came to an end much too soon. Leana held him, kissed him, and nursed him in the shade of the yew tree, mother and child discreetly covered by a plaid. Beneath the rough wool she smoothed her hand across the soft cap of hair that felt so much like Jamie's and wept afresh, soaking Ian's forehead with her tears.

Eliza met her in the nursery at noontide as planned and helped her dress in her claret gown, retrieved from Rose's clothes press.

"Och, miss! Ye look grand. As fair as any...as any lady." Eliza bowed her head as her cheeks turned the color of her mistress's gown.

Leana lifted the maidservant's chin to look her in the eye. "If you meant to say *bride,* I'll not take offense, for I mean to look my best today." This was how the household would remember her; she prayed the picture would be a favorable one. "I'm away to the kirk on foot now, for I must meet with Reverend Gordon on another matter. You'll make certain the others leave on time?"

Eliza made a slight face. "Mr. McBride would have it nae ither way."

Leana carried Ian down the stair, where Annabel stood waiting to take her turn with him. "Alas, I cannot carry you with me, lad." Leana kissed his forehead. "Be a good boy for Annabel. She has a new book to read to you. Mother will be home as soon as she can. You'll be watching from the window, aye?" Ian patted her wet cheeks in response.

Leana heard the door at the top of the stair open and watched Rose slowly descend, her green gown swaying with each step. *Another farewell.* They'd not seen each other since Leana ran from the stillroom and into Jamie's arms yestreen. Rose knew none of that; perhaps she never would, for Leana would not risk hurting her sister again just to ease her own conscience. When she left Auchengray, that secret would travel with her.

"I'm glad you are here, Leana." Her sister stood at the bottom of the stair with her hands clasped behind her, a familiar pose from childhood. "Annabel, might I have a moment alone with my sister?" With a curtsy the maidservant was gone and Ian with her. "I ken you are leaving to attend to your band and will not keep you. But I must…" She looked down at the toe of her new brocade slippers. "That is, I must ask your forgiveness."

Leana was stunned. "*My* forgiveness?"

"For the things I said yesterday. For the…foolish questions I posed. Nae, not foolish. Thoughtless. Insensitive. Cruel."

"Oh, dearie. You are but sixteen and a new bride." Leana gathered her in her arms, taking care not to crumple Rose's gown. "I am only sorry that I cannot bring myself to tell you what you need to know." She swallowed hard, knowing what must come next. "Will you forgive me, Rose?" *For all of it. For everything.*

"Leana, there is nothing to forgive."

"Nae, but there is." *More than I can say. More than you want to hear.* "If I have your forgiveness, my journey will be easier this afternoon."

Rose stepped out of her embrace, her eyes shimmering. "Then I forgive you, Leana. For on her wedding day, a bride's every prayer is answered. Away to the kirk with you now."

Reverend Gordon opened the door at her knock. "I've been expecting you, Miss McBride." Though he did not smile, he also did not frown, and his tone was as pleasant as the weather. "Come in, for the session clerk awaits. He's not had his dinner yet and so is a bit peckish. Don't let him rush you though. 'Tis an important task you have ahead of you, for 'twill be a matter of record as long as you shall live."

He escorted her into the spence, where Ian had been born. Memories of her confinement swept over her and tightened her throat. *Not here, Leana. Not now.* "I have fond memories of this room," she said simply, sitting at the small table where she'd taken a week's worth of meals. Mr. Millar, the clerk, adjusted his spectacles, then extended a pen to her, the book already open to the proper page.

"Miss McBride, unless you have a question, you are free to begin."

There was no need to hesitate, for she had composed every word on the road from Auchengray. Now she prayed her hand would not shake as she put pen to paper.

> I, Leana McBride, unmarried daughter of Lachlan McBride, do acknowledge with deep sorrow of heart my sinful behavior on the night of my sister's wedding.

She paused long enough to breathe a fresh prayer of confession. *Aye. That night and yestreen as well.*

> It is my earnest desire to be forgiven by God and by all of this congregation.

Some in the parish might not forgive her. But God had done so. *I have trusted in thy mercy.*

> It is my sincere resolution, through divine grace, which I heartily implore, that I will never again sin in so grievous a manner.

Never again. 'Twas harder to write than she'd expected. Harder still to mean those words, and yet she must. *Never again.*

> I am willing that this, my humble confession, be recorded in the session book and be counted against me as an aggravation of my crime if ever I shall yield to temptation again.

She would not yield. Nor would Jamie. Not if they were parted.

Leana leaned back and invited Reverend Gordon to read her words, lest they fall short of his expectations. She had never before written a band and prayed she would not be required to do so in the future. *Never again.*

"Aye," he grunted. "'Tis the very thing that's called for. Subscribe your name, lass, and 'tis done."

She hesitated a moment before writing her last name. *McBride* instead of *McKie.* A cherished habit not easily forsaken. The session clerk read her band, then added his signature as a witness.

Before she lost her nerve, Leana turned to the minister. "There is one request I would ask of you: a testimonial letter."

His thick brows rose in surprise. "Do you plan to leave the parish, Leana?"

"Aye." She prayed he would not ask her for details, for she had very few to offer.

"And you've somewhere to go? Somewhere they will not turn you out?"

"No one would dare turn me out with a letter in hand from you, Reverend. If you are willing…if 'tis not asking too much…" It was asking a great deal, so close on the heels of her compearance on the stool. He could easily refuse her, even punish her for asking. "Please, Reverend Gordon. I must leave Auchengray, for the sake of my sister and her new husband and their wee son. Life will be much easier for them if I am no longer under their roof."

The older man regarded her, his expression softening. "God forgive me for saying so, but Jamie McKie was a fool to have chosen your sister first." He stood, patting his waistcoat pockets as though searching for something. "Aye, I'll be pleased to provide a testimonial. We can't risk some pensie minister shutting the kirk door in your face, can we? I've paper in my study. A moment, if you please." He paused at the door and waved at the clerk. "Mr. Millar, make a note in the records that such a testimonial has been provided Miss McBride."

The clerk's pen scratched across the page as she stared at the bed where she'd welcomed Ian into the world. Could it have been only six months past? The most joyful day of her life spent in this room. And now this one. The most painful.

Reverend Gordon returned with paper in hand and borrowed Mr. Millar's pen and ink to draft a brief letter. Sanded and sealed, it was presented to her with a flourish. "This will do, I think." He peered at her for a moment, as if considering something. "Shall I omit mentioning this when the others arrive?"

"Aye." Only then did she realize how long she'd been holding her breath. " 'Twould be most appreciated. They will know soon enough, but I cannot ruin my sister's wedding a second time."

" 'Tis that very sensitivity I find most commendable. Suppose I have Mistress Gordon serve as the second witness and spare you that humiliation as well?" Her mouth fell open, overcome at his generous offer. "Aye, I can see that suits you. Come, might we take a short walk to the kirkyard? 'Tis a fine day, and the others from Auchengray won't be along for another half-hour. You'll have plenty of time to take the forest path home."

Leana followed the minister out of doors into the early afternoon sunshine. By a decision of the heart and of the will, and by the mercy of God and of man, she would leave her past behind and seek a new life. *A life without Jamie. A life without Ian. A life without Rose.* Not a true life then. A shadow of one. But their three lives would be better for it. That was all that mattered.

Looking up from her reverie, she realized he was leading her toward a familiar headstone. Made of red sandstone and carved with a wreath of roses, the marker stood two ells above the ground. The beloved inscription was still easily read: *Agness Halliday McBride.*

The two stood at the foot of her mother's grave in silence. When Reverend Gordon spoke, his voice was rough with emotion. "Your mother had the most unselfish heart of any person I'd ever known. I have come to believe that you, Leana, are her equal. May God grant you the strength to see your way through."

Sixty

Thou art mine,
thou hast given thy word.
EDMUND C. STEDMAN

Rose?" Neda's voice at her bedroom door. "The chaise is ready, and
sae's yer faither."

Rose spun round, making very sure the room was perfect. Candles,
linens, rose petals, nightgown. *Aye, perfect.* Deep inside her body, her
sister's tincture of valerian was hard at work. *Thank you, Leana.* Pressing
her hand against her belly, Rose whispered, "God Almighty bless thee
and make thee fruitful."

There. She had done all she could; the rest was up to Jamie.

"Rose?" Neda again at the door. "Dinna keep yer faither waitin'."

"Coming!" Rose touched her hair, styled on top of her head in a
thick, fragrant mass, with ribbons trailing down her back. She hoped
Jamie would approve. He'd not seen her yet this day, lost to his ewes and
lambs since before breakfast.

"Rose!" Neda's voice brooked no argument this time.

"Coming, coming!" Rose flew out the door, almost tearing her dress
on the latch in her haste. "Is Jamie waiting for me down the stair?"

"Jamie has already left for the kirk. Astride Walloch."

"Och!" Rose stamped the heel of her new brocade shoes. "Jamie was
to ride in the chaise with me."

"Sometimes plans change," Neda said evenly. "Hurry, lass, or ye'll
find Reverend Gordon none too pleased when ye arrive late."

Lachlan McBride was in a foul mood when she lifted her foot to
the lowpin-on-stane to be handed into the chaise. "Rose," her father
grumbled, "you'll be fortunate if anyone is still standing at the kirk door."

"Surely they won't mind biding a wee while." She dropped onto the seat with a blithe bounce. "What else is there to do on the last Saturday of March?"

"*Do?*" He snapped a command at the mare, who jerked the chaise forward and headed down the lane at a steady clip. "Lass, there are any number of tasks to occupy a man, your husband in particular. 'Tis why he rode Walloch, so he might hasten home to care for his flocks. Are you aware that his ewes are dropping naught but twins all o'er Auchengray?"

"Really?" she breathed, suddenly interested. "Is that Jamie's doing? Or the tups?"

Her father shrugged. "Jamie chose the tups and oversaw the breeding, so he certainly kens his husbandry duties. Duncan insists 'tis a blissin from God." Her father eased back in his seat, loosening his grip on the reins. A look of pride crossed his face, as if he were personally responsible. "I have my own notion of what brought such a blessing to my flocks."

"I pray the Almighty will...bless me as well," Rose murmured. When her father looked at her askance, heat crawled up her neck. "I mean..."

"I ken your meaning, Rose. 'Tis clear your sister can produce a son. We'll learn soon enough if you're her equal."

Her equal? Rose sagged beneath the comparison. Leana had a long list of virtues anyone in the parish could name. Rose knew her own list was short and her womb likely to be barren. She could only pray Jamie would love her for who she was and not spend the whole of their marriage measuring her against her sister.

Angling her shoulders away from her father, Rose pressed her knees together, folded her hands in her lap, and tried to look like a gentlewoman, even as she bounced along on worn-out springs. The dry road and light breeze made their journey tolerable, though no shorter. By the time they rode into Newabbey, a dozen or more villagers were loitering round the kirk door.

Rose stared at them, wide eyed. "Whatever are they doing here?"

"Seems your banns have drawn a crowd," her father observed, directing Bess onto the grassy glebe.

In the midst stood Jamie, Reverend and Mistress Gordon, and

Walter Millar. None of them looked very happy, and Leana was nowhere to be seen.

"Forgive us for being delayed," Rose called out. "I wanted to look my bonniest for my husband." She held out her hand for help in stepping out of the chaise. Three young lads from the village fell over one another to assist her, though her father brushed them aside and lowered her to the ground himself.

"Thank you, Father." She swept past the curious onlookers and hastened to Jamie's side, sliding her hand into his. How grand he looked in the new shirt she'd sewn for him! He'd also chosen his best embroidered waistcoat, new doeskin breeches with a rich, leathery scent, and her favorite blue coat. "At last." She squeezed gently. "You were kind to wait."

He did not look at her when he spoke. "What choice did we have, Rose?"

"None, I suppose." She wet her lips and glanced down, hoping one of the men might notice her pretty gown or the silk ribbons in her hair. "Where is Leana?"

Reverend Gordon cleared his throat. "After your sister subscribed her band, I suggested Mistress Gordon serve as your witness."

"Oh." Rose tried not to look disappointed, but she was. Had the meeting with Reverend Gordon been more draining than Leana had expected? When she'd spoken with her sister earlier, Leana had looked as if she'd not slept all night.

"Let us begin," Reverend Gordon said, his voice solemn, as though he were in the pulpit rather than standing on a slab of granite outside the kirk door. "With the understanding that this is an informal exchange of vows for the bride's sake and not an official wedding ceremony, I will begin with the usual question: Is there any impediment to this marriage? Any reason the two of you should not be joined together as husband and wife?"

Rose spoke first, wearing her brightest smile. "Nae. We are already husband and wife and wait only to be…joined together."

A snicker in the crowd sent her spinning round to locate the rude fellow until Jamie tugged her back in place. "Continue, Reverend."

"Since there is no impediment, will you place the wedding ring on your wife's hand?"

Rose slipped off the ring and tucked it into Jamie's palm in time for him to lift her left hand and slide it back on, though only to her knuckle. He held it there with a steady grip. Her own hand trembled at his touch and at the gravity of the vows they were about to speak. *Please mean what you say, Jamie. Please try.*

Reverend Gordon began without preamble. "Do you, James Lachlan McKie, take this woman, Rose McBride, to be your lawfully wedded wife?"

She held her breath and looked into Jamie's handsome face as he made his pledge.

"Even so, I take her before God and these witnesses."

She closed her eyes, shutting out the sorrow in his expression. *Do take me, Jamie. Please claim me as your own.*

Her eyes flew open when the minister spoke again. "And do you, Rose McBride, take this man, James Lachlan McKie, to be your lawfully wedded husband?"

Rose said as bravely as she could, "Even so, I take him before God and these witnesses." She held out her hand and pressed the ring home, though her fingers were so cold the silver band spun about.

"For this cause shall a man leave father and mother, and shall cleave to his wife: and they twain shall be one flesh."

One flesh. The words made her lightheaded. And more than a little nervous.

Reverend Gordon said with particular emphasis, "What therefore God hath joined together, let not man put asunder."

The small crowd mumbled at that. Whether for or against their joining, Rose could not say.

Finally the minister held his right hand over them to offer a benediction: "The Lord sanctify and bless you; the Lord pour the riches of his grace upon you, that ye may please him and live together in holy love to your lives' end. So be it."

"So be it," she said, then realized no one else had repeated it. *Ninny!*

Ignoring her blunder, the minister inquired of the others, "Shall we sing the wedding psalm? 'Thy wife shall be a fruitful vine—' "

"Nae." Jamie said firmly, stepping back. "The vows have been spoken twice, witnessed twice, and recorded twice. I am more than married, sir."

"So you are." Reverend Gordon stepped forward to plant a dry kiss on Rose's lips, as custom dictated, then nodded at Jamie. "Her next kiss must be yours, James. See to it, lad."

Sixty-One

What else remains for me?
Youth, hope and love;
To build a new life on a ruined life.
HENRY WADSWORTH LONGFELLOW

Rose turned toward her bridegroom, flushed with expectation. But Jamie did not kiss her.

Lachlan McBride pressed a silver coin in the hand of the minister, who strode off to the manse, his duties done. Mistress Gordon signed a fresh page in the kirk session records, and so did Lachlan, as witnesses to the vows, after which the clerk closed the book and disappeared into the kirk.

And still Jamie had not kissed her.

Whatever was the matter? He'd kissed her many times before. Chaste and proper kisses, to be sure, yet he'd seemed to enjoy them well enough. She touched his arm. "Jamie?"

"Forgive me, Rose." Without another word, he walked across the glebe and mounted Walloch with a single sweep of his long legs, then rode off, leaving her standing there, unclaimed and unkissed.

"Never mind, dearie." Mistress Gordon circled her arm about Rose's shoulders, turning her away from the villagers with their ill-mannered smirks and stares. "Give the man time. Mr. McKie will come round. His mind is elsewhere today, out in the fields with the ewes."

Rose knew better. He was not thinking of the ewes. He was thinking of Leana.

She rode home in the chaise with her father, her spirits sinking lower with each jolt of the wheels. Her bridegroom was nowhere to be seen when they clattered up the drive to the mains. The minute the carriage drew to a stop Rose leaped to the ground and made for the house, poking her head in each room, hoping Jamie might be found withindoors awaiting her arrival. Perhaps a kiss in so public a place did not suit him. Let him kiss her here at Auchengray then.

But when she reached the kitchen, her last hope, she learned the truth. "Jamie's busy with the lambing," Neda answered without being asked.

Rose breathed in the aroma of hare soup, which had been simmering on the hearth all afternoon. "I trust Jamie will join us for supper. 'Tis…'tis important that he…that we both enjoy your soup, Neda." Lillias Brown was a horrible wutch, but that did not mean the auld ways had no value. If the *gustie* dish, flavored with sweet herbs, peppercorns, and port, might help her conceive, Rose would happily consume the entire kettle.

"The man seldom misses a meal. I'll be sure tae ring the bell and call him hame whan the time comes."

"And what of my sister?"

"Not hame at present," Neda said, too busy chopping carrots to look up. "Ian is doon for a nap."

"Jenny Cullen, the maid from Glensone, will be here at eight o' the clock," Rose reminded her. "Leana will have Ian ready for her, aye?"

Neda's hands stilled. "The lad will be here, have nae dout."

"Fine." There was naught else to be done. Rose dragged herself up the stair, fighting tears. What sort of wedding day was this? No friends to attend her, no bridal feast, no sister to witness her vows, and no kiss from her husband. 'Twas not fair, not in the least. She slammed her bedroom door shut, pleased at how it rattled the pictures mounted on the walls, though it did little to ease the hurt. Rose looked about, realizing Jamie would not care what nightgown she was wearing or how sweetly scented the room was. Not when his heart still belonged to her sister.

Perhaps when they all gathered for supper, she might stake a proper claim on him and let Leana see that, despite all, she would make Jamie a good wife.

But Jamie did not appear at supper. Nor did Leana.

"Where *are* they?" Rose asked her father, sitting alone with him at table. She sensed something was amiss but feared what that might be. Surely the two had not run off together.

Lachlan offered little sympathy. "I've not seen your sister since noontide. You cannot blame the lass for avoiding you, Rose. 'Twas my understanding she was having supper with the Newalls." Lachlan put aside his soupspoon to toss down a glass of claret. "As for Jamie, I ken for a fact the man is halfway to Barlae Hill, up to his knees in lambs. One of the herds just came by with the latest count. 'Tis impressive what your husband is doing. Still all twins. Duncan swears he's ne'er seen the likes of it."

"Sheep, sheep, sheep!" she muttered under her breath. "Is that all this household thinks about?"

"At lambing time you can be sure of it." Her father's visage grew stern. "Jamie is laboring on your behalf, Rose. 'Tis your future at stake, and he kens it well. Be grateful, lass, and do not expect more of the man than he can give."

"Aye." Her father was maddeningly right, as usual. She glanced at the mantel clock. "Jenny Cullen is to arrive any minute. If I might be excused to see that Ian is ready for her?"

"Go, go." He waved his spoon at her. "And don't expect too much on that score either. These things are not as simple as they appear."

Alas, her father was right again. Jenny was a quiet young woman of twenty, with a bairn three months older than Ian and more milk than she needed. But Ian would have no part of her. Rose watched with chagrin as the child shrieked and waved his arms about, smacking poor Jenny in the neck, refusing to nurse, leaving the maid red-faced with shame.

" 'Tis not your fault," Rose assured her, following Jenny out the front door into the cool of night. Where *was* Leana? Surely if she'd been there, things might have gone more smoothly. "I'll see that my sister is here when you return in the morning. She may be of some help."

"I ken what tae do, Mistress McKie," Jenny said, ducking her head. "But Ian is a heidie lad, wi' his own notion o' wha's tae feed him."

"*You* are to nurse him. Once in the morning, once in the evening," Rose said firmly. "When he's hungry enough, he'll not fight you. We'll see he has porridge and juice and other bits of food throughout the day, but we're depending on you, Jenny. See you don't disappoint us."

"Aye, mem." Jenny curtsied and aimed her steps toward Glensone.

Seeing the young woman's sagging shoulders, Rose felt a stab of guilt. Clearly she'd been too sharp with her. " 'Tis a dark night," she called out. "Shall I have Willie walk you home?"

"He's gone, mistress." Annabel stood in the doorway behind her, holding Ian, her knuckle tucked in his mouth to keep his gums busy.

"Och, at such a late hour?" Rose threw up her hands. "Forgive me, Jenny. 'Tis been a most fretful day."

"Glensone is less than a mile awa, mem." The dark-haired servant curtsied again and was gone.

Rose trudged past Annabel and up the stair, pausing at the landing before her maid got out of earshot. "You'll attend to Ian's needs tonight, aye? Feed him porridge or applesauce or whatever the dear child will eat, as long as it will help him sleep through the night. I will be in my bedroom. If and when Mr. McKie returns, tell him his wife is waiting for him."

Everywhere she'd turned that day someone had disappointed her, Jamie especially. *Can you not love me a little?* Walking into their bedroom without bothering to close the door, Rose poked a stick of straw in the fire, then began lighting the candles round the room as the first tears began to fall, staining her green gown. She had his name and his fortune. But it still was not enough. "Please," she said aloud, her voice breaking, "I want more than that."

Jamie's voice floated in from the doorway. "More than what?"

Rose whirled about, trailing sparks from the straw. She quickly blew it out before the flame burned her fingers. "There you are!"

"I was told you were expecting me." He strode into the room, his shirt and breeches soiled from working with the ewes, and closed the door soundly. "What is it you will have from me, Rose? What *more* do you speak of? Don't you have enough? My name? My son?"

"Jamie, you ken what I want. Your…your heart. Your love."

"And this." He pointed toward her bed. "You want that from me as well."

"Aye," she confessed, drying her tears. "For 'tis the only means of having your sons."

"Wheesht!" He yanked his shirt over his head, throwing it onto the floor in a heap. "You want the children but not the man?"

"Nae!" she cried. "Jamie, please do not put words in my mouth." She tried not to look at his bare chest, sparsely covered with hair as dark as that on his head. "Of course I want you. Only you."

" 'Tis always what *you* want, Rose."

"Aye, but what I want is *you*." She held out her hands, imploring him with her eyes. "Does it not please you to be wanted, Jamie? To be desired, to be needed? To be…loved?" Her voice fell to a whisper. "Would that anyone felt that way about me."

"Och, lass, you cut me to the quick." His sigh was that of a beaten man. "I felt all those things about you once. But I cannot rekindle a fire that has burned out."

"Perhaps I can," she said, casting her modesty into the hearth. "That is, if you will let me." Her gaze darted toward the pristine nightgown hanging from the clothes press. Should she ask him to leave while she changed? Might he need to bathe first? She clasped her hands and tried not to wring them. "What…what shall we do…first?"

"Do!" 'Twas more of a growl than a question. "I shall scrub off the sweat of my labors. Leave the room or stay—it matters not to me. Then you shall remove your dress and put on your nightgown and join me in your box bed. 'Tis not a complicated process, Rose. Husbands and wives do this sort of thing on a regular basis."

She stared at him, stunned by the sharpness of his words. Was this how he'd treated her meek sister? Nae, she'd seen them together; he behaved like a gentleman with Leana. "Why, Jamie? Why are you being so cruel to me?"

"You ken the reason." He showed her his back, yanking off his breeches with little ceremony. "When you betrayed your sister to the kirk session, you betrayed me as well."

" 'Twas not a betrayal." One glimpse of his long, muscular legs and Rose turned away with a guilty start. "I spoke the truth," she reminded him, "just as my sister asked us both to do."

"Aye, but you did not tell the *whole* truth. Only enough to get what you wanted." His words were accompanied by the sound of water pouring from the pitcher to the bowl. "And now I am yours, Rose. 'Til death do us part."

She held her tongue, lest she infuriate him further, and gave him a moment to attend to his bathing. "Jamie," she said as sweetly as she could, "I searched the Buik for a special verse for you. For us. For tonight. Might you care to hear it?"

Water splashed near her feet. "By all means, Rose. If the Almighty can redeem this unco night, let his word be spoken. Though I'd prefer to see your face. 'Tis the only way I can guess what you're thinking."

She took a deep breath to steel her nerves and slowly turned round.

He stood before her, dripping wet, drying himself with a linen towel, not even blushing. "You were saying, lass?"

Flustered, she lifted her gaze so that all she saw was his braw face and his damp brown hair hanging about his shoulders. " 'Tis just this: 'The wife hath not power of her own body, but the husband: and like- wise also the husband hath not power of his own body, but the wife.' "

His eyes narrowed. "What do you mean, Rose? That you own me? Have power over me?"

"I mean that I am *yours.* That my body is yours to do with as you please."

"And mine as *you* please, I suppose." He tossed aside the towel. "Turn round, and let me see to your laces. Unless you prefer to have Annabel join us—"

"Nae!" She did as he asked, glad not to watch the storm brewing in his eyes. "Jamie, you ken that I am…innocent."

He snorted, tugging hard on the laces of her gown. " 'Tis not the word that comes to mind when I think of you, Rose. Once, perhaps. But not now. You've seen too much."

She could hardly disagree. *The betrayal of a sister. The spells of a witch. The death of a friend.* "Not innocent in all things, nae," she said softly, "but certainly in the ways of a man with a maid."

"Ah." He pulled her loosened dress off her shoulders, then began unlacing her stays.

The air felt cool on her back and cooler still on her face. "You will be gentle with me, Jamie. Won't you?"

Sixty-Two

Marriage is a desperate thing.
JOHN SELDEN

A ye." Jamie gripped the stays in his hands and closed his eyes. "I will be gentle."

'Twas the only promise he knew he could keep. *Do not ask me to love you. Do not ask me to enjoy this. Do not ask me to please you.*

When he opened his eyes again and saw her thick hair coming loose, he swallowed the shame that rose in his throat, sickened by a frisson of desire that had nothing to do with Rose and only to do with her being a woman waiting for him to teach her the ways of love.

Except this was not love. This was duty.

He released the last of her stays, and her clothes dropped to the floor.

"Jamie," she whispered, "might you fetch my nightgown for me?"

Stepping round her skirts, he reached for the delicate linen nightgown, then slipped it over her shoulders, letting her manage the rest of it. The less he touched her, the better. He would not build up her hopes only to dash them by the light of day. As his legal wife, Rose deserved his attentions for one night. His sense of duty stretched no further than that. Not when Leana, the woman he loved, slept in the next room. Though he'd not seen her since they'd spoken in the garden this morning, he was certain Leana would return from the Newalls soon and retire to the nursery.

Forgive me, beloved.

Nae, there was no forgiveness for this. The marriage law said this was good and right and holy. Yet, to him, this night was hochmagandy at its very worst.

Forgive me, Lord.

Darkness. That was what he needed. A veil of shadows to cover his sin. He made his way round the room, pinching out all but one taper perched on a bureau well away from their bedside. Flicking the soot from his fingers, he dipped his hand in the washbowl in passing and shook it dry, lest he sully her white gown.

Her gaze followed his every move. He sensed it, even when he wasn't looking at her. She waited until he'd finished with the candles before she spoke. Her request devastated him.

"Now will you kiss me, Jamie?"

He had no choice. He could not say no. Yet 'twas more intimate than any act that might follow, that kiss. His body would do what it must; he could disengage his emotions, if necessary. But a kiss was holy.

"Come here, lass." Jamie reached for her hand, helping her step over the mass of skirts and petticoats at her feet, and drew her toward him. Not too close but close enough. *I will give you my mouth, Rose. But not my heart.*

Rose lifted her face to his, beseeching him, not afraid to ask again. "Please?"

He squeezed his eyes shut to hold back the tears that threatened to unman him and slanted his mouth against hers. She responded at once, just as he'd feared she might. And tasted far sweeter than he'd remembered.

Oh, Rose. Do not ask this of me. Do not ask me to love you.

Long before the Sabbath dawned Jamie awakened and reached for the chamber pot, feeling he might be sick. The illness was not in his stomach; 'twas in his spirit. *Forgive me, Leana. Forgive me.* He could never say it enough.

In a few hours the household would set off to the kirk for services. To sit side by side in the family pew—Jamie, Ian, and Rose—with the curious gazes of their neighbors pinned to their coats like buttons. Leana would be forced to sit apart from them with her father. Even after her turn on the repentance stool, the woman would be held at arm's length by the parishioners for a long time to come. No longer a wife, no longer a mother, she would have no true place in the community. 'Twas the cruelest sentence of all, worse than the stool.

Jamie listened carefully to see if Leana stirred in the nursery next door. It was not unusual for her to be awake at odd hours of the night, caring for Ian. Though he could not meet her behind a closed door, they might speak briefly in the hall. He needed to assure Leana of his love, of his support. He well knew the reason she had not served as a witness at their wedding: She was ashamed of what had happened at the bothy, just as he'd known she would be.

'Twas naught but a kiss, lass.

Dressing in the dark, careful not to make a sound, he left his boots behind and padded into the hall, blinking as his eyes adjusted to the dim light of the setting moon. Jamie pressed his ear to the nursery door, wishing he could hear Leana's soft, even breathing. Though he could not enter, he could *look* within, could he not? For a moment? He needed to see her and let her see him. To let her read the truth once more in his eyes: *I will always love you. I will never leave you.*

He raised the latch, wincing at how loud it sounded in the empty hall. Pushing the door open as slowly as he could, he gazed at the tender scene, relieved. Ian was fast asleep, his thumb planted in his mouth. Next to his crib, buried beneath the covers, lay the familiar shape of a woman, with a tuft of golden hair showing near the pillow. He gripped the latch, forcing himself to stay put rather than follow his instincts, which would lead him to her bedside, to kiss her awake and pray no one would hear them.

When she turned in her sleep, brushing the sheets away from her face, Jamie fell back a step.

Eliza! Whatever was she doing in Leana's bed?

He backed into the hall, pulling the door shut as he went, not caring how loudly the latch sounded. *Why wasn't Leana there?* Then the answer came to him. *Of course.* Since Ian was now Rose's responsibility, one of the maids would sleep near the lad. Leana had no doubt been moved to his old room. Which was once Rose's old room. A very confusing household, Auchengray.

When no one answered his knock, Jamie entered the familiar bed-room, surprised to find the box bed curtains tied back. *Odd.* Though it was a mild enough night, Leana usually preferred to be closed in, for warmth. He stepped closer, then realized the sheets were freshly changed. And utterly empty. "Leana?" Ridiculous to say her name aloud as if she were hiding in the corner. But where *was* she? In the kitchen perhaps? Seeking Neda's counsel?

He eased down the stair in his stocking feet, aware of the cold stone against his soles and the loud beating of his heart. Not a sound came from the kitchen or from behind the spence door, where Lachlan slept. Jamie found a lighted candle in the front parlor and carried it about from room to room, growing more anxious by the minute. Her father had insisted she'd gone to visit Jessie Newall for supper. Had she spent the night at Troston Hill Farm? Would she stop at Auchengray before going to kirk or meet them there?

A sense of foreboding curled round him, like a mist rising from Loch Trool. Leana was hiding from him, or from Rose. He went into the empty kitchen, lit only by the glow of the hearth, and dropped onto a three-legged stool, setting his candle on the chopping block with a groan. "What have I done?"

"Ye've done naught, Jamie."

Startled, he turned round. "Och! Neda." If anyone knew Leana's whereabouts, this good soul would. "Where is she?"

Neda did not answer him at once, pulling up a second stool to join him by the hearth. The light played against the lines in her face, each one shadowed with a marked sadness. "She's gone, Jamie."

"Gone?" He bolted to his feet, knocking over the stool. "Gone *where?*"

"I dinna ken. She wouldna tell me."

Jamie stared at her, incredulous. "But you're certain she's left? For good, I mean, not just visiting the Newalls?"

"Aye. Leana told me while ye were at the kirk that she was leavin' Auchengray."

"But *why?*" Distraught, he ran his hands through his hair, yanking at the roots as if to punish himself. "Doesn't she realize that I love her?"

"O' course she kens ye luve her, Jamie. 'Tis why she had tae go awa. Tae spare ye bein' torn tae pieces. Which I see ye are oniewise."

Torn? He could barely breathe. *Leana, you cannot leave me. Not like this.*

Neda righted the stool for him, tugging on his sleeve with her other hand. "Come, sit wi' me, Jamie. Not anither soul kens she's missin', though they'll find oot soon enough."

Stricken as if by a hard blow, he dropped onto the stool, holding his head in his hands. "Why didn't she tell me? Why didn't she say good-bye?"

"Ye ken why, lad." Neda rubbed the back of his neck with a hand rough from years of housework. "Ye would've begged her tae stay, Jamie. And she would've stayed tae please ye, because she luves ye wi' all her heart."

"At least we would have been together."

"Thegither?" She glanced up at the floor above them. "Not mony a married man lives under the same roof wi' twa women wha luve him baith the same."

Galled by her words, he shook off the motherly hand on his neck. "Rose does not love me the same way Leana does."

"Nae, but she thinks she does."

"Aye," he grumbled, standing again and starting to pace the floor. Yestreen in their cozy box bed, Rose had told him she loved him more times than he could tally. He rubbed his hand across the stubble of his beard, trying to sort things out, trying to think. "Surely someone else saw Leana leave."

Neda rose as well, moving about the kitchen to collect what was needed for breakfast. Naught would be cooked—after all, 'twas the Sabbath—but a few cold items would be spooned onto plates.

He watched her and realized she was stalling, avoiding his question. Did she not have an answer? Or did she not want to tell him?

Finally she confessed, "Willie took her in the chaise, though I dinna ken whaur."

Jamie grimaced. She'd traveled some distance then. Or had too much to carry. *God help me, she can't have left the parish!* Nae, 'twas unlikely; she couldn't depart Newabbey without a testimonial from the minister, stating both her marital state and her moral one. After three Sabbaths on the cutty stool for hochmagandy, she'd be a long time wrangling such a letter from Reverend Gordon's righteous hands. "When did Willie return?"

"He didn't."

His heart thudded to a stop.

"Not yet." Neda shook out a fresh apron and tied it round her waist, eying him all the while as if deciding what else to tell him. "Jamie, there *is* someone wha may ken whaur she is: Reverend Gordon. Ye'll remember Leana went tae kirk afore the rest o' ye yestreen."

"To subscribe her band."

"Mair than that, lad." Neda's shoulders sank. "Leana asked the reverend for a testimonial. She showed it tae me afore she left."

Nae. Jamie stared hard at the floor. "There's only one reason why she'd need such a letter."

"Aye," Neda said softly.

Jamie pressed the heels of his hands to his eyes.

I will never leave you.

But she had.

Sixty-Three

We sleep, but the loom of life never stops;
and the pattern which was weaving when the sun went down
is weaving when it comes up.

HENRY WARD BEECHER

The bed was cold.

'Twas the first thing Rose noticed when she rubbed the sleep from her eyes. The second was more urgent: Her husband was gone.

"Jamie?" She sat up at once, her heart in her throat, and threw open the bed curtains. "Beloved, are you there?"

How strange it felt to call him that. *Beloved.*

Rose pushed back the covers and slipped her legs over the side, waiting for her vision to adjust to the meager light. Either 'twas a weatherful morning or an earlier hour than she imagined. She padded across to the window and peered out, frowning as she did. It was not only miserably gray but foggy and rainy as well. Dreich weather for a kirkin. Just as a newborn babe's first morning at kirk was cause for celebration, so was the first Sabbath for a newlywed couple. At last she could sit beside Jamie in the pew and hold her head up as Mistress McKie.

Claiming the single candle on the dresser, Rose turned back toward the box bed and her breath caught. *The sheets.* Faintly stained with blood, they were a stark reminder of all that had happened yestreen. She put aside her candle and gathered up the soiled linens, swallowing her disappointment. Aye, Jamie had made verra sure she was no longer a maid, and he'd been gentle, just as she'd asked. But when she'd whispered, "I love you," he'd only said, "I am glad." And when she'd asked, "Can you love me, Jamie?" his answer had been, "I will try."

"Please do," she'd pleaded, then hated herself for sounding so desperate. But she *was* desperate. With Leana living under the same roof and loving him still, Rose worried she might never win Jamie's heart completely. Her silver wedding band, gleaming in the candlelight, caught her eye, and she forced herself to draw a calming breath. "I am my beloved's," she said aloud, if only to remind herself of that truth. "And my beloved is mine." Patience was not counted among her virtues, but she could learn, couldn't she? And who better to teach her by example than her sister?

Her spirits buoyed, Rose tied her wrapper about her waist, then carried the bed linens down the stair, intending to deposit them discreetly in the laundry. Please God, she would not need to change her sheets again when the time for her courses came. After all, Leana had conceived on *her* wedding night. "Please?" was all she dared whisper now, for Jamie was right: Almighty God alone could bestow such a blessing.

Drawing near the kitchen, she heard voices. *Neda. Jamie.* "Good morning," she called out, not wanting to startle them when she crossed the threshold. They both looked toward her, their faces ashen, and Rose gasped. "What is it? What's happened?"

The two exchanged glances, then Jamie spoke. "It's Leana. She's… gone."

"Gone?" Her arms sagged beneath the sheets. "Where? To kirk, hours early?"

"Nae, she left yestreen." Neda collected the linens from her. "I'll put these in the laundry while yer husband tells ye what little we ken."

Jamie did not take her hand, as Rose had hoped he might, though his gaze did meet hers. "We don't know where your sister went. Only that she's left Auchengray."

"Left?" Rose pulled her wrapper tight about her neck, suddenly chilled. "To go where?"

"Hard to say, lass. While you and I spoke our vows, your sister took the forest path to Auchengray. She packed verra little, Neda said, and then left in the chaise with Willie soon after you and your father returned from the village."

"Willie…," she breathed, remembering Annabel's words. *He's gone, mistress.* Rose looked out into the hall, her heart already flying up the stair to the nursery. "But what of Ian? She didn't—"

"Nae. She did not take him, Rose." Jamie's face was grim. "Although I am sure she wanted to, the law would never allow it."

"Poor Leana." She dropped onto the stool beside him, her heart heavy with the weight of his news. *She ran off because of me.* Why else would Leana leave Ian's side? Or Jamie's, for that matter? "My selfishness drove her away."

He touched her elbow, his expression softening. "'Twould take more than a sister's ill treatment to do that."

"You do not ken the awful questions I asked her."

Jamie opened his mouth as if to respond, then clamped it shut when Neda returned, her cap askew, her eyes bleary. "I didna sleep weel," Neda confessed, stirring the broth that had simmered all night on the hearth. "I promised Leana I wouldna breathe a wird 'til this morn. Duncan and I sat up half the nicht worryin'."

Rose stared in the direction of the spence. "So Father has not heard." She prayed she would not be on hand when Lachlan learned of his daughter's desertion. For that was how he would style it, though *escape* might be a better word for it. "Who will tell him?"

"I will." Jamie stood, yanking on his frayed cuffs. He'd dressed in the dark, and it showed. "The moment he awakens, Neda, send one of the maids to find me."

A sudden tapping at the back door brought them all to their feet. *Leana!*

"Is it her?" Rose darted toward the door and yanked it open, only to find Jenny Cullen shivering on their doorstep, dripping with rain. "Och, lass!" She stepped back, making room for her. "You poor dear, come in and have some tea." Neda found a clean towel to drape round her shoulders. "I'll get Ian ready," Rose assured her, "while you get dry and settled."

She flew up the stair, grateful to have a task to occupy her thoughts, which at the moment were scattered all over Galloway. Where would Leana run off to? Their father had distant relatives in Annan, though they'd corresponded little. Surely she didn't go all the way to Glentrool? Then she knew. *Twyneholm.* Aunt Meg adored her older niece. 'Twas the most likely place, though quite a distance for a short visit. Or was it not meant to be short? Did Leana plan to stay away for good?

Rose tarried at the door to the nursery, letting the possibilities sink in. She would have Jamie all to herself, a comforting thought. But she would also have Ian all to herself, and though she loved him dearly, his care was daunting. At the moment both men in her life loved her sister more than they loved her. Could she weather their disappointment if Leana never came home? *And what of you, Rose? Would you miss her?*

When the answer did not come at once, Rose leaned her forehead against the door, her cheeks hot with shame. Of course she would miss her sister. It was Jamie's missing Leana that gave her pause. *Let me be enough for you, Jamie. Please let me be enough.*

Putting her misgivings aside, Rose knocked on the door, then entered the nursery. Eliza was already awake, with her clothes set to rights and Ian wrapped in fresh linens. "Is the wet nurse here, mem?"

"Aye. I'll send her up." Rose planted a kiss on Ian's cheek, still warm from sleep. *You are mine now, lad, and that's certain.* Ian blinked at her, not quite awake, looking a bit dazed. "I feel the verra same," she assured him, kissing him once more. Tempting as it was, she would not tell Eliza about her mistress leaving; Lachlan must be informed first, or they all would suffer his rebuke. "Have Annabel meet me in my room to help me dress for our kirkin," she said as she turned to go. "I'm afraid we've a difficult day ahead."

Rose found Jenny drying her skirts by the hearth, the young mother's spirits well revived by the fire's warmth and the saucer of tea in her hands. "Whenever you're ready, Ian is waiting in the nursery, Jenny. I...I pray 'twill go better for you this time."

"Aye, mem." The maid curtsied, then hurried off to her duties.

Jamie turned to Rose, a look of concern in his moss green eyes. "It did not go well yestreen with Ian?"

"Nae, it did not." Rose bit her tongue before she scolded him for being too busy with the ewes to notice. "Even Father said not to expect much the first time."

Jamie snorted. "As if your father had any notion of such matters!"

She glanced down the hall. "Has he stirred in the spence? The sooner he is told, the better, Jamie. If he hears the servants blethering about it…"

"Right." Jamie straightened his shoulders. "I'll not wait then."

"I'd best come wi' ye." Neda slipped off her apron and draped it o'er the chopping block. "I'm the ane wha let her go. If there's a price tae be paid for that *lealtie,* I'm the ane wha should pay it."

"Nae," Rose was quick to say. "I'm the one to blame."

"We all let her go," Jamie protested, though his tone was not unkind. "I was off minding the sheep, Rose was busy with Ian, and Lachlan didn't give the lass a second thought. He will now." Jamie eyed them both. "If you want to come, I'll not refuse the company."

Lachlan opened the door a full minute after Jamie's firm knock, plainly disgruntled at being roused early from his bed. He waved them into the room and pointed to the chairs, while Neda saw to the hearth, grown cold overnight. When Jamie did not sit, Rose hovered behind his shoulder. She felt safer there.

Jamie wasted no time telling him. "Leana left Auchengray yestreen. Probably bound for Aunt Margaret's cottage in Twyneholm, though we cannot be certain."

Rose watched Lachlan's jaw working round, as though he were chewing on the news, preparing to spit it out. "Is this your doing, Nephew?" he growled, his voice thick with sleep. "Did she leave because of you?"

Jamie leaned back as though he were slapped, his shoulder brushing hers. "N-nae, sir. She left without a word to either Rose or me."

Neda recounted her side of the story while the bonnet laird stared at his desk without comment. A silent Lachlan McBride was even more frichtsome than an angry one, Rose decided. When no more details could be added, the room fell silent.

Lachlan strode to his desk and reached for his wooden money box, throwing back the lid. "Guid," he said, nodding. "At least she did not fill her pockets before she left."

"Father! Leana would hardly take your silver."

He shrugged. "She's lost her market, as Duncan would say. None will pay to have your sister for a bride now. I thought she might have helped herself to my thrifite, but I see she has not."

Rose saw something too: a knotted gold cord stretched across the heap of coins.

The thorns which I have reap'd are of the tree
I planted; they have torn me, and I bleed.

GEORGE GORDON, LORD BYRON

A re ye sure ye won't come hame wi' me, Miss McBride?" Willie
tugged off his wool bonnet and worked it round in his hands
while his wet boots dripped on the cottage's flagstone floor. "They'll be
sairlie missin' ye at Auchengray. Truth is, I hate tae think o' ridin' up tae
the gate *wi'oot* ye." He hung his head, displaying his balding scalp. "Mr.
McKie will niver let me groom Walloch again."

"Now, Willie." Leana wrapped her fingers round the orraman's
hands, plaid cap and all. "You're not to blame for my leaving. I asked
you to help me, and you bravely did so. Neda will see that you're
treated properly when you get home." *Dear Neda.* She'd helped Leana
slip away unnoticed with a small case of necessities and no questions.
Leana had left behind everything but her sorrow and her tears, which,
like the late-March rain, had fallen without ceasing since she'd arrived
in Twyneholm.

She gazed out the small-paned window at the dreich sky. Gray and
damp, a mixture of fog and showers, 'twould make for a miserable ride
home for poor Willie. Even so, she envied him. *Home. Jamie. Ian.* To let
her thoughts wander there was to be crushed to the ground.

"I'll not send you back to Auchengray empty handed, Willie." She
produced two sealed letters from her traveling bag, written at Aunt
Meg's table in the wee hours of the morn when she could not sleep.
"You will give this letter to Jamie, aye? No one else? And this one to my
father to read aloud."

What she could not tell them in person, she would tell them on
paper. 'Twas the coward's way of doing things. A considerate person
would have left such letters behind in her wake to ease her family's

worry. Instead, she'd escaped by way of the stables while the family ate supper. Leana would not be surprised if her father tossed his letter in the fire unread.

"Fare thee well, mem." Willie pulled his cap on tight and tucked her letters in his coat, along with pickled mutton for the journey back. The two of them had arrived in Twyneholm nigh unto midnight, slept as late as they could, and attended the parish kirk with her aunt. 'Twould be six o' the clock before Willie saw Lowtis Hill and the last turn home.

"Godspeed," Leana whispered, a handkerchief pressed to her nose as she watched old Bess clop up the hill past the kirk and disappear from view.

"Come, lass." Her aunt edged her shoulders away from the window. "He's well on his way now."

"Aye." Leana tucked her handkerchief in her sleeve. "How can I thank you enough for taking me in, Aunt Meg?"

When Margaret Halliday raised her silvery eyebrows, Leana realized she was staring at a looking glass, seeing herself forty years hence. Meg's golden locks had faded to silver, and her eyes were more gray than blue, but 'twas the same broad face and full mouth that greeted Leana in her mirror each morning. More speeritie than she, her aunt smiled from morn 'til murk, if only to display her full set of teeth.

"Och!" Meg was saying. "Aren't I your mother's sister? And aren't you my favorite niece besides?"

Despite her heavy heart, Leana managed a faint smile. "I'll not tell Rose you said that."

Meg rolled her eyes, just as Rose did. "What a time I had with your sister under my roof for a week! And in winter too, when I couldn't shoo her out the door and borrow a minute's peace for myself."

"But I'll be here longer than a week," Leana cautioned her. Could her maiden aunt, blithe to live alone, bear her constant company? The cozy stone cottage had two rooms—one for sleeping and dressing, the other for cooking and eating and sewing and reading and everything else. "I pray I won't be a burden to you."

"A burden? Why, you're a welcome guest." Meg touched Leana's shoulder, then made her way about the cottage straightening her oft-mended curtains and tidying things as she went. Though Burnside was a humble place, no cottage in the parish was more neatly swept. "Don't you ken your auld auntie gets *lanelie* now and again?"

"Nae, I do not," Leana said lightly, standing to brush the wrinkles from her claret gown. "At kirk this morning, nary a soul came through the door without seeking your counsel about one thing or another."

"You ken why, don't you? They wanted a good look at *you*, Leana, my loosome visitor from faraway Newabbey."

She found herself gazing out the window again. " 'Tis not so far to Auchengray. Naught but two dozen miles."

"In Galloway, 'tis a world away. There are folk in Twyneholm who've ne'er seen any parish but their own." Meg lit another candle, made of beeswax from her own hives. "That's better," her aunt murmured as the room brightened, "for 'tis a gloomy day."

"I pray 'tis not gloomy at Auchengray." Leana turned away from the window. "Rose deserves a chance at happiness."

Meg's busy hands stilled. "Even though she never gave you that chance?"

" 'Tis plain why she didn't. Had you seen her face, Auntie, when she came home to Auchengray expecting to marry Jamie after her week here with you—"

"Hoot! You can be sure I heard about it." Meg released a noisy sigh and resumed her tasks. "Rose posted a very long letter to me while you and Jamie were in Dumfries."

"She'll not be writing you now, I wager. Now that she has Jamie to keep her company." *My Jamie. My love.*

Her aunt asked gently, "Will Jamie be happy as well?"

"I pray he will be." *Do you, Leana?* She bowed her head, ashamed of the truth. "Perhaps if I am not there to...to interfere. To distract him." *To tempt him. And be tempted by him.* "With me gone, 'twill be easier for all of them."

"Perhaps." Meg leaned over her and cupped her chin. "But not easy for you, Leana. It could ne'er be easy to allow another woman to raise your son."

Leana fumbled in her sleeve for her handkerchief. "Leaving Ian was the worst of all. The verra worst."

She'd held him until the last, standing with Neda in the barn while Willie brought round the chaise. Neda's words, though kind, had brought little comfort. "Ye're doin' what must be done, for the puir lad should ne'er have tae pick which mither he luves."

Leana had buried her sobs in Ian's blanket, lest someone hear them and put a stop to her departure. "I can't bear to leave," she'd said over and over. "But I must, Neda. 'Tis best for all of them if I do."

"Aye, lass," Neda had said, embracing her as the chaise drew to a stop at the barn door. " 'Tis."

Ashamed of her endless crying, Leana pressed her handkerchief to her eyes. "At the end…in my last minutes with Ian…I could not let go." A sob came out before she could catch it in her throat. "Had Neda not lifted him from my arms…oh, Aunt Meg, I might be holding him still!" She pressed her forearms hard against her breasts, dismayed at their fullness, even though she'd wrapped them with linen. "But I had to…wean him. I had to…let go. I had to…"

"I'm so sorry." Meg's eyes shone with unshed tears.

"I had to…" No other words would come. Grief, heavy as her mother's gravestone, pressed down on her, bending her over the small dining table until her cheek rested against the wood and baptized it with her tears.

"You're a good mother, Leana." Meg comforted her, stroking her hair. "You did what the law and the kirk required you to do. Ian cannot understand what you've done for him now, but he will. Someday his father will tell him what a wonderful mother he had."

Leana shook her head, her voice pinched with pain. "I could have remained at Auchengray, if only for Ian." Even saying it, she knew it wasn't true. "When Jamie moves his family to Glentrool in May, Auntie, perhaps then I'll return home." *To an empty house. With empty arms.*

"You did what was right, Leana. You've no need to doubt it." With some difficulty her aunt crouched beside her and wrapped her bony arms round her neck. "Now you must wait for the pain to ease. Wait on the Lord, lass. Be of good courage. And he shall strengthen your heart."

Leana's head sank back onto her arms. Her body felt like an open wound, leaking tears that would not stop, leaking milk meant for her son. *Ian, my sweet Ian!*

Ever so slowly Aunt Meg straightened and kissed the top of Leana's head. "There, now. Sit for a minute." The older woman moved quietly round the room, giving Leana time to gather her strength and dry her cheeks. After a bit Aunt Meg reached for a pot swinging o'er the hearth. "Suppose I make some tea to chase away the cold and damp seeping through my thatched roof." She eyed Leana's writing desk, still propped on the table. "You'll need to move that, dearie, or we'll have no room for our saucers. 'Tis a fine writing desk though. A gift from your father?"

"Nae." Leana took a deep, shaky breath and ran her fingers across the polished wood. " 'Tis from Jamie."

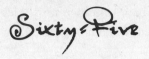

Sixty-Five

Thou bringest…letters unto trembling hands.
ALFRED, LORD TENNYSON

"'Tis for ye, Mr. McKie. Miss Leana bid me deliver it tae ye directly."
Jamie took the sealed letter from the orraman's weathered hand, relieved that in the fading light of the gloaming the tremor in his own hand did not show. Willie had arrived at the mains an hour ago, throwing the household into a stramash, even as he presented Leana's letter of explanation to Lachlan. Read aloud by the bonnet laird through clenched teeth, her missive was full of apology and remorse, begging her father and the others not to blame Willie or anyone else. No one but her.

Hearing her written confession only made things worse. *Oh, Leana. 'Tis my fault, not yours. I should ne'er have kissed you. I should ne'er have let you go.* Even now, Twyneholm seemed within reach. He could mount Walloch and arrive before midnight.

And then what? Run for their lives? Flee from their families, from the kirk, from the law? He'd entertained the notion for the last hour, always coming to the same bitter conclusion: *And then what?* He could not abandon his son or, in fairness, his new wife. Leana knew that. *Is that why you chose another parish, beloved?*

He'd come to the stables for a moment's peace. To think. And to grieve. "Would that you had brought me Miss McBride rather than this," Jamie told Willie candidly, fingering the letter. "Still, I'm grateful for your discretion."

Willie could not meet his gaze. "Miss Leana said tae gie it tae ye alone, sir. 'No one else,' she said. She's a fine lady, Mr. McKie. I'm…I'm sorry."

Jamie nodded, fearing his voice might betray him.

The moment Willie shuffled off, Jamie pulled a lantern close and broke the seal, rubbing his thumb over it first, noticing a faint print trapped in the red wax. *She touched it. Right there.*

He unfolded the stiff paper. The letter was not as long as he'd hoped. He wanted pages upon pages of her words, sentence after sentence of her voice in his head, in his heart. But he was glad for what he held in his hands, knowing it was for his eyes alone.

Sunday, 28 March 1790

My dearest Jamie,

Let me begin by telling you what matters most: I love you with all my heart. And I will never stop loving you.

I did not mean to leave in secret, for I fear I have hurt you greatly in doing so. Please, please forgive me, Jamie. If I had looked into your eyes, I would have stayed forever.

Was it only yestermorn we spoke in the garden? It seems days ago. Weeks. Every hour apart from you is agony.

If I were a stronger woman, I would be content to live quietly in a corner of my father's house. To watch Ian grow and to watch you fall in love with my bonny sister a second time. But I am not as strong as you may think. I am only a woman who loves you. And who knows that your future is not with me but with Rose.

Oh, my dear Jamie, how hard it is to write that!

You may say that you cannot love Rose again, but with time you will. She is young and has much to learn, but at heart my sister is a dear girl. And she loves you. Never doubt that. She has waited a long time and has risked much to be your wife.

I have come to realize, much as it grieves me, that I cannot be completely yours. Not until I hear you say, "I, James Lachlan McKie, do take this woman, Leana McBride, to be my lawfully wedded wife." A day I know will never come. For though you have proclaimed those sacred vows twice, you did not speak my name.

Oh, Leana. Stunned, he fell back against Walloch's stall. *I would gladly say your name, lass. Every day of my life.*

> If I could think of some way to be near you but not
> touch you. To see you without others seeing me. To love
> you without needing to be loved in return. Oh, Jamie, if
> I had a way to do those things, I would.
>
> If I could hold Ian every other minute of the day. If
> I could share him with Rose with a glad heart and not
> feel that a part of me had died, I would come running
> back to Auchengray. But I fear I cannot share Ian any
> more than I can share you.
>
> Promise me you will be my arms for our son.
> And my voice. And my heart. Hold Ian close. Say
> the words I would say. He needs you, Jamie. Even more
> than I do. And I need you more than I need air to
> breathe.
>
> I will always love you. And in truth, I will never leave
> you, for no other man may claim what is already yours.
> But I do release you, Jamie. To love my sister and to seek
> your future together in Glentrool.
>
> You will always be in my prayers and ever in my heart.
> Please forgive me.
>
> Leana

He read it again from the beginning to be sure, to be very sure he understood what she meant yet did not fully say. It was there again, and the third time as well.

Leana was truly gone. She would not come back to him.

Not because she did not love him. But because she did.

My love. My Leana. Jamie ran his thumb across her name. As if the word had texture, like the sealing wax. As if it held an image of her that he might touch. All at once her inky signature disappeared from the page, smeared by a stray tear on his thumb, now stained in black.

"You have marked me, my love," he whispered into the darkened stable. "I can never wholly belong to another. But I will love your son and mine. And I will honor my marriage vows because they cost me everything."

They cost me you.

Sixty-Six

There is none,
In all this cold and hollow world, no fount
Of deep, strong, deathless love, save that within
A mother's heart.
FELICIA HEMANS

I *will never be a mother.*
Rose sat in tears at her dressing table, dismayed to find her monthly courses had made an unwelcome appearance. Was it simply her body responding to the pull of the moon, like the Solway tides? Or was it the doctor's grim prediction coming true before her eyes? *You may be unable to bear children.*

This much was certain: Swallowing tincture of valerian had produced little but a horrid taste in her mouth. No wonder Jamie seemed loath to kiss her.

Jamie, Jamie. Five days of being his wife. Five days of being Ian's mother. And neither role felt one bit comfortable yet. She was trying hard to be cheerful and not complain, not make demands. But Leana's absence left a gaping hole in the household, one Rose feared she might never fill.

Thoughts of hardworking Leana, seldom seen without a needle in her hands, pricked Rose's conscience. She'd dawdled in her bedroom for most of the morning lest she be given more tasks to do. *Jamie's sark requires mending, Rose. Might you find his cravat, Rose? Ian needs his porridge, Rose. Have you changed his linens, Rose?* 'Twas endless, this business of being a wife and a mother! Leana's letter to the family had said nothing about how long she planned to stay in Twyneholm. Would her sister return in a fortnight? In a twelvemonth? Never?

Rose glanced at the clothes press, where a second letter from Leana had mysteriously appeared the day after Willie had come back from Twyneholm. A letter addressed to Jamie. Perhaps Leana had given *him* some clue to her plans. Her sister's familiar handwriting stared back at her every time she opened the oak door to find a clean shirt or smooth the creases from his coat sleeves. She was certain Leana's words to Jamie were vastly different than the ones written to the household. Did she dare pluck it out of the clothes press and read it? Jamie was away with her father to Edingham, calling on the Widow Douglas yet again. Since the men weren't expected home before supper, 'twould be the perfect day. The wax seal was already broken. And she would put it back just as she'd found it.

She eyed the bedroom door to make certain it was closed, then threaded her hand between the sleeves and hems until her fingers touched the cream-colored paper. She gingerly lifted it out, taking careful note of where it was hidden, then stepped toward the window for more light and opened Leana's letter.

Even before she read the first word, she noticed the signature was reduced to a smear of ink at the bottom of the page. Had Jamie tried to wipe it away, hoping to disguise the writer's identity? Anyone at Auchengray would recognize the hand that wrote it. Leana's salutation made it plainer still.

My dearest Jamie...

Rose's fingers gripped the paper. *Nae, my sister. You may claim him no longer.* She read on, alarmed by Leana's lingering affection for her husband. And when did the two of them speak in the garden? Then Leana's comments turned in her direction, and Rose's feathers fluttered back into place.

Fall in love with my bonny sister...

Rose nodded with relief. *Aye, Jamie. Please do.* He'd warmed to her a little. Yet whenever he gazed at her, Rose felt as though he were looking at her from a distance. Half a dozen parishes west perhaps.

Your future is not with me but with Rose.

She blinked and read the words again in disbelief. Could her sister mean that, loving Jamie as she did?

My sister is a dear girl…

The compliment heated her cheeks, though more from shame than from pleasure. How could Leana still speak so well of her?

She loves you…and has risked much…

Rose touched her damp brow, staring at the letter. Leana saw too much, understood too well what was going on inside her heart. For 'twas true: Loving Jamie, insisting that he honor his vows, all the while knowing he loved her sister and not her, was indeed risky. Foolish, most folk would say.

Except Leana would not say that. She had taken the very same risks.

Rose's mouth fell open. *Oh, Leana. You do understand.* Why had she not considered that before? *Because you only think of yourself, Rose.* She shuddered, knowing it was true. And hating that truth.

She focused on Leana's letter once more. *I cannot share Ian.*

Rose swallowed the lump rising in her throat. "And I cannot raise Ian alone," she confessed, addressing the paper as if Leana might hear her. Caring for Ian had proved to be much more difficult than she'd imagined. The child had settled down enough to nurse at Jenny's breast. But when Rose held him, he wriggled and fussed, obviously miserable. "What am I doing wrong, Leana?" she pleaded. "Is it because I am not you?"

The letter's silent prodding bruised her heart. *Say the words I would say.*

"I *do* say them!" Tears pooled in her eyes. "I tell Ian all the things a child wants to hear. That he's dear. That he's precious. That he's loved." Even saying those words aloud, Rose knew they were not what Ian needed most. "Is it because I am not the mother who bore him that he cries so?" She shook the paper, demanding an answer. "How can he miss you when he's naught but a baby?"

The same way you missed your mother, Rose. From the hour you were born. A fresh wave of grief swelled inside her. Undone, she collapsed on the nearest chair, the letter fluttering to the floor. *Mother.* The name she had never truly spoken. The name she might never hear. *Please God, may it not be so.*

The knock at the door was faint but enough to stir Rose from her painful reverie. Blinking away her tears, she stood, a bit weak kneed, and called out a greeting.

Annabel needed no further invitation, breezing into the room with a whimpering Ian in her arms. "The lad wants his noony."

"Nae," Rose sighed, "the lad wants his mother. His true mother, not a poor substitute."

Annabel's bright expression faded, and sympathy took its place. "Dinna fash yerself, Mistress McKie. Ian will warm tae ye in time. Bairns are hard tae please at this age. Always greetin' for this or that." She held the boy up. "Aren't I richt, Ian? Yer stepmither is tryin' her best tae see ye blithe and weel. As for ye, lad, see that ye honor yer faither and yer mither. 'Tis the wird o' the Laird, and I dinna mean yer *Granfaither* McBride."

Rose reached for him, both hands filled with hope. "Will you come to me, Ian?"

He did not stretch out his soft arms as he always had for Leana. But he let Rose disengage him from Annabel's grasp without protest and rested against her velvet bodice without squirming. How good he felt in her arms!

Annabel grinned. "There, ye see? Better already."

The maidservant spoke too soon. Ian suddenly howled as if stuck with a sprig of blackthorn and waved his arms toward the red-haired lass, his wishes clear. "Och! Come here then, and we'll see ye fed and put doon for a nap." She looked at Rose, clearly chagrined. " 'Tis all the child cares aboot at the moment: his noony and his nap. Ye'll help me, aye?"

Rose knew Annabel didn't need her help. The canny maid was doing what she could to boost her spirits. Grateful, Rose followed maid and child into the hall, closing the door behind them, determined to spend the day making herself useful. As her mother used to do, by Neda's account. As Leana always did.

The hours passed quickly, if not easily. While Ian napped, Rose was given the daunting task of helping Neda make marmalade. The Seville oranges, procured at market in Dumfries, were dear in cost and easily bruised. "Grate them wi' care, and see ye dinna lose a bittie o' the rind," Neda cautioned her. "After that, ye cut them crosswise and squeeze the juice through a sieve. We'll need lemons as weel, two lemons tae every dozen oranges. And whan ye boil the rinds, change the water *aften*. 'Twill take awa the bitter taste."

Rose did as she was told, wincing when she cut her finger and plunged it into the tart juice, yelping when she burned her hand clarifying the sugar. When all was finished and a fresh pot of marmalade sat cooling by the window, she hardly noticed her wounds for the praise Neda heaped on her head.

"I'll be proud tae serve yer marmalade wi' the boiled ham ye'll be havin' for supper," the older woman assured her. "Won't Jamie be surprised tae learn wha made it for him?"

The sun hung low in the sky when Rose heard Jamie and her father come through the front door. Her heart quickened at her husband's voice, at the sound of his footsteps heading up to their room. Perhaps she might keep him company while he dressed for dinner. She'd just wiped her hands clean on her apron and stepped toward the hall when she heard Jamie calling her name from the top of the stair.

"Rose?" His tone was less than cordial. "I would speak to you at once."

Apprehension slowed her steps. Had there been some mishap at Edingham? Had Jamie and her father argued on the journey home? Or was it something she'd done or not done? Exhaling to ease the tension building inside her, she climbed the stair, looking up at him waiting for her, his hands behind his back. "Jamie," she said tentatively, "is anything the matter?"

His gaze was even, and so was his voice. Unnervingly so. "Aye, 'tis the matter of a certain correspondence. Addressed to me, not to you. But which, apparently, you have read."

Leana's letter. She froze, her foot on the last step, picturing the letter discarded beside the bedroom chair. Forgotten until now.

Jamie held it up, waving it before her. "Am I correct? You found this in the clothes press and read it?"

"Aye," she said meekly. There was no use pretending otherwise. "I must confess, Jamie, when I spied it among your clothes, curiosity got the better of me, and I…I read it." She ducked her head. "Most of it, that is."

"Well, by all means come read the rest." He pulled her into their room, more gently than she expected, and aimed her toward the reading chair.

She stood rather than sat, wanting to be near him. "Jamie, I'm truly sorry. I had no business—"

"None whatsoever." He shook his head, clearly irritated with her but doing an admirable job of controlling it. "Do you nae ken what the Buik says, Rose? 'The heart of her husband doth safely trust in her'? How am I to trust a woman who would do such a thing?"

"I am…so sorry." She splayed her hands, at a loss for what else she might say to appease him. "Please, Jamie. Can a wife not be forgiven for wanting to read a letter from her own sister?"

"Forgiven?" His features softened a bit. "Aye. Of course you are forgiven."

He meant it. She could see that he did. When had he changed so? The Jamie who first came to Auchengray would have scolded her for an hour.

"The last line is the one you most need to hear." He held out the stiff paper. "Leana wrote, 'I do release you, Jamie. To love my sister.'"

Oh, Leana. "Do you think she…meant it?"

"You ken she did, Rose. When did your sister speak anything but the truth?" He folded the letter and slipped it inside his waistcoat, training his gaze on her all the while. "Because of my love for Leana, I am trying hard to love you, Rose. For all our sakes. But you…you make that very difficult sometimes."

"I do not doubt it." Grateful for his honesty and surprised at her own, she stepped closer. "I pray you will do as my sister asks and love me, Jamie. Love me, as I love you." When he did not flinch, she grew bolder still and rested her hand on his sleeve. "Please fill up the hollow place inside me," she whispered. "I die a little each day it remains empty."

His eyes searched hers. "Do you mean your heart?"

She bowed her head, ashamed to speak the truth. "I mean my womb."

Jamie started to say something, then turned away from her instead.

"Tell me what you're thinking, Jamie, for I cannot guess." A note of pleading threaded her words. "Is it wrong to want a child? To want someone who truly needs me?"

Jamie's voice was gentle. "Nae, it is not wrong, Rose."

Not wrong. But selfish. The word had dogged her all morning.

When Jamie turned back to her, the compassion on his face was unmistakable. "You *are* hollow inside, Rose, but 'tis not your womb that is empty. 'Tis your heart. Only the Almighty can fill that. Not me and not a bairn." His hands lightly grasped her shoulders. "Do you understand? Do you hear what I'm saying?"

She wilted beneath his touch. "You are saying you do not love me. And that no child of yours will e'er be mine."

"Nae, lass! You're not listening…"

Rose fled from the room, having listened to enough.

Sixty-Seven

God tempers the wind to the new shorn lamb.
SCOTTISH PROVERB

L ove my sister.
      "She is *your* sister," Jamie grumbled to himself. "*You* love her."
He heaved his water bucket into the trough too abruptly, making the
nearby ewes jump. "Sorry, lassies." He soothed the skittish animals with
familiar words and the calming sound of his voice. "Naught to worry.
'Tis only fresh water from Lochend."

The forenoon sun bathed the pastures in a warm yellow as he made
his rounds alone. There were too many ewes and not enough shepherds,
so the men had divided their duties. Jamie preferred to work alone, for
then he could imagine Leana walking the braes with him. Not an hour
went by when he did not hear her voice in the snippet of a ballad sung
by a passing shepherd or sense her touch in the caress of a soft April
breeze ruffling his hair.

To look at Ian was to catch a glimpse of the woman who had given
birth to him. Leana had always declared that Ian was a smaller version
of him. But Jamie knew 'twas not altogether true. Ian had his mother's
eyes. A clear gray blue. Unblinking. Trusting.

Jamie saw her every time his son looked at him.

Oh, Leana. Will you not come home to me?

'Twas a question already answered.

Love my sister.

"I'm trying, Leana." *But only because you've asked me to. And only
because I love you.*

Jamie climbed over the dry stane dyke and moved to the next pasture, steering clear of the muddy spots. He'd been up since before dawn,
seeing to the ewes, helping them deliver the last lambs of the season. All

twins, all healthy. Jamie shook his head, still astounded by it. "It seems I'm a better shepherd than I am a husband," he confessed to the lambs tottering round his knees.

"I'd have tae agree with ye there, lad." Duncan strolled toward him, a wry grin stretched across his weathered features. "Did I not once tell ye that Rose was a stubborn ewe and ye should handle her meikle the same?"

Jamie grunted. "Meaning what? See that she has a pair of wee bairns to care for?"

"Aye, 'twould keep her busy," Duncan agreed. "But ye ken verra weel 'tis not what the lass needs most."

"Is that so?" Jamie felt the skin beneath his collar heating. "Rose is my wife. I ken what the girl needs."

Duncan wagged his head, bending to pour more feed in the trough. "I'm not sure ye do, lad. Ye're thinkin' she needs yer kisses and sae forth. All weel and guid. But what Rose needs mair than a' that is what *ye* have, Jamie: the assurance o' God's luve and forgiveness for a' she's done wrong."

"*Wheesht!*" Jamie kicked the trough hard. "Let her get it from the Almighty then."

Duncan straightened, putting aside his bucket to fold his arms across his chest. "Was that how 'twas wi' *ye,* Jamie?" Though his voice was soft, Duncan's words jabbed like a stick. "Did ye seek after God's mercy a' by yerself and find it on yer ain? Seems to me Leana's luve for ye paved the way."

Jamie jammed his toe into the dirt, staring down at his boot as he did. Anything was better than looking Duncan in the eye. Or admitting the man was right.

"All right, Jamie. Ye dinna have tae confess it, for we baith ken the truth." Duncan lowered himself onto the dry stane dyke, crossing his ankles as if settling in for a bit. "D'ye see a strange irony at work here, young James?"

"Aye," he growled. That much he could confess. "I must do for Rose what Leana did for me."

"Guid." Duncan nodded in approval. "And what did the lass do, Jamie? Say it plain for ye ain benefit."

Infuriated, Jamie ground out the words. "Leana loved me when I did not deserve it, when I could not—*och*, when I *would* not return it."

"Ye were richt on the first, Jamie. Ye couldna luve Leana in those days, for a man canna gie what he doesna have." Duncan stood once more, clamping his hand on Jamie's shoulder. "Whaur d'ye suppose Leana found the strength tae luve ye, tae forgive ye whan ye were busy chasin' after her sister? Ye ken the answer now, aye?"

He that dwelleth in love dwelleth in God. Jamie groaned in resignation. "Aye, I ken the answer. But how can I love a woman who betrayed her own sister and me as well? Had Rose held her tongue when she was questioned by the kirk session, none of this would have happened."

Duncan studied him from beneath the brim of his bonnet. "Did it ne'er occur tae ye that this turnabout might be the will o' the Almighty?"

Jamie's chest tightened. *A blessing instead of a curse.* Was it possible?

"Forgive the lass, Jamie. Show yer new wife what it means tae be luved. And I dinna mean what happens in yer box bed whan the candles are snuffed. A' the other hours o' the day matter as weel."

Och! Jamie shook off Duncan's grip on his shoulder and stamped about the pasture, pretending to be getting the dirt off his boots. *Now* the man was telling him to love Rose round the clock! He spun on his heel and marched toward him. "Six months ago you told me to love Leana." He stopped inches away from the man and leaned forward. "Well, Duncan, I did! And I do. Can you not see 'tis Leana's love that matters to me, not Rose's?"

Duncan did not back away nor change his tune. "But ye already have Leana's luve, Jamie. And ye always will. 'Tis the way the lass was made by her Creator. The question is, what will ye do wi' that fine luve o' hers?" He waved at the boulders scattered about the pasture. "Bask in it all yer days, like an adder curled up on a sunny rock? Or will you do as Leana would have you do and care for Rose, who needs luve sae sairlie?"

Love my sister. "So." Jamie narrowed his eyes. "When did you read my letter?"

Duncan chuckled. "I ken naught aboot a letter. I've merely watched ye tryin' tae be kind round the girl, pullin' back on yer impatience, bitin' yer tongue. Things a man does if he's bent on doin' richt by his wife. Guid things, mind ye. But ye're holdin' back the rest o' ye."

Jamie flinched, as if Duncan had brandished a knife, so close to the bone did the man's words cut him.

"Let her climb inside a corner of yer heart, lad." Duncan thumped soundly on Jamie's chest. " 'Tis big enough now."

Jamie turned away, hiding his grief. But he could not keep it out of his voice. "You ask too much."

"I'm not the one wha's askin', Jamie."

Duncan's words trailed after him for days, then a week, then two, nipping at his heels like one of the collies. *Show yer new wife what it means tae be luved.* It was plain Rose was showering *him* with affection. His favorite ginger jam waited by his breakfast plate. A stack of neatly hemmed handkerchiefs appeared in the clothes press. She wore her hair down the way he liked it, with the braid curling about her shoulder. And—the most telling of all—she kept her sharp tongue well sheathed and her soft arms wrapped round his shoulders at night.

More than once of late he'd caught a glimpse of the Rose he'd kissed on the day he'd arrived at Auchengray. The charming Rose who'd stolen his breath and then his heart. *Sweet. Innocent.*

A sad irony, compared to how he felt. *Bitter. And guilty.*

Bitter over having his future decided for him yet again. And guilty for kissing Leana in the bothy, longing for more. *'Twas a temptation.* Aye, it was that. Knowing Leana as he did, he should have realized she would not simply rise the next morning as if nothing had happened. Nae, not his Leana. She had run to the kirk; then she had run to Twyneholm. *She ran to get away from you, Jamie.*

And left him to face the woman he'd wronged. The same woman he couldn't bring himself to forgive. *Rose.*

Love my sister. Aye, he was trying. Except it did not feel like love; it felt like betrayal. Even though he'd loved Rose before. Even though he cared for her now. Even though the kirk said they were rightfully wed. *Husbands, love your wives.* Could he do as the Buik commanded? Could he forgive Rose and love her again?

Sixty-Eight

A woman's love
Is mighty, but a mother's heart is weak,
And by its weakness overcomes.
JAMES RUSSELL LOWELL

Nae! Not again.
Rose washed the stain from her nightgown, drenching the fabric with her tears. *Why, why, why?* No matter how hard she scrubbed it with soap, the faint red outline remained. Reminding her. Taunting her. *You will never be a mother.*

Another four weeks had come and gone, taking her hopes with them. Still no bairn grew in her womb. Leana was so fertile she had conceived Ian on her wedding night. *But not you, Rose.* She threw the nightgown into a basket and quit the laundry room, blowing out the candle as she went. Following the dim passageway toward the main part of the house, Rose felt her spirits lift the smallest notch at the sound of a certain shepherd laughing in the kitchen: Jamie, preparing to head out for the morning.

With the lambing finished, the fruit of Jamie's labors gamboled o'er the pastures of Auchengray, twin lambs beside every woolly ewe. In mere weeks the flocks had more than doubled in size. 'Twas so remarkable a feat of shepherding even Reverend Gordon had given the Almighty praise for the bountiful provision during services: "Whereof every one beareth twins, and there is not one barren among them." Her father had beamed, as if 'twere his doing. After having his older daughter climb the repentance stool and then flee the parish, the bonnet laird of Auchengray needed a reason to hold up his head again at kirk.

Rose needed a reason too; she needed a child. Proof that she and Jamie had truly married and were living as husband and wife. Otherwise, the gossips would begin to blether that, while Mr. McKie's ewes were fertile, his wife was barren.

She emerged into the kitchen—the brightest and warmest room in any season—and found a flock of maidservants gathered round Jamie like so many ewes. But he was not looking at them. He was looking at her. Not with desire perhaps. But warm regard was a welcome improvement. After a long and chilly month together, Jamie was beginning to thaw. To look at her without evading her gaze. To listen to her without clenching his jaw. And, aye, to embrace her on occasion without seeming to hold her at arm's length.

The Jamie she had once known and loved was no more. This man was different. Older. Kinder. And wiser in ways she did not fully understand. Jamie did not love her as he loved Leana. But he no longer resented her, and for that she was grateful. Theirs was a marriage of compromise: She had stopped expecting so much, and Jamie, it seemed, had stopped expecting so little. He was hers alone, and in that she took what solace she could.

Jamie extended his arm to her, a gentleman in shepherd's garb. "Will you take a walk with me in the garden, Rose?"

She couldn't refuse so gallant an offer. They headed for the back door together, leaving the maidservants in their wake, and stepped into the fresh air of a late April morning. After a month of showers everything was growing in thick, green abundance. She couldn't begin to name the flowers, but the vegetables were easily recognized. Salad onions and fist-sized heads of cabbage, planted last autumn, would be carted off to the kitchen soon enough and a few stray leeks from last season picked before new seeds were sown.

"Now all the garden needs is Leana," Rose said lightly, testing the waters. Perhaps the more they spoke of her sister, the less Jamie would mourn her absence. Leana was not coming back; Jamie had assured her of that. Rose was chagrined to discover that nothing relieved—and saddened—her more.

"Your sister has a gift for gardening," Jamie agreed. His voice, pleasant but even, gave away nothing. "I'm glad Eliza has taken to poking in the soil in her stead." He gazed up at the sky. "It's been a fine April. Wet, as usual, but mild enough."

"Aye, mild." She could not seem to brighten her voice to match the weather.

They walked past Leana's physic garden. Rose pretended not to see the valerian, taller than it had been a month ago. If she stared at the soil long enough, she could almost see two faint indentations where Leana had knelt, pressing the plant back into the earth. *Forgive me, Leana.* She'd been unforgivably cruel to her sister that day. *Are you asking me how to please my husband?* Leana had fled to Twyneholm to get away from her selfish younger sister; that was the only possible explanation, for Leana would ne'er have left Jamie and Ian otherwise.

"What's wrong, Rose? You're entirely too quiet this morning."

When had Jamie become so perceptive? 'Twas a bothersome state of affairs when a lass could not keep her feelings hidden from a man. "I discovered…that is, I am not…" 'Twas too shameful a thing to mention. Rose aimed her gaze at a row of cabbages. "I'm not…expecting a child."

"Ah. I see."

Was he glad? Disappointed? Would he tell her if she asked? *Och!* She was married to Jamie and yet did not truly know him. Would he ever trust her with his whole heart?

"Perhaps 'tis best you're not with child just yet, Rose." He patted her arm like a sympathetic cousin. Not like a devastated husband. "I have some…some news I hope to share with you in the next day or so."

News? She swallowed a small knot of apprehension. "Will you not give me a hint, Jamie?"

"I've a few details to attend to first. But soon." He turned to her then, his eyes the color of the nettle leaves at their feet. "Are you well enough for a journey, Rose?"

He means Twyneholm.

'Twas all painfully clear. Jamie could not bear to be apart from Leana another hour. Or her sister had written Jamie, begging him to bring Ian to see her. Or Leana was coming home, and they would meet her carriage in Dumfries.

Rose tried to sound nonchalant. "A…journey? Of course, Jamie. Whatever you say."

Say it isn't Twyneholm. Please, please!

"Fine then. We'll talk more later, Le-…uh, Rose." She gasped. He had never called her *Leana.* Not once, not ever.

"Och, lass!" The look on his face was one of horror. He grasped both her hands, pulling her round where she could not turn away. "I am sorry, Rose. Truly, I am."

He was so polite, so genuinely upset, her disappointment soon faded. "I ken you did not mean to confuse us. We are sisters, but in few ways are we alike."

A flicker in his eyes, no more. "Very few," he agreed.

Too few, she heard behind the words.

"Rose!" Lachlan's loud voice startled them both. He strode across the garden, dressed in his riding clothes, his boots gleaming with fresh polish. " 'Tis good I've found you both, for I've news that cannot wait."

News? Rose looked up at Jamie. 'Twas obvious that he, too, was mystified. However, it was her father's expression that gave her pause. He was flushed, almost smiling, clearly pleased about something. As if he'd been awarded a great fortune or made some significant discovery. *Or perhaps…* Her hands grew cool. *Perhaps Leana has come home.* "What is it, Father?"

Lachlan's grin, seldom seen, was unmistakable. "I have decided to take a wife."

"A…*wife?*" Rose could not hide her surprise. "Whoever might that be?"

Jamie spoke first, his tone even. "I believe I ken."

"Aye, and well you might, lad." Lachlan nodded at them both. "Mistress Morna Douglas of Edingham."

"The widow from Dalbeaty?" Rose blinked, trying to imagine her father married to a stranger, to someone other than her mother. For that matter, married at all. "News indeed, Father." Jamie had met the woman and her sons, but the rest of them had not. "Will she come to live at Auchengray?"

"And where else would my wife live?"

Rose watched the questions that moved across Jamie's features and wondered if they matched hers. *Was it a marriage of convenience, or did he truly care for the woman? And what of the woman's three sons? Would they move here as well?* Rose dared not ask for such details; instead, she said what was expected of her. "Father, that is…wonderful news. I am happy for you."

"So you should be, for she will bring considerable…ah, skills to Auchengray."

And silver. She saw it in his eyes now. *And land. And cattle.*

"When will you marry?"

"Soon, soon," was all he said, brushing lint off his sleeve. "She is a woman of property. 'Twill take some time to sort out the arrangements."

Though Lachlan had made room for the widow in his thrifite, Rose was less convinced he'd prepared a space for her in his heart. Did the Widow Douglas know the man she was marrying? His pernickitie habits, his devious ways? "I wish you the best, Father." Rose reached for Jamie's hand, suddenly needing the warmth of her husband's touch. He might have married her out of duty but never out of greed. "Do keep us informed as your plans unfold."

"Aye, you can be verra sure I will." Lachlan departed as swiftly as he'd appeared, leaving the two of them adrift in the backwash.

Rose studied the wedding band on her hand for a moment, then met Jamie's steady gaze. If he was troubled, it did not show. "What's to be done, Jamie? Surely her sons will join her. I'm afraid we haven't enough room at Auchengray for four more people."

"Indeed we do not," he agreed, his gaze lifting to the vacant second-floor bedroom. "Though we certainly have room for one."

Sixty-Nine

Experience is guid,
but aften dear bought.
SCOTTISH PROVERB

That April evening another woman departed from Auchengray.
"Jenny, you've done a fine job with our Ian this month." Stepmother and wet nurse stood on Auchengray's lawn in the gloaming and eyed their mutual charge. "Hasn't she taken guid care of you, lad?" Rose cuddled the babe in her arms, bouncing him a little to see if he might smile for her. "Look how round your cheeks are and your little belly!" She lifted his chubby knee and kissed it. "Aye, and your legs, too."

"Ian will lose a' that whan he starts tae crawlin'," Jenny assured her. "My Davie is sleek as a trout, swimmin' round the house."

Rose smiled, though another thread of worry wound itself around her heart. Ian could sit and play without tumbling over now, content to stay at her feet while she mended stockings or carded wool. But how would she keep up with him, let alone finish her tasks, once he started crawling? Leana had warned her: *'Tis a great deal of work, mothering.* Rose had been too busy entertaining Ian at the time to mark her sister's meaning.

Rose walked a few steps farther before she finally confessed, "I'll miss you, Jenny. You ken so much about looking after bairns. I'm not…always sure…that is…" Her voice trailed off. What could she say? That the responsibility of mothering Ian was overwhelming? That she lived in fear of making a mistake? Leana had sacrificed everything for Ian's sake. Could *she* do the same? Could she be the mother Ian deserved?

Jenny's brown eyes studied her. "Mistress McKie, would ye care tae walk me hame tae Glensone? I'm thinkin' I might have a wird or twa tae help ye wi' Ian."

"Och, that would be grand. Wouldn't it, lad?" Rose positioned Ian more firmly round her hip as the two women started down the lane together, matching their gaits. Ian liked nothing better than an outing. "He has two more teeth now. Is that why he drools so?"

Jenny nodded, answered questions, and offered sound advice as they made their way toward Glensone, the sun taking its time sinking toward the horizon in front of them. Though only two years older than Rose, Jenny Cullen had grown up with younger brothers and sisters underfoot and knew all about rashes and fevers, about keeping bairns safe from harm, and about when Ian might start walking. "It may be a twelvemonth 'til he toddles off on his own." Jenny laughed, tweaking Ian's stockinged toes. "If he's like his faither, by his seventh summer Ian will be oot on the braes from sunrise tae the gloamin'."

"Aye." Rose gazed up toward Troston Hill, wondering if Jamie was anywhere close by. After supper he'd slipped back out of doors, lured by the lengthening days and his growing lambs. *But what about this lamb?* Rose bussed Ian's cheek, sticky with porridge. *He needs tending too, Jamie.*

The evening birdsong was at a fair pitch by the time the threesome reached Glensone. Night would not be long coming. Jenny pushed open the garden gate, then turned with a winsome smile. "I thank ye for the chance tae nurse Ian. He's a dear lad." She tugged Ian's blanket round his legs. "And, if I may say, ye're a better mither than ye think, Mistress McKie. Dinna be sae quick tae name yer faults. For I dinna see them, and neither does Ian."

Embarrassed by her praise, Rose planted a kiss on Ian's head. "If you say so."

The young woman waved them off. "Awa to Auchengray ye go, for the light is fadin' fast."

Rose moved Ian to her other hip and started toward home, her thoughts traveling north to the hills. If Jamie were there, just over the rise, would he welcome a visit from mother and son? *Stepmother,* she reminded herself, for whenever Ian said, "Ma-ma-ma-ma," surely 'twas Leana he had in mind.

She left the dirt lane behind and took off across the rough field, bouncing Ian as she went, making him squeal. "Come, young man, let's see if we can't find your father and bring him home with us." By the time she'd scaled Auchengray Hill, she was out of breath from carrying Ian and felt a bit foolish for making the climb with nighttime so near. Though Jamie was nowhere to be seen, she spied a familiar sight and could not resist. "Look, Ian!" Pointing to the bothy nestled in the glen, she started downhill toward it. "My sister and I played in that stone hut when we were just a few years older than you. Perhaps you and Rabbie Newall will do the same someday, aye?"

Moving down the steep hill with care, Rose swept aside her skirts to avoid a patch of gorse when Ian suddenly pitched forward, grasping for the yellow blooms. *"Nae!"* she screamed, bending to catch him. Thrown off balance, she tipped sideways. The uneven ground rose to meet her. *"Ian!"* She clutched him tight. The two hit hard and tumbled downward, rocks and sharp sticks tearing at their clothes and skin.

Her skirts finally caught on a bramble bush and yanked them to a stop. Ian was shrieking.

"Oh, Ian! Oh, my child!" Rose struggled to sit up, holding him close. "Are you all right, lad? Are you hurt?" His crying came in sharp gasps, and his face was scarlet.

Ignoring the searing pain in her leg, she examined the boy with trembling hands. "Ian, sweet Ian," she said between ragged breaths. "I'm sorry. I'm so sorry." She plucked twigs from his cotton blanket and brushed dirt from his cheeks. She could not feel any cuts or scratches. But that did not mean he was not bruised. And frightened out of his wits.

"My poor Ian!" Rose wrapped her arms around him, covering him with kisses and showering him with tears. "Can you ever forgive me? If I've hurt you in the slightest, I will never forgive myself." *And neither will your father. Oh, Jamie, I'm so sorry!*

Dazed, she stared at the lonely, darkening glen. What mother would bring her bairn to such a place at such an hour? *Not a guid mother. Not a true mother.* She must get him home at once. But when she tried to stand, she could not. She'd broken their fall with her knees, one of which hurt too much to move.

"Ian, whatever are we going to do?" She gathered him closer still, trying to calm him, to ease his crying, though her own tears flowed unabated. If Leana were here, she would sing to him. Could *she* sing? "Baloo…baloo." She could not. Her breathing was too shallow and her throat too tight. "Ian, Ian," she sobbed, rocking him back and forth. *What have I done? What have I done?*

Within minutes it was truly night. No stars dotted the skies, and no moonlight fell on the hillside. The herds and farm workers were settled in the steading by now. Jamie would be dressing for supper, wondering whatever had become of his wife and son.

Unless he was still on the braes.

"Jamie!" she cried out in a thin voice. Ian's wailing was louder. Surely his father would hear his son's cries above the bleating of the lambs. "Jamie!" She called his name repeatedly, begging the heavens between each one. *Let him hear me! Let him save us!*

Naught but the sounds of the night. Owls screeching. Nothing human.

"Come, Ian." Rose wiped her tears on her sleeve. "I must get you home somehow." She tried again to bend her legs underneath her, but her left leg would not be moved. Freeing one hand long enough to touch her knee, she was horrified to find it swollen to twice its usual size.

But she had to stand, she had to walk on it. She had to do *something*.

"Help!" she cried again, unashamed of the desperation in her voice. "Help us! Please, someone!" Her tears would not stop. "Please help!"

From a place deep inside her came words of comfort, learned long ago. *I have heard thy prayer. I have seen thy tears.* "Help me, Lord," she whispered. "I must get up. I must." *I will strengthen thee. Yea, I will help thee.*

Rose clutched her skirts in her hands and managed to shift her weight onto her one good knee, stiff and sore as it was. She pulled one foot underneath her, then the other, straightening as she did, clutching Ian to her breast. Though her left knee burned with a pain almost beyond bearing, she was standing at last. And shaking from head to foot.

Still, her efforts were for naught. She could never manage Auchengray Hill.

"Jamie! Jamie!" Rose shouted his name until she was hoarse, covering Ian's ear so she would not frighten him further. *Oh, Jamie, I'm so sorry. Your only son. Your dear Ian.* Perhaps she might continue a little farther downhill to the bothy. It contained naught but a slab for a bed, but at least they would have shelter. Until they were found. Until someone came. *Please come. Please.* Wincing with each step, she hobbled toward the whinstone bothy, little more than a shadow against the gray black night.

Jamie might rescue her, but he would never forgive her. *Never.*

Seventy

Who will not mercie unto others show,
How can he mercie ever hope to have?

EDMUND SPENSER

Forgive the lass, Jamie.

Jamie lengthened his stride toward Auchengray, as if he might escape Duncan's admonition. Instead it haunted him like a *bogle*, trailing after him in the pastures, invisible but palpable. *Forgive her.* 'Twould be easier if Rose admitted she was to blame for all that had happened. Easier still if she asked for his forgiveness.

Have you asked for hers? Jamie set his chin in a firm line, as if sparring with the notion. Rose knew nothing of his brief tryst with Leana. It was hardly worth bringing up, was it?

When Jamie passed Glensone, aglow with hearth light, he thought of Jenny Cullen. She might pass by on her way home, for wasn't this evening her last visit to Auchengray? With Ian properly weaned, all was in readiness for their journey. Naught remained but a letter he was expecting, and they would be on their way. He'd not told Rose yet and wouldn't until he was verra sure.

As he neared the steading, he heard the cows lowing and a horse neighing for his oats. Then another sound caught his ear. A baby crying. And a woman's voice, calling from some distance. He quickened his steps past the gardens and followed the cries coming from the direction of Auchengray Hill. He could hear the lass more plainly now, calling one word over and over. 'Twas his name.

"Jamie!"

Rose.

He flew across the steading grounds, his heart pounding. Whatever was she doing out of doors at this hour? She sounded in pain. Was she injured? Why was Ian crying so?

"Rose!" he hollered, letting her know he'd heard her.

"Jamie!" A little louder and more urgent.

He reached Auchengray Hill at a dead run, then scrambled up the brae on all fours, grabbing foliage to keep his balance. "Rose!"

"Jamie, we're down here. We...we fell."

We? She had fallen with Ian?

"Rose!" From the top of the hill, he heard her but could not see her, for the glen was shrouded in darkness.

"We're here," she called from below, her voice hoarse. "In the bothy."

The bothy. Guilt sang through his veins as he descended the hill, knowing the terrain all too well. "I'm coming, Rose."

He made his way toward her voice, wiping the sweat from his brow with his forearm as guilt gave way to anger. Of all the places for her to be. And with *Ian.* What was the woman thinking?

"You found us," she called faintly as he approached.

"*Found you?* I didn't know I'd lost you." When he stepped inside the primitive shelter, she was sitting on the stone bed, holding Ian tightly against her.

"Oh, Jamie. I'm so sorry. We fell..."

"*Fell?* What in heaven's name were you doing on Auchengray Hill at night? And with my son?"

"Jamie, I...please forgive me." Rose was sniffling now, and so was Ian, both their faces stained with tears. "I walked Jenny Cullen home, and then...then I was looking for you."

"Och!" Biting back his frustration, he sat down beside her and reached out for his son. "Come, lad, let's have a look at you." Ian fussed as Jamie ran his hands over the boy's limbs, then peered into his eyes as best he could in the bothy's dark interior. "We'll give you a thorough looking over when we bathe you, aye?"

He settled the boy in the crook of his arm, then turned his attention to Rose. "What of you, lass? Are you hurt at all?"

"Aye." Her voice was as bruised as her cheek. "I cannot walk. 'Tis my knee, I think."

"Oh, Rose. I should have asked you first." *Fine husband you are, Jamie.*

"Nae, nae." She waved a weak hand. "Ian matters more."

Holding the boy to one side, Jamie gingerly examined her knees, applying pressure to the joints with his thumb. One squeeze produced a slight wince from Rose. A touch to the other knee, swollen and misshapen, nearly made her swoon. He shook his head. She'd sprained it or worse. "You're in a bad way, lass. I'll not deny it."

"Jamie, please take Ian to the house. See that he's cared for at once. I'll wait here. You can send Willie along with a handcart if need be."

"Send *Willie?*" The lass must have hit her head when she fell. "What husband would abandon his wife in a bothy?" *The same husband who would kiss her sister. In a bothy.*

"Jamie, please." She gripped his sleeve. "Before another word is said, I must know if I'm forgiven."

"Forgiven?" *Och, lass.* " 'Twas an accident, Rose. A foolish one but not intentional. 'Tis clear you protected Ian at your own peril. His bones are supple and well padded. The boy will recover."

"Then you…forgive me?"

"Aye, Rose." *For this.* "Come, let's get you home." He placed Ian in her arms, then stood and slid one arm behind her knees, the other behind her shoulders. "Put one arm round my neck," he said firmly, "and hang on to my son with the other."

"Jamie!" She did as she was told, eyes wide with fright. "You can't possibly carry both of us."

"We'll see about that." Cradling Rose as if she were a wounded ewe with her lamb, he made his way across the rugged pasture. An owl hooted from an unseen perch as Jamie started up the hill, praying for strength. "Hang on, lass." Climbing was a slow process. Each step required solid footing before he could lift his boot and take them another foot higher.

Rose held on to his shoulder for dear life, cradling Ian between them, whispering soft words in the child's ear as Jamie struggled up Auchengray Hill. She was trying hard to be a good mother. Even he could see that. The damp night air grew cooler by the minute and seeped into his bones. At the summit he lowered Rose onto her good leg just long enough to catch his breath, then gathered her in his arms once more and started down the other side, aiming for the lighted windows of the mains, their glow diffused by the mist.

"You have quite a father, Ian," Rose told him as they neared the bottom.

Her trust shamed him. *A passable father but a poor excuse for a husband.*

When they reached level ground, Jamie got his second wind, striding past the gardens and toward the back door, where the aroma of the hearth and a simmering kale pot met them halfway. "Almost home, Rose." She did not speak, only pressed a kiss to his damp neck. When had his heidie wife become so tender?

Neda was the first to spy them coming in the back door. "Rose? Ian!" She hurried to help them through the kitchen, her supper dishes forgotten. "Jamie, whatever happened?" Neda plucked Ian from Rose's arms. "I thocht the twa o' them went tae Glensone."

"They fell," he said, deflecting Neda's questions for Rose's sake. On the long climb he'd had enough time to think through what must be done. "Neda, if you'll bring the necessary items from the stillroom— whatsomever Leana used for flesh wounds. Annabel, see that hot water, soap, and linen rags are taken to our bedroom at once and a fresh nightgown laid out for your mistress. Bring Ian along as well, for he needs a good bath and a careful going over. And something warm to drink for both of them. They've had quite an ordeal."

The women jumped to serve him, quickly bringing all that he required. Had he not tended injured sheep for mony a day? He could see to his wife's cuts and bruises. After carrying her up the stair, he waited while a clean sheet was tucked in place by a wide-eyed Eliza, then he lowered Rose onto their bed.

"Ian first," she pleaded.

Rose looked so forlorn he kissed her on the forehead, if only to assure her. "I'll have Eliza bathe him where you can watch, aye?"

Ian whimpered as the maidservant scrubbed him clean, though Jamie was relieved to find the child no worse for wear. "You guarded him well, Rose, for the lad has nary a scratch." He could see the relief in her eyes as she murmured a prayer of thanks. Jamie made certain Ian was given some runny porridge to eat, then saw to his wife's injuries. "I fear you did not escape so easily, Rose." He bathed her face with hot, soapy water, smoothing back the hair from her brow as he worked. Most of her scrapes were minor ones, except for one deep gash in her neck, which he dressed with comfrey. He unlaced her gown and eased it off her shoulders, pulling the fabric away with great care, and discovered her arms and legs were covered with more bruises than he cared to count. She would be some time healing. Perhaps their journey should be delayed a week or so, lest the carriage jostle her sore limbs unmercifully.

Unlike her other injuries, her swollen knee would require more than a simple poultice of shepherd's-purse to bring it round. He wrapped it in linen soaked in comfrey oil and propped it up with a pillow.

Neda peered over his shoulder. "What a fine surgeon you make, Mr. McKie."

" 'Tis more interesting than doctoring sheep, I'll say that." He handed Neda the herbal concoctions and Rose's *slitterie* gown, dripping with soapy water, then sent the women on their way with an exhausted Ian. Remembering a childhood fight with his brother, Evan, and his mother's concern for his own badly bruised head, Jamie cautioned, "Do not let him drift off to sleep, for he must be watched for the next several hours. If Ian's hurt his wee head, we'll ken soon enough."

Eliza, the last to leave, bobbed a nervous curtsy. "A-aye, Mr. McKie." She closed the door, leaving the couple in peace.

"Now then." He yanked off his shirt, sticky with sweat and blood, and scrubbed himself clean while Rose lay stretched across their bed, regarding him with a wary gaze.

"Jamie…" She tried to sit up but fell back on her pile of pillows with a grimace. "Jamie, I know what you are going to say, and you are right. I had no business taking Ian with me on such a foolhardy jaunt."

"Enough of that." He pulled a chair to her bedside, tugging the hem of her clean nightgown over her ankles in passing, then tucked another pillow behind her. " 'Tis forgiven, Rose. And forgotten. A mishap, nothing more."

"But you looked so serious just now. Is it about…what I told you…this morning?" She turned her head toward the wall. "About my not…expecting? Oh, Jamie, I so want to give you children. A quiver of sons that look just like you."

Touched by her sincerity, he leaned toward her. "Rose, I hope God will bless us with children someday. And that they'll bear the Almighty's image, not mine." His own words surprised him. Not that he wanted more children but that he wanted them with Rose. *Forgive the lass, Jamie.* Had it already begun?

"I pray the Almighty will remember me soon." She glanced down, her face a bonny shade of pink. "Despite my carelessness this evening, I do take my duties as a mother to heart."

"I ken you do, Rose." Jamie looked at her—truly looked at her— more closely than he had in weeks. *Nae, months.* The girl he'd fallen in love with long ago was no more; before him bloomed a woman. A woman aware of her faults, certain of her strengths, willing to work toward something that truly mattered. An honorable wife. *My wife.*

"Jamie." She lifted her head, her dark eyes shimmering in the candlelight. "I am grateful you are willing to overlook my blunder this night. But 'tis another evening that concerns me, a night when I used truth like a vengeful sword and left your marriage to Leana in tatters." Her voice thinned to a slender reed. "Oh, Jamie, can you ever forgive me for that? For 'tis a much greater sin."

This time, his head was the one that fell forward. In shame.

Forgive, and ye shall be forgiven.

"Aye, Rose, I can. And I do." Saying it aloud, he realized he meant it. That he *needed* to forgive her as much as she needed to hear it. That mercy was his only hope. In forgiving Rose he would find the freedom to move forward. *Love my sister.* Aye, and perhaps the strength to do that as well someday.

When their gazes met, it was as if they were greeting one another for the first time. Tentative smiles were exchanged as he wrapped his hands around hers. She whispered her thanks, and he nodded. And then he knew what must follow.

Tell her about Leana. In the bothy.

His conscience chafed at the thought. Could he not confess it another time when she was stronger? When she wasn't so exhausted?

Nae. Tonight. Before he lost his nerve. *Say it, man. Say the words.* He wrapped his hands around hers, "Rose, I have need of your forgiveness as well."

Her expression was pure astonishment. "Forgiveness? Jamie, for what?"

Seventy-One

Consider everything as moonshine
compared with the education of the heart.

SIR WALTER SCOTT

The hands that clasped hers were warm and solid. Jamie's face, though, was shadowed with regret.

"On the evening before our wedding, Rose…" He cleared his throat. "That is, before the supper hour…you and Leana had a…conversation. In the stillroom."

"Aye, we did. Though I wish we had not." Her heart sank at the thought of his knowing the particulars. She stared over his shoulder at the fire, wishing words once spoken might be sent up the chimney like peat smoke "When did Leana mention my *glaikit* comments to you?"

"Not long after you said them." He looked away for a moment, then turned back to her, though she could tell it was an effort. The candle on their bedside table brought to light all of his twenty-five years. Had she ever seen him so pensive? His voice sounded older as well, as though he'd aged in the last hour. "Leana came looking for me on the hills early that evening. In the mist. In the gloaming."

"I see." The memory of Leana fleeing from the stillroom and running for the front door flickered across Rose's mind. She'd paid little attention at the time, so elated was she to have the valerian. "Did my sister find you then?"

"Aye, she did." Jamie's grip on her hands tightened. "She was sobbing, Rose. Heartbroken. Looking for someone to…to comfort her."

Her breath caught. *Nae, Jamie. Please do not tell me…*

"So I…well, we…we kissed. Standing on the braes and…and then in the bothy." Before she could say a word, he hastened to add, "Do not blame your sister. The fault is mine alone."

Rose stared at him, fearing the worst. "Was there more to this… this…encounter of yours?"

"Nae…" His thumb rubbed a circle on the back of her hand. "But only because your sister had the strength to put a stop to it."

Rose slowly exhaled, gratitude mingling with her own sense of guilt. It would ne'er have happened if she'd not wounded Leana with her words. "I am to blame as well," she admitted. " 'Twas brave of you to tell me, for you might have kept it to yourself."

"A marriage built on secrets will not stand." He released her hands with a final squeeze, then rose to his feet, a look of determination crossing his features. "This morning I promised you some news, remember?"

"Aye." As if she could forget such a thing!

He crossed the room, then rummaged inside the clothes press for a moment before turning back to her, a folded paper in his hand. "Do you recall the letter Leana sent me?"

"The one I found?" *Or has there been another?* Leana's weekly letters to the family were read aloud at table, describing her quiet life in Twyneholm with Aunt Meg. Had her sister continued corresponding privately with Jamie as well? Rose studied the letter in his hand, dreading his answer.

"Aye, the same one," he said, putting her at ease. "I read the last of it to you, all but Leana's final words, which I'm sorry to say I kept to myself." He unfolded the paper and pointed to the last line, just above the smeared signature. "See what it says after 'love my sister'?"

Rose took the letter and leaned toward the guttering candle, skimming the lines until she found her place. Her eyes widened as she read aloud the closing comment, written in her sister's own hand. "Seek your future together in Glentrool." Rose looked up at him, speechless, but only for a moment. "Was *this* what you were hinting at when you asked if I was well enough for a journey?" Her heart, mended with hope, leaped inside her. *Not to Twyneholm…to Glentrool!*

His steady gaze warmed her. " 'Tis time we began anew, Rose, in a home that is truly ours."

Home. He could not have said anything that would please her more.

"Glentrool," she sighed, falling back against her pillows. The image of an elaborate stone tower house rose before her. Would she truly see it for herself soon? And call it home? She tried to take a deep breath and found her chest was too tight. "So...Glentrool...when?"

"I'd planned for us to leave on the first of May."

"May?!" She shook the letter, pretending to scold him, even as her spirits soared. "That's two days from now!"

"So it is." A faint smile creased his handsome face. "The lambs are growing steadily, and I've done all that your father has asked of me and more. We shall stay a few extra days and let you heal. But then we'll quit Auchengray. For good."

Just as Leana did. Perhaps 'twas best their father had chosen a new wife, or the house would be verra empty indeed. "You've told Father, aye?"

"Not yet," he said, though she heard no hesitancy in his voice. "I'm awaiting a letter from my mother, assuring us all is in readiness." He finished dressing for bed, pulling a clean nightshirt over his head, then poked at the hearth. "The verra hour that post arrives, I intend to corner Lachlan McBride in the spence, where his thrifite and ledgers are well within reach. The man owes me eight months' wages, and I will see it in my purse before we depart."

"My brave husband," she murmured, mustering her own courage as she held up the letter in her hand. Though she would go to Glentrool no matter how he answered her, she had to know. "Jamie, what say you of my sister's first request? That you...that you love me." She swallowed hard. "Do you?"

Rose wanted him to respond at once. To take her in his arms and say, "Aye, you ken I do," and kiss her soundly. But he did none of those things. Instead, he snuffed out the last of the candles and climbed into bed, gently taking the letter from her hands and resting it on the bedside table.

Jamie, please. Say something.

"I was sure I loved you once," he began, turning toward her, taking great care not to disturb her bandaged knee. "Then I discovered I didn't even ken the meaning of the word." In the darkness she could not see his face, but she could hear the sincerity behind his words. "I'll not lie to you, Rose. 'Twas your sister who taught me what it means to love someone."

Always Leana. Would it ever be thus? Trying not to sound discouraged, she said, "Tell me what it means then."

"Sacrifice," he said simply. "And patience. Two things that have ne'er come easily to me."

"Nor to me," she confessed in a low voice. "But I am willing to learn, Jamie. If you'll teach me." Dare she touch his face? Could she bear it if he drew away? Stretching out her hand, she rested it on his cheek, nearly crying with joy when he turned his head and pressed a tender kiss to her palm.

Oh, Jamie. "I have waited so long for you to love me again," she whispered. When he said nothing in return, she swallowed her pride and pressed on. "If I must wait longer still, so be it, for I will love you until my heart beats its last."

Seventy-Two

All is here begun, and finished elsewhere.

VICTOR HUGO

A n unexpected knocking on her door greeted Rose the next morn. "Dr. Gilchrist?" She watched in amazement as her father escorted the man into her bedroom, where she sat by the hearth, her leg propped up on a footstool. She'd not gone downstairs for breakfast. Too much trouble, for one thing, and her stomach felt a bit queasy. From her fall yestreen, no doubt. Ian had awakened ravenous, however, putting her mind at ease. "What brings you to Auchengray, sir, on this fine spring day?"

"I was in the neighborhood, attending to a patient—Mr. Bell of Tannocks Farm—and thought I'd stop here as well." He nodded at her father, whose scowl was less than welcoming. "Your father kindly honored my inquiry about your health by letting me see for myself."

Lachlan grunted. "As lang as there'll be nae bill for your services."

The surgeon's pointed gaze cut more sharply than a scalpel. "I've no need for your silver, Mr. McBride. Only the satisfaction of your daughter's full recovery from her bout of croup." His features softened when he turned to look at her leg. "Though I see you're dealing with a different malady now. Might I have permission to examine your leg, Miss McBride?"

"Aye, you may indeed." She smiled and flung the plaid away from her lap. "And 'tis Mistress McKie now. I married in March."

"I'm pleased to hear of it," he said, though she saw a flicker of concern in his eyes as he bent to study her injury.

Lachlan, standing inside the doorway, soon grew impatient and excused himself, taking the strained atmosphere with him.

"What say you, Dr. Gilchrist?" Rose prompted him after several more minutes. "Will I heal?"

"You shall, in good time." He straightened, yanking on his cuffs. "As to that…that other matter from my last visit, we shall soon have our answer, won't we? Now that you are married."

Rose thought of the slight stain on her nightgown yestermorn. "I'm afraid I already have the answer." Surely he would grasp her meaning and not ask for embarrassing details. But he was a doctor, he reminded her, to whom such details mattered. Her face heating, she described the dreary onset of her monthly courses. It was only then that she realized a curious fact: Neither her gown nor her sheets bore such evidence this morning.

When she told him so, he arched his brows. "Is that right?" He touched her neck, where her heart beat against his fingertips. "Other than your mishap on the hill, how have you been feeling the last few days, Mistress McKie? Lightheaded? A wee nauseous? Any tenderness?"

"Aye," she said cautiously, not giving hope any room to grow inside her. "A bittie of all those things." The notion of breakfast *had* drawn her stomach into a knot. And when Annabel had tied her stays that morning, hadn't she noticed some discomfort and assumed it was naught but her bruises?

"Well then." A smile twitched at the corners of his mouth. "The situation bears watching, I'd say. Wait a week or two and see if you notice additional changes. Sleepiness, for one. Changes in your appetite."

Rose could barely form the words. "Doctor, are you saying…"

He held up a cautionary finger. "I'm only saying wait and see, Mistress McKie. It could be nothing more than the trauma of your fall." He stepped back, glancing at the door as Neda appeared with a tea tray, then turned to give her a solemn wink. "Though I'd be pleased to see my original prognosis proven wrong."

"What's wrong?" Neda asked the minute the doctor took his leave. "Is it yer knee that's worryin' the man? Or that gash in yer bonny neck?"

"Nae, my knee will mend. So will my neck." Rose looked away, lest her jubilant thoughts be written across her face. *A week or two?!* Was Dr. Gilchrist daft? She'd be hard pressed to wait two days.

But wait she did, two verra long weeks. Her courses did not return, nor did her morning appetite. *It could be the tumble I took,* she told herself, then realized her knee was nearly healed. *Maybe 'tis the last vestige of the croup,* she decided, even as she winced when she held Ian tightly against her breasts. *Or it could be…it could be…* She could not bring herself even to *think* of such a possibility. Instead she hid her smile behind her napkin at table and dried her tears at odd hours of the day, praying fervently to the One who held sway o'er her womb. *Please. Please.*

The morning came when she could not lift her bleary head from her pillow, certain that her skin was the color of dried thistle and her stomach full of haggis. 'Twas the happiest day of her life. " 'Tis *true!*" she whispered to the ceiling over her box bed and the heavens beyond, tears soaking her pillow. "I shall be a mother! A *mother!*"

'Twas a gift, this child in her womb. Not from Jamie, and certainly not from Lillias Brown. Nae, 'twas from God alone. *Bethankit!*

Neda was the first to suspect the truth. "Ye're lookin' a bit fauchie," she said as they stood in the kitchen that forenoon. She grasped Rose's chin and eyed her closely. "Take ye a turn in the garden afore dinner, lass. Get a bit o' color in yer cheeks." Neda's gaze narrowed. "Or is there some guid purpose tae yer wan face?"

"Purpose?" Rose echoed, blinking innocently. "None that I ken."

Jamie was not so easily put off when they went walking in the orchard later that afternoon. Sunshine poured through the white apple blossoms, dappling his face with patches of light. "You're keeping a saicret from me, Rose," he insisted, though his tone was not unkind. "As your husband, I trust you will inform me of anything of consequence."

She stopped to look up at him, gauging his mood. Would he welcome her news or think only of Leana in distant Twyneholm? Might it spur him toward love or drive him away forever? *Och!* 'Twas enough to carry his son in her arms and his seed in her womb without bearing the weight of fear as well. She would throw caution to the Galloway winds and tell him.

"Jamie, I *do* have a saicret." Rose slid her hands inside his, reveling in their rough strength. "A canny lad like you has nae doubt jaloused what I'm about to tell you." Though he did not pull her closer, she had his complete attention. "You'll remember Dr. Gilchrist came in February and gave me some terrible news."

Sympathy shone in his eyes. "About your being barren?"

"Aye." She took a steadying breath, watching his face. "He was… wrong."

Jamie gripped her hands. "Meaning you're…"

Rose nodded, too overwhelmed to speak. Did the hope in his voice match her own?

He planted a fervent kiss on her forehead. "Rose, that is…wonderful news."

"Aye, 'tis." She could barely see him through a shimmer of tears. "Oh, Jamie, I hoped you might be…glad."

"*Glad?*" He pulled her into his arms. "I am more than that, lass. Whether son or daughter, 'tis a blessing from God."

She sank into his embrace, knowing he would not mind if her tears dampened his shirt. " 'Twill be another week or two before we may know for certain," she cautioned him, though her heart was as sure as if she already held the babe in her arms. *A son.* She was convinced of that as well. *Jamie's. And mine.*

Jamie leaned back to gaze down at her. "Shall we keep this our saicret then?" When she nodded, he said nothing for a moment, though his brow creased. "Your father must be the first to know," he finally said. "I'll not inform him until after we've made our arrangements to leave for Glentrool. Then we'll tell Neda, Duncan, and the others." He held up a finger in mock warning. "Not a word until I say so."

"Agreed." Rose bit her tongue before she asked, "But what of Leana? When shall I tell her?" There would be time enough to write before they left Auchengray. Rose imagined Leana unfolding such a letter, standing by Burnside's meager firelight to read it. Would her sister be happy for her? Or devastated at the news? *Leana, forgive me.* That's how she would begin the letter. *'Tis God's faithfulness, not my own. I will cherish this child as I cherish your Ian. For I love him dearly, my sister. As I love you.*

From behind them came the snap of a twig. "Ye'll forgive an auld woman for visitin' whaur she's not invited." They both turned to find Neda moving between the flowering trees, a fretful Ian in her arms and a look of chagrin on her face. "None of the lasses could make the boy happy. He's wantin' his mither and faither, is all."

Jamie stepped back and winked at Rose, well out of Neda's sight. "Here's the mother of the hour."

Her throat tightened. *My sweet Ian.* Was she truly his mother now? Ever since they'd tumbled down the hill, he seemed hesitant around her, and no wonder. Rose reached out her hands to him and her heart as well. "Will you trust me, Ian?" she said softly, brushing away the last of her tears. "Will you let me hold you if I promise never to let go?"

Please, God. Let him come to me. Let him forgive me.

Ian blinked at her with Leana's blue gray eyes. Bright and clear. His dear mouth, so like Jamie's, smiled at her. *Smiled!* And when she stretched out her arms, Ian stretched out his. "Ma-ma-ma-ma!" he squealed and fell into her embrace.

Author Notes

Give me but one hour of Scotland,
Let me see it ere I die.

WILLIAM EDMONDSTOUNE AYTOUN

An hour, a day, a week, a year—one can never get enough of Scotland. From Glasgow to Edinburgh, Skye to Aberdeen, Inverness to Dumfries, I have traversed my adopted country in every season, taken copious notes, and snapped endless photos, endeavoring to make Scotland come alive for my readers.

Alas, what I could *not* manage was a visit to the eighteenth century, so I depended on antiquarian books for my inspiration. A growing resource library of six hundred titles, including Andrew Edgar's *Old Church Life in Scotland* (1885) and John Watson's *The Scot of the Eighteenth Century* (1907), served as a valuable passport for traveling through time and place.

No matter which book I turned to, one truth resounded: From the Reformation to the early nineteenth century, the kirk held sway in Scottish society. No law was higher, and no voice spoke with more authority. The kirk sessions did indeed require the reading of *banns* to announce a pending marriage and the subscribing of *bands* to hold a sinner to his or her promise never to commit certain offenses again. I adapted Leana's band from one recorded in Mauchline parish in 1749 by a shoemaker who had insulted the minister and cursed his mother— grave offenses in his day. His pledge was signed simply *A.B.*

The Scottish *Paraphrases* is a collection of the earliest hymns of the Church of Scotland, though many congregations would have insisted on singing only the metrical psalms. Two hymns featured in *Fair Is the Rose* are from the 1745 edition. According to Douglas Maclagan's *The Scottish Paraphrases* (1889), the author of the hymn in chapter 7 is unknown, and the hymn in chapter 48 was written by the beloved hymnist Isaac Watts (1674–1748).

The descriptions of Lillias Brown and her eerie cottage were based on several accounts in J. Maxwell Wood's *Witchcraft and Superstitious Record in the South-Western Districts of Scotland* (1911). Despite their healthy fear of witches, rural Scottish folk celebrated Hallowmas Eve with wild abandon. Robert Burns's poem "Halloween," featured in *Poems, Chiefly in the Scottish Dialect* (1786), details various customs of that unholy night, including some of the divination rites that Rose puts to use.

Sweetheart Abbey, where Neil and Rose meet for their autumn tryst, still dominates the landscape of modern New Abbey, even as its ruins grace the back cover of this novel. Founded in 1273 by Lady Devorgilla in memory of her late husband, John Balliol, the Cistercian monastery was wholly devoted to the worship of God. The Reformation of the sixteenth century brought about the demise of Dulce Cor. In 1779 the roofless abbey was acquired by a group of local gentlemen who made certain Sweetheart would no longer be treated as a stone quarry.

The farms, towns, and geographic features in *Fair Is the Rose* appear on detailed maps of Galloway from the last two centuries. The spellings used here are based on Sir John Sinclair's *The Statistical Account of Scotland* (1799). Seldom did I write a page without turning to the volumes for Kirkcudbrightshire and Dumfriesshire. Truly an amazing resource.

Carlyle School for Young Ladies was patterned after similar establishments in Dumfries. Reverend William Burnside's 1792 entry in the *Statistical Account* notes that "two or three boarding schools for the education of young ladies" existed during Rose's time. As to the sort of instruction one might have expected from Mistress Carlyle, J. Burton's *Lectures on Female Education and Manners* (1799) and *The Mirror of Graces* (1811), penned by "a Lady of Distinction," were both useful and highly entertaining.

The *Dumfries Weekly Journal,* which Rose found so fascinating, was initially published in 1777 as the town's first political broadsheet. Conservative, provincial, and always in good taste, the *Journal* remained in print until 1833. Though Queensberry School is fictitious, Queensberry Square is indeed real. Laid out in 1770 as a public marketplace, the square later served as a ceremonial parade ground for the Royal Dumfries Volunteers during the French Revolutionary Wars.

The "auld alliance" between Scotland and France, to which Jamie alludes, dates to the 1295 treaty between John Balliol and Philip IV. Over the centuries the loosely defined alliance waxed and waned amid a steady exchange of soldiers, brides, bottles of claret, and culinary arts. The French language traveled north as well; many a Scot would have been conversant in the language of diplomacy.

The names chosen for the characters in *Fair Is the Rose* should ring true to residents of Galloway. First and last names collected from tombstones and census records of the time period were combined to create our fictional folk. In chapter 23, however, a well-known historical figure makes an appearance: Robert Burns (1759–1796) was very much a part of Dumfriesshire in 1790. Living as a tenant farmer at Ellisland Farm in Dunscore parish north of Dumfries, Burns was a ploughman, a poet, and an exciseman. The Globe Inn was his favorite *howff,* or public house, and the snuggery his usual haunt. In the brief scene included here, Burns is celebrating a birthday—his own—since the date in our story is 25 January. Rabbie Burns would have been thirty-one the night he met a nervous Rose McBride at the Globe, which was indeed owned by a Mr. William Hyslop of Lochend in Newabbey parish.

Sir Robert Grierson of Lag (1655–1733), Steward of Kirkcudbright, was dead and buried long before Rose met Jane Grierson in Dumfries. John Mactaggart, in his *Scottish Gallovidian Encyclopedia* (1824), declares Sir Robert "one of the most infernal villains Scotland ever gave birth to." A persecutor of the Covenanters, Grierson presided over the trial and execution of the Wigtown martyrs, was excommunicated as an adulterer, and later imprisoned as a Jacobite.

When Leana and Jamie visit Glensone, they are treated to fiddle tunes chosen from those described in George Emmerson's *Scotland through Her Country Dances* (1967). The jig "Johnny McGill" was named for an itinerant dancing master from Ayrshire who composed the tune. Burns would later add lyrics and call it "Tibbie Dunbar." An even older tune is "Green Grow the Rashes," first identified as "Cou thou me the raschyes green" in a book of Scottish music from 1549. Burns added lyrics to this tune as well, and his verses were amusingly autobiographical: "The sweetest hours that e'er I spend, are spent among the lasses, O."

"Croup" was an old Scottish name for a disease frequently found in rural Fife, Ayrshire, and Galloway, as noted in John Comrie's *History of Scottish Medicine to 1860* (1927) and as experienced by our poor Rose. Dr. Francis Home (1719–1813) was the first to describe croup in 1765 and to recommend a tracheotomy as the solution. The disease would be properly diagnosed and named a half-century later by Pierre Breton-neau, who called it *La Diphthérite*—diphtheria.

Leana had good cause for concern when Rose fell ill, for medicine was a primitive art in the eighteenth century, and bloodletting—phle-botomy—was a common practice. The few instruments described in Dr. Gilchrist's etui were often the only tools at a physician's disposal. No wonder Scottish folk turned to the old ways when illness struck! Saint Queran's Well—one of some six hundred Scottish healing wells—still exists near the hamlet of Islesteps. When the well was cleaned out in 1870, coins were discovered from the reign of Elizabeth I. Today rags left by more recent visitors can be found tied to the nearby bushes.

Rose's recipe for marmalade was adapted from my favorite book of Scottish recipes, F. Marian McNeill's *The Scots Kitchen with Old Time Recipes* (1932). A tourist soon learns that no "full Scottish breakfast" is complete without a rack of toast served with a huge slab of butter and a pot of marmalade, as well as a bowl of porridge doused in rich cream. Of marmalade and porridge McNeill writes, "These two dishes are Scotland's chief culinary gifts to the world." Scottish porridge is smoother and paler in color than the hearty, lumpy oatmeal served in America. Raisins, however, are not served on the side; quite a few eye-brows rose round the breakfast table when I requested currants and dumped them into my porridge!

The herbs in Leana's physic garden and stillroom were chosen with care from two recent books: Tess Darwin's *The Scots Herbal: The Plant Lore of Scotland* (1996) and *Scottish Plants for Scottish Gardens* (1996) by Jill, Duchess of Hamilton. Mrs. M. Grieve's recently reprinted two-volume set, *A Modern Herbal* (1931), is a grand resource for those of us who want to learn about wild arum, cowslip, shepherd's-purse, comfrey, and valerian. The list of medicinal herbs is endless and ever fascinating.

I am grateful to be surrounded by editors and friends who cherish such details, as I do. Heartfelt thanks to my editorial team at Water-Brook Press—Laura Barker, Dudley Delffs, Carol Bartley, and Paul Hawley—and to Benny Gillies, my favorite Scottish bookseller, cartographer, and proofreader. His well-tended bookshop near Castle Douglas in the village of Kirkpatrick Durham is brimming with Scottish books, maps, and prints. Do visit him online at www.bennygillies.co.uk. I am also indebted to several "specialist readers": Blessings to Madame Susan Thompson for her command of French, Barbara Wiedenbeck for her shepherding skills, Velma MacLellan for her expertise in spinning and carding, Leesa Gagel for her eagle eye, and Ginia Hairston for her exceptional horse sense. Finally, I can never thank enough my agent and friend, Sara Fortenberry, who read the manuscript more times than I can count and offered ongoing encouragement and wise direction. Bless you, dearie.

Kindly join me on a virtual tour of the Scottish countryside featured in *Fair Is the Rose* and *Thorn in My Heart* via my Web site: www.LizCurtisHiggs.com. You'll also find there my complete Scottish bibliography, additional historical notes, diaries from my trips to Scotland, readers' comments, links to my favorite Scottish sites, a discography of Celtic music and soundtracks that inspire me as I write, and some uniquely Scottish recipes.

If you would enjoy receiving my free newsletter, *The Graceful Heart*, printed and mailed just once a year, please contact me directly:

Liz Curtis Higgs
P.O. Box 43577
Louisville, KY 40253-0577

Or visit my Web site:

www.LizCurtisHiggs.com

Do join Jamie, Leana, and Rose once more for *Whence Came a Prince*, which brings their story to a rousing conclusion. Until then, dear reader, you are a blissin!

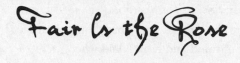

READER'S GUIDE

In books lies the soul of the whole Past Time.

THOMAS CARLYLE

1. *Fair Is the Rose* begins with the very scene where *Thorn in My Heart* ends…but this time we see things from Rose's viewpoint. She soon tells Jamie, "What is *right* and what is *fair* are not necessarily the same." Is that a true statement? Does Rose have a rightful claim to Jamie's heart? Does he treat Rose fairly in this difficult situation? If you could advise Rose at this turning point in her life, what would you say to her?

2. Lachlan McBride cautions Rose, "Your bonny face may open doors better left closed." How do Rose's fair face and figure work for her, and how do they work against her? Does charming Rose elicit sympathy from you…or jealousy? Do you find yourself rooting *for* her or *against* her? Which of the following quotes best describes Rose McBride: "A rosebud set with willful little thorns" (Alfred, Lord Tennyson) or "That crimson rose how sweet and fair!" (Robert Burns)?

3. In *Thorn in My Heart*, Jamie's behavior is often less than honorable. In *Fair Is the Rose*, we find him becoming more trustworthy. Describe the positive attributes you find in Jamie McKie. And in what ways might he disappoint you? What are Jamie's weaknesses, and how do they affect his relationships with Rose and with Leana?

4. Is Leana "too good to be true," or can you relate to her struggles and flaws? What incidents have most influenced Leana's life to date?

In particular, how has motherhood changed Leana? When she stands up to the kirk session, what thoughts and feelings run through your mind and heart? And when she flees to Twyneholm, are you proud of Leana or disappointed in her? Could she remain at Auchengray in such circumstances? Could you?

5. What do you make of the disciplinary actions of the early Scottish kirk—the session meetings, the repentance stool, the jougs, the subscribing of bands, the testimonial letters? How might conventions like these create a better society? And what are the dangers inherent in such practices? How would you compare the role of religion in today's culture with its role in eighteenth-century Scotland?

6. Each of the three main characters—Jamie, Leana, Rose—would be justified in echoing Rose's oft-stated claim, " 'Tis not fair!" In what ways have they been wronged and by whom? Which one of the three has the most cause for complaint? Describe how each person handles unfair treatment and what that says about his or her character. How else does the concept of fairness play out in this story?

7. The epigraphs that introduce each chapter are meant to foreshadow the action that follows or to capture the essence of a character's struggles. Chapter 55 opens: "For every rose a thorn doth bear." What thorns press into Rose's tender heart in this chapter? Choose another epigraph from the novel that strikes you as particularly appropriate, and explain its significance to the story.

8. Rose tries everything to heal her barren womb—from cantrips and herbs to a predawn pilgrimage to Saint Queran's Well. Think of the various reasons she is so desperate for a child of her own. Which ones ring the most true to you? In what ways might modern women define themselves by their childbearing abilities?

9. In his poem "Halloween," Robert Burns describes "the principal charms and spells of that night, so big with prophecy to the peasantry in the west of Scotland":

Some merry, friendly, country-folks
Together did convene,
To burn their nits, an' pou their stocks,
An' haud their Halloween
      Fu' blythe that night.

Do the Scottish traditions of dunking for apples, building bonfires, and carving faces in turnips conjure up fond memories of your own childhood autumns? How has your view of Halloween changed over the years? What do you make of Rose's many divining rites? Are they harmless diversions or risky forays into a darker world?

10. Do you consider Jane Grierson the "bad girl" of *Fair Is the Rose*? Or might that title belong to Lillias Brown? How and why do these women make a mark on young, impressionable Rose? Perhaps you've found yourself drawn to such risktakers at one time or another. What is their appeal? Might they serve some divine purpose in our lives? in Rose's life?

11. When they share their testimonies before the kirk session, Rose, then Jamie, and finally Leana strive to "speak the truth in love." Review their statements in chapters 40, 41, and 42. What truths do you find there? And what untruths do you discover? What one word might you choose to describe Rose's testimony? and Jamie's? and Leana's? Was the outcome of the session meeting what you expected? Why or why not?

12. Reverend Gordon undergoes a significant change of heart throughout *Fair Is the Rose*. Compare the man we first meet in chapter 4 with the man we see in chapter 59. How might you explain such a transformation? Can you pinpoint one or two places in the novel where his behavior shifts? What conclusions might you draw about the difference between a religion based on law and a religion founded on grace?

13. Jamie's uncle, Lachlan—like the biblical Laban after whom this character is patterned—depends on devious words and clever deception to

accomplish his will. Can a person simply be *bad*, without explanation or justification? What do you make of Lachlan's relationship with the Widow Douglas of Edingham Farm? How might life at Auchengray be affected if Lachlan McBride suddenly became a happily married man?

14. The scene in which Rose asks Leana for the valerian Ian has pulled from the garden, then hurts Leana's feelings and sends her fleeing into the gloaming in search of Jamie, parallels the account in Genesis 30:14-16, in which Rachel offers Leah a night with Jacob in exchange for a fertility plant pulled from the ground by Leah's son. However, what was common practice circa 1900 B.C. is hardly acceptable in either A.D. 1790 or the present! I decided young Rose would never make such an offer, nor would Leana throw aside her band and all that preceded it for one night of passion with Jamie. Had the story followed the biblical account to the letter, how might that have altered the lives of Jamie, Leana, and Rose in the days that followed? How would their relationships with one another and with God have been affected? And how would it have changed your opinion of Rose? of Leana? of Jamie? What might this pivotal scene suggest about choices and consequences?

15. Though our story comes to a meaningful close, clearly the tale is not yet finished. How do you hope things will conclude for Jamie, Leana, and Rose in *Whence Came a Prince*? All three of them long to love and to be loved, but that is not all they need. What do you think Jamie needs most? And what of Leana? Finally, what might Rose require above all things? What is your definition of a "happy ending," in novels and in life?

Scots Glossary

a'—all
aboot—about
aften—often
ain—own
ane—one
anither—another
argle-bargle—argument
athegither—altogether
auld—old
awa—away, distant
bacheleer—bachelor
bairn—child
baith—both
baloo—used to hush a child to
   sleep
bauld—bold
bethankit!—God be thanked!
bittie—small piece
blaeberry—whortleberry
bleeze—blaze
blether—babble, gossip
blissin—blessing
bogle—ghost, specter
bothy—small cottage
brae—hill, slope
braisant—shameless
brak—broke
braw—fine, handsome
Buik—the Bible
burn—brook, stream
byre—cowshed

bystart—bastard
cantrip—charm, magic, trick
clack—gossip, idle chatter
cleck—conceive
clootie—piece of cloth, rag
close—passageway, courtyard
compear—appear before congregation for rebuke
cutty stool—stool of repentance
deasil—sunwise or clockwise
deid—dead
de'il—devil
dochter—daughter
dominie—schoolmaster, teacher
doocot—dovecote
dook—to duck
doon—down
dootsome—vague, uncertain
dout—doubt
dreich—bleak, dismal
dry stane dyke—stone fence without
   mortar
durstna—dare not
eldritch—mysterious, unearthly
ell—a linear measure, just over a
   yard
faither—father
fash—worry, trouble, vex
fauchie—sickly looking
feeing—engaging as a servant
ferlie—superb, wonderful

flindrikin—flirtatious
flit—move one's household
flooer—flower
fowk—folk
freshening—refreshing
frichtsome—frightening
fu'—full
gairden—garden
gie—give
glaikit—thoughtless, daft
glaumshach—greedy, grasping
gley—avert the eyes, look away
glib-gabbit—gossipy
goud—gold
gracie—devout, virtuous, well-behaved
granbairn—grandchild
granfaither—grandfather
granmither—grandmother
green—young, youthful
greet—cry, weep
grush—crush, squash
guid—good
gustie—savory, tasty
halie—holy
hame—home
harn goun—coarse linen gown; sackcloth
hatesome—hateful
haud—hold, keep
haud yer wheesht—hold your tongue
hauflin—adolescent boy
hearken—eavesdrop, listen
heidie—headstrong, impetuous

herd—shepherd
het—hot
hindberry—raspberry
hizzie—hussy
hochmagandy—fornication
hoose—house
hoot!—pshaw!
howff—public house, or pub
howre—whore
hurlie—trundle, move about on wheels
ill-deedie—mischievous, wicked
ill-kindit—cruel, inhuman
ill-scrapit—rude, bitter
ithers—others
jalouse—imagine, presume, deduce
jougs—iron collar used for punishment
kell—headdress worn by a young, unmarried woman
ken—to know, recognize
kenspeckle—conspicuous, familiar
kimmer—godmother
kintra—of the country, rustic
kintra-side—countryside
kirkin—first appearance at kirk
kittlie—itchy, sensitive
kittlins—kittens
knackie—funny
lade—millrace
lanelie—lonely
lang—long
lealtie—loyalty
leuk—look
limmer—prostitute

loosome—lovely
losh!—lord!
lowpin-on stane—leaping-on stone, used to mount a horse or a carriage
luve—love
mainnerlie—mannerly
mair—more
maun—must
mebbe—maybe, perhaps
meikle—great, much
mem—madam
michtie—scandalous, disgraceful
misbehadden—improper, unbecoming
mither—mother
mony—many
morn's morn—tomorrow morning
mutchkin—$1/4$ pint Scots
neeps—turnips
nicht—night
nits—nuts
niver—never
noony—late morning meal
och!—oh!
oniething—anything
oniewise—anyway
oo aye!—yes! (from the French *oui*)
oot—out
orraman—odd-jobs man
parritch—porridge
peerie-winkie—little finger or toe
pensie—pompous, self-important
pernickitie—cantankerous, touchy
pittin' the brain asteep—meditating

pou—pull
praisent—present, gift
puir—poor
richt—right, authentic
roarie—noisy
rummle-gumption—common sense
run-line—psalm sung one line at a time
sae—so
saicret—secret
sairlie—sorely
sark—shirt
scoonrel—scoundrel
scuil—school
shortsome—amusing, enjoyable
sic—such
sleekit—smooth-tongued, deceitful
slippie—slippery
slitterie—messy, sloppy
sonsie—substantial, appealing
speeritie—energetic, spirited, vivacious
spleet-new—brand-new
spurtle—porridge stick
stane—stone
stayed lass—an old maid
stramash—clamor, disturbance, uproar
suin—soon
swick—to trick
swickerie—trickery, deception
syne—ago, thereafter, since
tablet—a sweet made of butter and sugar
tae—to

tairt—tart
tak—take
tapsalteerie—topsy-turvy, upside down
tassie—cup
thegither—together, concerted
thocht—thought, believed
thrifite—moneybox
tup—a ram
twa—two
ugsome—gruesome, horrible
unchancie—unlucky, dangerous, risky
unco—eccentric, odd, strange
unheartsome—sad, melancholy
vennel—alley
verra—very
wabbit—exhausted, weary
waddin—wedding

walcome—welcome
wame—womb
waukens—awakens
weatherful—stormy
weel—well
wha—who
whan—when
whatsomever—whatever
whaur—where
wheesht!—hush!
wi'—with
wickit—wicked
widdershins—counterclockwise
wi'oot—without
wird—word
wutch—witch
yestermorn—yesterday morning
yestreen—yesterday, last night

Leana, Jamie, and Rose
will return in...

Spring 2005

WATERBROOK
PRESS

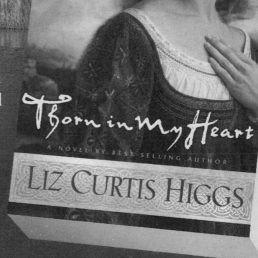